# UNCLE BROTHER

# CONTENTS

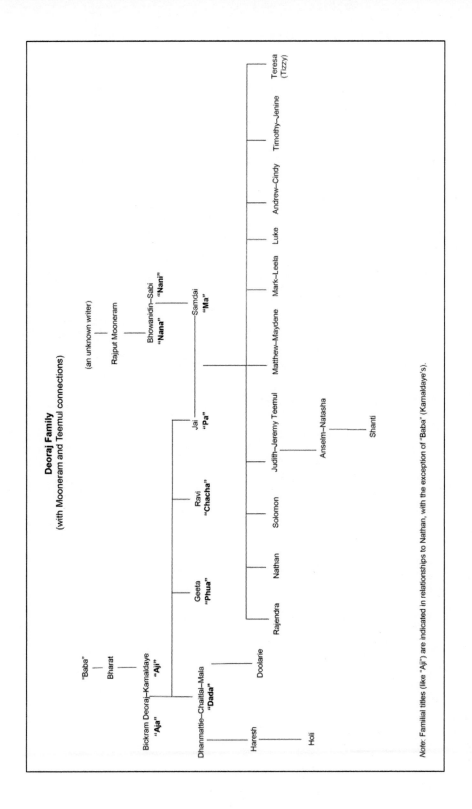

**Deoraj Family**
(with Mooneram and Teemul connections)

*Note:* Familial titles (like "Aji") are indicated in relationships to Nathan, with the exception of "Baba" (Karnaldaye's).

PART

1

# BROTHER

## *(misplaced)*

## Nathan

The phone lies dark and mute on the hospital pillow. No more can be done tonight, so I force my eyes away, my gaze now powerless to avert calamity, and I drag a screen between my mind and the pain: *sufficient unto the day is the evil thereof.* Somehow my heart throbs on, stubbornly etching green waves on a monitor the size of my TV.

*You cn do better than that, at least a twenty-two-inch. And you gotta get a flat-screen.* I hear the child as if she is at my bedside, irrepressible, infusing my mind with the possibility of tomorrow and lifting me beyond these ravages of time. *You're only just catching up with DVDs, but they're lame already, you know – it's Blu-ray now and 3D and all that kinda stuff. Right?* Twelve years old and determined to bring me into her century, her eyes sparking with mischief. *You gotta dump that old TV, Uncle Brother. Look, don't worry, I'm gonna tell you what to do.*

Once there were no screens, only books. Once there were no books, only voices.

I still feel it in me – how, almost eighty years ago, the stories carried me away. Some bore me up, then set me down so gently it was only then I realized I had been floating; other tales lay hold roughly and manhandled me along, leaving me breathless and wounded. Arithmetic was a game I mastered easily, but the stories surged in my veins like blood whether they called them history, literature or religious knowledge. What could they ask me that I could not answer – and it was not only, as they thought, because I listened more closely than the other children; it was because I didn't just listen to the stories. I entered them.

Till I began to think, perhaps *I* have one to tell.

From habit, pondering the right or wrong of it, I start to raise the forefinger on my left hand, but the tug and pinch of the needle and tube for the drips makes me think better of it. Tomorrow they will take those away again, but tonight, immobilized as I am, I constrain my thoughts to one path at a time – specifically, the ethics of telling it. A serious thing, inventing your own version of people you care for, for what if your version takes over? On the other hand, what if one day there are no versions left? You would be, in a way, responsible. Correct?

In the night the softest noises of the hospital resound in the small ward where I lie. Then a phone jangling sends a wash of hot and cold, fury and terror, along my skin, but it's outside, outside; the tension recedes, leaving me spent in the sudden silence. Govern this. Force my mind from the sullen silence of that other one on my pillow. Pick up my thoughts. Aaha. Whether I've had a story of my own to write. What became of that?

Where do they go, the lost books? Those secretly authored, lingering in oblivion. And then there are the ones not yet set down. (A soft footfall and someone turns the monitor, so I no longer see the green waves. Just as well, I tell myself sternly: *they* know how to read those things.) Young people communicate in their own way now, messages hurtling back and forth, but out there, even beyond this cyberspace she tells me about, there must still be some dimension for aborted books, those not yet accomplished, still unformed fragments in boxes like those from under my desk in Mission with notebooks and unbound leaves that have anecdotes or bits of essays, letters and legal papers, quotations, an insight jotted on a paper napkin, a prayer journal. And these scraps preserve, precariously, shreds of the past so momentous on a personal level, tattered clues of actions and circumstances that were incoherent at the time, although now their unfolding may seem fully achieved in the minds and hearts of some of us who shared in the events – events too private to let slip into the world.

These are the books not yet set down, demanding to be written but forestalled by a sense of duty to the living or the dead, and the possibility of them sends out echoes into the void as they hang there, suspended in eternity.

But on my pillow something warbles gently and a new text message lights up:

SEPTEMBER 12, 2010 – 3:45 A.M.

> *they let me send one more raelly last one Uncle Brohter they have me ereh . . . help me Ullni they say money. no police or they willl do it like htey said they have an axe*

# CHAPTER 1

# BIRTH PAPER

| When Born | Name (if any) | Sex | Name and Surname of Father | Name and Surname of Mother |
|---|---|---|---|---|
| *October 24, 1928* | *Gahadar Deoraj* | *Boy* | *Illegitimate* | *Elizabeth Deoraj* |

## Nathan

How not to tell it – this tale pounding in my head for a way out. *Dear Lord*, I used to pray, *please to help me keep my mouth shut.* Is not like I know how to tell story. Not like Pa.

Even earlier, when I was five and we lived in the area people called Anlévé (although Pa said the real name of the cocoa estate was Dessalines), even then I knew: it had no one else like Pa.

That must have been 1933 or so, and years later I still hung on his voice, and if I close my eyes I hear it now. Pa's head was crammed with stories from wakes, from the rumshop where the griot might sing in patois, and from nights in the forest with Papa Bois and the bamboo creaking round them and the fire they huddled round – the fire self snapping, *krik krak.* And Ma – no, I was not like her either. She never went to any of those places but she could still tease a little yarn out of nothing, pull a thought out the air and twist and knot and weave it to brief accounts of her parents or other old people, tales that settled things in their place, light and binding like her orhni.

Mostly it was Pa who told stories of La Plus Belle or Compère Ananci or even people like ourselves. That was when you had settled down in the evening with steaming roti and baigan, the smell lingering even after Ma had taken it off the fire, the garlic and pepper stinging your eyes. And the roti you juggled hand to hand because it was too hot to hold when you tore it open to pinch up the baigan chokha in the urgency of getting it in your mouth even if it burned.

"Take you time, beta." Ma took it easily in her own fingers, opened it in her unflustered way, closed it on the baigan and blew on it before popping it in my mouth. Then Pa would begin the story. The flambeau threw shadows that flitted from the dark wooden walls and pitched back again across our faces, and Pa's hand swept out and caught up the patches of light and dark as he wove his tale.

Ma was a woman of few words, her eyes habitually cast down, but just now and then she raised them to me, and behind her veil of quiet I glimpsed fire and steel.

I was still a little fellow when it began to come together, this vast unwieldy tale I cannot simply relay – not because it is shameful (quite the reverse) but because . . . "Because people does be faas," Ma said when I was older and asked why I mustn't write in my essays about Aji making roti and alu or how Dada get a bust head from Sunita father.

"But Radica and them – plenty children in the class – they ent have *no* lunch," I objected.

Then I saw from her blank stare that it was not that she was ashamed of roti and alu. It was that family matters must be kept to ourselves.

"Whatever else you do or doesn't do" – Pa set his mouth in determination with that dangerous light in his eye that an evening rum invariably kindled – "you protect you family. And you protec them from talk. You feed you family and you protec them."

Even in the early days, early as I can remember, there was always food. I was small and Pa still working on Papa Jacques's estate when I opened my eyes in the dark to find Ma standing over me, hands floury, urging me to make haste and fetch the water. By then she would be in the cooking area at the back, before the chulha, a clay fireside open at the front with wood pushed in and lit already, and the tawa resting on top, so I would go out for the rain water we had caught overnight and get it to her as fast as I could. Later, when I had stumbled about our room sweeping out beetles that had flown in at

night after Ma lit the lamp, I would go back to her. By then she would be taking up the loya, wheeling the soft dough hand over hand, fingers and palms
working it thinner and wider until she lay it on the hot tawa, and even there
spinning it slowly near to one edge of the iron till it began to swell first on
that side, then all over, so the smell rose too and enfolded me.

By now the birds were waking up, sleepily at first, whistling, chirping, fluting as the cool damp of early morning dried up. Ma helped me wash myself
but she would be dressed already, her hair smoothly coiled in place. She wiped
the cooking area, with an eye on my awkward efforts to drag on a shortpants
and with a calm that spread order and quiet however fast she worked. Ma
moved deliberately and things fell into place around her.

After taking Pa his food, then completing her own weeding, she came
straight back to cook again. Things hard all over the country, I heard Pa tell
her, all over the world it look like, and she said yes, for she get to hear from
her old people way off in Central that pay was low on the sugar estate. So Pa
said sugar wasn' so sweet after all then, and sometimes he came home with
songs people made up about low wages and how to save money; and what
could these people be like, I wondered, with names like Growler and Roaring
Lion. Most times though, Pa didn't joke about money; he clenched his jaw
and his mouth tightened to a straight line.

On good evenings Pa lifted me on his shoulders and danced with me. He
told us how what he called *other kind of people* were making music on old pan
they hit up to get different notes, and the ping-pong not sounding bad at all,
but when I asked Ma for a tin she kept under her bed, so I could make a music
too, she said no, for then where she would keep her two three piece of
money? Still, from as early as I can remember, I listened to everything. Keeping my face turned away from bigpeopletalking, I listened.

For there was another life I had glimpsed. Now and then Pa took me with
him in the evening along the dim winding path under the trees till the bush
opened up. I suppose there would have been no real building to speak of. At
any rate, all I remember is a long room with oil lamps and stools and a big
paper spread on the table in the middle and men gathered around it curiously.
It had marks on it that seemed to mean all sorts of strange things. There were
stories that the man who brought the paper never lingered over, only mentioned – stories about trouble and adventure. People were talking a lot about
a man named Hitler, people were amazed by another man who had flown
around the world, people were flocking to see what they called a moving

picture with a thing like a big monkey, big like a tree in the forest, they called King Kong. Then, the bad rains that the paper called a hurricane had hit the tip of the island, and now there were thirteen people dead and a thousand homeless.

Pa put me on his shoulders afterwards to carry me home and I sat up there, fingers locked in his thick black hair, with my head spinning with hurricanes and monkeys bigger than the tallest trees and wicked men in faraway armies and children who got washed away and people who flew or sang and had dangerous-sounding names like Lion. Only, when I questioned Pa he could tell me nothing more, and when I asked Ma she said, "That nice, beta. Eat now."

And I would fall asleep dreaming of the paper that mysteriously held the full stories and wake up trying to work out how to get a paper like that and learn to decipher it.

It was barely light when the conch blew for lineup and the overseer allocated tasks. In dry season the hard, stony path under our feet was riddled with cracks, but in some places the grass lay squashed down or strewn with large flat leaves from trees I did not know the names for – not like Pa who knew those things. Still, it was not thick underfoot as it would be if we stepped farther from the path where there might be centipedes or scorpions. Or snakes. Pa had laughed at the overseer for warning the workers not to kill snakes they found in the cocoa. "He sit up on he horse and say snake eat pest." Pa regarded the gleaming edge of his cutlass with satisfaction. "Let he talk. When I see snake I hitting he one lash."

"What name *pest*?" I asked, and he rubbed his rough fingers in my hair.

"You think you alone like cocoa tea? Boy, everything like cocoa – bird, rat, and don't talk bout squirrel. I tell you, monkey and all come for he share."

Early in the year we would go in the cocoa while it was still cool, sheltered under the immortelles, though I only learned their name afterwards. Now these huge trees were dropping their leaves and putting out fiery blooms the sunlight touched and set ablaze. The cocoa pods hung bright and heavy, and the donkeys were tied waiting with open panniers, and Pa's gullet reached for the high pods, rugged red, yellow, or shades in between, while Ma put down her pallet to dig the beans out with her fingers and spread them on banana leaves. It was still cool that time of year, though not cold cold like other places I heard people talk about. In the mornings, hurrying to keep up with Ma, I began to think that far as we had to walk there were places more far than that, all them place I never see. Like where she came from, for so far I had never met my nana or nani, who were her pa and ma.

"Ma," I blurted, my bare feet scurrying to keep pace with hers, "where you live before you get big and come here?"

"Get big what? I born and grow in Couva, beta, but I was a child myself when I come here."

She grew quiet then, and I was much older before I got further into her thoughts.

Her name was Samdai and although she could not say what year she married my father, I later worked out that it must have been 1924, and she was not yet fourteen. "And before I have fifteen year I done make child," I heard her say years later, "and the child born and dead."

Before that, when Pa's people came to ask for her she was outside with some other girls playing pat-pat. She heard them calling, "Samdai, Samdai," just as the young goat her father had given her jumped about and shook his tail so fast she laughed out, right by the door. People she didn't know were sitting there with her parents and her father's brother whom they called Roop. "I used to fraid this Roop, for he was the biggest uncle and he bring up my pa and them when they own father dead. So when I laugh out and they send for me I get so frighten I partly couldn't breathe."

She couldn't watch them. She had to keep her eyes on the floor not to shame her pa (much less Roop), and after they all looked at her a little they sent her back outside. So, she never knew what this thing was about. Later her Ma said that if the boy was now getting a work on the cocoa estate, Samdai too would have to do hardwok and live in barracks, and it sound like was some bound yard. But her father said Samdai was getting big, and Roop and he decide to settle she one time. "Then Ma start to say how no girlchild of hers suppose to live in any bound yard, but Pa call one lash cross her mouth so I couldn't ask nothing unless I want lash too."

Time passed though, and Samdai forgot the visit. Her mother kept her close and with all the work she hardly played outside anymore, except to run round with the goat before putting him up. Then one evening her father told her to stop playing up with the goat. "That goat have to kill soon, because you going to married."

When they said she musn't cry about getting married because Jai was a hardworking boy and would mind she good, she said, "Is not that I studying

– is the goat." And it was true, Ma admitted later. The goat concerned her a lot more than this vague idea of marriage.

"But you is a chupid child" – her father laughed at her – "that is what goat *make* for!"

So she married and left Couva, coming almost across the island to the cocoa estate when she was a child herself. Thank God, she always said, that her mother-in-law turned out to be a good lady. She had not known what to expect. Mother-in-law does beat you if you don't wok good, other girls had told her. "And afuss I frighten for licks," she said, shaking her head at her own foolishness.

The day came as a complete surprise. She had been to weddings in the village so she had vaguely expected her pa and his pardners would one day start cutting bamboo and setting up a marava. "I say I must know when tent putting up for me self to married." Her mother would put out kurma and sindoor and thing on a tray. She never stopped to think where her ma would get these things, let alone a tray. Long after, when I heard Ma talking to other women, she said she remembered when Indrani did marrieding and how the girl cried and said, "But I don't know what it is I must do." Then the big women had said, "You go see soon enough," and they laughed behind their hands and whispered about matikore. Running behind her mother every day she kept an eye out to see sohari leaf cut and brought in to wash, for at weddings that is what they would put the food on to eat.

Now that I have been to so many weddings, I suppose she must have dreamed of tassa going in front of her to the well and the wild dancing of the older women, but whatever drums beat in her heart, nothing like that was going on, no saffron on her skin or mendi on her hands and feet, not the thud of the knife cutting through mango and pumpkin to the board, or the smell of rice parching for the lawa. None of it happened. Only one morning her ma made her put on her good dress, and out on the road her pa's big brother, Roop, called out, "Barat." So her father went out to greet the boy.

That was when the whole village should have been singing to him and she should come out in a yellow sari like the girl she knew in the next village, and the boy should be in kurta and dhoti. Perhaps he was. But she couldn't raise her face to see what this boy had on or even how he looked, this boy from so far away they hadn't even had the brief meeting she heard parents arranged, and she kept her eyes on the floor. The pundit said prayers but there was no music, only the food her mother had cooked. Even after the pundit left and they brought out the goat meat she couldn't swallow it – although it was only Roop and his madam who normally refused to eat meat.

Her pa's face got serious and the people who had come with the boy were leading her away. "Ma? Stop," she whispered. "Ma, you not coming? Come nah, Ma?" But her mother had fainted away and her sister was fanning anxiously, saying, "Never mind." Samdai's pa kissed her and shook his head. "Hush, child. You is Madam Jai now." Even he began to cry. And the boy, Jai, stayed quiet as if he didn't know what to say.

So then she found herself on the bull cart bumping down the cane road away from everyone she knew, till the cane fields fell behind and the land changed. The stoney track led onto a road with bush on both sides. Bush all day, and it was still far to go, past Biche, they said, outside a settlement they called Impasse. They must have stopped and eaten, perhaps even slept, but when she looked back all she could remember was shivering with dread. "For this road keep going deep into the bush, and was not like Couva, like the estate. Was tree and more tree."

Forest like it going on forever and, and all overhead the tree close over them so evening barely come on but was dark and the branch reach down like they go strangle who on the track, so she shut up she two eye tight. "Then a thing happen I coulda never forget. Far above we, something start bawling, yelling." And another call came from someplace else, echoing, howling all around, and a boy helping to drive the cart said, "Rain go come." He saw her shuddering and he said, "Is just monkey, gyul, howler monkey." And still the boy they had married her to stayed quiet, quiet.

When the noise passed there was only the crunch of small stones and dry branches under the wheel of the lurching bull cart, and the thump of the hog cattle hooves. Then rain. *One* rain. Water trickled down from her head so she squeezed her eyes tighter still and held the side of the cart, telling herself they had turned back and her ma was waiting for her at their own door. Till she heard them say, "Watch, gyul, we reach," and she opened her eyes.

Standing in the doorway, a tall, dark, slim lady with a long face held up both hands, and when they lifted Samdai down from the cart, trembling too much to stand, the tall lady came out in the rain and wrapped her arms round her. "Yes, Dulahin," she said. "Come, child. Come in out the wet."

There was a girl too, a few years older than herself, and a big man behind them, blocking out the dim light of the house. He was older than the boy she was married to, but still young. "This is you, Barka," her mother-in-law said.

"He name Chaitlal." Late in life when she was slipping in and out of consciousness Ma let drop something she would never knowingly have said to anyone. "I find the boy big brother, this man, Chaitlal, did watching me like he buying a fowl."

The girl beside him was not Ma's barki but the boys' sister, named Geeta. Geeta's husband was the one who had first gone to Couva to ask about Samdai. He worked on a truck and knew people all over the country so he had said he would get a girl for his wife's brother and he arranged, with Roop to begin with, to marry Samdai to Jai. But before he could get to see them married, Geeta's husband drowned at Mayaro.

Geeta said their youngest brother, Ravi, who had helped with the bull cart, did not live with them, because the man he worked for (who owned the bull cart) lived far away. It was the big brother, Chaitlal, who lived with them – only his madam had taken her son and gone back to her own family in Piparo, and *her* father said if Chaitlal only crossed his door again he would kill him with his own hands.

Geeta's mother threw her a stern look before turning back to Samdai. "So I too glad you come, Dulahin," she said, stroking the girl's face and bringing talk of Chaitlal's madam to a close by sending Geeta for hot tea in a tinnen cup. But later Samdai's mother-in-law told her how Chaitlal child di' so nice and, when Chaitlal and Dhanmattie live with her, she self would mind this little baby. They named the child Chaitlal too, for the father, but when Dhanmattie took the baby and went to Piparo, her father made her change the child's name altogether even though the pundit warned them against that. But Dhanmattie's father said the child go be more curse if he keep the name Chaitlal, so they called him Haresh. One little grandchild in the place and the girl di' take he and run away, her mother-in-law said. Was a good thing Samdai come now to bring more child in the place.

But Samdai's first baby died right away. "And too besides it was a boy child. Rajendra we was going to name the child, and he dead." But Geeta's ma said, "Hush, beti. You soon make another child."

To Samdai, who was to become my ma, everything on this side looked strange at first. In Couva the cane field spread bright and open. Even between the cane rows was hot and noisy – mill working, cart loading, driver shouting. Here was quiet. Soon she and the boy moved onto the estate, to a room in the barracks, not far from his mother and Geeta. It was a good walk on the Biche road, but she was always glad to go and see them.

"Time pass, land clear and more cocoa plant, and what plant before we married start to flowers and the next year it bear fruit, but no more baby come. That time, a girl that live near Biche and used to like this boy I marry to, this girl start to talk and say, Jai Deoraj look for that – how he leave good good girl in he own village to marry a bahila. Well, I cry too bad when I get to hear someone calling me cow that can't make no young." Some things Ma told me or I overheard years later; some slipped out towards the end when she grew confused. "Chaitlal laugh sly sly and whisper to me, say he know that not true, but is because they send a boy to do a man wok. But he never say dem ting in front he brother."

It was Geeta who suggested they consult the missionary, and although Ma talked little and the Reverend was a white man, it turned out to be easy because he often came to the estate to speak to the workers. The Reverend's voice was kind but serious. "You see how that child died and no more came?" She needed to marry properly, he said. There was a house where he held church on Sundays, not so far away. "So we go and married again, Christian," Ma told me.

Her mother-in-law, Kamaldaye, who was like her own ma now, drew out cloth she had bought for herself and made it up in a dress for Samdai so she and Jai could be married all over again. "And in truth the year ent pass before this boy born." Ma added that, right away, her mother-in-law said she did always feel this thing they call *Christian* have something in it, and she get baptize one time.

Only, when the Reverend saw the child's birth paper and read out the name, he asked, "*Gahadar?* What is that?"

They smiled at how he sounded out the name. "Gajadar, Reveren'," they said.

So it was spelt wrong, he replied, but even so, why – after all that had happened – were they still keeping those heathen names? They must give the boy a name from the Bible. "He's the first in a whole tribe," the Reverend said, and he laughed. "Call the boy Israel." He even insisted the young parents take new names, like John and Elizabeth instead of Jai and Samdai. Ma liked the name Lizbet, "but this child father did never comfortable to name anything but Jai."

Next thing, when the father took the child to be baptized, there was a creole fellow with his dougla child and, somehow, the two names got mixed up. "The creole mister gone home with he child name Israel while we child come back name Oswal. I so vex I never know what to do, and you aji di' roasting damadhol on the chulha and she stop just so." Chaitlal said this fool boy, Jai, couldn't get nothing right – not even his son's name, for look how he name him *Gadaha* to begin with (and you know that mean jackass) and now he end up get him baptize with a creole name.

There was no time to go back now to change anything because soon they would have to set off for the estate. But Ma Kamaldaye said they would fix the thing right there, for the Reverend had said to get a name from the Bible and she remembered one she heard in church the last Sunday. That was how they decided on Nathan. Chaital said he had never heard a name like that, but the child's father said if it was from the Bible it must good. Then his ma announced that it had damadhol ke choka ready with hot roti. "And we well eat before we leave and go back to the estate. And no time pass before we forget this child ever have any other name but Nathan."

Even then Ma must have looked like a child herself, for when Papa Jacques, who owned the cocoa estate, saw her walking on the track with me on her shoulder he shook his head and said, "Baby making baby."

"Nathan?" people asked. "Eh? What kinda name that?" But she paid them no mind.

"And this child – from he small he ask all kinda thing," Ma said later. "And the more I tell he the more he want to know. He want to know about my pa. He want to know why Roop bring up my pa, and where dem father was why he never bring up he own child, what happen to them father. Dead? How he dead? I had to search me head to find answer to them thing."

Ma's father and big brother had said their father, Rajput, was born in the old country, and came to Trinidad and died this way: Rajput worked in Vista Beya, a place creole people called Border Town, and it would have been sometime around 1902 that he got a job to dig manjack from deep in the ground. So Ma's grandfather and the other men climbed in and out on a ladder, and under the ground was a tunnel. This tunnel was dark and they used a lamp to find their way.

But it happened one day, Roop had told them, that men near the top heard a noise and other workers bawling "Fire," and those were able to get out, but the men down the tunnel got burned or fainted from the gas, so only one or two could be pulled free. They said it was like a wind drove through. But anyway Rajput died in the mine and the only big child was Roop, who was eighteen. Roop said the company offered to pay for a box and a hole to bury his father, but when Roop insisted he had to burn him, they just gave him twelve dollars to take care of things. So Roop made his mother and the children move to Couva and they took work on the sugar estate.

But what made Rajput come to Trinidad to start with? I had to ask several times before Ma found the time to answer, and after that I would beg for her to tell me again and again.

According to Roop, Rajput had grown up in the old country with his adopted father who was a halwai: he made sweets. Rajput learned the work from his father, and in the 1880s they had a good business and were comfortably off. How he really landed up in Trinidad was this. One day he was just married and sitting with his madam reading to her from some book of verse that his mother or someone was supposed to have composed. "Some book with a poetry, nah. Well, then a white man come up and talk to him and say how he is captain of a ship right over there, and all the place he go and all what he see." Then, Roop had said, the man offered his father the chance to look around on the ship and Rajput agreed. And the captain said to let the lady wait for him on shore while he took a look.

But while Rajput walked about on the ship he began to feel dizzy and when he looked at the shore it was moving away and his wife was there with her hands stretched out to him and her mouth opened wide in a cry he was already too far away to hear, and from that time he never heard anything about her again. "So Rajput come Trinidad with nothing in his hand but a poetry he di' reading, and land up here only to meet hardwork and to dead in the mine. Then he big son do what he can for he small brother that was my pa," Ma said. "And is so I grow up fraid this Roop too bad."

I think now it must have been about 1933, when I was only five, that Ma's story started gathering in my head, not through any one fluent telling but in scattered droplets, sometimes a perfunctory answer to my questions, sometimes overheard in some soft exchange with my phuwa, Pa's sister, whose name was Geeta. But that was later, when we saw more of her. Besides, Phuwa was the one who talked most, especially when she and Ma huddled together, their hands cupped over their lips, shielding laughter. Even decades later details new to me occasionally seeped from a past that was misty even to Ma. It condensed and trickled together over the years and collected in my mind, and I cannot tell whether the shape it takes now is its own form or just the form her understanding accommodated. Or perhaps it is merely how it seemed to me that it seemed to her.

But even as a small boy I was overwhelmed by how much Ma had seen, how far she had travelled even before I was born, and I made certain in my mind that I would travel too, and farther, to places she had never heard of. Sometimes I pestered her with questions, tugging at her skirt till she slapped me, for she needed her breath for the work. Now I know she must have been constantly managing several streams of thought at once, but despite all that went through her head she hardly talked – except to me. I alone knew when the message came to her that her pa and ma, my nana and nani whom I had rarely seen, had set out to go back to India. Later she expanded on it.

Her pa and his older brother, Roop, had decided: their children were married and would stay with their families while the brothers went back to India. Their own father, Rajput, had never intended to be here anyway: Aja just get ketch, Ma reasoned; and she was right if, as they insisted, the captain had simply caught and stolen him away. "And Pa say India did always call 'pon Roop," because her big uncle was a strict Hindu, "for look – he never eat meat like us and he did have a kutiya by he door and all." Not like her pa, she said, though she remembered my nani, her mother, gathering flowers to place on the little shrine a few steps from their own house, white flowers with yellow centres strewn before the murti. But there would be bigger mandirs and grander murtis in India.

At any rate, Ma told me that her pa and ma, and this big uncle and he madam, sell they two piece of land and the animal and thing, and they buy four ticket, and the big brother gone in front with he madam onto the boat. Only Nana and Nani didn't get to board because, they were told, no one else could hold on the ship. Like the company oversell ticket and so, nah. They never expect everybody who buy to turn up. You ever hear anything so? Ma pondered it. "I mean, what is *that*?"

So, she said, her pa and ma had to turn back and get refund for the two ticket, but then they had to find another place to live and with all what go on they would never get up the money to buy two ticket again. "The one who get to go on the ship never expect to separate from he small brother now as he getting old," Ma told me months later when the next message came. "He must be never know what happening. The letter that come tell them he di' looking for he brother all over the boat. And this boat well leave land before he understand what take place. And they say he take it on. Anyway, I now find out Pa say he get to hear how Roop dead."

Ma wiped an unaccustomed tear hurriedly, then passed her hand roughly through my hair. "Best you don't tell you pa nothing about nobody going back India, you hear, beta?" There was a strong note of warning in her voice. "Because he never believe in that. He feel it have wok here. Is to keep you tail here and work and mind you chirren."

Work. Work was what we understood, the frame that supported us so our lives inched up from the ground. Work was what the sun rose for, what we woke to, breathed in, slept from. To work was to exist, to buy oil and flour, to cling to a vague sense that others yet to come might also survive.

Others.

We lived in the barracks and, at first, stories were all I heard about my own aji (Pa's mother) and phuwa (Pa's sister, Geeta). I couldn't remember them at first because, a few months after I was born, Aji had left her own house in the small settlement called Impasse not too far along the Biche road, and had gone instead to live with Phuwa, who was moving back to the house in Sanchez Village where she and her husband had spent the brief years of their marriage before he died. It had been only a few years after my parents moved to the estate that Aji began to find it impossible to live with her oldest son. I remember hearing talk about Pa's big brother, my dada. "That Chaitlal not easy," Ma confirmed under her breath.

Aji would never turn her own son out of her house so she had left "for now," as she said, just to help Phuwa set up on her own in the place that had been her husband's and that had been locked up too long for Phuwa to clean by herself. Sanchez being fifteen miles from the estate, I did not know them in my first years.

All I knew of the world was our room on the Dessalines Estate, one in a long row in the clearing. I had measured the ten feet of the room with my steps as Pa had taught me when I asked him how people knew where their land ended and someone else's began. At every three steps I allocated space for one of us. Then I stood still, halted by an understanding: that must be why the baby before me had died. There was nowhere to put Rajendra, so God had taken him back. I tried to follow the idea further – and what had God sent the baby for in the first place? Unless people were meant to have more space. It was barely a thought, more a formless glimmer on the edge of my mind that faded before it could occur to me that the people in the next room had six children. I only thought of that later when I heard Pa say that was bhaat alone them people did cook and sometimes they fried up what was left over with onion, but most time they didn't have no onion and they partly never have anything leave over. "Is that why you have to plant ting for yourself," Pa said. "Otherwise, how you go mind you child?" But our world was not built to accommodate prolonged reflection.

Who built it? I was not sure. Inside my head I seemed to have a little box that did not snap shut. Questions and half-formed thoughts popped up and spilled out. I accepted unquestioningly that it was God, but I groped for some tool I could see, or someone He used, a manager or . . . or something, I reasoned. Papa Jacques? He owned the cocoa estate. The morning led up to Papa Jacques's arrival and once he had gone nothing momentous was expected but his next coming. And his eyes. They were grey-blue like the sky in between rain and dry season, different to any other eyes I had ever seen. I noted how the men arranged their lives to his schedule, bent and accepted the lash if they failed to meet his appointed times, and even Pa, who feared nothing on earth, showed some awe of Papa Jacques, for the work was ordained by him.

I wondered where Papa Jacques had come from, and whether all the people from there had eyes like his. Wherever it was, that was another place I would travel to one day – and I would have to go by boat, I supposed.

But all that water, with all those big, big fish.

# CHAPTER 2

# CHANTEY

*Codfish girls they have no combs*
*Heave away, heave away!*
*They comb their hair with codfish bones . . .*

## Nathan

THIS IS WHERE I MAY COME to the story of Jacques, if I ever get it straightened out, and only because I must have been about six when I began to wonder about one of his descendants, Papa Jacques, who owned the Dessalines Estate. It was much later, when I was a grown man, that Papa Jacques himself sent for me and turned over to me the old journal that had been rotting away in his family for generations, and he asked me if I could get someone I knew, a history professor at the university, to have a look at it. It was scraps of French and English from another time and damaged by water, time and neglect, so all that could be gathered were fragments of a boy's disorganized record, but it prompted me to read a little background history. By the time I put together what I could, Papa Jacques had passed on and no one else cared. Perhaps this would be the place for it.

Jacques's life was tied in, entangled even, with codfish, and to understand what became of Jacques one has to understand a few basic things about the cod – because you could almost say it reeled him in.

So. The cod. It seems a good-sized fish might live twenty-five years left to itself, browsing for herring and shrimp, and spawning million after million of eggs. But it was too succulent for its own good, sixty, even a hundred and sixty flaky pounds of it, especially dead and salted. So you see where I'm going: it dried well; it could be stored. That was treasure of a kind in the 1760s and, as my historian friend likes to say, anything perceived as treasure can reshape history.

Cured fish. Unknown to Jacques, who, I imagine, would have been little versed in history anyway, the cod had sustained the Vikings on their raids, inspired improved fishing boats, and supplied protein Friday after Friday to any number of Catholics inland. Fish on the table, any distance from shore, all year round. This thing had a market. Correct? Hunger, yes, but also profit, adventure, religious observance. Ostentation, for don't forget the need to demonstrate piety. Then, there seemed to be a growing greed for luxuries from across the sea, and from the sea itself. The sea is an ordinary thing for us, but over there, back then, it offered an escape from home for daring boys, and men with something to run away from or nothing behind them in the first place. It was a way to another world made of rumour and fantasy where anything might happen or be said to have happened. The call of the sea was exotic, as if one could swallow up the great wide world in one's own body.

The cod trade. Nothing could have stopped it – not the Black Death centuries before, nor wars in Europe since then, nor power lust that exploded in political crises. In truth, the trade made competition fiercer. My same friend, the historian, insists that the British appropriated the cod just as they claimed Asian tea and the African lion as English. (He seemed quite annoyed about it.) Anyway, William Pitt argued in Parliament that the cod was British gold, there at the centre of trade between New England and the Caribbean, as contraband in French business arrangements and currency for American settlers dreaming of rum to be drawn out of molasses from the French Caribbean. The main point is that the cod intersected with other markets, and with trade in other types of flesh. And this is how we get back to Jacques.

The flesh trade was almost a family tradition in Jacques's past, but his family seems always, with a sort of stubborn carelessness, to have been on the wrong side of it. Everything is out of order in the journal and there is a note near the end that in Ireland, a century before, the boy's great-grandmother had been spirited, as they called it, and her people who had heard rumour of how such things worked had hoped for her return in seven years. But she stayed gone, although perhaps she may have broken away because my friend traced a notice in the *Pennsylvania Gazette*:

> Run away on Thursday last from Johan Teegs a lusty Irish servantmaid named Kiara past her first youth but still firm bodied only pock-fretten. Speaks good English well-cloath'd. Had on red quilted calico petticoat and striped apron, good pair shoes stolen and blue silk handkerchief stolen. Whoever secures the said servant so that her master can have use of her again shall have 30 shillings.

There is no other record of her.

Elsewhere, though, Jacques records the story of Kiara's daughter, too small for a father to mind and, so, left at the convent door. But she would not stay indoors with the nuns and was always running to the seaside to look for her mam so she was snatched too and the nuns heard nothing more of her for years. It turns out that on board she ate dry biscuit and salt meat and water, and a castrate watched over her to keep her safe. When they approached shore, before the sale on shipboard, she could see Barbados and said it was beautiful like Tir na nOg, or like Eden. Like Eden, it changed hue. She was bought, three years later traded for a pig, two years after that gambled away. As the end of her time approached she grew less valuable, more ill-treated and more determined to get back to Ireland. That was when she wrote a barely readable letter to the convent, recounting it all and begging to return – but there was no further news of her either.

Her da did contrive to keep her brother with him and this boy built a good life and kept his own children safe. One of his girls married a Frenchman, a good Catholic like herself, and their son, Jacques, could read and write, pray in Latin, do sums and play the accordion. From what Jacques said of himself in the journal, it was a well-connected family in a major salt-producing area of France and the boy seemed destined to do well.

But the little fool ran away to sea.

It seems that an eighty-ton vessel with two masts, and no chaplain or surgeon (apart from the able seaman who knew how to perform a bleeding) required a ship's boy. Jacques and his accordion set sail with them early one March in the 1760s and drove west for a month till the water changed colour. He said the temperature dropped and strange birds he had never seen before flocked overhead. The ship lowered its sounding lead, furled sail and drifted mildly with the wind on the port beam. The men secured themselves in the wide-based barrels for stability, covered up in tarred cloths, greased aprons and leather mitts to haul the lines. After cutting out the cods' tongues to keep track of numbers, they would slip the fish along the conduit to the header, the splitter and, then, the nautier. This was Jacques, the boy who detached the air bladder for separate salting before the cod went to the hold. It was not the life he had expected but he learned fast and became popular by accompanying the men chanting their work songs.

At some point (there is no indication when) he changed ships. He wrote down some new songs he had learned, but many were the same. He drank in the tales of storms, of hailings on the route to Marseille by Barbary pirates, of overcrowding and violence on the saques that bore the seamen back to port when their own boats were too laden with fish to carry all hands, of all the chants, jokes and stories through which he gradually came to take in the vast triangular system of workers, fish and freight in which he had enmeshed himself. A year later he somehow drifted from one system to the next, finding himself at last in a British seaport, still little more than a boy, barely sixteen but with three years' experience. Of course, he does not describe himself – except once. Contrasting himself to another man for whom he was mistaken, he says his own eyes were grey, and on a later page he says blue. He talks about handling the ropes even while they tore his flesh until he became accustomed. I imagine him as skin, bone and sinew, with eyes grey-blue like rough water and hands hard as stone.

What is certain, though he does not seem to have known it at the time, is that the more competent he became the more valuable a commodity he turned into, and that proved to be his undoing one evening outside a seaside tavern.

Jacques was, after all, not such a fool. In fact, I suspect he was an intelligent chap of whom a good teacher might have made something, given a chance. He drank only at places where the landlord served in glass-bottomed tankards so a customer could see whether a king's shilling had been slipped into the drink so as to press him into service. He wrote that he kept a keen eye on strangers and avoided places where officers stalked recruits. Yet it came to him on the street, a cudgel swung at his head – an impact, he says, and darkness. By then the press was essential to the navy that enabled Britannia to rule the waves, and Jacques writes how he learned to accompany *that* song on his accordion as lustily as the rest.

What the press sought were experienced seamen, and if they could not be made to accept the shilling, the officers found other ways. A patrol could set out, not with guns or cutlasses that would maim but with good stout clubs. Jacques writes that he came to on the press smack, restrained by iron grates and bolts like the other men, lying in filth with rats running over and between them. From shore came the sound of women wailing, but he knew it was not for him because only his mother, a world away in Le Croisic, would have clung to the belief he was alive somewhere.

Elsewhere, I read that closer by, in England, Samuel Johnson described tenders like that smack Jacques occupied as "prisons with the chance of being drowned". The chance of being blown to bits was added when they transferred him to his ship in the navy, because the journal contains a sketch of the hull during broadside firing, a tight smoke-filled space between decks. Here he could make out nothing, and a wrong move in the dark might end in being blown to death or having an arm or leg torn off. Jacques dodged enemy fire, exploding ammunition and recoiling guns, and when the boatswain rapped him with his cane the boy was just thankful to avoid a real beating let alone stranger punishments like death by rolling. The Quaker had been sentenced to be *roll'd*, Jacques wrote, shut in a cask with nails pointed inwards and rolled to death, but at the last minute he was unaccountably spared. Rumour even had it he was discharged, and that was a relief to Jacques because of some way in which the Quaker had once been decent to him. In fact, just when the man thought he was going to the barrel he had emptied his pockets in the boy's hands. The the man was released, then gone.

But that was how a pocket diary passed from the Quaker into the boy's possession, and now and then Jacques added to it and tied on other notes of his own, bits and pieces about life between shores, a record of flotsam. One note was that he had seen a black man, all black from head to toe just like the schoolbooks said, only he was not from Africa but some other place where sugar grew on trees. A good strong cover that had come loose from a ship's log turned up and Jacques used it to keep together what was turning into a disjointed journal.

After the jotting about the black man who was not from Africa, Jacques noted that he remembered when he was a child and Mamam had stirred sugar in his cup of chocolate and she said it was all from the same place, the sugar and the chocolate, a faraway island. He had sipped it and closed his eyes and thought, *One day, I'll sail away and have that whole island for myself.*

And look where that had got him.

*Codfish boys they have no sleds*
*Heave away, heave away!*
*They slide along on codfish heads . . .*

CHAPTER 3

# CONTRAC

Between the undersigned . . ., and the natives whose names are hereunto affixed, the following agreement has been entered into by the several parties binding themselves to the observance of the conditions thereof:

The natives agree to proceed to the Island of Trinidad, to work as labourers there, upon a cocoa estate, the property of Ronald de Jacques, and to remain there, if required, for the time of five years. . . . The passage of the natives to the West Indies shall be paid by Ronald de Jacques who shall also provide a passage again to this country. . . . In addition to the pay as above fixed, food and clothing shall be supplied to each as follows – Fourteen chettacks of rice, two ditto of dholl, two ounces of salt, and some oil and tamarind, daily; and annually for each, clothing as follows; two dhooties, two blankets, one jacket, and one cap. . . .

## Nathan

Papa Jacques's name was really Jean de Jacques, but they called him Papa and from the time I was five years old I had wanted to know why. It seemed no one could tell me, although Pa usually tried to answer my questions once we had eaten and he had had time to himself. On a special evening it would be roti with saltfish and tomatoes, and sweet sweet chocolate tea that only Ma could make. In deep thought I ran the forefinger of my left hand round the inside of the tinnen cup to scoop out the residue of sugar, keeping an eye on

Ma, because in those days she was still trying to encourage me to use my right hand although she never gave in to neighbours who advised tying the left behind my back. At the same time, I concentrated on the problem. Now I was six, I was certain that behind the awe accorded to Papa Jacques there must be a story.

It seemed to me that every living thing on the estate listened for his step. Everyone knew a part of his history too, but in different versions. Mr Manny who ran the rumshop in Mission, a village south of the estate, pieced some of the tales together and told Pa much later, when I was big enough to wait for Pa outside the rumshop, straining to overhear their talk. Sometimes the men sat on a bench outside and the proprietor leaned in the doorway. One evening, Mr Manny stood there under the sign that said LICENSED TO SELL INTOXI-CATED LIQUORS, and he told Pa and his pardners the story as he knew it.

"They say some big navy officer name Jacques, or de Jacques, di' sell out and gone into business in Canada. Years later he sell that business – was some fisheries or something – and move through Louisiana and down to Haiti, getting richer and richer along the way. So he have this big property in Haiti but when trouble break out over there he pack up he family and he slave and jewel and everything, come over to Trinidad. And the government stay just so and give him a set of land even though some Spanish people say was theirs. Anyway, de Jacques come in with he people on the track that cut in north from the main road.

"Was Lezama the Spanish people name, not them Lezama round here, unless these is some pumpkin vine family. I mean white Lezama. Real Lezama. So they wouldn't let it go just so. Was a big case, but in time old Lezama lose the case and he take to drink, crying that people seize he property unlawful, and after a while he disappear somewhere. After that, people call the place Anlévé, even though the new owner name it Dessalines that he say was he family old name. And the old rough road that wind in from the north on the east side of the estate through bush and stone – that never call anything but Tiefin Trace.

"Meantime, the son and them in the French family keep adding thing to they name. Longtime they used to call themselves de Jacques and say they from Salines, then they claim it had some Jacques Dessalines was a hero and must be they family, until they find out more about he. So the estate remain Dessalines but they keep the Jacques as they family name. The longer it get the more important they show they is, man. Must be was the grandfather did stick in what they call the particule – so they like to call it – and they refuse to sound they whole name. The end, nah. If you ever call old Raymond's name with a "d" he woulda curse you in the worst way. And you better make sure you don't make it sound like *Raman*, because that is Indian now, that is a next thing, a heathen thing, he woulda say."

I believe now, putting together Mr Manny's account with bits I overheard from my own aji, that it was old Raymond who put up this thing Aji called a *coataraam* on the gate. This I eventually discovered was a coat of arms, and they called in my aji, who was the nearest thing to seamstress in the area, to sew it on handkerchiefs, table sheets and other things. After a time, however, they started to send the cloth to Port of Spain to get it done and she lost that work. Afuss she vex, according to Ma. Anyway this coat of arms was a shield with a dark blue background, under a helmet with plumes, and light blue running across it in waves. "With one green or grey colour fish in the middle," Aji said, for she used to be sewing it all the time. It also had other things on it people never understood. Mr Manny said that when they asked old Raymond de Jacques, *he* said the other patterns showed the arms of a Chevalier. So they asked what that meant and he said his grandfather was an important officer in the regiment of Monsieur – which took no one any further, and Pa would steups because that was long after we had left the estate. He no longer felt quite the same awe for Papa Jacques.

Certainly there were other people called de Jacques and some were related and some were not. Papa Jacques liked to say his own great-uncle was Father Claude de Jacques, a Dominican priest who drew East Indians, especially Madrasees from other parts of Trinidad into the Roman Catholic Church. All over the place he went, riding a donkey, gathering children into school and making them sing hymns in patois, Hindi or Tamil, this tall white man on a little donkey. When people asked him why he didn't ride a horse, a big man like him, he said a donkey was good enough for Our Lord and would do for him.

Some of that explained a question I had asked Pa: "Why it have Indian that not Hindu and not Presbyterian?"

But he would only say, *"Zafè kabwit nè pa zafè mouton."*

"What that mean, Pa?" I insisted, for I did not know patois.

"It mean sheep business not goat business, so mind you own business."

As far as Pa was concerned in those days, his business and therefore mine was work on the de Jacques cocoa estate, Dessalines, and it might have been so for me forever, because nothing was built into our lives to prompt change. Even Papa Jacques's footsteps never changed. On gravel, wooden flooring or loose dry leaves, the uneven scrunch of his brisk limp ground painful but determined. Ahead of him a way parted between the men, who approached him only through the overseer. Yet, curiously, we loved him, for he gave us everything we had – work for shelter from rain, snakes and centipedes, work for hot fragrant roti. Papa Jacques provided work, and work was life.

With a nod at a labourer or a benevolent wave at children hurrying by with feed or manure, he turned away, back to his other life that set him apart as intrinsically superior to us, yet spread in full view of ours. His big airy house on Morne Esperance stood at the end of the steep drive lined with royal palms, overlooking the estate. Sometimes the Magistrate took lunch with him, and people said yes, that was as it should be. Together Jean de Jacques and Magistrate Marchand arranged things as they alone knew best. If Mr Manny was to be believed, cases were tried and decided over their after-lunch drinks.

One morning, my pa limped in late for work. The lull fell in expectation of a whipping. There was no malice in the buzz of interest, for my father was popular among the men; it was only how things were. But then he did a thing that changed our lives forever. He walked straight up to Papa Jacques, shrugging aside the driver, and pulled up the leg of his pants to show the swelling. Is chinnee sting him, he explained, the little furry black son of a bitch curl up so small he never see it, how black and hard he flesh get and how it blaze all night so he fall asleep only in the morning and is that how he miss the time, and Papa Jacques can whip he because is his right, only Papa have to see for heself that is not that Jai Deoraj don't take he work serious. But this chinnee is a hell of a thing, man.

And the morning held its breath, the workers frozen in awe that he approached Papa Jacques directly, and the driver tensed, incredulous, then smouldering.

"You've come to me like a man, John," Papa pronounced. "Don't they call you John?"

"Jai, Papa."

"No, no, man. You have a good Christian name. John is a good name, the best there is." The men chuckled obediently. Jean de Jacques was pleased. Now, he said, we would all see that he was approachable, that he was a fair man: Pa was allowed to go straight to work. That was the beginning of many things: Pa's status among the men, his godlike heroism in my own eyes, and the driver's lust for his blood.

The driver was a tall, lean, hungry-looking man selected by the overseer from the ranks of the workers, and he had no one to laugh with, but gave only a wry smirk when the whip sliced down, so he guarded his power with savage jealousy. Pa had pushed past him to Papa Jacques, so the man waited, coiled into himself. Weeks passed and still he waited, watching Pa with his sidelong unblinking stare. "Like some damn mapepire," Pa said later. "I know he hold me in mind for that."

When the Reverend dropped in, his visit wiped the venomous driver from our minds. The young missionary had just arrived to replace the white-haired one recently returned to Canada. "I see your boy started Sunday School last week," Reverend Innis began. "Good. His teacher says he's bright. He should be in school too, during the week."

Pa shifted uneasily and Ma, startled in the midst of cutting up long mango for amchar, drew a deep breath and held it. The Reverend's eyes shifted to her.

"What do you say, Madam John? I want your boy in school."

She looked directly at his face, then dropped her gaze again. "Reveren, I would like that too bad."

Pa stared. Ma so rarely spoke out that her answer stunned him.

"A wise mother." Reverend turned hurriedly back to Pa. "He'll get a better job and be a help to you when you get old." He leaned forward. "Don't keep the boy back to help you now, John. Send him to school."

"Reveren, every day I work is for my family."

"I know it, John. And the best thing you can do for this boy and for yourself is to school him."

So Pa agreed he would make the sacrifice, and in the next few days Ma sent me off in a group of other children from the estate to a house half a mile away where the missionary's wife held school.

But all this time the driver watched Pa. Every day, Pa said, all day.

The sun was blistering hot, not directly overhead any more but glaring as if the few hours left of work time would never pass, and the laden fig tree on the way called to mind that bunch they had put away under a jut of rock where it was dry and cool. "We forget bout them fig in truth," the men agreed when Pa reminded them. "When we done here we go meet up with that." But the fig was firm gold in Pa's hand, the fruit letting go the stem obediently and the skin peeling back easily to give up the plump mouthful, so much sweeter than regular bananas.

The story came back to us from others besides Pa. Then and there he had handed round the fig, and for a minute there was only the odd muted word or sigh of satisfaction or heckling comparison between the fig and other things. And work paused.

"Forty cent a day and like you could spare ten cent." The driver's eyes glittered, darting between the men and back to Pa.

"You haul you tail," Pa responded. "I does work every day, rain, shine, sick, well."

"I going check you though," the driver said, thrusting his face forward viciously. "You is such a big man, you is. You bitch, I checking ten cent." He flourished the rod and Pa grabbed it, wrenching it from his grasp and swiping it across the man's chest, his face and, as he cringed away, his back, shoulders and raised arms.

"I say, check some of this, and I give he five good rod," Pa said, repeating the tale excitedly next morning, a bit feverish as the blankness of the future loomed up while Ma gathered up the little we had in an appalled silence. We followed him hurriedly along the tortuous path people called Tiefin Trace, east from the estate, then south to join the main road.

But the afternoon before, something else had happened, insignificant perhaps to everyone else, but for me, momentous: I helped Pa send a letter. I had been home when Pa stormed in, catastrophe on his face along with fury that made him impossible to question. Yet he called me quietly, and I was not afraid, standing in front of him and memorizing the message for Teacher to write down. Someone would take that written message to Pa's mother, my aji, who would find another someone to read it to her.

I have no memory of going to the schoolhouse, but I can see myself now, running back to our room holding the paper with Teacher's writing, clutching tight so it could not blow away but trying not to crush it. Even now I relive the feel of it between my fingers, fragile and powerful, a thing of wonder, this paper carrying thoughts to far places and across time, words that had come out of my mouth, though Pa had put them there. Someone would read this aloud and Pa's family would know all that had happened. By night the message came back by word of mouth. "She say allyou must come."

So we left the barracks and took shelter with Pa's mother and sister, my aji and phuwa.

Aji was tall and lean, darker than Pa, and Phuwa shorter with round, soft arms. On evenings, sitting on the front step when we had eaten, Aji smoked her pipe while Ma shelled peas with her mantle of calm spread over us and Phuwa told the latest news of the village. And sometimes my dada, Pa's big brother whom they called Chaitlal, would be there too. From what he said he worked very hard, but Pa grumbled that Chaitlal got into one scrape after the next, shifting what responsibility he could to everyone else. Ma addressed him as Barka with what show of respect the situation forced from her. Then Pa steupsed and muttered, "Bahanaa," but he said it under his breath for his mother's sake, since she allowed no one but herself to comment on Dada's propensity towards trouble. Pa's own position was shaky and sometimes Dada would drop comments about a grown man like Pa not having a wok.

Ma set her mouth stubbornly, put her hand on my head, and said the child father force to leave the estate and she glad he never take work in the forest now it have so mucha people getting bite by poison bat. Phuwa nodded staunchly and no one questioned the connection between our circumstances and blood-sucking bats that carried rabies.

"But in my day," Aji pronounced, holding her pipe away from her lips temporarily, "they woulda kill you with licks." Pa was her favourite son – what with the youngest, Ravi, having lived far away in Moruga up to recently, and Chaitlal, her oldest, being incurably wayward – but Aji did not mince words. She had moved into her daughter's room to make space for us and Phuwa's house was not a long-term solution for us.

Pa was silent and short-tempered, and I was angry too, wanting to know how I would reach to school. "He feeling a how," Ma explained when Pa had snapped at me for asking about school over and over and Phuwa had protested softly on my behalf. "The man have no wok and no house of he own," she reminded Phuwa. Phuwa herself was not rich even though her husband had died leaving the shop, for how many of her neighbours were so well off as to buy much from her? Of course it was property. Ten or fifteen years before (no one could remember now) her husband had bought it from a Chinaman for three hundred dollars and a deer, and it barely kept her and Aji.

"So how all you go live now?" Dada demanded, though he seemed pleased in a way I could not define. My chacha (Pa's younger brother, Ravi) had arrived to talk it over with Pa and Dada, but he had nothing to suggest.

Chacha was a gentle jovial fellow who dressed with care and wore his hat at a rakish angle – not like Pa who flung on whatever was necessary to get out of the house and be about his business. Chacha always had sweets in his pocket, or a joke or riddle stored, sometimes for weeks. He had moved back from Moruga a couple months before and lived in Aji's house in Impasse with Dada. Pa's two brothers got along well, but Chacha's madam looked harassed and wretched. Phuwa did not think they would stay long in Impasse, for Chacha was not only jolly but kind and his wife too (my chachi) was a gentle, generous woman he would not want to see unhappy for any length of time.

"Why she don't like it there, Ma?" I had a feeling something was wrong with Aji's old house because it was nearer to the estate yet we had never gone there. I liked being with Aji and Phuwa well enough, but as usual I was on the track of a story. Why we come all this way if it had place there? I probed.

But Ma cut off my questions abruptly. "You Pa di have to come here" was all she would say. It could not be helped, Pa insisted, telling again the best parts of his tale. In my head I too told and re-told it, including bits Pa no longer mentioned but never putting these into words because they were no business of anyone but ourselves.

Ourselves? There was an ourselves that covered everyone in the house, and there was an ourselves that was just Pa and Ma and me. I learned the difference when they were deciding what to do about my hands. Aji worried about my using my left hand and Phuwa argued that if they didn't tie it back I might never learn to use the right, but Pa said, "Leave the boy hand."

"Once he use one hand good, that no nothing," Ma agreed. There was Pa and Ma and me.

Only now there were to be more of us, because that was when the next baby came – suddenly in the small hours of the morning, well before the expected time. Certainly I had had no idea, but everyone else seemed equally unprepared for Solomon, my brother.

And he died too. Unlike the baby who had come and gone before me, Solomon was not just a passing reference, a tale overheard, but an actual pale, wrinkled, tiny form swaddled in blue cloth, and my mother so exhausted she could only gasp *no, no.* Over and over for hours or days, *no, Oh Father, have mercy. No, man, no no nooo.* Like Rajendra, the first brother, Solomon was gone so quickly I was afraid I would forget he had ever been there. When Ma's cries died away out of my head (*nooo, no, noo*), I might forget. And I thought: if I could just put it down on a paper. It would keep him somehow without holding it in my head, the pale little clenched hands and tight lids that had never opened. And Ma's howling. And when the *noo, no nooo* tightened my throat and forced tears I could not account for except that Ma was crying and there was nothing I could do, I thought: if I could put it down on paper it might keep yet go away at the same time.

But I couldn't write. And why would Pa have paper? Pa was occupied morning till night with contractors who might give him one odd job after the next. In the evening, before bed, Pa would sit staring out along the trace that vanished into the surrounding night and he would mark out the day to come in his head. In the morning he sat in silence with a cup of coffee and worked out the days beyond that – all that must be done for us to eat and, one day, have a place of our own to live in.

Ma dragged herself out of her grief to hold my face between her hands and say quietly to me, almost in a whisper, "Come. You is my one child. Watch. It have another school not so far. I going try to make him send you. Ask your Phuwa if the shop have any book and if when time come she will trust you one. Don't bother you Pa with this at all at all."

"I want the same school," I grumbled.

"We ent going back." There was no questioning the finality in her voice. "We go find you a next school."

I wondered whether Papa Jacques even knew we were gone, and then I wondered again why they called him Papa. But I thought it best not to ask about any of that either.

"You see longtime?" Aji flourished a boney arm. "I tell you – this boy, Jai, woulda dead from licks. Watch the three of you now, with nowhere to go. When I did small like you, beta – I mean small-small – is so we almost lose my pa when he leave the place where he did working. Bharat, he name. He woulda be your pa nana if he did live."

It was all in Aji's head – like a hunter's mark on the trail, chipped into stone – all she had seen and overheard as a child. There were no dates for her to hold onto and she gestured time away with her dark thin fingers as she reached deeper into what she had heard of her own father and grandfather. In between puffs of tobacco she passed it on, etching it on my mind, the story of Pa's grandfather, Bharat. Aji drew up the memories of her father from the century before, when she was a little girl called Kamaldaye.

In those days if you had no work, even if you were trying to get it, once you wandered too far and you found yourself where no one knew you, they would pick you up. Bharat was walking in search of work when they held him for vagrancy (wandering about because he had smoked gunjah, they declared) and they brought him before the Magistrate. The neighbour ran to tell Bharat's madam that the Magistrate wanted to send him to the madhouse. "Savagery" was what the Magistrate had called it, watching the woman and children, including my aji, little Kamaldaye, huddled up in the doorway. "Gunjah making the lot of them mad. Gunjah at the root of all the coolie-wife murder happening all about."

When Bharat's wife and the children started to bawl, the officer drove them out for disturbing peace. So they bawled harder still, for if Bharat was going to the madhouse, how were they to live? Yet somehow the Magistrate let him go. No one knew why.

Aji remembered when her father got too sickly to work any more and sat around the house. That was when he told them how he came to Trinidad when he was young, with *his* father. Aji called her grandfather Baba, and said Bharat had come from India as a boy, with Baba. I think now it must have been in the 1870s. Aji could not say.

Her Baba was – she didn't know – like a police? "Some one of them," she said. "Nice nuniform with brass button and braid, but it don't pay good." So when Baba first spoke of going on the ship, his little son heard the old people laughing, calling Baba a stupid boy, for the government had banned that travel years ago. That was true, but when Baba inquired he found it had started again. He had no idea how to go about getting on the boat, but he knew first of all he had to reach Kolkata – a place so far from Uttar Pradesh that people only dreamed about it. When he asked the way to catch the boat, people cursed him and said if he wanted to leave he own country to dead in a strange land where nobody would know the prayers, then he deserve to dead so. And Bharat's mother – worse again. Woman don't business on ship, they tell Baba.

But nobody could change Baba's mind, so he set out for Kolkata with his child, Bharat, and the boy's mother. They had little to carry and Aji said, "They make sure to take the nuniform because they don't know what work he going to get in the new place. And too besides, is a nice clothes." In Kolkata, a man called the protector of emigrants asked whether they knew what it meant to pass over the sea and advised them to go home. "But it didn't have no home again," Aji said, "for Baba done sell partly everything to get where they was."

Among the few other scraps of memory was Bharat's recollection of a woman who was just bones, begging someone to buy her child for a rupee even while she was hugging and kissing the child and it was only bones like herself. Rich people passed on the street in fine saris and gold jewellery, but they didn't bother with Baba and his family. Waiting to board, Bharat heard music and there, outside, was a man holding something like a pipe to his mouth, with a monkey chained to his waist, and people going by threw money. "Bharat was a child, nah, so he go watch all like that," Aji said.

On board, after the land shrank from sight and there was only water, Bharat's mai started to rock back and forward and say, "Aaah, bhai. Aaah!" Bharat said he would stare at the sea, how it tilted up to one side, then the other, but Baba said, "Nah. Don't look on the water." In the evening, after the food, there was singing and drumming. "Is all like that he look to remember," Aji said. Three months on the sea, but Bharat had felt it would go on forever.

Bharat's mai had some trouble that Aji felt he was too young to understand. "From what he say, my mind tell me somebody on board did advantage she," she whispered to Ma. "And like she begin to suffer with she nerves and she get the sickness easy." When the sailors said they were nearing Africa even those who were accustomed to the boat huddled below, vomiting. The sea tilted high above them, dark and heavy, then the front of the boat rose over it till the boat plunged once more and you could see the sea ahead again high, black, boiling over. Bharat's mai weakened till she lay still with closed eyes, drawn down small, like a child. When she died they said what prayers they could but there were no flowers and no fire. Only water, water. They had to put her over in the sea. The water stretched out everywhere they turned, Bharat said. It met the sky. In front the boat tore it apart so the white spread away behind, and was lost again in black.

This place they came to was hot year round, not like the old place where the mountains reached up into snow, but Bharat had no one here with whom to remember that. Even on board many of them had never seen snow, but, however different their pasts, they landed as if they had all come from one place. "The ship, nah," Aji explained. When they left the ship and separated and went their different ways, Bharat had said, "Was like when we di' give Mai body to the sea."

In the barracks they shared a room with a man and woman with two children, and after a while Bharat's father met a woman he liked. But she had trouble with the Sadaar. I recall Aji breaking off and glancing my way, then taking a long drag at the pipe before resuming in a low voice. It was only the Sadaar you could complain to about certain things, but he was the trouble. Baba complained to the immigration agent who visited the estate and drank with the owner, but it was Baba who ended up in jail, and they added that time to his contract. After he had earned his passage home he accepted ten pounds to stay on, but he packed away the uniform in a trunk in case he went back in truth.

Meanwhile, Bharat grew up fighting, first other boys in the barracks, then men over their wives or daughters. In between he learned to play the bansuri and Aji could remember his fingers moving from one hole to the next in the bamboo. He would be different then. "Quiet, nah." But, while he lived in the barracks, he never stopped complaining, running away, and cursing when they flogged him. When his back was cut raw from the whip, they told him to rub saltkine on it to make it heal. "I remember like yesterday how Pa tell me that," Aji said. "I was small-small and I could never forget. I surprise they say he was so wild when I see how he get sick and weak. And even when he die I keep he father clothes good in the trunk. Is there, good still. And I take care of Pa till he dead; nobody can't say I never mind he good."

My own pa scowled as Aji finished, but he said nothing. He was in a better mood these days now that he had steady work with a contractor. He sat outside with us cleaning his gun to hunt, while Ma shelled pigeon peas.

"Pa, you know all them people Aji tell we bout?" I asked him.

"She must be forget I di there when Bharat dead after he never do nothing for she." Pa scowled. "Same Bharat that was my grandfather. He knock about and he chirren scatter, and this one that is my mother get leave on she own when she find sheself alone with four child. Was like she have no father when trouble come. He could find he tail back to her when he sick though. Ma one – with four children. Three, for Ravi he di' still in the belly. You phuwa and me – seven, eight years old – and you dada, although, he hustling from he young and he never think bout anything but heself."

"Pa, what bout *your* father? *My* aja."

He turned a smouldering eye on me, and I backed away.

Eventually I found that Ma had gathered the essentials of it from Aji and Phuwa but it took years to reach to me, bit by bit. It came together roughly along these lines.

Aji's pa, Bharat, lived with them till he died, just as Aji had said; but for a while she had lived with her children, Chaitlal, Geeta, Jai and Ravi. Before that she lived with the children's father, Bickram. Aji's mother had died long before, and Bharat had no dowry to give for this little child, Kamaldaye, to marry anyone worthwhile. Who had dowry in those days? So she ended up marrying Bickram (it must have been around 1902) and the two of them had nothing.

One miserable little shelter Bickram make, Aji said, flat flat, open on the side, and centipede and scorpion and thing could walk in. Then one day she hear like something crackling in the forest, and a set of insect and thing running out before it. Aha? When she *do so*, she see is a set of ant, chasseur ant, like is a army of them spread out along the clearing and coming at the house. She grab up she baby – that was Chaitlal – and she pick up the young goat and she run. She had was to stay by a neighbor till the ants pass through the house and gone. But she say after that the house clean clean, not a pest leave behind. Only Bickram say is how she did keep the house nasty why the ants come. Ma and I knew my aji, though, and we agreed that couldn't have been true.

Bickram was miserable the whole time. He complained that this woman and her children were sucking him dry and he going dead if he have to take it any longer. Then, Ma told me, one day when she was huxing corn to grind Kamaldaye stop just so and realize she ent see Bickram come home, and she say, take care he dead in truth, and she start to cry. And is when she bawl out, the neighbour come and say, "No, never mind, the man well, for look we see he gettam on boat to go back India." That was when she found out he had sold everything they had – the piece of land, the brokendown house they were living in, the one old goat, everything – and he had bought his passage.

"Like he done plan out he life for heself alone." Ma hacked the pumpkin with extra force as if it were Bickram's head. "So she get leave with these chirren and, next thing, she have she own pa to mind."

As the oldest, Chaitlal remembered his father, and retold anecdotes of the early days. But Pa never mentioned his father once. It was as if he had wiped his mind clean of him.

I was thinking about that when Ma cast a swift hard glance in my direction. "Best you don't ask you pa nothing bout no Aja." As an afterthought she added, "And you see right now? Don't talk bout Dada neither."

That was because I had asked her what Phuwa meant when she said Chaitlal, my dada, had a son that didn't know him. I could not work out how some-one could not know who his father was, or even how Dada could have a son I didn't know. Phuwa said Haresh knew very well who his father was, but that didn't mean he knew him. When she wondered what sort of man Haresh would turn out to be if Chaitlal went on that way, I made sure not to catch anyone's eye or turn my face to them because then they would send me out-side (bigpeopletalking) and I wanted to hear the rest. "Because you see it have a thing name example," Phuwa went on. Everybody in the village knew everyone else and the thing had happened right outside Mr Manny's rumshop. "Haresh big now," she said. "He must be have twenty, twenty-one years, But this thing happen years back when the boy di' only a likkle older than Nathan now." She waved her hand at me, a tragic gesture, and Ma observed me sorrowfully as though it had all happened to me instead.

Haresh had been growing up with his mother Dhanmattie and her parents, and since the old man died the child's mother had never let any man in the house. "I does know this child father too good," Dhanmattie told people. "Don't mind Chaitlal don't care bout you, he wouldn't make nobody else mind you."

One day when Haresh was just nine and life was so hard his mother could not see how she would feed the child in the coming week, she waited with him by the roadside until Chaitlal came by. He had just met up with a friend over a petit-quart and he didn't make them out till she called him. "Man," she said, and he stopped. "I bring you son for you to see. I never ask you for noth-ing before, but I come to find out if you can give we likkle help." She kept her eyes down and talked quietly. I had no picture of her in my mind; it was the first time I had ever heard of Dada having a wife in those old days. It seems she had run off even before Ma and Pa were married, but Phuwa said the lady was desperate now and trying not to aggravate Chaitlal. "See if you could give the boy something, nah?"

"Is you leave me, you bitch."

"But is you child this, man."

Chaitlal walked across and regarded the boy looking up at him, then leaned forward and spat on him.

Haresh had not known to close his eyes or shield his face and he stood there speechless as his mother took her skirt in her hand and cleaned his skin gently and held him to her. He threw up right there in front of the rumshop. "Oh God, Ma," he gasped, heaving, vomiting again, "oh God."

And now, Phuwa say, this same Haresh grow up and marrieding and next thing he go have child heself. "What I want to know is how *he* child go make out," Phuwa demanded. "Ma study talk to Chaitlal about minding he son – till she was tired, but Chaitlal so harden. You make children, oui, but you doesn't make they mind."

Inside my head as a boy of seven I groped for these half-drawn pictures I could not fit in any frame: Bickram, who would have been my aja, who ran away and left his family. And Dada, whom I saw so often, with a son he didn't want. The uncle I knew seemed almost as much a stranger as the grandfather I had never met.

So then I saw Pa, suddenly, with a new, almost unnatural clarity, as if I had never glimpsed him before. Now I look back he was a young man, not even thirty, but he seemed worn as well as strong. I saw the strain of wiry muscle across back and chest, the hard hands and stubborn jaw and the impatient dismissal of anyone who spoke to him when he clutched his coffee, when he was pondering work to be found, looking past us all, staring down the future. I had thought that his mind was not on us, but it was. Providing for us was an obsession that drove out any alternative.

Or did something fester there? As I grew up I wondered whether sometimes he dipped deep into some crevice of his memory to look for his father, when he was alone in the forest at night burning wood so as to sell coal. Did he never think of setting us down and making his way into some other life with only himself to see about? When he slept on the wet ground where scorpions or snakes could have got him. What did he do about the poison of neglect backed up inside? What did he see in the glow of charring wood deep in the forest?

Over the years I came to think he deserved some monument, marks chipped in stone or even just set down somewhere on paper. True, there was life sustained in his family, but it always seemed there should be something else as well, something more permanent than flesh and blood. But for the time being flesh and blood was all we could grapple with.

When he had laboured all day and left the house again at night to go into the forest, he would call over his shoulder, "Boy, see bout you mother." And his words seared their way into my brain.

SEPTEMBER 11, 2010 – 10:45 A.M.

*Uncle please send money. Don't calll police. They will know they know everythign abuot us. they say they cn get more for me, sure money frm some esle if yu donn't pay fast. help me unlce*

# CHAPTER 4

# PAGES BY FLAMBEAU

## Nathan

I could not work out what it was, only that the calm seemed gone out of Ma, leaving an edginess, a glance of something . . . hunted. A while after Solomon was born and had died, just after my seventh birthday, I had heard Aji tell Phuwa how she worried bout Samdai for she look like a churail. And this terrified me because that was what they had called the neighbour who died having her baby.

I began to dream Ma was being washed away. A flood roared through Sanchez tearing apart Phuwa's house and gulping Ma under, her arm stretched for mine, but only my awkward right hand was free. Her fingers reached for me, but I could not grip them before they too sank out of sight. I woke sweating on the paal Ma had put down clean and dry for me the night before and soon the rough fibres seemed damp, then unravelling on wet planks. Dark water lapped on wood. It was a boat, hurled high on boiling black water and plummeting deep into a trough before the huge wall of water toppled over us. Then everything was still and Ma was pale and stiff, Pa crying and sliding her over into the water as the boat sank beneath us and swirling water sucked me away.

So began my recurrent nightmares, and so I became aware of my terror of water – stealthy water, rising, creeping forward, darting at my foot like a snake; angry water rushing, ripping and thundering, crushing breath away.

In the day, though, I was simply and unaccountably terrified for my mother, sensing some undertow I could not locate. I sometimes woke up while it was dark, before she did, and lay listening for her. "Oh Father, have mercy," Ma sighed as the night greyed to morning, the full day ahead rolling out in front of her, and she forced herself up on her tiny feet with the wide splayed toes flat on the clammy ground. I became anxious about leaving her even to go to school, but that seemed to give her comfort – my setting out with my slate and, later, my copybook, and my lunch of roti and alu. She regarded me with what I now remember as her single-minded, obsessive zeal, pushing aside whatever else haunted her.

"Listen to the teacher, eh," she whispered urgently. "Learn, beta."

My education had resumed some months before when Aji insisted I attend Sunday School. Pa caught sight of me bathed and dressed in the new short-pants she had made, standing at the door holding Aji's finger, and he laughed out. "But this boy dress up like Papa Jacques self," he said. "Yes, boy, go with you aji."

In the early 1930s Sunday School was serious work. I must study the Bible and write exams, Mrs Jattansingh said. She was a broad pale lady with eye-lashes so short and thin she seemed to have none. She was flat back and front but wide across the hips, so I could not see around her, only gaze up into her anxious eyes with their bald lids. On the estate I had started out making my letters in a tray of sand, but I never got beyond that stage. Mrs Jattansingh looked frankly alarmed and said something must be done.

So the Reverend came to our door asking for John Deoraj, and I scampered to find Ma and hung behind her as she explained my father was at work, and she was now come in from the garden why her hands were dirty, and she was so sorry. But the Reverend said, never mind, just tell John he had come to say the boy must be in school, and he would talk to him after church on Sunday.

The teacher was in church too and we knew who he was, a great man named Peter Mangalsingh who eyed me with concern and said I must be in school. What could Pa do but agree, muttering about where money would come from for books, but they assured him it would be a while before I needed any. First they would give me a slate to write on at school, so we had time to save for books.

Save what, was what Pa wanted to know when he got home, but at Phuwa's suggestion, Ma planted man-better-man bush "with a money" to bring luck. "And braps! The thing work," Phuwa said, for almost at once

Pa found steady work with a contractor who remembered him from an earlier job and set him to supervise a small team, so Pa contrived to get work for Dada too. "That good," Phuwa said. "It go keep he from knocking about." The lines around Aji's eyes relaxed at the thought of Chaitlal spending less time in the rumshop. Ever since that mysterious story about Dada having a son he didn't know I had been watching him curiously for clues. But there was nothing about him that seemed to account for anything I heard. There wasn't even a pattern in the way he drifted in and out of Phuwa's house.

Dada was dark like Pa but heavier, yet he never seemed as powerful, and although he talked more I couldn't always work out afterwards what he had said. "He like to waste he breath," Pa said. That was because of a thick, spreading tree root in the way of a drain they were to build. By evening, without a word to anyone, Pa had it out, but Dada had been cursing it for a week. So Pa would be paid for clearing the drain, while Dada never seemed to have money however hard he said he worked. Now that he was working with Pa, though, he passed in on weekends, sometimes with a few sweets. "Too mucha sugar not good for chirren," Ma grumbled, but she could hardly object if he brought packs of channa or, now and then, a bottle for Pa, Chacha and himself, although Phuwa said, "He self go finish that now for now."

What I looked forward to were his stories, the old tales his father had told before he sailed away, back to India, tales no one else remembered because they were from India too. Then there were stories about creatures in the forest and river nearby, sometimes Anancy tales of trickery and cunning. "He go know bout that," Ma said under her breath. Occasionally she would shoo me inside, if she thought the story was going to be cruel or vulgar, but I crouched with my ear pinned to the door.

Sunday School had stories different to Dada's, stories that answered questions I had had since I could remember, stories of how the world was made, and then lost because people were disobedient and ungrateful, and of how life was given back because God forgave. *"Thy word is a lamp unto my feet,"* Mrs Jattansingh explained, and I took it in gratefully. And there were stories at school, of countries far away, of how England and other great places had found us and brought order and light to a situation somehow confused. I was not sure how it had become confused, but was glad to know something had been done.

That was about the time that Dada produced his new wife, Mala, who was tall but fragile looking, younger than Ma, not twenty yet. Her wide timid eyes darted about and seemed to search each corner for a hiding place. Dada and Mala lived in Aji's house in Impasse, but Mala said she felt frightened there. She worried about snakes coming in from the forest and rats from the cocoa and beetles from . . . wherever beetles came from – from the night. She looked anxious when Dada was around and lost when he wasn't. She hurried about searching for things to do, something that would please him, I thought, but she didn't seem sure what that would be. She stuck close to Ma and got under her feet, but Ma's spirits seemed improved and she was gentle with Mala. "She ent know what to do," Ma said, "and she does be frighten."

Pa had no patience with Mala's whimpering. "What you supposed to do for she? Cry? Tell she to band she belly and mind she house. Let she watch you and see how woman does conduc theyself."

Ma said no more, obviously pleased but not ready to give up sympathy for Mala. "And she making baby too," Ma observed later to Phuwa. But that was not news to me for now I was big enough to recognize the signs.

The work Pa had found, clearing bush and drains, and cutting roads, was in a village that had been called Mission Number 2 until the other Mission was renamed Princes Town. Our Mission was partway between where we lived, at Phuwa's house in Sanchez, and Aji's old place in Impasse where Dada and Mala lived. Dada worked hard once something turned up, though it was always Pa who hunted it down, first in his head as he cradled his coffee in both hands.

"Samdai, girl," he said to Ma one night. "One day I go buy you a bera."

"How gold go feel on my hand? Like I might have to stop making roti," she said softly, her mouth tightening to forestall a smile and her eyes snapping with mischief.

"You mad or what?" he said.

But she had smiled, or as good as smiled. The house was lighter.

Dada still drifted in every few days looking for food. "What happen, boy? You madam doesn't cook?" Phuwa asked pointedly. Occasionally on a Friday Pa and Dada would come home together in the evening and sometimes their younger brother, Ravi, would pass in, so we would fall asleep to the sound of laughter and ole talk. Then Chacha heard of a job as a night watchman in Moruga, where he had lived before, and he moved back there again with his wife; but even before that Pa had found a way to work overtime and he began to come home after dusk. Dada might disappear for days, even weeks, till Aji sat rocking back and forth in distress and moaning, "What happen to this boy now?"

Afterwards Pa would grumble about his brother's lack of consideration. Next thing he loss the wok, after Pa self beg the contractor to hire Chaitlal. "And he can't even send and tell he mother or he wife he living?"

"He go come back," Ma would remark in her most resigned voice, and so he would.

Pa shrugged it off because he was busy clearing a piece of land in Quick River Trace, a good bit west of Sanchez, on the edge of Mission. He was going to build a house, he said, and Ma's eyes lit up but all she said was "That good."

By the time the old carat house that had served as a school for the children in the village was replaced by a wooden building, our own house was going up in Quick River Trace. By now Pa knew people in the area and they gathered to stamp the mud and grass mixture for the tapia – to dance mud, as they said – so the walls rose steadily. Between each phase of the work Pa patrolled the trace and other roads in Mission, observing houses of all sorts, and came home with a look of sly satisfaction to adjust his plans for laying the carat palms for a roof. Every penny was for the house, he said, and we spent little, eating what we reaped from the land. One day Aji came home with chataigne seeds and as soon as she was out of earshot Pa laughed and said, "Farting pills for dinner, oui." But that was just fatigue he was throwing, and the house glowed in his good humour.

The neighbours came to lipay the floor of the new house, mixing clay and cow dung and water to plaster smoothly. Then our house was up and we moved in, its grey-brown thatch sloping steeply over us. At dusk we could hear the deep, long, rattling groan of red howler monkeys in the forest. "If my pardner, La Borde, ever catch one of them in he pot he wouldn't have to bawl so again," Pa chuckled. "What you say, boy?" I hurried over to sit by him and he gave me a sip of his coffee. "We go plant pigeon peas and corn, and put a stand in front the house to sell," he announced. "Every weekend you go sell peas, boy. You going to school now so you could count money."

"Is good he going to school," Ma agreed. She was in better spirits now we had moved, although she still talked to Phuwa about having two children dead and what life would be if she had no more. Then Ma would catch herself, and take Phuwa's face in both hands and say, "But we have this one."

I was ten, some three years later, when the baby came. It was a girl, but Pa said it was a good sign and he made a shak-shak, lovingly whittling and smoothing the wood. They christened her Judith almost immediately, although they called her Sabita for a while. She would be the last to have an Indian name, even briefly. Big jobs like teaching, or even police work, were only for Christians and it was because she was a girl that she was Sabi for a couple months. Soon even Pa called her Judith.

Pa worked harder than ever. With all the talk of war, he wondered whether that would affect people being hired. Despite the worry and uncertainty, though, his face lit at the sight of the baby, and he put up a hammock with cross-sticks to keep the cloth from closing over her but allowing enough depth to prevent her falling out. Aji arrived to misay and santay, massaging Judith's limbs with oil and drawing them gently back and forth, but Dada visited less because he said he couldn't take the bawling. As for Ma, she became a living soul again.

On the other hand Aji soon reported that Dada's wife, Mala, had run away, taking their baby daughter, Doolarie, to live with her own parents, and that Dada had arrived at Phuwa's house in the night crying and threatening to kill himself. Ma made no comment on it and I wondered whether she would have thought it such a bad thing if he did. "And he should accustom to that now," she muttered. "She ent the first one." But she said it so quietly I wondered if I had misheard.

"At least he not about to kill she," Phuwa comforted Aji.

But Aji still worried. "Next thing the stupid boy really do heself a wickedness." And she decided he must stay with them in Sanchez for a little.

"That is a good thing," Ma said, but I suspected she was just glad he would drop in more rarely. There was a look she had when he turned up. It was like the time she had flipped aside rotten wood in the garden and jumped back and when I asked why, she said, "In case of snake, beta." Now she sat on the gallery sometimes on evenings, though she had more to do than ever, never letting Judith out of her sight (because, she said, a girlchild is another thing again). I told her I would look after Jub Jub, for I had never felt anything in my life like the flood of warmth that suffused me when Judith's fist closed on my finger.

Yet I was home less than before. I went to school in Mission because it was nearer than the one on the other side of Sanchez where I been going while we lived with Phuwa. Even so, Mission CM was three miles' walk from Quick River Trace to the Junction, then left at the police station, and another half-mile up the hill. When Dada first heard I would be going there he warned me about the police station. "Boy, you see when you reach the Junction, you must run fast fast past the station, or police go catch you and lock you up in they cell with the rat and thing."

"Nah!" Aji said. "Don't tell the child that. Beta, watch. Nothing like that, you hear?"

At first I dreaded passing the police station but after a while when nothing happened I decided Aji must be right, though I remained cautious and never quite lost my sense of unease about policemen.

After Sanchez, Mission seemed a big town, although Sanchez had been bewildering at first to a five-year-old coming from the estate barracks. Mission had not only a school and police station but a post office, shops, wooden houses of different sizes and a few buildings of red clay brick. At the junction, roads went in all directions, one north to the Dessalines estate and on past Aji's old house where Dada had lived before, all the way to Biche. Another road led from the Junction south past Troyville, and bad road too, through the bamboo to some oil fields. That was the Hilton Pinto Road that went off left from the main road before I reached the turn to the school. The main road went on west to Princes Town, but it was hard to imagine anywhere larger than Mission, where many other roads, like Balata Trace and Seukeran Trace, turned off from the big road along my way, well before I reached the Junction.

No one called this intersection anything but the Junction except for that corner of the Junction where the Hilton Pinto Road turned south. This corner was occupied at night by fellows playing cards, and it was called Flambeau Corner. On mornings I would pass the coconut man, whom we knew only as Nuts, setting up his stand at Flambeau Corner, and I hurried on past the stalls where vendors sold vegetables and provision, before making a left uphill to school.

Then, the books. The feel and smell and promise of them. I stayed after school to read books the teacher kept in the classroom. The best was one that had tales of the knights. If I had lived in those times, I decided, I would have been a knight. Teacher Mangalsingh, who had been shifted from Sanchez to Mission, read my mind and asked which knight I should have liked to be, and I fell silent, tongue-tied. But a couple days later I loitered under the mango tree near the door waiting for him to notice me, and when he said, "Yes, Nathan," I said, "Percival, Sir," and ran away.

My life revolved around the schoolhouse. As soon as I had cut the grass and put out feed for the animals, I ran as much of the way to school as I could. Our road ran north to meet the main road, across Quick River, which was shallow at the crossing except in heavy rain and I bounded over it from one large flat stone to the next. Quick River passed closer to our house before the crossing but was deeper there and had no stepping-stones, and the bamboo met across the top making it dark and threatening, but farther on the crossing was bright and open, with a faint gurgle of clear water around the stones.

I barely paused, skipping across it, as I went over whatever home lesson I had at the time, reciting tables, poetry, Bible verses, for the big new schoolhouse was not only a school during the week, but Church on Sundays and, two hours before service, Sunday School. The schoolmaster taught us that there was a world outside our own and the Reverend that there was a life after this one. It was all one to me, the *beyond* that my mind fluttered over in the alternating light and shadow of what I could see and could not see and what I could conceive of or only try to imagine.

On Friday and Saturday nights the schoolhouse became a meeting place, an exhibition room, a lecture hall. Here the Agricultural Exhibition would be held, important visitors of all sorts (people Teacher Mangalsingh taught us to call *dignitaries*) addressing a crowd packed tight into the room. Weekdays, though, it was the domain of Teacher, whose ordered life and frugal means went into preparation for class, leaving over next to nothing for himself. Not only our first adviser but our parents' most accessible lawyer, doctor, nurse, this was a learned man the whole village held in awe, the man I would have wanted most to be in all the world, if only my mind could have formed such a thought. But even the more modest horizon of primary education seemed to be slipping from my reach. Ma's belly looked the same as usual but she and Pa talked as if there was going to be another child and they would need more money.

I composed my face to give no sign that I was boiling inside, even before Pa said, "This boy have to leave school and do real wok." It was a damp gusty evening with rain blowing in every direction. "It have no money to buy book," he shouted. I stayed quiet, for what could I have to say? "Two boar rat can't live in one hole" was what Pa would say, and it was not him I was furious with – it was all kinds of other things, like the bush that spread back as fast as he could clear it. It was the blade that fell off his cutlass and lay in wait to cut the workman's foot, leaving Pa shorthanded. It was the endless grinding labour that would be his whole life, and mine as well. And so, yes, it was Pa too who did not understand I needed school the way I needed food.

"Let he stay in school," Ma pleaded. "Don' worry bout book and ting. I could still do a little weeding and the boy self will get up earlier and do what he could. Something go wok out." I held my breath, and, after a prolonged silence during which Pa clutched his enamel cup of cocoa tea and glowered at the months to come, he said we would watch for a couple weeks.

Still, he muttered about us needing land of our own. "Is so people does build theyself up." He coughed and rubbed an aching arm irritably." Then what? I go sleep in the delki and burn coal for me whole life?"

All Ma said was "Man, put on you clothes. You go get sick if you sit bareback in the dew."

It may have been coincidence that Teacher sought out Pa after church that Sunday to say how well I was doing, and how much help I would be to the family one day if I kept it up. But I had seen coincidences like that before, usually after Ma had scurried through her work, set out mysteriously in her best dress and orhni and returned tight-lipped and never, at such times, to be troubled by questions. "Go do you home lesson," she would say sharply. "You too fast."

Teacher Mangalsingh went further than praising me. He reported to Pa that the School Inspector had noticed me. The Inspector never had before, threadbare and barefoot as I was like the rest, but I had answered his question directly in a voice as much like Teacher Mangalsingh's as I could manage, and before leaving the room the Inspector had glanced back at me and murmured something to the teacher.

Most of the children were not like me. They read when they had to. I stayed, reading, until they shut the door, until the old cross-eyed caretaker called my name kindly and closed me out. "Go home, boy. Go help you mother get firewood. It getting dark early now. Next thing, night ketch you on the road."

Ma had thought of that too. Pa was so often late himself that he was not aware of my hours, but Ma questioned me carefully. Later I found out she had been to see Teacher. She was standing over a heap of dasheen bush, studying me in silence as her hands moved, automatically stripping the purple film off the long stalks. "He say is very good – so mucha reading." There was another silence. "So you must read all them book he have." Ma was troubled though. "It have a book he want you to buy too and I can't ask you pa for no money."

By morning she had worked it out. I was to leave early and gather limes along the way. "It have two three tree by the road," she reminded me. "Don't forget dem bag for the lime." I was to sell them and take Teacher the money daily. "He go tell you when it nuff." She hurried away so she could get on with my chores before moving to her own. "I say go, boy. What you standing up for? Go fast, and sell the lime."

It was my first real book. It had a red cover with black writing on it. It was filled with stories about people all over the world. I could read it at home on the weekend in between gathering eggs, chopping wood, cutting podina and bandhania from the land behind the house, and scattering corn for fowls. And I would save stories for Judith in my head, for when she was big enough. I stayed in school, and if Pa kept me home two days Teacher Mangalsingh himself came to the house to know why, so I took note of the fact that the schoolmaster was not just doctor and lawyer but policeman when necessary.

"Now you could read," Ma said one day with the air of one who had been waiting on something for years, "it have a book my pa give me to keep. He say he own Aja or somebody di' have it. I want you read it to me." And she brought out a worn volume, shredding at the corners. A page or two from the front there was a picture.

"What you picture doing in a book, Ma?" I gasped.

She stared at it. "That not me, beta." She peered at it again. "You find it look like me? Nah." Then she got back to what she wanted. "Beta, watch. I want you read this book to me."

## खोया

Dark clouds seemed driven here and there over the cover. I opened it but could make nothing of what was inside. "Is not English, Ma," I explained. "Only curly curly marks, not real letters. That can't read. . . ." She stared at it blankly. "Where it come from, Ma?"

"I don't know what it is Pa say. I feel he self wasn't sure." She gave a deep sigh, then put it aside. "That ent nothing, beta," she said. "Right now it have roti to make. Hand me the baelna."

During the week I still stayed after school to read whatever the teacher brought to the classroom, and he made me report what I had read, and he said, "Good. That's good."

Pa made me take Teacher Mangalsingh an agouti and Teacher sent back his thanks, saying he and wildmeat were good pardners, because his own name was Peter and St Peter was the patron saint of the agouti.

"But what he means, Pa?" I asked.

"Well, boy, when you hunt gouti and ketch it, it does squeal out. If you listen good you hear him say 'Pierro, Pierro!' That is the sound he make."

I was glad of the understanding between Pa and Teacher Mangalsingh, but there remained the issue of books.

"I don't have nothing, boy." Ma's eyes were fierce behind her tears, and I was trudging away when she called me back. She was holding Pa's best white hen against the curve of her belly. "Watch. Take the hen and sell it." I stared at her horrified. "I tell you go fast," she said. "Matter fix."

That evening we helped Pa search for the hen. "Is a hell of a thing, dis," he pondered. "I leave this hen here good good, and it just stop so and gone. Like somebody tief me hen in truth."

"What going to happen now, Ma?" I whispered. "You don't see how Pa getting on? It have blood in he eye, man. Next thing he kill somebody and is my fault."

"Nah!" Then she raised her voice. "Man, watch me! Next ting is a macajuel come in from the forest." She planted her hands on her hips and studied Pa. "Or you think the fowl sick and gone into the bush to dead?" Pa insisted he leave the fowl good good. "But, man, you sure you check under the house good? I feel I go look again."

This was nothing we could try a second time, so I stayed in school as long as I could to read the teacher's books. Sometimes I copied down a story I particularly liked, word for word. Each day I hurried home, cutting through the edge of the forest to avoid the long way that would take me in after Pa arrived. It was impossible though to tell direction once the light dimmed, and as the year wore on the shadows darkened before I left the trees. "Ma," I said, "don't Dada have a camp in the forest for when he go to hunt? Ent he could find me if I lose the path?"

That was when I found out why Ma had been collecting white stones for weeks, bending carefully to pick them up as she held her belly with the other hand. She spaced them out along my shortcut through the trees so I would not miss my step and wander deep into the forest. Then, when Teacher asked me if I was getting home before dark after all that reading, I told him it was all right because Ma had set out the white stones through the trees, and he sat there and said nothing for a long time. He said, "I'll lend you one book to take home every week, but leave earlier. Hear?" But first he gave me a book to keep as my own, not a school book but the kind of book people read just because they read.

It was called *A Tale of Two Cities*. I read it to Judith, although she was too small to understand and only clung to my voice, relieving Ma, who tired more quickly now the bulge in her belly was clear. A few month still to go though, she sighed – but she looked pleased. She was up early as usual, grinding corn to mix in flour – because of the war, she said, because the government was allowing only so much flour per family for each day, so we had to find ways of making do.

The workmen were chasing down iguana, Pa said, but he preferred to shoot birds or squirrels, and occasionally he brought bigger game like agouti or manicou. "What about if you use you camp to hunt meat, instead of the stupidness?" I heard Pa ask Dada when the two of them were outside and didn't know I was around. Dada said something I didn't catch except for the word *meat*, and Pa said, "You is a ass or what? One day somebody go shoot you."

Sometimes I had to stay home from school to stand in line for bread at the bakery for hours, from before lunch to late afternoon. Ma could not do that now and we had to buy bread to save flour for roti. Still I did well enough in test for Papa Jacques to stop Pa in the road and say he had heard his son was a real scholar. That was the word Teacher Mangalsingh had used to Papa Jacques after church on Sunday, and Pa tried it out on his tongue. Soon he was rolling it off with a flourish.

This was a big thing, to be recognized by Papa Jacques, and Madam Ramjit whose son was in my class and going nowhere hastened to remark that if people like to feel they is big just because they child could cheat in test, then let them feel so. Madam Beharrysingh, the seamstress on Oceanview Trace (which overlooked the cemetery), made it her duty to visit Ma and console her for having only the one boy child after all these years. "*So* Madam Beharrysingh does know how to jook fire," Phuwa grumbled.

Those days, Pa was working late and coming in tired and irritable because Dada was only running away early to the rumshop. Pa said it was the rumshop when he talked at home but when he caught Dada by himself and did not notice me close by he said something altogether different. "I catching my arse on the job while you gone by Madam Fleur," he said. Madam Fleur was so famous that the area where she lived, just two roads up from us, was called Fleurville but it was a while before I knew what she was famous for. Dada had been sitting on the gallery all the time, smoking and waiting for Pa to come in, and when Ma and Phuwa withdrew – to blag, as they said – Pa thought I had gone with them. Dada grinned at him.

"What happen, boy, you jealous me?"

Pa gave a loud steups and responded was not *he*, Jai, that people know to be *robust*.

"And who say that? Who the hell say that?" Dada burst out in his boisterous way. "Show me him. I go eat he raw without salt."

Ma came out instantly to send me back for water from the drum, but Dada said, "Let he hear, let he hear. Is a boy child."

But Ma looked through him and the tapia wall into some clean space no one else could see, as I scuttled away.

When Dada left, Ma murmured something to Pa I could not hear, but Pa shouted, "I don't want to hear nothing bout that. I go deal with my own brother. You mind you house and child." And a deep silence fell over her.

But the next afternoon she gathered her things to leave home, and all my crying and pleading resulted in Phuwa setting out in search of Pa. When he arrived, Ma was at the tawa, still in her going-out clothes with the packed bag on her bed.

"What all this about?" he demanded. "Where you think you deck off going?"

"You see?" Dada muttered to Phuwa. "He never put he foot down. Nobody could ever say a woman have *me* in grip."

Ma concentrated on the roti swelling nicely on one side, and spun it round. "Is this boy beg me to stay," she said, without glancing up. "Ent I does mind me child? You ever see my child limping with bette rouge in he skin? I does see and hear everyting that happen in my house."

I frowned over my book and made a few hurried notes. Ma had whispered to me from the beginning that I must run after her and bring her back whatever she might say. Pa stared at us suspiciously and muttered savagely and went down the back steps to the barrel for his bath. Dada laughed, but Phuwa said what happen was Samdai need a cooling and she (Phuwa self) would give her some burn-bread water.

"I does walk on glass, you see me here," Ma muttered. But when they had all gone and only I remained in earshot, she raised her head to me and smiled – right there in the midst of some turmoil that was a mystery to me. It took my breath away. Then she lowered her glance again to the next roti. "You know, beta, I hear before he get the job in the mine, my aja did make little money doing bottle dance?" There it was again, like the ruined book she had preserved, then tossed aside, a shining fragment of a story lost, the glimpse (gone in a flash) of her grandfather dancing over smashed glass, a chapter slipped down through a crack between the generations, throwing back a reflected gleam.

How did such bits and pieces hold together and were they connected with or through me? Was all that was to come like what had gone, strewn somewhere just as carelessly? Perhaps there was some other place, one I could not imagine – but real – where everything was not where big people thought it ought to be, where I could turn into something no one I knew could ever imagine. Even I could not imagine it – the me I could become. I searched in books, not in fairy tales but in stories of real people in other lands and other times. I turned my mind into a map, and all the people and places and events I read about found a place on my map and in between was space for what and where I could be, although I could not precisely locate it yet, and that *yet* hung there too, and the map unfurled in my head with all that had been and was and would be and could be. Sometimes when I walked home from school through the edge of the forest I was also walking along a track on the map in my mind. But it was a track that faded away to darkness and there were no white stones.

The next Saturday Ma was away for hours until I grew afraid she had really left, especially since she took Judith with her. "You crazy?" she asked when she got back. "Gone and leave *you*? You mad or what?" She had offered to pay a driver but he had insisted that he would take little or no money from her because she had been good to his wife once after they lost a baby. So he and his wife had driven her all the way to the monastery at Mount St Benedict and met some holy person who had prayed with her. The driver was so amazed at her going so far to pray that he would not accept payment at all.

And now she was home, roasting tomato on the fire as if nothing had happened. Pa had gone to cricket, cheering on Papa Jacques's team, for the warden and his officers, and the engineer and civil servants living in the area made up a cricket side called Jacques's Boys.

"Gone where?" He stared at Ma on his return. "Who take you?" The idea of her leaving the village alone and finding her way so far stunned him. He stared at her belly, then at her face as if she had suddenly become someone else.

"How prayer does hurt anybody?" She shrugged, then turned on me. "Boy, you better finish bathe now for now, you hear me?" She kneaded her hand wearily in the small of her back, pushing her belly forward, and suddenly bent over and clutched it in both arms. I was terrified and cried out even before she did.

It was a boy at last, a gift for my twelfth birthday, Ma said. Aji and Pa insisted that some of the names people used from the Bible might be bad lucky, and although everyone agreed that I had prospered they felt we should stick with the people in the Bible that they heard about all the time. So the new baby was Matthew.

Pa and his friends disappeared into the forest to hunt and brought back a deer. Only it was a female and they had not realized she had young till they saw her dripping milk, and they looked for the little one lost in the forest. "I feel somebody going like what I have here. Where Mother?" Pa had taken to calling Judith *Mother*. "Come, Mother. I bring you a baby." He set down the bundle he was carrying and it was a little deer still wobbly on its legs, and Judith jumped up and down, her hair a mop of long bouncing curls.

"Boy, you go help she mind it," Pa told me.

"Where Chaitlal?" Phuwa asked. "Ent he say he gone to hunt?"

"Not with me." Pa's face was expressionless.

By the following evening though, when no one had seen Dada, Pa looked tense. In a day or two there were anxious whispers, things no one would say in front of me, but I came to understand that Dada was hiding. Aji was frantic.

"Boy, you can't talk to the fellow?" Phuwa asked Pa.

"Tell he *what*? Is the man sister." Pa lunged off the stool with a force that threw it down. "But I suppose I wi' have to talk to him."

"Wait," Aji pleaded. "He say if he can't find Chaitlal he glad to kill anyone in Chaitlal family."

"Boy," Ma said sternly to me. "You ent sweep under the house yet? What you doing here?"

The following day word came that whoever was looking for Dada had actually shot someone else in the forest by mistake and the man was dead. "Police hold he one time," Phuwa reported, "so at least he safe inside."

Soon enough Dada reappeared. "Ent I tell you I go be all right?" He stared at Ma irritably. "What wrong with you, madam?" he asked Pa.

"She friend, Madam Kalloo, bury she one son yesterday," Pa answered. After a while he added, "The fellow that take you bullet, nah." He walked inside and lay on his bed to finish his cigarette, blowing the smoke up to the ceiling.

Ma went outside to the latrine and I could hear her sobbing. So I sat on the step till she came out. When she saw me she rubbed my head absently – I don't think she realized she was speaking aloud. "This Chaital is like a sickness that does just spread," she said. Then she went in and nursed Matthew.

Matthew was not two years old, and Mark, who had followed swiftly, was only a few months when the rains came heavier than I had ever seen before. It was school holidays and when the rain held up I was desperate to get out the house.

Phuwa and Aji had come from Sanchez for a few days, and we left Matthew with Aji so as to go and buy goods. As we walked back from the Junction the rain poured down again, and Phuwa and I clutched the disintegrating bags of rice, the salt and what little provision the garden was not producing at the time. Ma tried uselessly to shield Mark from the pounding rain while Judith ran alongside holding tight to Ma's skirt. Then we came to the river, and I stopped.

It was not the curling stream with the fine silt smooth and clean around my jumping stones. It rushed fast, brown and angry, almost covering the rocks. "We have to go back," I said at once. "We can shelter till the water go down."

"Good thing we reach now," Phuwa said. "Next half hour so we wouldn't able get 'cross."

I was fuming but no one noticed me.

Judith held Ma's skirt and sobbed, and Ma said, "Child, stop the crying and hold you brother hand." But I was afraid too.

Ma stepped forward to the edge and Judith wailed louder, and the baby, startled, took it up. I felt my own cries edging up from my belly and gulped them back because it would have frightened Mark more, because it would have driven Judith out of control, because I was ashamed of being more afraid than Phuwa or Ma.

"No. Not to frighten," Phuwa encouraged us. "Watch me. You could still see the stone and dem. We crossing, man. Beta, give me you big bag so you can help you mother. Don't watch at the water." Phuwa hoisted up her skirt and took my bag bulging with pumpkin and sodden rice, and she edged in. The water sucked round her ankles but she made good headway, stepped up on the first stone and went across, from one to the next, pausing at the gap where I always pretended there was deeper water. Now it was no pretence. Phuwa threw an apologetic look at Ma and dumped the bag of food to spring over safely, and then she was on the other side.

"Now," she shouted. "But you must come now."

So Ma tugged Judith, who was screaming by this time for she was tiny, no more than four. Ma dragged her into the water frothing at the edge and soon against Judith's chest, and she held Mark to her shoulder, his cries lost in the noise of the brawling river and Judith's terror, and I could only follow with my belly churning, prodding Judith forward so that Ma could keep hold of her as they scrambled up on the first stone. And so we went until we were almost across, but at the second-to-last stone the gap was wider and the water fierce and muddy in between, and although we were now close to the other side I shouted, "Ma, we can't get over. Leh we go back."

Torn between terror and fury I glanced behind, but one by one the stones had disappeared under the torrent, so Ma shook her head and she froze there on our flat rock in the widening river, with the baby's stranglehold on her neck and Judith literally trying to climb her, and I could only try to keep my legs from giving way and clench my teeth, and I dropped my small bag with the oil so I could hold Judith and prevent her from sliding or dragging Ma down into the water.

Phuwa shouted at us over the tumult, and Ma stared at her incredulously because Phuwa could not have said what it sounded like she said.

"Throw the baby!" Phuwa yelled again, her arms opening wide. "I go catch he."

I steadied myself and hugged Judith as tight as I could.

"Throw!" Phuwa yelled.

And Ma wrenched Mark from her neck and pitched him with all her might to Phuwa, his scream drowned by the water or just the air knocked out of him as he tumbled through the air, legs splayed, hands beating wildly, spinning down to Phuwa's outstretched arms, which grabbed and locked around him with his head down, arms still flailing till she swung him right way up against her bosom.

And in the same instant Ma grabbed Judith with both hands and shouted at her, "Shut you mouth *now*." She stared straight into me, her eyes blazing through the terror that shut down my brain and her lips spreading and she howled "Jump" with a force that propelled me so we came down together on that last rock clutching Judith, who clenched her arms and legs round me like a vine. Suddenly the stranglehold relaxed and Judith braced her feet on the rock, and even as Ma shoved me on into the water on the other side, Judith was scrambling down into it as well with her eye on the bank, although the water was almost at my waist and Ma and I had to keep her raised between us, her mouth squeezed tight so it could not fill with the water that was sucking at my legs, and Ma's other hand clamped down on my arm thrusting me on till we scrambled up onto the bank where Phuwa was waiting with Mark curled on her shoulder.

We kept going, drenched as we were, straight from the river along the path without comment or pause for breath, or sign that a baby had been hurled over the river or anything else that could not have happened – other than Phuwa's passing Mark back to Ma and Ma's answering glance at her, that exchange of something more between them now, something almost blindingly bright and durable.

So we reached home. I don't know whether Pa ever knew, because Ma had little to say and he came home so late, working gayap as he was, every day the men clearing land for a different member of the group till everyone could have a place to plant.

But that night after I said my prayers I thought, when the thing was happening it didn't even have time for me to pray. Then I thought, one day I might forget how frightened I was, and how we got across. Next, it occurred to me that one day if something worse happened and I could remember how we got across, this would help me. But then I couldn't think of anything worse that could happen.

Still, when Phuwa gave me a new copybook she had brought me from the shop, I put it in a place only I knew about, and I began to write things down. I decided I would only write down things that would not hurt anybody – should in case anybody find it who could read, I thought. First I wrote down a line from a hymn they had sung that Sunday. *I'll be waiting by the river.* But I thought better of it and rubbed that out. *I come to the garden alone,* I wrote instead, wondering whether it was a garden with orange and plum trees, or if it only had bodi, pumpkin and other food.

I started to get mixed up sometimes about whether I was praying or only thinking and it worried me a little because I seemed to have so little control. Sometimes when I went off exploring inside my head I found things I could not understand and I wondered how they had got in there. Sometimes they were things I could not tolerate, unthinkable things, and the question was, if they were unthinkable what were they doing inside my head. So you see I could not have made them up. There was a shadow, for instance, in tall boots caked with mud and at the side of the shadow was the gleam of a machete, only the shadow had disappeared and the machete leaned at the door, but the shadow was there, always somewhere, and it was evil.

The world in my head was laid out precisely as far as right and wrong were concerned. There was good and there was evil. When the hard line between these blurred and bewildered me, I walked out of my head and back into the usual confusion of life, but sometimes I made a note of the questions I was leaving unanswered. Some were questions about Dada. The man who had meant to shoot him was on trial and Dada said he hoped the lawyer and dem wasn't going to let go the murdering likkle bitch. I didn't know who to feel sorry for.

I also wrote down some of Aji's stories so I wouldn't forget, which reminded me to ask her something I had thought of over and over, and she said, "Yes, beta," and showed me the uniform her aja had brought from the old country. From then on, when we visited her, I sometimes went and pulled out the box and looked at it, but in later years when she died there was so much activity that I forgot it until long afterwards when no one knew where it had gone. Once, though, while I was still a boy, looking on my own, I saw a scrap of paper in the pocket (perhaps Baba himself pushed it in there for safekeeping during the voyage). I couldn't read it and just slipped it between the pages of the copybook, but soon the copybook was bulging with scraps of loose paper and I needed a box, especially since I decided to add some of my own essays.

I had many essays by then, collected over the two years before, and sometimes I would look at the earlier ones when I had to practise writing for an exam.

That was when they had needed my birth certificate and it couldn't be found. Over and over I went through the papers Ma and Pa kept on the spike. I had to do it because I was the only one who could read. Even now it is so clear in my mind I smell the coffee parching over the fireside.

We took all the papers off the spike one by one. "Call it out," Ma had said, "call it out hard," and I went through reading one paper after the other in search of the birth certificate. When I read out "Gahadar Deoraj," Ma said, "Aaha!" But I already had another paper in my hand and I read out the baptismal certificate for Oswald Deoraj.

"But who those people are?" I demanded, and they laughed. I was annoyed (for there they were, treating this thing for my exam as if it were a joke) but I could only wait for them to explain themselves. After that we had to go and speak to a lawyer to get another paper called an affidavit to say that Gahadar was Nathan, and that there was no Oswald.

One of the first things I had written was the story of a knight and a lady, and right afterwards I followed it with a prayer for my mother because it was a prayer I needed to keep working on. I wrote it down even though I did not yet know how to pray properly. I hadn't known how to write a story either, let alone a real essay, but I kept that one because it was one of my first.

### The Princess Treasure

*Once there was a beautiful lady who was very young but had many important duties. She had not always been a great lady in a castle, for she was the eldest daughter of a fisherman. The most important duty was to keep a certain treasure safe from the touch of Evil Hands. The treasure was really the cup that Jesus has used to serve the first communion, but the lady had magical powers and could disguise it as other things.*

*Although the lady was young she was married to a great knight who was very busy building castles and roads and bridges, and he was brave and went hunting deer and agouti when he had time. When he came home in the evening he was tired and sometimes he shouted at people in the castle but it was only because he had been working all day even when he was in pain, for he had a wound in his chest from an old ~~war~~ combat and it had never healed properly. He did not complain about pain because he was a true hero.*

*The lady's treasure was usually disguised as a little princess, and unless the knight or the lady's faithful page was there she kept the princess with her always.*

*One day when her faithful page went home from his lessons, the lady was quieter than usual and although she went about her work (for the knight would soon be home) ~~she could not~~ she was p r e o c c u p i e d. When she gave the knight his cocoa tea in his special mug it was cold and he lost his temper and boxed it away. And for a moment, with the tea staining her dress, she looked ragged and tired, but she shook her head and smiled and became again the most beautiful of all ladies. That night after she had hung up the sheets around the water barrel she bathed for a long time and the page could tell she was crying because she was so quiet.*

*The next morning the lady was as beautiful as ever but very stern. She warned the page to study hard and become a great knight too, because the world had Evil in it and she needed his help to protect the princess. So the page swore an oath. However, all the time the princess laughed and played and did not know she was really a treasure.*

The prayer afterwards was the first I ever wrote down and I was so anxious to get it down I never worried about what Sir called style.

*Dear Lord and Father,*
   *Please help Pa find plenty work so he wouldn't worry and get vex and send up his pressure. Please make Matthew and Mark mind Ma, and keep Judith safe so Ma could relax a little. Please help me know good from evil. I don't know what to think about the fellow who got hung this morning. I didn't want him to get out and kill Dada but I sorry he hang.*
   *Amen*
   *Thank you for the wildmeat Pa catch yesterday.*
   *Amen*

When the neighbour called across the fence to Ma that the man had been hung, Ma shook her head, and I barely caught her whisper: "He di' worth three of Chaital."

That was about the time that, in my head, I began to build a house, an upstairs house with a gallery full of Ma's flowers and around the house were trees laden with fruit. Where that house stood, in my mind, Judith and the boys were busy about their schoolwork and the boys would get good jobs. Pa kept the garden but no longer needed to work so hard. Ma tended her flowers on the gallery. I could not fit Dada in anywhere. I was getting on a boat to study abroad. But in between that space in time that I drew up in my head and the place where I sat was a dark gulf with sharp stones underfoot and deep churning water and I could not see where land or sky ended and the sea began.

As usual that night, by the time I put out the lamp, my nostrils were black with soot.

CHAPTER 5

# AFFIDAVIT

This is to certify that the attached affidavit declared before me on the fourteenth day of August 1939 concerns the birth certificate which gives the date of birth of Nathan Deoraj who is registered as Gahadar Deoraj.

I, Ravi Deoraj, of #18 Fellowship Road, Moruga, declare as follows:

1. That I am the declarant herein.
2. That I am a citizen of Trinidad and Tobago.
3. That I am the uncle of Gahadar Deoraj also called Nathan Deoraj. I am his father's brother.
4. That Gahadar Deoraj and Nathan Deoraj is one and the same person.
5. That the name of his father was not entered in the relevant column of his registration of birth and should have had "John Deoraj" thereon.
6. That his mother's maiden name was omitted and should have had her complete name as "Elizabeth Deoraj formerly Mooneram."
7. That I have known Gahadar Deoraj also called Nathan Deoraj since his birth.
8. That the name Oswald on his Baptismal Certificate has never been used and he has never been called by that name.

## Nathan

It was some years before I met the other boy – the one Phuwa said should have been Oswal but had been christened Israel instead, the name originally intended for me. Phuwa was the one who told us that that Israel had lived with his aunt, who was half Spanish and married to a Chinee because she disdained black people, her mother having been mainly white.

They say that when Israel's mother died, this aunt took him even though he was almost as dark as his father (whoever *he* had been). The truth was, whether or not they were right to call her *racial*, this Tantie Annie loved children and had none of her own, and her much older husband (the Chinee) felt the same way. They had left Mission and lived in Port of Spain for a little but Tantie said Nelson Street was too hard, not to mention too low, and so they were getting ready to move back to the country when Tantie died. They brought the body back for burial in the cemetery at Mission and Phuwa attended the funeral, taking a natural interest in the circumstances of a boy who had been given the name originally selected for me. It seems Israel's Tantie had died several years after her sister's disgrace had brought down confusion of the most embarrassing sort.

The sister who was Israel's mother had taken up with a mister who may or may not have been the child's father, but he managed to take for baptism a baby everyone was already calling Oswal and come home with him named Israel. When the man moved on to the next stupid woman he could find, as was inevitable, the young mother took refuge from heckling neighbours and preaching family by running to her older sister in Port of Spain, who took her in and nursed her through a mysterious disorder until she died leaving behind a healthy boy child. It was not long after that that Tants, the elder sister, died too.

Tantie's husband kept the boy and was kind to him, and they moved back to the village as planned and opened a chinee shop. So Israel picked up school again in Mission. He was a thin, wiry, coffee-coloured boy with impulsive movements and a ready grin.

"He bright too bad," boasted Old Chin, his foster father who was neither old nor named Chin but who was always called Old Chin. "Time they put a sums on the board he done eat it up aready. But he does like to play, you see. He is a real boy; you cyan' help for that." Old Chin was an admiring and undemanding pa, and Israel, bright as he was, was growing up the usual way, tolerantly described as playful, which meant he got into mischief that rarely harmed anyone but himself and would, eventually, drink a bit and chase girls. Meanwhile, Old Chin recounted his exploits proudly. "You know this boy take me whole meat I bake for the Christmas and chop it up to hand it out to he friend?" He smiled broadly.

So Israel left school at thirteen with a good mind but nothing to show for it on paper, and he went to work in the Contract. Part of the Contract work was to clear the way for roads through areas of virgin forest. The men had to fell trees anyway, so it was an opportunity to burn coal at night in order to make a little money on the side. In the day, though, they worked as hard as Papa Jacques's men had on the estate, only they worked for Baas who had a whip he called The Hunter that he used on horse, dog or workman. Outside of the hours put in for Baas, the men cultivated nearby land with pigeon peas, ground provision, corn, cocoa and, in some cases, ganja. "No harm in dat," they pronounced. All around them the forest was full of wild meat.

Israel was still small when Old Chin first introduced him to Pa, as one of the men working in the Contract. Pa had gone to the shop to pay off a minor debt. Later Israel encountered Pa again, working in the Contract, and Pa hailed him out as if he were a big man. Flattered, Israel more or less attached himself to the older man, and it was actually through Pa that Israel began to hunt. By the time Israel was fourteen, cheered on by Old Chin he acquired a couple hunting dogs. Old Chin reported the boy would be almost dancing with excitement when he came home with the stories of how the dogs had raised a beast and the men had run fast behind it. "The lappe get away because he reach water," Israel explained to Old Chin the first time, when he returned empty-handed. "He love water too bad, you know. Is he house."

The next time they followed an agouti, which bolted into a hole in a long, thick log. They corked it up at one end leaving just enough room to push in a rod so as to drive the animal him out through the other end, but the log was too long. "Smoke he out, man," Pa commanded. But even then the animal was too confused to make its way out, so they cut the log short and the dogs held him easily. Then Israel was able to hand over some of the precious meat to his foster father. "And don't mind my hand skinny and can fit in the space," he said. "You can't push in you hand because sometimes it have mapepire in hole like that." This was a deadly snake and Old Chin thanked Pa for looking out for the boy, enthusiastically adding hunting exploits and near escapes to his bragging about Israel.

I felt Israel must have wondered why I never hunted with them even though I was his age, but now there were three smaller children and Ma was big with the next. Once, when Israel passed by the house on the way into the forest, Pa did call me to come with them, and I said, "But, Pa, I can't come, because who will help Ma?"

"Come, son," Pa said, his voice quieter than usual, "I go teach you how to talk to me." And he hit me a stinging slap on the face. "I is you father. You want to argue with me? You feel you big. I wouldn't give you no more but don't talk back to me again." There was nothing to say but "Yes, Pa."

Israel stared – I suppose he wondered how I would react – but I knew Pa was Pa so I waited to hear what he decided, and when he nodded I went back to chopping wood for the fireside.

It was as well I stayed in earshot of the house because the next baby came that same night, May 2, 1944. It was a terrible birth, and I heard that the midwife I had fetched talked of little else for weeks, saying how Madam Jai nearly never make it, but look how it come good in the end. I was in the shop when Pa told Old Chin he was going to name the boy Luke, and Old Chin nodded genially and went on weighing cheese.

I wondered what a fellow like Israel thought of me, hovering near my mother instead of going out to hunt, for Israel seemed to be in the thick of everything. He composed and sang calypsos, and his lean supple body took to dancing in a way I could never achieve – even if dancing had been the sort of thing that happened in our family. He beat drum too, in season. I watched him, eaten up with envy, then went home to my books. He was everything I was not, daring and spontaneous, but there was nothing I could do about myself. By now I was a monitor in the school and on a different path to Israel.

Old Year's Night found me running to the chinee shop for help, trying to make myself heard over the yowling and snapping of the dogs behind their fence of galvanize.

"Like he Pa take in," announced a man they called Pitch who had come to beg for more time to pay Old Chin for goods and was standing, as best he could, in the doorway, his swaying form barely visible against the night. "Deoraj ha' pressure, you know." Pitch cradled his current nip of rum, barely able to support himself with the other hand. Israel ignored the unsteady figure gesturing vaguely at me near the shop door, and ran to untie the hammock at the back of the shop. Then we pelted out into the night and picked up Pa from the roadside where he huddled in the dust, raising him in the hammock between us.

Since it was Old Year's, the hunters were firing off their guns for midnight while one or two villagers with cars drove around honking their horns. Israel was strong despite his thin frame and between us we stumbled along with Pa in the hammock, till the sawmill truck pulled up alongside. But now we were nearly at the Junction and it would have been too hard to pull a sick man up in the truck and bring him down again, so Israel begged the driver to go for the doctor, who generally saw out the old year in the area anyway, drinking with the Magistrate and his friends. The truck rattled away, still honking, but these sounds of merriment were barely audible above the clanking of its ramshackle body. We had got Pa home and cleaned up by the time the doctor arrived.

When Pa recovered, Ma went with me to Old Chin's shop to see Israel. "When you passing we house you must stop and eat. Now you is my son too." She smiled faintly. "I di' suppose to have a son name Israel." That was all she said and he had no idea what it meant. Later I explained it, telling him how, years ago, we had had to get a legal paper to change names, and Israel laughed about how easily Nathan could have been Israel and he, Israel, would have been someone else called Oswal. But he grew serious as he studied the words. Don't mind how we look like different sort of people, he said, the difference was thin like the paper self.

He grew closer to us. We played cricket on the same side but he was always the better player, a leg spinner I watched breathlessly. He was a riveting storyteller at a wake too and, eventually, a stirring preacher – not in the Presbyterian Church, but one of the smaller groups – and he became deeply devout. Not blind though, he insisted, for he worshipped with one congregation for three years, then dropped them abruptly when they started calling up the dead. Not him in *dat*, he said. You mad or what? Me who wash in the blood of the Lamb? And he started over with a more moderate set and, gradually, became even more fearless than before. When he went to hunt in the early days he had carried a Belgian blackstone in case of scorpion bite, but after a while he gave it to Pa because once he, Israel, had wash in the blood of the Lamb he had nothing to fear from bichhi. Yet even the word for scorpion he had learned from Pa.

In fact, sometimes he and Pa worked alone. In that rough lean time coal was $1.20 a bag, and to get money as fast as they could burn coal they sold it for seventy-five cents. That meant burning almost twice as much, so once again Pa spent nights in the forest to supplement his earnings in the Contract, for now he wanted to take us out of the carat into a fine board house.

Israel later said that all the time there were people who said Jai Deoraj's big son shoulda put down he book and help he father with the work, while others said, "You don't see the boy is monitor? When he turn teacher, he go have money to help he father more." A few laughed and said, "Teacher what? You believe that?" But others insisted, "Nah, nah. He go make it. And a teacher is a big man." I held onto my books like someone grasping a branch in the flood.

That first night, as we waited for the doctor to come, then for Pa to respond to the injection, I told Israel that one day I would go for real training. I would be a trained teacher. Israel was not the sort who would laugh. Judith leaned forward to hear more, and I said, "Yes, Mother?" So she scampered away leaving her expression of wonder reflected on Israel's face. As if he knew in that moment that it was going to happen, he stared at me, stunned, for a trained teacher was rare. When you saw one you marvelled at how one man could know so much. Even a provisional certificate seemed to mean writing exams for years before an official from the Ministry of Education examined you.

Israel said, "You have belly, oui!"

Inside, Pa's ragged breathing knitted again to allow a relieved whisper. "Tell the boy outside – Old Chin son who help me get home – tell him thanks too, Doc."

The next time it happened, Ma sent at once for Israel, who ran to beg Teacher Mangalsingh to drive us. The rains had started and Teacher Mangalsingh's car inched through pools of water in the road, but when we roused Dr Harris, he came out to administer the injection. Israel and I had jumped out to make room in the car for the doctor and waited, peering through the water beating on the car window at Dr Harris holding Pa's wrist.

"You know, Doc. This Israel is a good boy." Pa's voice was still low and husky. "He ent in no bacchanal. It have some boy doesn't want to work. They only live by tiefing." Dr Harris laid a quieting hand on his arm, but Pa was feeling more himself and no one could silence him. "What? Tiefing like Bajan. But this boy is a good boy. And he can read and write, you see. If you know anyone can give he a better wok, I would glad."

So in time it was Dr Harris who got Israel a job doing pen work for a man named Thompson, who owned the dry goods business in the village but could neither read not write. After work old Thompson took Israel along to church meetings. Then, Israel told me, he started to go with the boss on Sundays. Was there he hear the Apostle preach and testify, he said, till time come he was saved.

While Israel was a lad still working in the Contract, however, he would help us drag material to the next trace, where a balata tree marked the spot on which Pa would build the wooden house. On Balata Trace, just a half-mile down from Quick River Trace in the direction of the Junction, the wood for the house was piling up because Pa could average how much he would need for each room and every stick of furniture. He had bought all he could from Thompson when the old man cut down two poui trees whose roots threatened the foundation of his store.

Pa would call Israel out to hunt as we grew up, but when they shot a quenk and shared up the meat, the older men took the hog head and boiled it in a pitch-oil tin set on three good stones, with split peas and dumpling and plantain, but Israel laughed and waved it away. "Look, I cooking my food right here. When I was in the world I woulda damage him, but now I can't eat hog again." He was strong without it, he said, because the blood of the Lamb keep him in power, and nothing could hold him down, because of the key.

When he was baptized they had given him a key, which was "Jesus thou son of David, have mercy on me," and Israel insisted that whenever he found himself in trouble he used that key and came through: the surgery for the boil, the time he fell in the river, the night he went astray in the forest. There was that time he decide to go sentry, he said. He check where have fruit that the beast bite up and set himself on a strong branch nearby with his gun. He coulda set a trap gun but was a thing he never like to do after he see a man lose his leg when he accidentally trip he own gun. He could hear the tattoo grunting as it ploughed the leaves in search of fruit and roots; he glimpsed the dull plated body and took aim, but it so happen he slip and fall out the tree. Yet he never break he neck or shoot heself or nothing – because of the key. That was why, when he realized how worried I was about Pa, he urged me to find out what was the key for me, because light does break different on different people.

One night in '46, when Israel and I were eighteen, the men had started home from the forest when he got the news that Old Chin, who had complained of nothing more than a discomfort in one arm and a little dizziness, was dead. This thing was a blow that struck Israel to his knees and in the shock of it he held onto Pa around the ankles and cried like a child. "And the boy right," Pa told us. "Chin was father to him more than plenty people to they blood chirren. And I never hear one bad word bout Chin since I know he. If I say, 'Mr Chin, I have to trust the goods this week,' he say, 'Don't study that.'"

Everybody came out to help with the wake, to put up the shed; and they sent for the carpenter to make the box. Nobody asked anything about money. Ma made coffee and shared it out, and when they were lifting the box, I was in front across from Israel. And so we buried Old Chin.

"Allyou is the only family I have now," Israel told Ma.

"I tell you I was suppose to have a son call Israel," she said.

Years later he had sons too. But one was Kenny.

SEPTEMBER 11, 2010 – 9:10 A.M.

*Uncle I heard them tell you on phone they wuold cut off my head they MEAN it please ask unlce luke for hte money please uncl*

# CHAPTER 6

# PRESCRIPTION

## Judith

Now that everything around me shimmers with this sense of the unreal I can only turn back to what it was to have been that age, hanging on the stories Pa told at night and those Brother read by day. I did not know all that while how our lives were coming together to bring us here. Together. And only now I see how Brother made us up as he went along – but not for this. Surely not for *this*.

Sixty-plus years ago, of course, my situation was unique. I was the *one* girl-child.

Matthew arrived while we were living in Quick River Trace and I was only two, then Mark was born, which I don't remember either. But Luke had been two years ago. "Just before this kitchen finish build," Ma said, for she had her own way of dating things. How I remember it is because of the way Ma screamed, but let that stay right there.

Minding Luke was on my mind while I waited on Pa one Sunday, biting my nails as he argued with Teacher Mangalsingh and Dr Harris on the way from church. Dr Harris had said 1946 would be remembered as the year the country was set on the road to confusion, but Teach said something called *adult suffrage* was a good idea. Pa get vex one time.

"What make that good? Nothing new in that. Ain't I know suffrage from I born? What good bout that?" All this time Pa was getting more and more vexed, the work I had to do was piling up.

I knew everything about the house already from helping Ma before and after school and seeing about the boys. In fact Pa used to call me *Mother*, and Brother and all took it up. Phuwa was a godsend, for she lived near us once she had sold the shop in Sanchez and moved to Mission. Aji said she and Phuwa had moved to Mission Number 2, as she still called it, a little after I was born, and I did not know Phuwa's place in Sanchez and had only heard vaguely of Aji having had some old house on the road to Biche. Now, Phuwa and Aji lived in the heart of Mission, just past the turn after Flambeau Corner onto the Mission Hill Road. The path to their house led off from Mission Hill Road before it continued up to Mission CM School.

Sometimes it was hard for Ma to send me to school, but she would tell Phuwa, "Nathan go vex if I keep she home." Dada would steups if he was in earshot, but Ma seemed not to hear him.

Brother had been living at Phuwa's house for a few years and said it was convenient being close to school. According to Phuwa, though, Ma had arranged it so Pa could not fly into a temper and command him to forget the stupid books and help on the land. I was not sure about the truth of this because Pa seemed proud of the time when the School Inspector had insisted Brother be made a monitor, and I was there when Teacher Mangalsingh explained to Pa and Ma that the boy was going to be a fine teacher if they could just hold out a little longer. That was more than a year ago and now Brother was a force to be reckoned with and insisted I must not miss a day of school.

Pa was out working almost all the time, so Brother made more and more decisions. Brother was seventeen when I was seven, with Matthew, Mark and Luke making trouble non-stop. Ma and Pa hardly had time to think, so they said, "When Brother talk, hear him." It was later that I understood the other forces at work. The sheer range of his knowledge on matters beyond their experience and unimaginable to them made them throw up their hands and say, *send for Nathan*. Pa's brothers did not wield that power over us. Dada worked with Pa but sometimes he could not be found. "He and I going to get away one day before one of we dead," Pa grumbled, "and then I hope one of we don't have to dead."

Ma cast him a glance that said *make sure is not you*, and she spoke up. "Don't take he on, man. Don't make youself sick over he."

Sometimes Brother hired a car and went looking for Dada to set Aji's mind at rest or to remind him Pa expected him to turn out for work. Dada lived in the old house in Impasse that had been Aji's, and in those days we never saw much of him. Pa would see him at work, but by evening Dada hardly bothered to walk past Mr Manny's rumshop to reach our house.

When I was smaller we lived in the carat house far inside Quick River Trace, almost in the forest, before Pa built this one in Balata. I remember seeing the walls of the new house going up and thinking, I going to live in a house partly all wood, instead of mud. Of course the kitchen was outside, down the steps. The house was crowded, Ma and Pa in the one bedroom, and the back gallery partitioned for Brother while the children slept strewn here and there in a common room. At night if it was hot we propped the window open with the stick.

When Brother went to stay at Phuwa's house, though, I took Luke to sleep in the back room Brother had cut off for himself, announcing it was quiet and "the baby go sleep good there, outa the noise." I don't remember us having much in the house then – except for Luke's hammock, and Ma was always reminding me how to prop the cloth apart with sticks, but she never needed to tell me that. Luke was too nice. "I does mind he real good," I said, vexed that she would even question it.

Still it was in running along beside Ma that I absorbed secrets no one else cared to know, like how much water to mix with flour, how to clean dasheen bush and children's ears and a wound made by a nail, how to support a baby's head and keep cloth from settling over his face – how to keep life going. The knowledge came just from being at Ma's side, watching her hands, catching soft exchanges with Phuwa, but there was their conscious teaching, too, enforced, when my attention strayed, by a slap. For it was only when I concentrated that I could sweep and watch the boys while listening in case the rice boiled over.

All the while, Pa was studying how to get the contractor to give him more work. "You have to keep youself in front the contractor," I heard one of his friends say, "or he forget bout you, oui, and he gi' the work to someone else."

"Forget bout me?" Pa threw him a grin of pure ridicule. "What? I ent need to be in front he, nah! I dere in he tail. How he go forget?" It had all kind of thing Pa could say that nobody else could say.

Ma would smile behind her hand and say we better listen to how Brother talked, and every evening Brother would come and read for us. Pa told tales we hung on breathless for every word about the creatures in the forest, but Brother read us other stories and poems that brought faraway places into the room. We knew we were to speak like Brother.

Everyone in the village knew about Brother. "He passing he exam one shot instead of taking them over and over like some of them," Ma explained, "and it have people training for teacher that don't like that."

"To hell wid them" was what Pa said, because, however much he had needed the help Brother could have given in the Contract or on the land, this first son was shining beyond anything Pa could have foreseen and a precious source had opened up to let in a thin but steady trickle of money.

With things going more smoothly, Pa made us laugh in all sorts of ways. Sometimes, unexpectedly, he would crook himself into the posture of Blows, the shoemaker, with his crouching walk, blundering through the house calling for us roughly, heels turned out, toes in. He would put down his coffee cup, pick up a spoon from the table and begin to pound himself on the chest or arms like Blows.

Blows lived in the same shack along the main road where he mended shoes, sleeping on a couple bags in the corner. In the evening he sat outside in his shortpants and hit himself with the hammer rhythmically on his chest, arms, thighs, upper back, chanting in time to each thud, "Baap, baap, baap, baap," over and over. And Pa coming out of his thoughts and finding the house too quiet would knock the pot spoon on his chest, and (if he was sure we were watching) on his head, and chant, "Baap, baap, baap, baap." And we came tumbling over each other to reach him first and clamour for a story, while Brother observed serenely.

Brother was taller than Pa and heavier set, his face fuller too like Ma's and lighter skinned as she was, but his eyes were Pa's, direct, steady, openly evaluating. It was a calmer face than Pa's and didn't look as if he was always about to do something urgent. Brother would sit watching, intently, as if to get to the bottom of things. He had more patience that way, though none at all for what he called *flagrant nonsense* – and whenever he said that everyone scattered out of reach. Brother was more likely than Pa to listen before making a decision even though there was never any question about who was going to make that decision or of anything being said about it once he had. Ma said it had too mucha children to see about for Brother to have to hear a set of stupidness.

Ma spent hours in the garden, growing almost everything we ate. While I jumped about kicking Ti-Marie to see it close up, Ma bent over her plants. Sometimes Pa and his friends would catch wildmeat in the forest that spread beyond the rows of peas, corn and orange trees, but I never strayed so far. "Help me make garden, child," Ma said, in those weeks before Andrew came, and I needed to bend low over the soil to distinguish food from weeds. Pepper, bandhania, sive, pudena, damadhol. Sometimes she called on Pa to clear more land. Watch this. I get a garden fork. Pumpkin, karile, bodi and seim. And then, since it ha' fence, I go make the bean run on it. No, child. The gobar is to lipay the new chulha. And don't throw 'way that dry leaf and rotten tree trunk.

Outside our own small piece of land where we had the house, we planted where we could. Then Ma might talk to me or to herself. "Is Nathan help me put this bamboo to bring in water. You see the wet place? Plant greens. No, beti, we wouldn' clear that; is good grass for cow. Eh. Eh! Dasheen bush growing up for heself. Leh we give he space."

Some mornings Pa was gone by the time I awoke, and some evenings he came home when I was going to sleep. One evening the first patter of rain had sent us running outside to pull the slanting galvanize cover in place over the coffee. The beans were laid out, ripe red mostly but occasionally green, to dry for parching and grinding, but we had to be on the alert for rain. When we came in Pa was back, telling Brother it didn't make sense to work for no contractor all he life. Better he contrac for heself, he said, and he and Dada work together. Brother glanced at Ma but her face was blank.

The only thing was he couldn't read, Pa said, and how he would sign he name on the contrac? So Brother said, "Good. I'll show you." And he told Pa not to sign his whole name because that was too hard to start with. Just sign *J Deoraj*. He held Pa's hand and made him practise, and just like that, Pa started to work as a contractor himself. When there was a contract to be read he sent for Brother, who would come back from Phuwa's and read it out so Pa could decide whether to sign. But next, Pa said he must read the contracts for himself, so Brother taught him his letters and brought him a reading book, and Pa began to call out the words. That is how Pa learned to read after I did – only I got to go to school.

School was near to where Phuwa and Aji lived. Up the hill, past their trace, then up the wooden steps we arrived at the big room with its wooden walls and the wire mesh at the top for the breeze to pass through. When it rained we ran this way and that shifting tables and benches nearer to the middle, but all that mattered was that I had got away from scrubbing wares and floor and clothes and I could sit in the classroom where something new might happen, and then one day I had a slate to use and it was so wonderful I could barely touch it. "You have to press harder than that, child," Miss said.

After a while when I was too big for the slate I had a copybook and a pencil to write with, but Ma cut the pencil in two and put away half of it, then hung my half on a string round my neck so I would not lose it. One of the girls whose parents had money asked why my pencil was short, but what was I to tell her, when she had not only a whole pencil but an eraser as well? I never answered, but she was not a bad girl – she just didn't understand. She was in another class, a group facing a different teacher to ours but part of the hum of our unpartitioned room. I never minded the noise, the humming; I thought that was how classrooms were. The best days were those in dry season when we sat outside on the grass around Miss Ragbir under the mango tree and she read stories, but inside was good too.

School was a release from sweeping the kitchen, grating corn, fetching water. I was taking care of the boys too, and the stand pipe was a good ten minutes away, so I often ran along the track to Quick River instead. Matthew was no help with Mark; the two of them argued and fought all the time. "You see he?" Matthew complained about Mark. "He is a man go damage you top just for so. You playing with him good good and he go give it jiggers. Every-ting is a joke to he."

Ma was too occupied peeling vegetables, grinding masala, geera, garlic. "Judith," she would call, "what happen? You not minding them children or what?" Under her breath she would continue, "Is to plant more corn. What it have there not nuff." A glance or slight movement of hand or head would be enough to issue directions to me as she went about the unrelenting stream of tasks. Sharpen the machete and put a handle on the hoe. Clear more land, and bring good goat manure. Wait, child, wait. If you put you foot on that plant you go bust out in a rash. Oh Father, but like this baby coming now for now.

I was eight in 1946 when Andrew was born. John was supposed to be Pa's name, though he wouldn't use it, so Ma had wanted to call the baby Paul because she said Paul was a next one the Reverend always talked about. But Pa said all he hear bout Paul was that he study ketch he tail with shipwreck and, worse still, police, so he want he child to have a more luckier name. Dada say James, Phuwa say Philip, and Aji say Andrew. Ma smiled and said, "That good." Pa say that is the name for he, and I told them, "We going to call he Andy."

Over the jooking board as she scrubbed clothes she consulted Aji, who had come to spend time when the baby came, and Aji advised Ma to plant fever grass and tulsi. Aji felt weak these days or she would have planted it herself.

"I can't do no more hardwok, beti," she sighed.

"Don't forget man-better-man bush," Brother teased, as he always did when he felt they were playing doctor.

"Let he talk," Phuwa said good-naturedly. "He never know when that save allyou skin." *That* was hard time, they agreed, and it was the man-better-man they planted that had changed things. Now work in certain areas belonged to Pa and Dada alone, but Pa knew he would do still better when he could read properly.

"I feel one day I go build a bridge," he said.

Everything went quiet.

"When Pa say something, why it is everybody stop talking and just watch at him?" Matthew asked, tugging my dress.

"Is because when he say dem thing they does really happen," Ma replied.

Pa. I look back and I can see him now. Pa was lean, dark, sharp-featured with a severe set to his face. He had a square jaw and straight thin lips, and a direct, almost bold stare. This hard look could crack into laughter so his eyes lit with mischief, but he was mostly serious and to us he seemed strong as if the years had beaten some invisible armour over him. Hands work-hardened, feet scarred but toughened beyond bruising, back stubbornly unbowed, he forced his way forward with a sort of petulant independence, a fearless self-confidence bordering on arrogance that broke out in spontaneous response to anything that took place in his presence or reached us by word of mouth. He was uninhibited in expression, irrepressible. "And when I can read good," he continued, "nobody going to fool me with nothing."

"They can't fool you now," Brother replied, observing him in his calm way, eyes bright with laughter.

"True."

Day by day Pa brought in papers to do with his work and Ma punched them down on the spike, one on top the other. Periodically, Brother checked through them, and one day he noticed that someone was trying to trap Pa into clearing an extra lot of land without additional payment. "I go cut he tail," Pa raged, until Brother convinced him they should handle it quietly.

"You don't want people to know you're not reading the contract good yet," Brother reasoned.

So Pa agreed to let him take care of it.

Brother came back with a letter saying the other document was a mistake and apologizing for the inconvenience. "So it's all right," Brother said.

"All right? And that tiefing bitch running loose and we ent even bust he tail? How that can be all right? Ent he go tief someone again? At least he should lost he wok." But Brother said he couldn't make a man lose his work, for how would that make him stop tiefing? And Pa said, no, but it might make he starve. In the end it went Brother's way.

Alongside his work as a contractor, Pa reaped cocoa he had planted years before and we spread it to dry on a balisier mat because, as Pa said, we wasn't big people with cocoa house. Ma told Phuwa how different it had been on the estate where the big women would dance cocoa, bare feet shuffling the beans and keeping rhythm with the music, laughter bursting out as the songs got . . . *hmm*. Still, cocoa tasted better when it came from our own tree, according to Ma, and the milk from our own cattle. One Friday night, she showed me how to make dahee, boiling the milk and skinning off the cream. "Put a few drop now, beti. That nuff, that nuff. Is just to bust the milk." Now she was strong again she was mostly in the garden, planting not only food but medicine, and other things of no apparent use. "Some border plant have leaf allcolour," she reflected, "and croton does brighten up the yard."

Pa still took his time, evening and morning, to work out the day ahead. "Leave him alone," Brother commanded. "It's because he plans that you have a roof over your head and roti to eat." It was true that now, besides the food Ma grew, there were fowls, pigs and cattle – hog cattle and all, for the hard work. First it had been one, and later two hog cattle. These water buffalo were huge tough animals that plodded methodically in the wet grass, dragging out wood, their backs shining with moisture, then crusted with dried mud, their heads strained forward, tilting back the wide sweep of curved horns. I pitied them, not because of the work but because their eyes seemed blank of thought and sensation.

The more we had, the harder we struggled to maintain it. Longtime, Ma said, Brother would leave early on his bicycle to sell milk, then come back and change to go to school. "But first," she recalled, "he reaching home with a bundle of grass, and before he bathe he graze them animal and tote water to the house." But now he get big, she continued, it have plenty chirren to do them thing.

More than ever, Ma referred to him in every emergency. The day she and Phuwa prepared a purge for me, senna and salt – so bitter the smell drew tears to my eyes and I refused point blank to drink it – they sent for Brother. We waited for him to explode as he surveyed the cup grimly. "I don't blame her," he pronounced. "That thing not only tastes horrible – it gripes the belly." He threw a last look of loathing at the mixture and stomped off, so Ma turned away and there was nothing Phuwa could do but throw it out. He became my hero.

Brother did things no one could predict. One day Dada reported that Brother had started to buy a newspaper every day and people who saw him laughed and called out to ask whether he thought he was Papa Jacques. One of them voiced a tirade about people who tried to make out their families were better than others, some of whom had great-grandparents who had been fierce Spanish fighters. "Hey, Papa!" Old man Lezama would shout.

"Lezama and he Robber Talk don't frighten me." Brother's slow deep laugh started out quiet with his shoulders raised and shaking and his eyes squeezed tight until it burst out, his head thrown back and his hands up in the air to clap down on his knees. And the whole house was lifted and set down again refreshed. He made me read from the newspaper too and told me to try and speak the way people wrote in the papers. No, he never bothered with what stupidy people said. He just rolled up his newspaper and waved it at Lezama and he said, "Right, man, right," and he brought it home to read. Let them say what foolishness they wanted. He grinned. When they needed news he was the same one they would come to.

But it was not all laughter with Brother. A workman turning his back on bush burning near the house, or Matthew perching precariously on the railing around the gallery drew down a roar of fury; and even Pa and Ma avoided crossing Brother by interrupting home lessons for chores. At the same time work had to be done in the house. What if Mark were left to get up to his pranks, or the clothes not hung out, or the chickens or cattle not fed? The order would go out, "Cut a whip," and the lash would descend swift, cutting, indiscriminate. "How else we go sell milk?" Ma said. "It have thing to do, and I can't do all."

The cattle had to get water with molasses and coconut meal as well as the feed if we wanted the best milk to sell and to drink ourselves. Then Ma would grate the chocolate and sweeten it for tea. We breathed in the smell, and we tasted it and our eyes would meet over the rim of the cup because it was even better than we remembered.

By the time I was eight the rest of us had taken over feeding animals and selling milk. Ma said that longtime even Old Chin at the chinee shop would buy, and now he was gone his son Israel and others wanted only our milk.

Some with no money to pay, like Guitar, would hold out a tinnen cup and beg a drink. "And how you go refuse him? Just make sure he hand don' touch the bottle," Ma said. Even the Lezamas would buy when they had money.

The way the Lezamas lived was different to us. The big brother, Badjohn Herman, was only fighting, fighting. Afus that boy bad, Pa would say, and even Dada confirmed it: "Bad no tail." When he started as a stickman people said his father had been bad same way, and he grandfather bad same way. Only the youngest brother, Francis, was a little quiet. Pa and Ma shook their heads when they spoke of the Lezamas.

Them was real poor. We wasn't like them. Their flooring was rough dirt and Aji said it had nothing in they house to speak of beside chalchattaa (which is what she called cockroach). The only thing of value, she said, was a big water jar Lezama call he demijohn that he have for twenty-five years. They live vie-ki-vie. They never buy oil. They get light mainly from the cooking fire, and was only sometimes they light a flambeau. They never grow nothing neither – they only know how to waste, Pa said. He said all like them would cut down a whole tree to suck one fruit. Brother would carry produce and things from the garden for them; and some nights, when we could spare it, he would take the mother some of Ma's sancoche. But he said at night if Francis dropped food and was feeling for it in the dark, he would eat it from the floor. Scrape it up with the dirt and all.

We always had food. "You see that is why I does make garden," Ma said. But there were neighbours who didn't and sometimes they would simply miss a meal. Brother said Lezama's wife shared food for whoever was there at the time, then she would eat what was left in the pot, and if Francis came in late he had to wait till morning to eat.

Brother knew things like that. He taught at our school, which was growing steadily and had several teachers now, some living in the area and some in Princes Town, and he said sometimes Francis couldn't reach to class because he had no food to eat that morning. I was going to school by then and I knew well enough too. When the Lezama children were going to school each one would carry a tinnen cup with coo coo. If they didn't have food they didn't set out but, once they did, as they got to our balata tree we would see them sit down and eat it out and put the pans by the tree root. So they went to school without anything to eat for lunch. A few minutes before lunchtime each one put up a finger to be excused, and they would go out and take some other child's lunch and eat it out.

"Ma," Matthew said, "bell ring and children crying because they have no food. Someone eat they lunch. Teacher give them a money to go buy anything they can get. Brother does study do that too."

"*So* these people live," Ma sighed. She had her own way of operating. She packed our food and told us to stop at Phuwa's house on the way to school and leave our lunch there. When I was nine Matthew and Mark went with me at lunchtime, back down Mission Hill Road to Phuwa's house, and we sat there and ate roti with turn sikiye fig or maybe alue choka. When we had a piece of curry, wildmeat or so, I would have been glad to eat it in school so the other children could see. But that wasn't often and Brother said not to lose that lunch for any reason, because the only way a piece of wildmeat would be left back for us to get the next day would be if Ma had gone without.

"And when Brother vex he eating like barbwire," Matthew whispered. So we made sure we swallowed whatever Ma packed for us because Pa said it have a thing call sacrifice, and we better understand it good. Brother added, "Unless you want to be like Francis Lezama and them." He shook his head. "I don't even want Francis to be like Francis and them," he added. So he started to make Francis come early to school for lessons, to catch up.

When Matthew and Mark quarrelled, Matthew would run farther along Balata Trace, then down Fishing Pond Track to Quick River Trace looking for someone else to play with. So one day he came home with the tale of how Francis had found himself in real trouble with his foot, "because it had chigger," Matthew said, "and swell up big big." And as Francis was limping round he stumble and make a mistake and grab at the nearest thing, and was he father water jar. He throw down the water jar and it break; and he walk round the broke-up jar bawling, "Oh God! What a cut-ass I go get!" And, Matthew said, *so* he cry till he fall asleep on he crocus bag on the floor. And when his father come in, the man tumble Francis from off the crocus bag and beat him with the bag on the swollen chigger foot and that boy bawl till we hear him in we house.

Francis mother like she break down under it all, according to Phuwa. Madam Lezama did use to say she was saved, but it never take her through like how it take Nathan friend, Israel. Must be she get sick in she head, because she say she come to know treasure bury behind they house and she begin to dig. She dig one hole like a well, was ten foot deep, Phuwa say, till the fork wear out and Madam Lezama go on with her hands.

I remember when Ma felt sorry for her and sent an old fork that was missing one of the middle prongs. Ma said that Francis wasn't a bad little fellow for he try to take he mother inside to calm her down but it never work, and one day she wander away and nobody hear about her again. Ma said it was a sad thing. Too besides, what Lezama would do with all them children now?

Pa was not so sympathetic. He said old man Lezama was wotless not to give he family the care he give he beast, the one old donkey that survive all he bad treatment, and Lezama get to hear about it and say how he going to give Pa some real licks. But, as usual, Pa say he ent fraid nobody. That was true, for Pa talked his mind to warden, doctor, teacher, reverend. We couldn't imagine someone not listening to Pa. He was thin but sturdy, and at first we all thought him tall. Only as we grew up we realized he was average height and it was some force in him that made him seem bigger and stronger than everyone else, invincible against flood and drought, bad dogs and strangers. His outspokenness made me a little nervous until I realized how many people respected him. When Pa felt ill Teacher Mangalsingh would drive him to the doctor in Mayaro and Dr Harris would come out to take care of him at any hour.

It was always something though. By the time Mark was five he was getting in more trouble every day. "It have rain outside?" I complained to Ma. "He gone out and come in the house dress down in mud, singing, say is Jouvert. All year is Carnival for he and he jumping like dirty people in ole mas. And nobody else causing problem. Matthew have Andy watching outside and Luke don't care nothing once it have jub jub for he to suck. Is always Mark."

Ma had other things to think about. When Pa was too ill to work, she pulled a meal together from nothing while Brother and and his friend Israel talked about anything that might distract Pa. Israel was pleased that Pharaoh's calypso had won the 1947 Road March but Pa said nothing had come out for years that could touch *Matilda*. While Israel and Brother were belting out how *she take me money and run Venezuela*, Ma shared food for everyone, then scraped the pot and gathered the rice that had stuck to it for herself. Brother broke off in mid-line and dashed into the kitchen. "How could you do that?" He sounded as if he was in pain. "How could you share it all out and not leave for yourself?"

"Chupid boy." She shook her head. "The bu'n bu'n is the sweetest part."

"Lord, Father," he erupted. He closed his eyes and stood there for a minute with his jaws clenched, then he grabbed a bowl and began pouring stuff in and stirring. He mixed egg nog and held it out till she drank it, silently, without taking her eyes off his.

It was what they called hard time. "Water more than flour," Ma said. But Pa still practised his reading every night. Phuwa visited and brought pone, so, as Ma observed, "everybody quiet, licking finger," while Brother sat beside Pa. Even while Pa's pressure was high and he felt too ill to get up he insisted they call out the new words. "I go come good just now," he said. "I hardly pass forty – how pressure could keep me sick?" Sometimes, though, he just stared through the window with his mouth tight. One Saturday like that I had climbed up on the table and was sitting there scrubbing it, so I could see out to the street as the man they called Guitar wandered by and Brother glanced sideways at Pa with a smile like he had a secret. Pa stared at him like he felt to laugh.

"You know why they does call him that?" Pa asked.

"Who, Guitar?"

"Guitar, self."

"They say" – Brother half covered the smile – "well, they say he does strum he instrument."

"Is truth," Pa confirmed. "I see him myself."

Brother laid his head on the cushion by Pa and laughed till he was breathless, and Pa rested his hand on Brother's head, the tension easing from his face. "You is a good boy. A good man." But I never saw the man carrying anything like a guitar, however many times I glimpsed him on the road, so it was a mystery to me for a long while. Meanwhile, though, our attention was diverted by Pa's younger brother, Ravi, who had heard Pa was ill and arrived to see him.

Chacha brought us news about the rest of the world. He was enthusiastic about Port of Spain, its big shops and office buildings, about new roads being built and people he knew that had gone to New York and come back. He said one day he would go to New York but before anywhere else he would go to the old place, even though he knew now he would never be able to find his pa or know what to do with him if he did. He would go to India. But one day before that, he told me, when I was big enough he would take me to Port of Spain. "We go take out a picture," he promised. "You go make a nice picture." He smiled, stroking my hair. Ma watched carefully, but she never minded. "You chacha is a nice gentleman," she would say.

Chacha was the first to have a radio, and he brought it to Mission with him and left it when he went back. But first he spent the evening showing us how to work the little shining knobs. Pa sat apart, his face turned away and watching us sideways, suspiciously, but soon he was as anxious for the news as Brother, and shouted at anyone who spoke when he was trying to listen.

It would never be long before Pa was up again, and after one such bout he and Brother called Dada and sent word to Chacha and they were off to cricket. When Chacha had left them for his own house and the rest continued back to Mission, they passed by Mr Manny's rumshop for a nip. Pa and Brother left Dada there and came home laughing about how Lezama got to the cricket ground late, looked around in surprise and announced, "It has beguns!"

"Big man getting on so stupid!" Pa was vexed and amused at the same time. Then when Brother asked him what he really thought of Lezama, Pa shook his head. "He does get on like bad behaviour sailor in the rumshop. He study drunk and disorderly. In fact he life is one long ole mas, but, poor fellow, I feel he even more bad-lucky than he bad. Watch he head – bald like bam-bam – and inside it must be clean same way."

Ma had cooked up pembwa, because it came off the tree right there on the land, but Brother's friend Israel had just dropped in. "I bring allyou a piece of wild," he announced, and he had brought it clean and seasoned, so now she was kneading roti after all. "Don't move from this house till the food cook," she said sternly, and Israel's face broke into the grin he kept for her, a flash of perfect white teeth that lit up his lean, bronze face. The boys had been to the sawmill for wood chips and some larger pieces that Brother cut up with the axe, and the fire was ready and the tawa hot.

Things grew easier as more people sought out Pa as a contractor, but still, cradling his coffee, he stared into his mind and pronounced, "La Tout Saint." All Saints' was coming up, and he would secure the contract for cutlassing weeds in the cemetery so relatives visiting the graves could light up their candles in a clean place.

On Sundays after Brother had lined us up for church, then brought us back, Ma would give Matthew money for juice and ice. At the Junction, Bisnath took daily delivery from the truck that passed with ice, but his best sales were on Sunday. When Matthew left we might be chasing down a fowl, and by the time he returned, ice balanced on top the tin of juice, Ma would have cleaned and seasoned the fowl for simmering in the round iron pot.

Brother too brought in more and handed over almost everything to Ma, but once he said that Ma should have better dresses and showed her two pieces of cloth he had held back some money to buy. Then he drew out one more, yellow with specks of white. "And Judith must have a dress too," he said. "Use the end of the blue, Queen, to get a shirt for one of the boys. Mark must have torn up everything he has. Miss Beharrysingh will sew for you in a few days. Right now, she says, she have nara and she Tantie come to rub it. So give her till Saturday."

The next weekend Ma took me with her to Miss Beharrysingh, a tall, wide lady who lived alone because her husband had died long ago, Ma had told me, so no one knew why they called her Miss Beharrysingh. She measured and made notes, her businesslike scrutiny stripping and exalting me at the same time, before sweeping on to leave me forgotten. When she was done she said Madam Jai must take something and brought out cups of steaming lime-bud tea. I sipped and listened. It tasted stupid but had to be swallowed so I focused on the talk, the warm tea gentle on my stomach, which felt sore inside.

The story she went on to tell made my mind heavy too so my head seemed to fill with darkness punctured by sharp points of light. In a quavering voice, Miss Beharrysingh said her son had come in late, drenched with sweat and blood.

"What happen is this. He coming home with he pardner and dem, and they meet with a lagahoo. No, is true, Madam Jai. Is not a boy does make up story. And is not he head mix up with no drink. The whole of them see this thing. They cross Seukeran after they pass what was Ole Chin shop and they turn like they going up to Fishing Pond Track by Lezama and them, but instead they decide to take a path through the cemetery and meet the Balata farther down. Yes, going out by you – is why I telling you so you go know. So, as they round the big stone where de Jacques and dem does bury . . . yes, just by the hole for Madam Ramnase fineral, they hear chain shake and this thing rise up right there in the way.

The thing foot big like a tree, wide so and tall and it cover in long hair, but it back was to them, so they try to back back and duck behind the big stone. Then they see how de head tun backway for the red eye light up watching them and fire flowing out of it. Aaha? Before it swing on them, they pick up the shovel by the grave site and some pole for lowering the box and they start to beat it. Afus they beat that beast. And it change and come down small and start to bawl but they know what it is and they beat it till it turn into smoke and they couldn't see it no more.

And if I tell you, Madam Jai. How that boy get on when he reach home, and how he breathing hard and he eye red. Red like the lagahoo eye. After I see bout he I gone on me bed, yes – you know I does suffer with me nerves, nah. But I come good now, you will get them dress soon. Don't frighten for that." She leaned forward for my cup. "What happen, beti? Talk alone frighten you? What woulda happen if you did meet the lagahoo self?" She was laughing at me as she saw us through the door.

"Stupid little boy and dem," Pa raged later in the evening. "You know ole Lezama donkey – the one old donkey he have? It get loose and stray in the cemetery and they find it dead this morning. He self ready to kill somebody. He say he lost one jackass – he go bring in another just as dead. Stupid little bitch and dem frighten to show they face on the road. Like they forget who they was dealing with. They does watch he in stickfight, but they only now remember: he ent use he balata just for stickfight. What? Lezama could crack head like a police. They frighten like hell now. Anyway they friend only making joke at them, jumping out from behind tree, shouting, 'Bois! Bois!'" Pa laughed in the midst of his vexation.

I fell asleep with Lezama's donkey hiding in the trees, just two blazing eyes in the bush, and next morning I felt dizzy and the way to school seemed longer and hotter than usual, the boys louder and more unruly. I liked to read but that day I was glad to finish for my throat felt dry and rough. Then, outside was so bright I couldn't play. A battimamselle trembled on the top wire of the fence, iridescent in the sunshine and wavering against a wind so light it hardly stirred the mango leaves, and I felt shaky and transparent too. I leaned against the school fence, biting my nails, and hard, sharp light pierced my head so I wished I were at home and I wondered how to get back. Brother came and asked if I was well and I just said yes because my lips were too dry and uncomfortable to explain. "You didn't get into trouble?" His voice was stern and pricked tears from me instantly.

"No, Brother. Teacher say I read real good."

"Never mind then." He softened and took my hand to press something into it. "If you have a problem you must tell me." As he left, I saw the paper in my hand had two coconut drops. Brother, who was big now – a great man who didn't have to remember I existed – he had come looking for me to give me coconut drops. The sunlight sparked and sizzled, pain shot through my head and I closed my eyes sucking the candy, and his presence hovered over me calming, smoothing like the sugar, melting like my legs as they slid beneath me.

When I opened my eyes he was carrying me.

"Juds? You should have told me." His eyes swam. "After I left, I wondered if your hand hadn't felt a little hot." He had turned back, and caught me before I hit the ground. "How you didn't tell Brother?"

I had never seen him like that.

"I sorry, Brother. I will tell you next time." I was confused. "But what I must do now?" With the back of my hand I wiped away blood from under my nose.

He gathered me against him and began to run. I wasn't sure what happened for a while, just patches of light and dark, yellow fabric for a dress lost somewhere, and fiery eyes drifting in the shadows under the trees, then the doctor and Ma whispered over me, Brother holding me all the time.

"Lord Father. Hospital?" Ma's voice, afraid. Other voices.

"But people does study dead in hospital," one said.

". . . and the child father at work . . ."

"No time," Dr Harris was saying. "She must go straight away . . ."

"Juds?" Brother. "You'll get well, but we have to go where there are plenty doctors and nurses."

I grabbed at his hand and when he squeezed back I didn't care if he cracked my fingers because his grip held off the iron crushing my head.

I never knew about getting to San Fernando. It must have been weeks later that I opened my eyes in the hospital, an old wooden building. Strangers on bed after bed stretched down to the other end of the room with an old lady in white, knitting under the window. People came to see me, not rough, just strangers. Swabbing and probing, staring into my mouth. I looked past their hands and instruments into every corner. They spoke kindly but I burned and shivered searching the room, my eyes unable to close, until one took my face in her hands and turned it to a doorway where Brother leaned forward, waving. Then my eyes could close and I slept – but it was not restful, just empty.

I was in hospital for months it seemed, and even when I woke up I watched the open doorway until he came. There he stood, smiling and nodding, or placing his hand on the space in the doorway till I could raise mine too, to press it against the space between us. Afterwards Ma said she thought I had died and they were afraid to tell her. They wouldn't let her travel with the next child heavy in her belly and a cloud of grief weighed her down more, even though Brother insisted he had seen me and I was doing well. Brother studied at night to make time for his visits, and Pa worked harder and longer to buy my medicine. But the cost was impossible for Pa meet and long after-wards I learned Brother had borrowed the money or I would have died, though he never told Pa that. As for Ma, she mourned on silently in her head.

In San Fernando Hospital the nurses were kind enough, and one in partic-ular helped me to my feet, while they still crumpled under me, until I could hold the bed and walk around it. But that was not the end of it for I caught chickenpox, and blisters covered my arms and face so I was too miserable to swallow and I could feel my life draining away in the hunger and the distaste for that mush in front of me and then I realized it was all there was and what would it have been for if I died of hunger so I closed my eyes and shovelled it into my mouth and it started to come back up and I felt dizzy, mixed up as if I was coming through the river and mud had got into my mouth, but I told myself it wasn't mud and gulped hard and I was so angry that all I wanted was to get it from in front of me and I kept swallowing till it was gone. And there I remained, eating minced meat and mashed potatoes until one day Nurse Jenkins noticed me with my eyes squeezed tight, forcing it down, and she spoke to people in another part of the hospital and they brought rice and chicken with pigeon peas and I knew I would get better after all.

Then came the day Brother was allowed in, and I woke to see him sitting beside me. He was bigger and stronger than I remembered and his face was smooth and glowing with pleasure. He hardly said anything, and in the feeling of well being that surged over me I fell asleep again, almost at once.

Another day, he came to take me home. But I saw it immediately.

"Now *you* are in trouble." I perched on the edge of the bed watching him. "And you must tell me."

I could see him considering for a while, then he took out a piece of paper from his pocket and turned it over and over without giving it to me. "Some-times," he said, "a person who pretends to be your friend doesn't want you to get ahead of him. He doesn't try to get ahead himself, but you musn't get ahead of him. So. Someone has been writing things about me to make me lose my job."

I held out my hand.

*TO WHOM IT MAY CONCERNED*

*Nathan Deoraj looking quiet quiet but do not trus because he is a snake. He pretend to reading all the time but does he knows what he read? What paper cer-tificate do this man have to show. This man cannot edicate your child do not put your son or dauter in his care.*

"Is a big person this, Brother?" I could not believe it. "But I write better than that."

"I should hope so. I think it's the father of one of the teachers, but the fellow himself must know about it. The man himself is spreading stories, and that is more serious."

I felt like a big person because Brother spoke to me openly about such a thing, and I asked for his pen, and on the back of the paper I wrote my own circular and gave it to him. It was short and simple because I was still very weak.

> BROTHER
>
> *Nathan Deoraj is my Brother. He is kind to everybody if they do their work. He knows a ~~lot~~ a great deal because he reads so much. Whoever doesn't know that is a chupidy.*
>
> *P.S. I know the word is fool but Brother says it is not polite for a child to say, especially about big people.*

I still felt too ill to do any better.

On the way home I glimpsed big buildings I had not seen when Brother was bringing me to hospital. The streets of San Fernando were busy with cars and buses even on the new bypass and the tram bore down on us now and then when we bumped over its tracks. Soon the road grew quieter and the cane fields gave way to bush and trees. Banana and plantain leaves opened sometimes to a glimpse of pineapple in neat rows, until different trees soared up, flashing deep purple-pink pomerac blooms or trailing vines. Then I knew I truly was going home.

When I got out of the car, Ma cried. She could hardly speak; she just stared at me with her eyes streaming. Was like this child come back from the grave, she said. She cried because my face was thin and pale and my body just bones and my hair thin and clumps of it still falling out, but mostly she cried from the shock of relief. When she realized it was really true she stroked my face and looked at it as if she could never see it enough. "You must take this child to Mayaro," she said. "The sea breeze go do she good." But Brother was too afraid of one of us drowning.

In any case the excitement brought the next baby early and the pains started in the night. Pa was in the forest and Brother got Ma to bed, then leaned through her window and stopped two cars on the road to send their drivers for the midwife. "It don't take two of them to find she, boy," Ma protested.

"Yes, yes. In case one stops by the rumshop or something," he insisted. "At least one will get the message through."

"Oh Father have mercy," she said, and left it up to him.

The arrival of the midwife, a broad, solid woman who began giving instructions in the doorway, brought the house to order. I was too worn down by the fever to be of help, but Phuwa had finished cooking and took over Andy and Luke while Brother moved into the next room to pray. He stopped to eat the food I had taken out for him, steaming rice and dhal with dasheen bush bhaji, and he called the boys together to ensure we had all eaten, then went back in and prayed and read for hours, till the baby cried and we heard that Ma was safe. Aji had not been strong enough to come and Ma said weakly that it was the first baby to arrive without Aji's help, but Phuwa was there preparing fish tea for Ma and me both. For days afterwards Brother came directly home after school and made eggnog, and watched till Ma had drained every drop.

"I go stay with you." Phuwa stroked Ma's hair and sopped bay rum on her head. Phuwa had got a young girl from the village to sit with Aji. The girl's father, they said, was the coconut man. "You don't remember Nuts? The fellow who does sell coconut at the Junction?"

"Yes. Nuts selling there years now."

"I go stay," Phuwa repeated. "So much child you have to mind, and I have none."

"All my child is your own," Ma said softly.

And Phuwa nodded, gently oiling the baby's legs.

Timothy, they agreed.

The new baby meant extra expense and more work, but for a long time I was useless. My hair had gone thin, making my face ghostly, and my arms were too frail to be trusted with Timmy. I could hardly steady my hand to carry the posey from under my bed to empty it, but I was ashamed to leave it for anyone else. I was ashamed of being an ineffectual trembling thing in the hammock, and since I couldn't help it and had no cause to berate myself I was even ashamed of being ashamed. So I climbed out of the hammock and made myself walk around and ventured out when the sun was not too hot or the rain not pelting down, and I tried to pull out some weeds from between Ma's plants when no one was watching. But mostly I ate everything I could get.

As usual Pa and Brother carried us through, bringing home the money to put in Ma's covered pan, for there was no bank those days – or I suppose now there must have been but we never knew about it. A few weeks had passed before it dawned on me that Brother had not lost his job because of the thing he called the poison pen letter, and I told him shyly it must be because of the letter I wrote, poor as it was. I knew better, but he smiled and said that was why he had brought me a new dress all made up already by the seamstress.

When I put it on and had the ribbons tied I could hardly stand still.

"It fit me, Brother? I looking nice?"

"What? Nice too bad. *Elegant.*"

Brother and I loved words. When one of us learned a new word we would save it up as a gift for the other.

One day Matthew said, "Bro, what you go do with all them word you collect in you head?"

And Brother said, "I wonder. Sometimes, you know, I think I have a book inside me."

"What that means?" I pushed through the others who were crowding round him in excitement. "You mean you going to write a book?"

But he laughed and shooed us away. Ma paused to look up, her hands automatically popping peas out the speckled pods, tossing aside shells, then dropping pearly green beads into the bowl. Her glance flickered over us, lit with the satisfaction that we were all there together, eating, laughing and bickering. Later I crept up alone and asked Brother again what he had meant about the book.

"It's a funny thing," he said. "I don't understand it myself. It's like something writing itself inside me, but I don't know how to stop and pull it out." It would be like fishing, I thought, like what his friend Israel talked about – patiently waiting on a hard tug at the line, then drawing it up out of deep strong currents. But I forgot that for a while, for new things were always happening.

It was about that time that Pa discovered someone in the village had put up a shack at the back of our land, to sleep in on the edge of the forest instead of walking back and forth to the village, and Pa walked all around the shack looking at it, then took one of the poles in his two sun-baked work-roughened hands, shoved once and leapt back as it crashed down. The next day he sent Matthew with a message for the man to collect his material before Pa burned rubbish on the weekend. A day or so later the heap of wood and galvanize had vanished.

Things like that created a brief stir, then fell out of mind, but not every-thing worked out that way. Two weeks before I went back to school after the fever, Phuwa set out for her house because Aji had resolutely taken to her bed and driven away Nuts's daughter. "Go," Ma urged. Only Phuwa came hurrying back in no time, insisting that Ma call Brother home fast fast.

"Nathan at school. The boy working," Ma protested. "You go see him pass to come here, and you can stop him and talk." But Phuwa said it couldn't wait and only Ma could call and make him leave school. Then she whispered what she had just heard in the street and Ma flew downstairs and sent the message to Brother. Once that was done they agreed that the first question would be how to find Pa and Dada and the next would be whether Brother would be able to prevent them from making a jail.

When Brother arrived, Phuwa burst into tears and announced that Dada's second wife, Mala, who had years ago gone bawling back to her parents with their child, had now take up with a mister and move into he house. Mala mother dead and she father get sick and can't mind Mala and she child no more. And, after what pass between Mala and Chaitlal, she wouldn' come back to he. Chaitlal did beat she for giving him rice without surwa because although he like he curry cook till the sauce dry down he di' still want surwa on he rice, so he did beat she for the surwa and she hand break. So she say she wouldn't come back to he. But now no one to mind she and the child – and is all of that why, when the mister put question to she, she follow him onetime, even though this man short and thick and have a set of button on he face so people say he look like a canal frog.

When Dada arrived, fully informed, dangerously drunk and supported by Pa, Brother was there to insist that no one should be chopped nor any house burned down. He got Pa to agree they wanted no licks put down on Mala neither. On one point, however, both brothers were fixed: a man child can't live in a house where the man wife take up with a horner-man.

And that is how it happened that Dada's daughter, Doolarie, came to live with us when she was thirteen and I was not quite ten. Dada and Pa had hired a car, found their way to the place where the mother now lived, and watched the house. Chacha, having been sent for, joined them obediently. Phuwa reported, after talking with the driver, that just as Mala bring Doolarie home from school and as the horner-man self open the door, the three brother rush out of their car and grab the girl and push her in the car and bring her home.

"He ent coming to fight with we," Chacha had said, "whatever he bawl out. That is just grand charge."

But the detour to drop off Chacha at Mathilda's Corner, where he could get a drive back to Moruga, delayed Dada and Pa for nearly an hour. They no sooner reached home than Phuwa reported that the man Mala take up with had sent to say he go come after them and trow some good chop in they tail. Is when they hear that, she told Ma (as they both stared at the car swerving away from the house again), is when they hear *that* that Dada and Pa take up they gilpin cutlash and gone back for the man.

"But why you tell them?" Ma's eyes were wide with fear and she shook her head in disbelief. "What make you tell them what the man say?"

In no time they were back, though. They said they only planass the fellow with the gilpin, and after they well beat he they leave him and Mala alive but too frighten to follow them home for the child. After that we heard through Phuwa that the mother had gone bawling to police, but the police say was the man child – so what to do? They say the child father and he family didn't kill the horner-man – they just use the flat side of the cutlass to beat he, and he well lucky he get off so light.

Over the next week Phuwa brought further reports. First we got to hear that the mother take in. Phuwa said she hear Mala stomach stay just so and get alterated and she wouldn't go doctor. She only bawling for she child, and was when she stomach rupture that she finally gone doctor. Not long afterwards we heard it was too late: she did gone hospital but she dead. So Doolarie couldn't have gone back even if Dada would have let her.

Doolarie was a tall, lost-looking girl who cried and cried. Ma told her, never mind, for sheself would mind her good good like her own child. "Don't cry, beti," Ma said. "And you don't take it on," she added more sharply to me, sniffling in sympathy as I washed the wares. "When she done cry and it don't change nothing, she go settle down and eat roti, and cut grass for the cattle and go to school with all you."

That was precisely how it was. When I went back to school at last Doolarie walked with us, only she had never attended very regularly before so she had to go in a class with smaller children and she resented it. "She'll catch up," Brother said, and set her extra work. But that made her cry harder, and Dada said to leave her if she wasn't interested in books, once she could clean and cook and wash good.

Doolarie was about three years older than me and sometimes we went to the pipe together, she with the large container on her head and I with the smaller one in my hand. As we walked back the water lapped and splashed over. "You wetting me," I grumbled. Doolarie shot me a fierce look and said nothing but I was quiet and we went on, the water slapping over onto her head, soaking her hair, trickling into her eyes, running down her back.

When we got home she was drenched, the sodden clothes clinging to her, and Ma shook her head. "Oh, oh!"

"You was to bring some of it home, gyul," Dada said. "Like you think we send you to bathe." His voice sounded different, raw and hoarse, as he stared at her from under heavy lids.

Ma wrapped a bedsheet round Doolarie and drew her away, rubbing her hair. "Don't fill it so much next time. Is not good to walk on the road like that. It have wotless people."

Eventually life returned to normal, and Ma to her garden. "Man, what you think happen? Goat coming in and eating me crops," she complained to Pa with her eye on the tawa, showing me again how to turn roti directly over the heat without scorching it.

"If the neighbour don't control he goat, best you make a barracation," Phuwa advised.

"Nah, nah!" Pa grinned, "Best we curry the goat."

"No, man," Ma murmured. "That have chop up in it."

"Is true," Pa called back over his shoulder as he passed through the door. "Goat must chop up before it curry."

Even Doolarie laughed. She was one of us now.

Before we could stop to wonder whether this was a good thing, something new happened that filled us with wonder and knocked everything else out of our heads. Pa built a bridge over Quick River, just where Ma had thrown Mark for Phuwa to catch. There were people who had schemed and bribed for the contract, but everything Pa had ever built had lasted, so the contract came to him and he built the bridge. How did he know how to build a bridge? He couldn't say. Only, he said, is years now he gone to watch every time he hear bridge building, and he listen to the men talking about how they do it.

But a few people were jealous. A boldface neighbour with skin the colour of abeer resented Pa getting the contract when her son had not managed even to get work on the team. This Madam Ramjit announced that she woulda never eat by Madam Deoraj after the last time, when Madam Deoraj food did give she bad stomach. She gave details on how often she went off and the pain involved. Not she again, she said. She ent able wid *dat*. Phuwa said the woman should have tried absent salt, but all Ma said was not to tell Nathan nothing, because the boy had better thing than that to study.

Meanwhile, the same teacher whose father had written the letter about Brother said that if Deoraj was making so mucha money a week and he satisfy to build everything except a good house for he own family then to hell with he. Ramjit agreed eagerly. Let Deoraj keep he family in a house that lean to one side, he said.

"Lean like he foot." Pa steupsed, and poked fun at the neighbour's knock knees and mimicked his awkward posture by twisting one leg to make it stick out to the side. "I need a man look like capital *K* to tell me how my house supposed to look?" In no time Ramjit was widely known as Capital K.

Christmas came, with the smell of hot bread and the squeal of the pig – the meat Ma would season and send Matthew with to the baker, who would drive it deep into his oven till it was shiny brown and sizzling. The fellows from Cabal Trace came strumming quatro and as usual Pa gave them rum so they sang parang deep into the night. No one home had time for Ramjit's views, especially since Brother had come out first in his exam and if he kept going that way he would soon get to training college in truth.

Meanwhile, Brother took me out of the class I was in, which was the class with the jealous teacher, and he put me in his classroom with bigger children and taught me a separate syllabus alongside the rest. I had his full attention, and that was not an easy thing.

# CHAPTER 7

# COPYBOOK

## Judith

"Study you book good," Ma would say between grinding geera or mending Mark's pants, and her glance gathered in Doolarie as well. "My two girlchild must be able to put they hand in they pocket and feel they own shilling."

I needed no urging. I could not wait to get away from scrubbing wares, floor or even babies, and into sums and stories. Brother insisted we do other things as well, like singing. "The Ashgrove" was a song about trees, flowers and scenery none of us had seen and it ended sadly without explanation, but I belted it out because here I was singing instead of washing clothes. Schoolwork was an infinite relief.

Most of the other children never felt that way, and one or two of the bigger boys actually closed their mouths mulishly during "The Ashgrove" till Brother flourished his belt. "I have no voice myself," he said, "but in case you do I'll see that we hear it." The belt was really for other lessons though, like grammar. "Speak the way you are to write," Brother insisted. "That way you will write well automatically and get a good job one day. You want a car or a bike?" he asked the boys. "If you don't work hard you will have a car like Mahal."

Mahal was from a nearby village that had actually been smaller than ours but was growing rapidly. He had a serious, focused expression as he steered to avoid other cars, children, potholes and pothounds. He changed gears seamlessly, mashed brakes gently and reversed into narrow spaces with impeccable accuracy. The only problem was that there was no car.

Matthew said that once when Pa sent him out on a Sunday to buy the usual grapefruit juice and ice, Mahal drew up in front the shop and Mr Haseley asked him whether he was going as far as Mr Manny's rumshop that day. Mahal said yes, so Mr Haseley gave him a small parcel to drop for Mr Manny. "It don't matter whether it reach morning or evening, Mahal. Once he get it today self," and Mr Haseley turned away because Mahal was absolutely reliable and went wherever he said he was going to go. Mahal accordingly threw the parcel in the back seat, mashed the accelerator hard and swung off directly to Mr Manny's.

In the evenings Brother would read to us and then Pa would read to Brother, all Cutteridge had to say about the geography of the West Indies. The rain beat on and on, soaking Ma's plants, filling barrels and overflowing drains and rivers, and tearing away land. Inside, Pa read on about ways in which people irrigated crops in dry places, and about how farmers in other places needed barriers to protect cocoa flowers from the desiccating effect of wind. What was that now? Pa asked. Brother explained *desiccating*. Pa was awed, not only by the knowledge but by the words, and by the fact that Brother knew them.

Brother read continuously – Shakespeare, Sir Walter Scott, Burns and Hardy – and passed me every book that came into his hands. Brother was a window through which to look at a world so different from our own that even when we used the same words they might not always mean the same thing. One day I asked what made the gardens in these books so beautiful. How could karaile and pumpkin and all the other things that grew in a garden like Ma's be pretty? He said those were flower gardens. Pa dismissed the idea of a whole garden just for flowersplants as a waste of good manure, but Brother said he wasn't so sure. In fact, he said, we had gardens like those in Trinidad and perhaps we should go and see them.

Now that Brother was a teacher he put together with Pa and bought a piece of land near the Junction, putting not only Pa's name on the title with his own but the boys' names too. "We go put a brick house on that one day. I telling you the truth, as man," Pa said, contemplating the area of bush and old wood affectionately and proudly. "For now we go fix back the best board house this village ever see."

On the land was what had been the first wooden house in the village.

Boards of different lengths stood side by side so the top of the wooden wall was irregular and had a gap between it and the roof. "Dat good." Ma surveyed it as Brother watched her reaction. "Dat mean air go circulate." She was adopting words as fast as we brought them home. "Too besides, you pa go study pull down room and put back. In no time that whole thing go build over."

"It going to have a kitchen inside," Pa told her.

"I feel I go try me hand with some dahlia in that garden," Ma said. "And you see where the bamboo dripping? I go plant fern. And over there I making a machan and put buttercup to climb." I already knew those yellow bells were not real buttercups like those that grew with flowers like Wordsworth's daffodils, which stayed obediently on the ground instead of clambering up and rioting all over the place, but I was caught up in the wonder of it.

"Flowersplant?" Pa scowled, and Ma said no more. Who knew better than Ma that the garden was a place for growing food? But when she slipped a tin with dahlias in a corner of the gallery or stuck in buttercups to shoot up beyond the bodi, Brother shrugged tolerantly and said, "Leave her. What harm can it do?" Then he grew very serious. In front of Pa he plonked down a brown paper bag from the pharmacy and said, "You stopped buying these tablets Dr Harris told you to take, but now I've paid for them make sure you swallow one every night and don't waste my money."

Pa glared at him but it was no use and he turned away to hide the smile edging up round his mouth.

"You see this boy, Nathan?" Pa said that night to Dada and Chacha. "That is a good boy. Not like how some people chirren does turn out."

"They all doing good," Dada agreed, his glance scooping me up greedily before flicking over Matthew and Mark glowering at their homework.

Every morning Brother came by and cast around an eye that noted a scrappy copybook, hanging hemline, flush of fever, callused hand pressed absently to the chest or a protruding wire at eye level. And he would wag a left forefinger in that direction, a silent command, *fix that*, before stepping out back to the street.

Ma watched him with fierce intensity and swept her finger to gather up the gaze of every one of us and point it at Brother. "Take pattern," she said sternly.

But not everyone cared about his example.

People say the boy Reds ran errands in the big house on Jean de Jacques's estate, Dessalines. Reds was a rough sort – not the type whose house Ma would send me to, even to sell eggs. He was friends with some of the older Lezama boys, and with Fingers, whose father was the tailor, Ramjit (Capital K) – another one whom Pa said was too wotless to mind he own chirren. I asked Ma why Papa Jacques kept Reds there if he was so wild, when Pa self lost his work for just standing up to the driver. How come, was what I wanted to know, but Ma said I was too fast with myself and I must mind my business or the roti wouldn't swell.

Whatever Papa Jacques had felt about Pa once, he spoke well of him now – of how he had survived and provided for his family. "And imagine he built that Quick River bridge," Papa Jacques said. An engineer who was Magistrate Marchand's friend had seen it and said it could not have been better done. Papa Jacques had said it was he, Jean de Jacques, who had taught Deoraj the value of work, for everyone knew Pa worked day and night. Dr Harris warned that it was aging him prematurely, though, and he must slow down.

In between all he did as a contractor, however, Pa was busy rebuilding rooms in the house at the Junction, little by little. He passed the most strenuous labour to his workmen, but keeping track of lumber and galvanize, and watching the comings and goings of the labourers tried him sorely. Even with Ma helping at every turn it was a continuous battle in mind and body. He looked strong to us, but Dr Harris said Pa's pressure was high and the pains in his chest were not good. When Doc drank with Papa Jacques and Magistrate Marchand on Fridays he mentioned that Deoraj was working himself to death. The conversation came right back to Ma through Madam Jasmine, the lady who ironed Papa Jacques's shirts.

Madam Jasmine came to the house when Ma had hurt her back, and Brother paid her to help so I would not miss school. She was there when we got home, a tall, full-bodied woman squirming between rows of washing to haul bedsheets and clothes off the line and up the steps, her eyes darting around curiously all the time. When she caught sight of Brother she waggled away hastily, trailing her long tail of green cloth like a startled iguana. As soon as he left, she poked her head round the door, then brought in the dry clothes to fold, and resumed her story.

Papa Jacques had asked Dr Harris what was wrong with Deoraj, who looked strong enough. "He in real monkey pants," Doc responded thoughtfully. "Heart, pressure, the works. But he could go on for a good while if he slowed down a little."

"What choice the man has?" Papa Jacques had demanded. "All those children to provide for."

"He make them," the magistrate pointed out.

"The big son was always bright though," Jean de Jacques said, "and they
say he's doing well."

"Actually, with a little help that young fellow could do very well," Doc
agreed. But that was as far as they got. Papa Jacques grumbled that Reds was
a lad who could be just as able if he put his mind to it.

People said Reds's mother had been Papa Jacques's housekeeper. They
said it with a knowing look that I knew better than to question. "When she
mister get vex and say she must look another wok she leave he right there.
Then story jump out," they whispered. When that housekeeper died, Jean de
Jacques instructed that Reds go on living on the estate, but when Reds was
sullen or impertinent de Jacques said no one must lay a hand on the boy
beside himself. Madam Jasmine said Papa Jacques had pointed out Nathan
Deoraj and told Reds that if he applied himself he could be a respected young
man in the village, just like young Deoraj.

But what did Reds care about Deoraj and hard work? All that meant to
him was that Brother didn't know how to enjoy himself – which was stupid,
to Reds way of thinking. He was under fifteen, at least six years younger than
Nathan, neither of them with any interest in the other. But it turned out Reds
had noticed that Deoraj had a sister.

Nothing like that sort of thing was in my head at all; at twelve I was still a
little girl. I can see it now: Reds walking up Balata Trace one Saturday with
his hair sticking out and the sun behind it so it was like fire – you couldn't
miss it when he was still at the bottom of the road. He slowed down and
craned his neck to see into our yard. He would never have dared turn his eye
if Brother was there, much less Pa. But I was alone, scattering feed for fowls,
now and then stooping to look under the house for eggs.

I can see it now: two boys from school were passing on the other side of
the road, must be to cut across to Quick River Trace and follow it up to Fishing Pond Track so as to meet up with Francis Lezama, and the boys nudge
each other and stop. And they lean on the wall as if it had cricket or fight or
something, and they settle down to watch. So now Reds look like he want to
walk on but he can't. I see he squeeze a pimple on he chin and wipe his hands
on his pants, then pass them quick quick over his hair. It make no difference
because the stiff curls flame out round his face same as before. He looking all

about with the strange grey-colour eyes he have, watching me and watching the window and the road.

"Ey! Ey, gyul!" He call to me in this hoarse whisper that make me jump even though I was seeing him all the time through my hair that fall over my face when I bend down for the eggs. So right away I duck behind the water drum.

Ma come out from nowhere and slap her hand on the door loud so he jump, and once he look up she fix him with her eye he couldn't move. And she watch him like a cockroach she mean to mash.

"You?" Ma flash one look at me, then back at Reds, like she can't believe her eye. "You ent even fit to carry she posey."

The boy haul he tail back up the road with the pothound barking after him and the other two boy running behind, one of them laughing and making *shwshwsh* sound like wee-wee coming down and the other calling out all kinda rude thing, and is after that some of them start to call he Posey.

The real problem was that Phuwa had seen the whole thing, for she had brought cassava pone and was there out of sight, standing behind Ma. That evening, while Ma gathered in the clothes downstairs, and Brother and Dada were talking, waiting for Pa to come home, Phuwa settled down to tell the story and Doolarie laughed out hard. And Dada exploded. "Is a joke?" he roared at her, at the room at large, swinging towards the door and glaring through it as if expecting to see Reds lurking outside. Then he turned back, his hard gaze stripping and impaling me. "I go kill she. Watch here." He flexed his arm threateningly and I shrank back against the wall. His fist rose like a hammer over my face. "*So you does carry on, eh?*"

"But she never called him," Brother objected. He thrust me behind him. "I should have got in before."

So it died down, Brother insisting he should have been there to prevent it and no one, not even Dada, capable of blaming Brother. It passed quietly and Ma only knew about Dada's rage because Brother whispered it to her later. I was curled up tight in Pa's Morris chair, still cold and distracted, when, to my horror, Ma erupted.

"One thing I doesn't want is people saying my girlchild bright. You see? You see how that does just invite wotless people to interfere with she? Let she step outya line, I go blaze she tail. The first skin on she body not she own."

"Ma, she didn't do a thing."

"But if she was minding she work better, he wouldn't fast with her," Ma observed, her face taut – but she had not been angry with me when it happened and I crouched petrified, trying to work out what had changed.

"You see this? She doesn't deserve licks for this," declared Brother, the first one to raise the tambran rod for bad schoolwork.

"No. Is truth." Ma subsided and the terror drained from me so swiftly I needed deep deep breaths to recover. "Much less licks from Chaitlal." After a moment Ma added, "Imagine this wotless boy land up outside my house calling my nice little girlchild for that bahanaa to think he must touch she."

I crumpled with relief that her fury had turned elsewhere but with a gathering resentment that it had come my way at all. "And what Pa going to do?" I whispered afterwards to Brother. "Next thing Dada tell Pa, and Ma agree with him now." I managed to keep down the mutinous tone threatening to surge up into my mouth and Brother just rubbed my head and said, "Don't study that. *Sufficient unto the day* . . . Go in your bed." But the bludgeon of Dada's fist hovered over me in my sleep, now metal black, now bloodied, so I could not tell whether it was clotted with my gore or someone else's. When I started up I realized I had always shrunk from him.

Next day Brother bought me a pallet, and I licked the sweet frozen milk wishing it would never end. Doolarie sulked and moped. "Like I must wait for a boy to farse with me, for me to get pallet," she grumbled.

There was something grander in store though, a secret that took two weeks to arrange. Brother was taking Doolarie and me to see the gardens in Port of Spain. To my amazement she said sulkily that she didn't care to go all that way to watch no garden, so we went without her, just the two of us one Saturday, by train, and found our way to the place. THE ROYAL BOTANICAL GARDENS, said the sign.

Inside was nothing I could have foreseen. I visited far grander gardens later in life, but coming afterwards they were nothing to this – not so much because of the plants I had never seen but because of how those I knew well were set out as if each had a value all its own. An old cotton tree with its huge twisted trunk reached out gnarled branches hung with vines and some flowering creeper the sun shone through like a sheer curtain of fine strands brightened by tiny blooms – yet it was just an old old tree. The wonder of the ordinary laid out in mild slopes and curves of close-cut grass, palms that fanned out or gushed up green, and walkways of clean stones edged with bushes flat-topped or rounded, green and white, or red streaked, then a round pond with flowers like floating stars. Beyond, rows of other flowers lifting out of dark soil with the deep green hills behind and, in between, trees I recognized but had never seen standing so proudly with the grass manicured between their roots, branches hung with tough cords that swayed pink flowers, clustered like the grapes I had seen in a picture but never eaten. On other trees the flowers were shaped in long tubes like pale baigan, orchid-shaped blooms or glowing spumes of lilac.

I realized I had been quiet for a long time and glanced anxiously at Brother lest he think me ungrateful, but I saw it was all right. He had known how it would be and brought me here so that even when we left, though it would fade from my mind for a while, it would bloom again, drawn up again and again in the schoolyard, the kitchen or, years later, in the chill of a far grey city.

It made him still more godlike in my eyes, for although he had not made the garden he had placed me in it however briefly and it in me forever. And now something awoke in me – it was like how reading woke things up – something stirred in the chaos of growing things inside my head as if there were patterns I could draw out, some order I could define to impose balance and harmony. Yet it would be something I would have to *do*, just as others had had to do things to make this garden – for this was not real, this carved and ornamental place. It was a picture made of pieces of nature, each exquisite item lifted out, teased apart and reassembled according to size and shape and colour, according to what plants matched or stood out against another. Placed, just as Ma placed her plants where she wanted them.

Then I began to see Ma and her garden, how she laid it out to use the fence for climbing plants and the trees for shade and the open spaces for plants that craved bright sunlight and the stubbornly wet places for those that had to soak up moisture, and she had ordered every inch of land she could without torturing the plants, almost by giving in to them, and they were clean and moulded too. And beautiful – bright red and yellow peppers and rich purple-black baigan and velvety green pods of pigeon peas. I thought of what Pa had said about whole gardens for flowers being a waste of manure, and of how hard he worked, and I tried to say something of what was confusing me to Brother but I could not get it out for I was part of Ma's garden but was touched beyond words by this one.

We sat on a bench as he slipped off his shoes, peeled off his socks and rested his bare feet on the grass. "Ma would like this too," he assured me. We both knew she could never have left the house and the boys for so long. He may also have been thinking about Pa, for after a while he said, "There is more to nourishment than food." He smiled. "But food comes first." He unwrapped roti and baigan, and when we had eaten we found our way back to the train.

At home there was always something new. Another surprise came when Pa dug out a pond in a place at the back of the land where the ground had sunk down and was always wet. "Once you have water you does get fish," he reasoned, "and if not we go catch some and put in. So we going get fish to eat. That boy, Israel, go learn we how to fish good."

In a few months he reported that not only was it true and the water full up with fish but, eh, eh, no sooner the pond fill but alligator and all find it. We ran behind him to see for ourselves. Only, Pa's acquaintances included Warden Green as well as his officers, Mohip and Nandlal, and Warden Green had travelled to America and told Pa that some people in Florida ate alligator.

"Now that is plenty meat," Pa said to Ma, only she responded, "Nah, dat nasty. Don't bring it by me to clean." And fortunately it dropped from mind, because next day Mohip was fixing his roof, lost hold and rolled off. People all over the village had something wise to say about his death, but Pa just set off down the road to help Mohip's family. Then he got caught up in preparing for the wake and forgot all about the pond and the alligator, which by now we had learned to call a caiman. Ma said she was too sorry bout Mohip but the poor fellow do her a good turn because she believe Pa woulda really bring that nasty thing into the house for her to cook in truth.

Now Mohip's wake was another story that Pa told us when he got home.

"I never see a wake like that in me life! You know it turn out that Mohip first wife dead and he remarry, but he never tell the new wife that he di marry before. So he have a son is a big man and the son come to the wake with he madam. And he madam say Mohip house suppose to leave for she husband, and the next thing is the two lady ketch fight at the wake."

"Oui, Papa!" Ma said under her breath, a grin almost breaking away before she caught it, but it was no use and she dropped the spoon to cover her mouth.

"The box was on the gallery and one of them push the next one hard, and when they bounce the box, the two bench they have it on tilt so the box slide. So Pierre, the same old creole tailor, shout, "Gardez!" But no one couldn't hold it, it have so mucha weight, and it slide down the step and bust open and fire out Mohip and he land prop up against a tree, right in front of Nandlal, who work with him for years and owe him one set of money. And Nandlal bawl out, "Modder arse!" and leap back and put he foot down in the fire. So the wake mash up. They had was to get Mohip back in he box and treat Nand-lal foot for the burn. But Nandlal get such a fright he say he bringing the money for Madam Mohip tomorrow and Pierre start to laugh and say but which of the Madam Mohip? And everything turn ole mas all over again. Any-how Mohip get bury in the end and I don't know how Nandlal going solve he problem. Serve the bitch right," Pa added. "He does study borrow and never pay back."

We stopped laughing suddenly to stare down to the road from the gallery, because Mahal was just passing our house and slowed down. While he braked, we watched with interest because he had never stopped there before, but he had obviously just forgotten something because he reversed into the entrance of the yard and swung back out the way he had come.

"Bro, ent one day you go buy a car?" Matthew asked.

I wanted to say that one day I would, but I held my tongue. I was still trying to avoid attracting too much attention. In fact, weeks after Dada erupted because of Reds and even a little after our outing to the gardens, Brother had noticed I was quiet and walking with my eyes to the ground and asked me what was wrong.

"I too afraid anyone say I bright," I confided, but Brother shook his head.

"No, no, don't think like that. You're not that type of bright," he said. "You're smart." I twisted uncomfortably as his eyes narrowed, holding mine. "A friend of mine has a sister who runs a school in Princes Town."

"Oh no, Brother. Don't send me away."

"No, no. I'm just saying that this lady teaches and directs her staff. She dresses beautifully, and she drives herself everywhere. And she doesn't come from any rich family either." He put up his left forefinger and shook it sternly. "My sister can do just as well."

He would have drawn in Doolarie too, but books bored her. He taught the school leaving class and Doolarie made slow progress, but there was noth-ing he could do about it when Dada set no value on sums and essays. "Let she learn to make a good roti and talkari," he steupsed, his voice roughened by puncheon to a coarse rasp and his bloodshot eyes shifting from one of us to the next. He had joined Pa and Brother on the gallery after a session at Mr Manny's and Ma had driven us inside to bed, but their voices died away shortly after that and through the window to the road I could see Brother holding Dada's arm and coaxing him along. After that, Brother never talked about any course of action regarding me or Doolarie when Dada was around, but to Pa and Ma he spoke of girls who went through school and found good jobs that made their parents proud. In Doolarie's case Pa and Ma talked of having to find a boy for her in a year or two, though Dada seemed strangely uninterested in that, but I was three years younger and had all the time in the world to improve myself, according to Brother.

"This Judith is as smart as any boy I know," he insisted, and announced that one day when he had some money and bought more books, I would read them too. Meanwhile, every one was an event in my life.

Brother himself was in no hurry to settle down to a family of his own; he would finish training first and keep an eye on me. He began to reflect on girls who had been in Mission Presbyterian with him when he was small. Ramjit's big daughter lived way up Hilton Pinto Road now, clear up in the bamboo, with twelve children and a husband who practically inhabited Mr Manny's rumshop, sometimes passing out in front and lying there all night on the curb. Ria, whose father did teeth in the village, had been a smart little thing, sitting in Teacher Mangalsingh's class, and now had twenty-one children. What was to be done for any of twenty-one, let alone all? Brother counted out the girls from that class, some overwhelmed and crushed now, others more carefully married off and comfortable enough. But he wanted something else for me, he said. Pa was puzzled, and Brother could not say what he had in mind. The strain of trying to work it out showed in his face.

One night he came home with the news that he had won an essay competition and the prize was a ticket to St Vincent or the equivalent money. He claimed the money, set off for Port of Spain and came back with purchases from Muir Marshall – books, he said. Boxes and boxes. Matthew did not care and the other boys were still too young, but this thing took my breath away so I grabbed Doolarie's arm. She patted mine, vaguely glad for me, and turned away.

We were different – even I could see that. Doolarie was moody and tense. At school she barely did what was required – it was that or the belt – yet she hardly played either. At home she was skittish, cleaning and cooking as a matter of course, but sulky. Her father's visits intensified the moodiness. She was dizzy with pleasure when he brought her a hair ribbon and bragged about it for days, but she hid it when he returned. She fawned on him and feared him, clung to Ma but made cutting comments about her behind her back. "She don't mean nothing. She getting big and she don't know what go happen to she. Is that," Ma said. "We go find a good boy for she." It went without saying they would find one for me too, and I would fall in with whatever they arranged, certain they knew best. Brother, however, seemed to view it as more complicated.

He had no hold on Doolarie. There were so many of us, he said later, too many of us to drag along one who had no interest and over whom he had no authority. I did not need to be dragged. I read and read, and in the evening there might be a precious half-hour when Brother and I talked about the malice or bravery or impudence of one character or the other. Sometimes we talked after one of Pa's tales too and I asked Brother if he believed in douens, spirits of children not born and baptized, not living, not dead, wandering in the forest.

"Nah!" he said.

"Boy!" Phuwa broke in, scandalized. "Of course it have thing so. You know how mucha people see dem thing?"

"I think it's true that if people throw children away or lose their . . . spirits, in a way they can turn into demons," he said. So everyone was satisfied.

When Brother was to start Training College he sat with us before he left and waited to see whether Pa would come in. Perhaps Pa would be vexed now Brother was to be away during the week; it looked as if he would stay away till Brother was gone. We heard him trudging heavily up to the door and held our breaths trying to read the sound of each footfall. Brother walked slowly to meet him at the top of the step.

"I'm ready, Pa." He gazed around at us as if he felt guilty about leaving, even for the weekdays.

Pa fixed a stern eye on him, but when their hands clasped there was a crackle of paper before Pa turned away. Brother opened his fingers, and Pa had given him twenty dollars, a magnificent sum. Brother was speechless.

If that was the way Pa felt, Brother said, he had nothing to worry about except what would become of me. By next weekend when he came back he had begun to work that out. First, he approached the headteacher, Mr Boodram, to make me a monitor. But this was a new dispensation, not like the old days with Teacher Mangalsingh, and the headteacher refused. I was not surprised. I had come to think that pale, stocky Mr. Boodram looked as if he had swallowed stone and tried to pass it without success.

There were few people in whom Mr Boodram showed any interest. One of his friends had a son, Brother said later, duncy as they come; but all

Boodram cared about was that it was his friend's boy, so the foolish little fellow was to be a monitor. "Not some young teacher's sister," the head teacher reprimanded Brother. A girlchild? Before a boy? Just because she is family to somebody on staff? Cleaning up in the kitchen, I could hear Brother on the gallery talking to Israel. Their voices were low but it was a quiet night and I turned the wares silently. When Brother reported what Mr Boodram had said I could just see the headmaster's tight eyes and clenched lips. "Another one they have in mind for monitor has an uncle who sells cars," Brother said. "I sure money pass."

Israel did not read or study much, but Brother always said he had a good mind and practical sense, and after a thoughtful silence Israel agreed. "It have bobol in them thing, oui." Brother lowered his voice and told Israel that the man who was now headteacher was the same man who had once tried smearing him through his father's anonymous letters. Whatever trace of guilt I had felt about disliking the constipated-looking little man evaporated. "You see? You shoulda deal with he one time," Israel replied. "Now he get a more senior position he can take it out on you family. Watch. This man is a ass – you could show he up."

"No. No cause for that. I just need to move her out his reach. I'm thinking of Ragbir's, past Sanchez there?" My heart sank. Ragbir's was a private school a good few miles from Mission and I would know no one. "The thing is I hear it's not so good. Poor results." I could see Brother through the wide doorway to the gallery. He stretched, tilting his face to the ceiling and squeezing his eyes shut as he did when he was straining to think things out. "This girl has a good mind. I can't make the set of them understand. No, I suppose they understand." Something beyond his comprehension thinned his voice to a whisper. "They just don't care."

"Wait, boy." Israel's voice was charged with excitement. "Don't get downcourage. You ever think bout sending she to San Fernando? She a little big to start, but don't study that."

Naparima High School for Girls, far away in San Fernando. The pot slipped from my hand and clattered on the ground but no one noticed. I snatched it up and rested it down noiselessly, wiping my soapy hands on my dress, then creeping nearer them, settling on the inside of the door to the gallery. I opened a book in my lap, *Far from the Madding Crowd*, one of Brother's new ones, but for once I had no interest in it. Brother was staring at Israel as if seeing him for the first time.

It was a breakthrough that propelled Brother into a fury of activity. He set out at once to see his old teacher, and Brother told us later that Mr Mangalsingh hired a car (since he no longer drove himself) and met him in San Fernando the following Monday so they could go together to see the Principal. I would have to write a test, and then there was the money. Teacher Mangalsingh offered to lend a part, to be paid back somehow.

The next evening when Brother travelled home after his own class and unfolded the idea, Pa stared, speechless for once, as if a branch from some tree had snapped and fallen on his head. They sat for a while looking out into the night. After a while Pa said, it so happen he join a susu and expect to draw the hand that month, so that might do the books and uniform. Both Pa and Ma were confused and frightened, but there was a sort of rebellious pride in Pa and fierce loyalty in Ma that hooked them fast into the scheme. I was shocked, exhilarated but confused, and I was alarmed that they would not be able to afford passage for me to come home regularly. Only in those nightmare months of the fever had I ever been to this new place, bigger and farther away than Princes Town.

Brother took me aside. He was wearing shortpants and I noticed for the first time that his knees were cut and badly bruised. "Juds, I'll tell you what it is." He looked away, through the wall and into a place I could not see. "You could be frightened and stay where you are. Or, you could decide what road you have to walk, and say, 'If I perish, I perish.' That is in the Bible, you know. 'If I perish, I perish.'"

"What happen to you knees, Brother? They purple."

"Don't bother about that now." He waved a hand irritably, unaccustomed to being questioned.

"I can't help it. I can't think until you tell me."

"Initiation."

It was a new word for me so he relented and explained. I already knew he had begun at Training College, having passed at first try examinations that older, experienced teachers had sat repeatedly. He was one of a few accepted for the accelerated training programme and resentment had backed up in some quarters. New people generally had to take a little pressure, he told me, but he and a few others had had to climb the steps on their knees and gravel had been scattered on the steps before him, so his knees were puffy, raw in places but mostly just an angry blue black, mottled with red. But all that wouldn't last; he fanned it away like a fly. Those fellows would come round, not that they mattered: bruises healed.

He looked back at me directly, straight into the inside of my head, and he said, "Juds, if you do this thing your life will be . . . beyond anything you can dream of now." His eyes wandered past me and I followed them with mine. I looked at the wall he was staring through and I couldn't see anything but old wood, but I knew he really could see through things that looked hard and blank to other people and I was more afraid of going nowhere than of going somewhere I did not know, so I went with him and I wrote the test.

And I passed.

When we got home, Pa surprised us by coming in early. He made light of it but he had been keyed up after all. "This is a big thing, Pa." Brother pursued it softly. "You see if you send the child to this school? When you do that, is like when you build that bridge."

Pa nodded, but we could see the calculations churning in his head.

"Watch me," Ma said. "We go save more money than before. Right now we growing partly everything we eat, but we go save more again. You don't see zaboca bearing?" Avocados hung full and heavy on the tree outside the kitchen window.

"In fact," Brother said, "why we don't have some now?" Think, eat, pray, sleep – his formula for mapping our way through problems we could see as well as those lurking round corners. We cut up the ripe zaboca with onion and pepper and ate that with hot sada roti and cocoa tea.

By next evening, Brother was back in Mission with material for uniforms and I went for Miss Beharrysingh to take my measurements. If it had been a dress for them to marry me in, to some boy I had never seen, I would have gone even if it nauseated me – in which case I would also feel I was ungrateful to be nauseated when everyone who knew what was right was doing the best for me that could be done. This had to be better. Brother said so, yet he had tried to find out how I felt, and I was frightened but grateful. And, inside, something else edged in on the fear. I felt sinfully glad to be cracking out of their sheltering care and unending chores, mutinous about every lurking obstacle, exultant about feeling the way I felt and not necessarily the way I was supposed to.

Then I wondered how *they* felt. What would it be like for the house to go on without me? I asked Ma who would help her when I left, but she said, "Doolarie is a nice child." Doolarie was leaving school, for she was not interested and Dada said it made no sense to force a girlchild to study book. It was true that she was of help to Ma. Sometimes Ma seemed reluctant to let her out of her sight, sometimes anxious to get her settled. "Besides," she said, "dem boy quite big enough to do some good work you see them there."

"Certainly," Brother said. "Look at all I used to do before going to school. What? Tired? On a Saturday morning? Flagrant nonsense."

Matthew and Mark could grate corn and Timmy could shell it. Even Timmy could help collect wood from the sawmill for Matthew to chop up into pieces for the chulha. Matthew was big for his age and strong enough to wield the axe. "It have plenty chirren here, beti," Ma said. But it was disorienting, just the thought. There are things that women tell only to women or say only in the presence of their daughters, things that women learn only from women and that can pass the men in the family by altogether; and now here I was stepping out of that meshwork of wisdom passed from mouth to mouth and I felt strangely exposed.

Before I left the village for San Fernando, I went to see Aji, who was getting quite low, Brother said, and he didn't know if she would be there when I came back. The missionaries would walk the short track in from Mission Hill Road to Phuwa's house, to give Aji communion, past the land her neighbours cultivated with pigeon peas as the forest receded year by year. But I would not be able to come often, all the way from San Fernando, because of the car fare.

"That is *you*," Doolarie said. She woulda never want to go so far from home, and for what? Yet I wasn't sure. Sometimes she looked as if she wanted to go as far away as possible and sometimes as if she couldn't bear to leave the house. Sometimes she begged Dada to take her away. One was never sure what Doolarie felt.

Yet San Fernando was not all that far when one considered it. I knew that where Brother wanted to go was England. "The mother country," he confirmed reverently. He would see places we had read about, and the tombs of poets and kings. He also spoke with longing of places I knew nothing about, like the Lake District and the Cotswolds. Yes, he was interested in India, but he would see England first. I knew that he had saved enough for the fare and I wondered why he hadn't gone already. Perhaps because he would have to go by boat and the thought of all that water made him postpone it. But *one day*, he insisted.

I went with Brother in the car he hired, to the school in San Fernando where I would live in dormitory and he would visit. "Didn't I visit you in hospital?" he insisted. "You know I did." He unwrapped roti and curry Ma had made, but he warned me sternly to eat whatever they served in dormitory. He put down a few coins and a little brown paper package and left me there. When I opened it I saw he had bought me sugar cake and bene balls. I licked every sesame seed that strayed from the bene balls and clung to my fingers. Then I put away my things where they had said I should, and I went down to eat. When they served the food it was different and I had to use a knife and fork. I blinked rapidly to forestall tears, because for tonight at least I had Ma's roti on the shelf beside my bed. When I got back home, I thought, they would ask whether I had cried, at least I hoped they would, for Brother would believe me when I said I hadn't. I felt safe because he was in my mind and I in his wherever we were, even if he went to England.

Then I remember, suddenly, right in that dining room, seeing it with blinding clarity. It was as if the big room was torn apart and everything there – the people and their polite chatter – were sucked away from the centre of my vision, and I saw it. The money for the uniforms, the car fare, even some of the fees could only have come from Brother's savings for his passage to England. It could only be that, because we were too many for Pa alone to do more than feed and shelter from the rain, and Pa could not open up that path that led through books. I had thought myself so close to Brother, but I had not even glimpsed his mind.

Years later, when I faced him with it, he told me he used to ponder that gap in age between him and the rest of us and he decided there must be a reason. "It meant I was big enough to do . . . something," he said. "I actually had no idea what to do" – he was matter-of-fact, as if he was stating a point of grammar – "only that if I did not it would not be done and everything Pa was breaking himself to accomplish would be utterly lost and Ma and the children, all of you, would disappear in abject want, sucked out into howling emptiness. If I did nothing, if I turned aside even for a while, made a trip, took a course, divided my time, if I even shifted my eye away you would all . . . simply vanish."

SEPTEMBER 11, 2010 – 6:35 A.M.

*Ucncle 1 of thm tried to hold me down only the ohther stopppd him. Please plse get me back*

# CHAPTER 8

# LYRICS

## Timmy

What I remember best of those early days was Mark, always in one set of confusion.

Like that business in the cocoa. The way he tells it, he was always to blame for everything. *Mark do this and Mark do that.* Where they were when Mark was getting licks? Matthew and Luke looking on with satisfaction and Andrew hiding under the house, that's what. I was the only one who would get vexed and shout, "Stop it!" I wasn't afraid, even of Pa, and from then I had Pa's temper.

Pa had repaired the big wooden house near the Junction, room by room over the years. Still, it was old and talk of rebuilding it with bricks came and went. On a reasonably sound roof of galvanize the rain thundered but then poured off to guttering that led down to two barrels, and the roof projected over most of the gallery. A few leaks persisted but you pushed a bowl under them, and nothing was damp about the house itself, set high on pillar trees of strong poui that left underneath airy for drying clothes or swaying in the hammock. Not that children were encouraged to lie around in any hammock or that Ma or Doolarie had the time, especially now Judith was away at school all week. Dada used the hammock more, for since Aji died the old house they said she had in Impasse had finally fallen apart from neglect, and even before that when it became uninhabitable Dada had found a place farther along Mission Hill Road, past Phuwa's house and beyond the school.

"Then he couldn't fix it while he di' living there?" Ma grumbled under her breath. "Good good house leave to rotten, so he move out just before it fall on him. Allyou father woulda never do that." Once Dada had finished work and made the rounds by Mr Manny's he would pass home to get a drink from Pa before finding his way to his own place. Sometimes in the morning when you were scattering corn for the fowls or passing the cocoyea broom under the house you found he had got no farther than that hammock.

So just about everyone was around in the evening to report to Pa on where Mark was or what he wasn't doing.

It wasn't that Mark didn't appreciate how hard Pa worked, but he said, "This toting of cocoa is a hell of a thing, man."

So after they spend the day reaping it (and Pa watching every pod of he own cocoa from he own crop) and they have to carry them bag now, all Mark want is for the day to done so he could go home. And every bag heavier than the last, so Mark decide to lighten it up. Only, he forget all about the fellow Pa employ to help with the bull work. "Tonnere!" The workman swore, then bawled out. "Mr Jai, watch the boy pelting you cocoa!"

Well, when Pa charge at him, Mark scatter. Pa shout out, "Boy, find you tail home and when I get there make sure I don't see you." So Mark get to go home, but later Pa well cut he skin.

Next day when Brother heard about it, he told Pa it was the same thing at school. Brother was back from Training College full of ideas for getting children to learn, and here was his own brother showing no interest in the books. Staring at Mark in disbelief, Pa breathed hard, his nostrils dilating. "You mean is playful this boy playful why he losing marks in test and all? And he mother breaking she back to feed he? But this boy is a waste of skin in truth!" Pa nearly beat him all over again.

This was why the Friday after that Mark said he had to slip out the house easy easy to reach down to the cricket ground at all. He know he go get ketch when he coming back in, but he never study that. Licks, what? He never fraid licks. So he play all day, and later he tell us how he run near the edge of the ground, fall down bladdam, roll downhill and get condense milk tin slice into he knee; and then he pull it out and wipe the blood with some grass and he bowl again. And I couldn't wait to be big like him and do all them wickedness.

So limping home now with the darkness pressing round, Mark began to run over what he could say. He told me later that he knew Pa might still be out and Matthew had gone to help him, but Brother could be there. It was Friday and near month end so Juds would be coming home from school, and she might beg for him. Only, when he reached the door he saw no sign of Judith and all he could hear was Dada voice, roaring like he mad. That was when I ran up to Mark and grabbed his shirt, for I had been hiding outside and it was a relief to see him come so we could go in together. "Dada must be fire a good few before he leave the rumshop," he said.

But as we pushed the door, Brother waved us back out the house. "Go over to Phuwa," he ordered. "Get over there right now."

"But what the hell is this I hearing," Dada shouted, Doolarie backing away in front of him, the colour in her face washed out to grey, and Dada eye blood-shot, rolling in he head. "My friend tell me in truth – he say, 'Watch. You have cocoa in the sun.' But is only when I land up in Manny's," Dada went on, "that I get to hear this thing."

"Out," Brother shouted at us, his eyes on Dada. He was gesturing to calm him, hands palm-down stroking the air, but even as Mark tugged me back out the door Dada lunged, his fist smashing Doolarie against the wall.

At Phuwa's house, neither Luke nor Andrew had any idea what was happening because they had been there all day, but Judith sat crying wordlessly, rocking back and forth. She would say nothing and Phuwa uttered not a word to any of us, only shared out roti and pumpkin and, later, went to the house, and returned to say we could go home. By then Dada had taken Doolarie away to his own place where he said he would keep an eye on her himself.

"Is the man child" was all Ma said, her face carefully expressionless, but later she cried when she thought no one was watching. She seemed relieved when Phuwa said they had found a good boy for the girl, but before it could be settled the news came that Doolarie was gone. Dada arrived at the house by the Junction, all but collapsing in the doorway, incoherent with grief and rage. After all he do, he sobbed, for she to go like that without a word. Ma said nothing about it then, but later she pulled her orhni across her face and shook silently.

As for Mark, his knee swelled, "Big big, if you see *dat*!" Phuwa reported to Madam Ali, at the fence. "And after even the aloes and thing don't make no difference this boy had was to go to doctor. No cricket for he, week in, week out. He Brother and all get sorry for him and buy souse and pudding and bring to the house."

Worse still, Mark nearly went mad over the school books because, as he recounted later, when he ketch heself he find he in the class before Exhibition and he see Brother watch at him. "Right. You. You need special attention," Brother said. The lifting of that left forefinger halted Mark on his way through the door. Brother's gaze bored through him, that way he had that skewered you so you couldn't move.

That was when Ma chose to put her mouth in. "Allyou pa ent go through all he go through to see *he* boychild do hardwok," she said. So they better listen to Brother, or she self would give them some good cut skin. And as for Mark? "All day all day this boy only harassing the rest of we. I talk till I tired but he too hard-ears. Nathan boy, *gi'* he work to do." And Mark's face fell as if his heart had sunk down into his feet.

But nothing stopped his mouth. "I woking from morning to night already, you see me here." And like he just catch heself before he steups too.

Brother's eyes opened incredulously. "Who do you think you are? And work? You haven't even met work yet." Before Mark could budge, Brother grab him with he right hand, twist the pants waist to tighten the cloth over he tail and call two hot lash on him with his left. "And you don't answer back. You understand?" He put Mark down and smoothed his clothes with irrelevant gentleness. "Now you don't write badly, but you have to do much better. You see how you spoke to the doctor? Talk like that all the time. Practise speaking the way you want to write. And you see this 'Ah woking'?" He raised his left again but Mark was quick.

"I *am* working." He leapt back.

"See? You know very well. I'll be watching you" – Brother leaned forward, his broad face inches from Mark's – "and listening. Closely."

He extracted Mark from a classroom near to his own and brought him into the group preparing for the Exhibition Scholarship to take them to secondary school, and Brother planted him in the centre of the front row. On the weekend, Judith explained that some teachers were jealous of Brother's performance at Training College and of his students' results since then, so Brother wouldn't entrust Mark to anyone else. Mark steupsed loudly, so Judith shrugged and turned to her own work.

Later, as celebration or crisis brought us back to reflect on the old days, Mark would recall how he had felt at the vortex of an encircling chorus of Exhibition students under meticulous preparation, in between the lessons Brother drilled into him as a foundation for his own Exhibition year. "You have it in you," Brother insisted. Brother established Mark, in the midst of the older students, as a class of one, and *when* he merged into that bigger class he could never say. It just absorbed him.

Yet many of Mark's other concerns persisted.

"This Matthew could only make a half-side kite," he said. "When breeze take it, it ducking to one side." He was telling Luke, who was just eight, so Luke and all would laugh at Matthew.

"Stop playing the ass and do you home lessons," Brother cut in. "You not going to brimble you way out of work in my class, you hear?" Then he added almost gently, "You have brains, you know. Use them. Mash the X, man, and you will reach the top and get the Exhibition."

Mark had passed that exam and found himself in college in San Fernando when, on one of his weekends home, we overheard Phuwa telling Ma that Doolarie was married and living somewhere around the Dessalines estate. "But how that go feel," Phuwa wondered, "to married so, with no family and thing. But I suppose *she* make she bed." Later on she was still pondering it. "Nimakharam," Phuwa said, focusing on the ingratitude and falseness of young people. "Imagine allyou take she in, and she get on so. I never see more." She went on to reflect that it was a good thing her own mother, Doolarie's Aji, was dead and gone. All Ma would say was how often she wished Ma Kamaldaye was still living, and that they should try to have a prayers. She told Pa she wanted them to sing "Karo Meri Sahai" at the prayers because he Ma had liked that song. She was a nice lady, she said, and in truth she missed her more than her own Ma. Pa grew quiet. "Yes," he said. "And it have some woman that remember people who treat them good."

Mark seemed to care little about these finer feelings and I concluded they must not be any concern of ours. If we even wondered about Doolarie it was not the sort of thing Judith or Ma would talk about. On weekends Mark occupied himself making mango chow, turning the hard, pale, yellow-green slivers with salt, pepper and garlic, and keeping out of the way of real work yet getting underfoot. Regardless of the fare, he had to return to Mission on weekends to be under Brother's eye. On Sundays Brother marched him to church with the rest of us, but Mark expected that; Saturday was another matter. It did not help that Brother had built a bookcase along a whole wall of the back room that was still officially his, filled it with books, and invited the whole of us to read them. To make it worse, Judith had been working her way happily through, one by one, and chatted with Brother about what had compelled characters to do what they did and what would have happened if they had done something else. "What have *you* read lately?" Brother swung around to ask Mark, who clearly found himself at a loss for an answer.

Brother said he realized that a boy needed to be active, so he began to take Mark around with him, even to an evening with the debating club. "But you can bring your little friends," he had said kindly when he was warning Mark to be ready on time. I could almost feel Mark's scalp prickling. "I mean, Oh Gaaawd, ease me up," he said when he trudged into our room to put on a shirt before Brother came for him. Like Brother couldn't even see what ridicule would be heaped on Mark's head if he proposed an evening of debate to the cricket side. But there seemed no escape for Mark. Luke was ill with high fever and muscle pains, and Ma more tired and irritable than we had seen her before. She insisted Mark go with Brother so the house could to be quiet. But what was the point to weekends if he had to live in the damn school house every Saturday, Mark grumbled. It was all very well for Brother.

It was not what he had expected, Mark said when he described it later.

"Be it resolved that the Federation is in the best interest of the West Indies," Nathan announced, all eyes riveted on him. In training college Brother had learned to prepare all kinds of topics, as he had told Mark on the way. "I'm ready for them." *Ready*. It was decades later that Mark told me how this set off something inside him that he hadn't known existed – a deep resonance. Suddenly he realized how, again and again, Brother must have debated in front of this packed schoolroom, under the lanterns, hardly seeming to glance at the notes in his right hand while gesturing occasionally with the other. The whole village gathered there early. Warden Green chatted with Father O'Neil and Griffiths, the new doctor from Mayaro. A buzz of attention rose as the magistrate entered, and a hush fell. *Papa Jacques, man, Papa come.*

Jean de Jacques was heavier now, red-faced and leaning on a cane. He was the sort of man people talked about and we were accustomed to hearing the reports. People said he suffered horribly from gout and on some days he could not walk at all. Others said it had nothing name gout. Papa Jacques had trouble with his feet, yes, but what really happen to he was he crack a vein. Another explained that Papa suffered from what doctor and them call bellicose vein. Whatever his problem, though, tonight he had come. Then as they about to start – a further burst of activity, less subdued. It was Pa, with a following of his pardners from Balata Trace.

One of the Warden's Officers, Nandlal, who seconded Brother, fumbled and lost his place, stammering to a halt. His fiancée fidgeted in the second row.

"That is the kind of man you go married?" shouted one of the Lezama brothers. "Next thing he go lose he place again."

"I done with this," Nandlal retorted. "I don't have time for dotish people."

Brother took over and order was restored.

According to Mark it was just the same as at home, only at home Brother depended more on the tambran switch than on words. The fact was, though, that he was felt to show great forebearance with Mark. "Good thing you big brother so pationate," Phuwa would say. "Anybody else woulda cut you tail every day, don't mind you nearly tall like he." But Mark did not think Brother at all patient, and once when Mark was smaller he had run away from home and got as far as the sawmill – but what to do next? He had hidden under the building till it got dark, then crept home defeated, only to notice the cow had dropped a calf and the first milk must be in. That depressed him more, because now he had missed the paynoose Ma would have made with it. As he slipped in, Ma had called quietly, "Mark? Find youself here." But it wasn't more licks. It was a saucer she had hidden for him with a share of the sweet gingery paynoose. "Little Jab-Jab," she grumbled. "Now find you bed before I pepper you tail instead."

It was these unexpected things Ma did that came back to him again and again, he said later, and there was something like that in the searching flash of her keen eyes when he and Brother returned in triumph from the debate. "Like you well enjoy that," she said. Ma noticed everything even in the midst of her anxiety about Luke.

Phuwa had said the child body was heated and he needed a cooling. "And you see that kinda pain? You need a jaray lady to rub that pain. Hospital? You mad? Hospital go do for he. You don't remember how long it take for Judith to get better when she did go hospital?"

At the mention of Judith, Brother sprang from the Morris chair. "Mark boy, come. If we can get a car we could overtake Dr Griffiths on the Mayaro road." After the sprint to the Junction in search of someone with a car who would stop for them, it was a mad race to overtake the doctor's car, a race Mark would have enjoyed if had he not been alarmed by Brother's reaction. It had never occurred to him that anything major could be wrong with Luke. After examining him, though, Dr Griffiths explained that Luke was actually recovering from a terrible illness that killed many people, especially children.

However mildly Luke had had the polio, the rest were to stay away from him. After the doctor left, Brother called them together to pray that Luke would be able to walk again. He sent Phuwa home, but she returned directly with clothes in a shoulder bag and settled in with Ma to nurse Luke. As usual she relayed the news of Mission and the surrounding villages, although Ma was too preoccupied to take in much of it.

"But who Haresh is again?" Ma asked, hardly pausing for the answer.

"Chaitlal son, nah. You forget he married before allyou, and he madam leave and gone home? " Phuwa massaged Luke's legs gently without losing track of her tale. "Long before Mala and Doolarie, Chaitlal di' married and he have a son. That same boy grow up and married, but the wife die as the child born and now I hear Haresh and all dead. So who go take care of the child?"

It was not a question Ma would linger over at Luke's bedside. "The boy mother living," she said. "Is she grandchild – she go see bout that."

"But that is what I telling you. Dhanmattie gone in the madhouse."

Ma stopped and stared. "In truth?"

When Brother arrived it was all unfolded again and he too paused because he had recently driven old Dr Harris to see a woman named Dhanmattie in Piparo. The neighbours had been beating her to get out a spirit that they said had taken her over, and a parent of one of his pupils had spoken to him about it. After her son died a slow agonizing death, she had broken down and started talking to a lamp post at the corner of the road, so it became clear that a spirit had taken her up – perhaps Haresh, the son who died. The report luridly relayed how she ran bawling in her nightclothes, hair flying, breasts flapping, as she dodged the neighbours chasing her with sticks, belts and pieces of rope – anything that came to hand. So Brother had intervened, convinced them that she needed treatment and organized them into packing her clothes for the hospital. "And this Dhanmattie is some family, you say now?" he asked irritably.

Once more Phuwa explained patiently that the woman had been Dada's first wife, and had run off before Ma and Pa married, but before she finished, Brother had turned away in search of quiet. What he craved was silence, so he could concentrate on Luke. He called us together for a short group prayer. "But ent Luke getting well?" Matthew whispered, puzzled by Brother's tension and a little impatient. Brother paused and stared at him and, big as he was, Matthew clapped his palms together and squeezed his eyes tight. After the *amen*, Brother regarded Matthew for a few painful seconds before withdrawing to the back room.

In a quarter of an hour Brother rejoined us in better temper, turned a commanding stare around the room until someone scurried off with a plate to take out food for him, and he consumed an impressive quantity of roti and bodi. For there would be another problem waiting for you the following day or week or month, he reminded them, and you needed to be ready. Mark closed his eyes and you could see he was letting his mind drift. We had long lived amid the philosophy through which Brother took charge of his own life and of that of those around him and led them firmly for their own good. Mark yawned.

It was actually the sort of situation in which, when Mark was a little fellow of seven or so, I vaguely remember him holding a katha, praying loudly in his imitation of the old language, what they called Hindi, till he broke into a Presbyterian hymn or a bhajan while he took up a collection. After a while Ma had objected: "Is not to make a joke of serious ting. Next thing, when trouble come and you decide to pray, God say, 'Nah, he just a joker,' and He don't bother with you." Right now Luke's thin weak frame made it obvious to us all, even to Mark, that praying for him was serious business.

Luke's recovery dragged on as the rains passed, and dry season wind rattled leaves over the hard cracked ground. Ma was exhausted, balancing Luke's care gainst the battle to keep food crops alive through this shattering drought. Matthew, who was tall and broad now, almost like a man, set up gutters to lead water out from the kitchen to the garden, but usually it was only Andrew or me around in the week for small tasks. Even when he could raise himself from bed Luke barely managed to move his body from the couch to the table.

Eventually, after Mark had returned from school weekend after weekend to find Luke only minimally better than the Friday before, Andrew and I were able to run out and greet him with the news. "Come fast. Watch how Luke walking almost good like before, and Brother say we will have to have a prayers for that." Matthew added, "You see? Is because Brother bring the doctor. Hey, you small man." As Brother strolled in through the gate Matthew snatched up Andrew and spun him around on his shoulder. "Best we send you away to study people instead of frog and you come back a doctor. Brother, ent we go save money right there?"

"Good plan," Brother said.

So it was, every crisis. When Pa and Ma agreed that Judith must start wearing an orhni and she protested, they called Brother. Ma was making bake and fry dry when he arrived and the smell of the peppery little fish had even Luke bobbing around her eagerly. All the rest of us wanted Judith to settle down and do as she was told while the fish were still cripsy, but Judith caught Brother's hand and squeezed hard. "Please, no." She was getting on like the heavens were ready to fall. "I just can't. Is only old people wearing that."

"That's true," Brother agreed. "Give her a chance, Pa. The young women don't wear that now, man. What about a hat?"

Judith sighed but was quiet, and Ma looked thoughtful. The new teacher at the school, Amani Manniram, wore no orhni, just a hat that she took off inside the school house. "When they have a little education, is different," Ma agreed reluctantly.

"So, now education time soon done, is getting time for married." Pa was glad Judith was doing well, but looking forward to seeing her settled. "How it will look, this big girl with her head bare on the street?"

"Not bare, Pa," Brother reminded him. "The hat. And she needs a new bodice and all, man." And where Brother had come by any knowledge or interest in women's clothes was another question to be juggled in Mark's lively brain, as he glanced at Matthew and glimpsed an answering twitch of ridicule at the corner of his mouth.

"Well, I doesn' want she to dress up like no Dame Lorraine either," Pa said, delivering a sour corrective to frivolity, so that the younger boys smirked and nudged each other at the idea of the overdressed carnival character trailing her swelling skirt, and Mark immediately pushed two grapefruit into the front of his jersey and a pillow at his bottom, and flung a bedsheet round him to flounce up and down.

"Now there's another thing." Brother fanned Mark aside impatiently. "You know we said we would start work again on the house this crop time?" Brother unfolded his plan. Instead of marrying as soon as she left school Judith could start work at the Warden's Office. A position for a payment clerk offered seventy-two dollars per month, which would help buy material to rebuild the house. Brother had already found out where to get a good price on galvanize for the roof. This would be a proper brick house, with an inside kitchen and toilet.

The news found its way to Manny's rumshop. "What?" Old man Lezama scoffed. "Latrine inside house? What sort of nastiness that? I suppose Deoraj get big big now he son finish Training College, and girlchild and all gone to school and ting. I tell you one thing. I would never have a latrine inside my house."

"Tell he to get a house to begin with," Pa shouted when he heard about Lezama, "living year in, year out in the same kaba kaba yard. Tell he one step at a time – get a house. He well frontish to put heself in my business. Tell him *he* daughter better study she book than up and down in the street, walking as if she does mess ice cream."

Phuwa tried to cool him down. "Don't botherate with ignorant people, man."

Brother has his own system for letting off steam. His friends were more than drinking parders – the sort of people, he said, with whom one could exchange ideas. "This same Dr Griffiths," he told Pa, "he is the sort of man you could talk to about all kinds of things." It seemed to Mark that Brother viewed an evening discussing Shakespeare or Wordsworth as one of mild dissipation. "Griff reads everything. He meant to do a degree in English but at St Mary's they pushed him into the science class and he got the scholarship to do medicine. But he is . . . he is an altogether different kind of fellow. And he could sing you know. He sings the way I always wished I could sing."

Pa came home one night with the news that this thing was true. Passing the doctor's house Pa had seen Nathan sitting on the Griffiths's gallery with a set of friends and they called Pa in for a drink. Doc was teasing Nathan about having lost his heart to the beautiful new teacher, and Nathan just shrugged sheepishly.

"Guilty as charged." Israel laughed, and demanded a song from Griff. Then Doc said he would sing on behalf of Nathan, and he sang, *Drink to me only with thine eyes and I will pledge with mine.*

"This man voice," Pa said, "it does fill you up. People stand still on the street, I tell you. Everything stop right there."

"Then like you son go married soon," Dada remarked. "Is about time – he pushing twenty-seven. But what you doing about the girl?"

One evening Dada brought home two old people who were trying to find a girl for their last son. "Good night! Good night, neighbour," they called. They had come to talk about Judith, and Ma came to the door. "Sita Ram," Madam Rita said politely, putting her palms together so her fingers pointed up. Pa was still out, and Ma spoke with them. Not yet, she said. They wasn't ready for Judith to married yet, but Madam Rita must come back one day, please God, and they would blag a little. So eventually the people left. Afterwards Ma muttered that it must have someone better for she nice child than that boy who never do a good day work, and he so fat and greasy too. She well surprise, she said, that Chaitlal could think he friend could help she or she child.

In fact there were whispers about some of Dada's friends. One was a policeman who, people said, took bribes; others were hunters who included a couple desperate characters. Most colourful was the pardner whom people called Firedance, because he would do banaithi on Hosay night, dressed up in white, dancing and whirling a long stick with fire at both ends. Ma was not impressed, muttering, "Don't mind he wife and child and them have to band they belly. He there dancing with fire."

"Salaam!" It was the neighbour from across the way. November rain was giving way to clear cool weather and everyone was coming out into the street. "Salaam, salaam," Mr Ali called again. "Madam Jai, I just want to pass you little sawain for the season."

"He have son to married too, or what?" Mark dug Judith with his elbow, and Ma glared at him.

"Thank you, neighbour," she called and hurried to the door.

"Show some respect," Brother snapped when the neighbour had moved on up the road. "And what's the meaning of that stupid haircut? Your business is to mind your books. You think *saga boy* is a profession? You will end up cutlassing Tiefin Trace for your living if you keep this up. Judith is an example for you to follow." He broke off as Judith scrutinized her nails, which she had started biting again. "What is it?" Brother asked. "What?" A little irritable, unaccustomed to repeating a question.

"Brother, don't be angry." She squinted outside into the sunlight as if trying to discern something that darted and wavered in the distance, fragile like a battimamselle.

"What?"

"I want to study some more." Now she hurried on impetuously. "Cecile, my friend from school, got a . . . a grant, they call it. She's going to England to write Higher School Certificate and . . . and get a degree, and . . ." And it came out in a rush. "She and I applied together and the British Council agreed to help us. Brother, make me try, nah?"

England.

It took his breath away. Then his face relaxed, his eyes glancing far off, and we could see that was the dream of his life, studying in England. And now (as Brother described it later) the endearing impudence of this girl. "England, eh?"

"But what the France is this?" Pa held his head when he heard. He discussed it with his brother Ravi but Chacha had no light to shed on it. Brother only said they had to help Judith all they could. Even when he found out that she had tried to slip Doolarie a few dollars that no one could spare, he held his peace. "How did you find her?" he demanded.

"She was selling right there in the market." Judith took a deep breath to steady her voice. "Nobody had told me anything. When I saw her I ran over, and she turned and . . . she saw me look at her and she turned away. I told her I would write to her, I would try to help. I asked where to send it. She wouldn't say a word. She wouldn't even look up."

Months later, rain poured into every crevice, lingering in pools or high grass beaten down to mush, swelling wood and mildewing surfaces, seeping into areas without the drainage to accommodate the rise in water edging forward to flood streets and stop traffic. Yet we squeezed together in the car that sputtered north, then west to Port of Spain, bumping through widening puddles of uncertain depth that hid bulging stones or squelshing mud.

At the port we went with Judith as far as we were allowed, and she went on alone, walking very straight among the other passengers who were older and bigger. The original departure date had shifted without explanation, and Brother had learned on inquiry that the ship had had an old welding repair that had fractured and needed to be welded again for it to sail a straight course. This was terrifying in itself, and when the new date came and all was ready, the troop of family, Pa, Ma, Brother and the rest of us filed anxiously to the area where they could see Judith board. The older ones tensed when nothing happened. How was one to account for the delay but by imagining holes in the hull, seams opening in unknowable places.

Yet the ship loomed above us, solid and powerful, black at the base and white above, scooping up higher to the front and long beyond our expectations, its sides punctured regularly with what Brother called portholes. Heavy ropes looped up and, above, rails gleamed, shafts slanted this way and that, flags fluttered, a massive funnel banded dark and light like a tiger cat, belched copius black smoke. But then, between the dark cracked edge of the place where we stood and the base of the ship, murky water sucked at black metal.

Nearby, a man seeing off his brother demonstrated his superior knowledge by pointing out the captain boarding, the bosun and his mate, the cook and several others. Then passengers surged up the walkway and eventually Judith came in sight, the distance to the deck seeming greater as she ascended. Brother waved a red handkerchief he could only have bought for a pre-arranged signal and she stopped near the top and waved directly at us a red cloth of her own.

Yet the boat stayed rocking in place and at length two men scurried down the walkway. An hour and a half passed before they returned, and still there was no announcement. "If something wrong with the boat is best she come off now," Pa said at last, and it was what we were all thinking. Ma nodded, her face pale and drawn.

"No, Uncle!" The man nearby had been back and forth, seeking an explanation. Now he told the forlorn group huddled around Brother in the rain that some member of our crew had been sent to buy cigarettes and liquor for a group of other staff but had stopped to gamble and ended up with . . . well, a lady, and he had returned on board without the money. So the master had had to come back ashore for funds to reimburse a number of men who were murderously angry, but it was all settled at last. A deafening blast from the ship confirmed this and the steep side began to draw away, the water widening in between as the ones on shore staved off tears by arguing about which of the dwindling figures could be Judith, and then she was gone across the heaving grey water that stretched away without end.

Mark had squeezed his eyes tight as if some shock reverberated through him. Opening them again, he caught me looking at him and jabbed me with his elbow. "What about if I go away too, small man?" That thought led to others that penetrated unobtrusively like sunlight through cane arrows, the sort of seasonal gleam so familiar that it was easy to overlook yet left a shimmer in the memory. What if I . . .

Not England though. Canada. That was it. Canada.

Mark glanced sidelong at Brother, who had closed his eyes too, but we both knew Brother was not thinking about himself. For Brother, it would not be one less to take care of, just one beyond arms' length but lodged securely in the forefront of his thoughts. The reach of Brother's mind occurred suddenly, unsettlingly, to me – sudden bends to be negotiated, depths we might never penetrate.

Perhaps infected by Judith's resolve, Mark began to work in earnest. As his grades improved, Ma's sighs of relief continued to alternate with groans of despair and regular explosions from Pa or Brother. For Mark was as much in trouble as he had ever been, every day that he was home. I produced my own type of confusion but that was different. It was true that I blew up when anyone around me interfered with my things – a green stone, a bird nest shaped like a bag – simple things no one would see the use of. But the disruptions Mark brought resulted from what Brother denounced as sheer folly.

He ran away from the weekend chores to play cricket and bust a neighbour's window with his slingshot. He tried to get into the village steelpan side but before Brother found out, the group had put him out anyway because he showed no sign of being musical and less of being inclined to practise. "Don't be an ass, boy." Brother grabbed him by the front of his shirt when he found out and shook him soundly. "Your brain is designed for something else. Mind your books." Brother was strong, even stronger than Matthew, whose build seemed more powerful, and he had actually lifted Mark off his feet. Now he dropped him.

"You wouldn't mind if was 'The Ashgrove' I was playing on a violin though," Mark returned sharply. "Is because pan is poor people music, ent?" And he bolted before Brother could lay hold on him again.

Mark answered back everyone who was older than he, and teased the rest beyond endurance, yet I wanted to be him for he had something to say about everything and even when there was nothing to be said, he said it anyway. Late at night when it could be borne no more and our parents were dying to sleep, Pa bawled through the partition that separated their room from that of the older boys, "Boy, close that hole in you face."

CHAPTER 9

# LETTERS

## Timmy

That was one kangalang – Mark and school. I ent in *that*, I decided. I go study but take my fun quietly, so people not always in my business.

After Judith left for England, though, we boys helped Ma even on weekends and had little time to ourselves. No one minded doing Luke's share, but Matthew and Mark passed the chores down when they could. In Mission, shops were spreading out from the Junction and more and more bustle and noise rose up to the gallery. There was the hammering of new buildings going up, not only pounding on wood but clink on steel, honking of cars and loud voices on the street. At the corner, Nuts sold more coconuts than ever at his usual stall, but the bakery had moved east from the Junction, where a new hardware had sprung up, so our errands spread out over a greater area.

Brother might have shared the work out more evenly, but something had happened that changed up everything again, only this time it was nobody getting sick or going away. It was something just stupid. It had this new lady teacher in the school. She may have been at Naps still while Judith was there, but it was only later that the family heard how well Amani Manniram had done in School Certificate before she went back home to Mayaro. Nobody in Mission knew anything about her before she came to teach at the CM School. And right away it was one set of confusion.

Big strong fellows like Matthew and them stopping to watch how Miss Manniram comb she hair. Anybody could see how it sweep back to this big black bow where it gather up then fall just beneath her shoulders, but what it have to notice in that? Matthew and Mark whispering about her on weekends, and the girls at school watching every shade of she clothes, and some of them vex because they know they could never look like her and some of them in a dream that they look like her in truth. Fareeda Talib say watch how Miss wear colours that go together, and start talking about "mint green and beige," and Fareeda say her brother only watching how the fabric swirl around Miss legs when she turn around.

And all that, all *that* woulda be nothing if it wasn't that Brother of all people get caught up in this same madness – because I glimpse him in school passing her classroom and I could see like Brother couldn't watch nowhere else. Only he couldn't look in her face and he eye stop somewhere about the hem of she skirt. Now this skirt was made up from some soft kind of cloth that flowed round her and stopped under her knees so you were only seeing smooth smooth calves curving down to these shoes these women would wear with high heels. And if they shine? Shine is joke.

Then, one evening, just as if he hadn't been watching for her on weekends himself, Mark asked Brother whether he had seen the new teacher yet and if she was really as pretty as people said, and Brother just slid down in his chair. "Oh my Lord!" he said, like he didn't have strength even to pretend.

"Like he and all gone through." Matthew's mouth fell open as if he couldn't believe it, even though he was grinning and knocking Mark with his foot, but Mark left it alone now because he was soft-hearted underneath all the playfulness, and although Brother was brilliant when it came to books who could say whether he had the lyrics to get anywhere with Amani Manniram.

It was nothing Miss was trying to do. She was a quiet quiet lady just going to teach her class, but when she reached school there would be this flutter of some ribbon or skirt hem or some flash of floral something and children would crane they neck or start to talk behind they hand. And it must be so she wouldn't feel uncomfortable that Brother would keep his head straight. People who didn't know him might not guess, but it was different for me. Even Andrew was out of Mission Presbyterian and off at secondary school by now but I was still in Mission, in Brother's class – which went without saying – and I could see Brother *not* turning his head. Only, when she was in the next class, through the space in the partition, you could see her arm, you could tell it was hers – slim but, you know, *round*, and her hand with the chalk gliding across the board and leaving this trail of handwriting, even the hand-writing curving round and smooth. And you could hear her. Brother would lower his voice so that, while you listening to he, you watching him listen to her. I can't say how Brother manage to teach, but he manage somehow and I very well manage to learn because otherwise it woulda be licks.

In between the dramas with Brother and Miss, a letter would come some-times from Judith. The letters would come to Brother but he would bring them in the evening, and Ma would say, "Read it out hard." The first letter from Judith had also been the first letter ever to arrive home from abroad.

*Dear Brother,*

*Thank you for the sweater. I had to put on almost all my clothes one on top the other and the sweater on the outside and then I was just warm enough to go out and buy a coat. I didn't want to spend all that money on a coat but I couldn't study or even think; it was so cold. And please tell Pa what he heard is true: it does rain all the time here and I carry the umbrella he bought me every day.*

*I made contact with Cecile and yesterday we got together and made roti and alu. I can't tell you how good that was. I've got a part-time job in the Library, the best place in the world to work when one has to study too, so you needn't send as much money. Please keep some for the house . . .*

Other evenings, Brother's friends, Mr Israel or Doc Griffiths, might be there. One evening, trying to keep a straight face, Doc mentioned that Miss Manniram had come in that afternoon to pick up a prescription for her father. Doc shot Brother a sidelong glance of pure merriment and asked whether he had noticed the lace collar. "Noticed!" Brother shook his head, faint, like a dying man.

"Is a life sentence he get, you see him there," Pa said. "The fella fall without a struggle, and like he can't even pretend." It was true enough, for Brother had no practice in concealing his feelings.

The problem, according to Phuwa, was that Amani Manniram's parents had money because old Mr Manny's rumshop had done well and his son, Amani's father, had opened a good business, a dry goods store. Brother said, never mind all that; and Ma said, what sort of people wouldn' glad see to get a boy like he for they daughter. "Well, anyway, I live to see Nathan get basodee over a gyul," Pa chuckled, but he was pleased. It was time and past time this boy give he a grandchild, he said.

We fellows began to speculate about what it would be like for Brother to be married with his own house to see about, but meanwhile the house near the Junction went along much as it always had. As Ma said, Mark's departure to school in San Fernando five years ago had not really made the house more peaceful, for I was quick to get vexed and on weekends Mark liked to *raise* me at every opportunity he got. No one would torment Luke and it was no point teasing Andy because he didn't care, but Ma would say that when I was around, Mark was like a phukni – the little pipe oldtime people used to blow into in order to light a fire.

Later, as grown men with our own families, we might huddle together in a hospital waiting room trying to think of anything else but what it would have been like to be alone in trouble at that age and suppressing our anxieties about what Judith and Brother were going through by dredging up memories of past quarrels that had seemed important to us at the time.

"I go zop he," I remember threatening when I was still a little fellow, only recently plucked into Brother's class. In marble pitch, zopping meant hitting another boy's marble directly, so I positioned myself up on the press in the boys' room, ready to land on Mark as he came through the door. But he had headed off to the cricket ground, and after a long frustrating sojourn on top the press I was more furious than ever. And I was afraid of no one.

"This child, Timmy, mannish already." Phuwa shook her head. "Always have something to say and he ent laughing at all. If you tell him he rude, he more vex than you. I never see more."

With Mark away during the week, I had turned my attention to other things. I was flying my kite when I encountered Selwyn, from my class, and began to fight him with Dada egging me on. What did I care about Selwyn being creole? I never noticed before Dada pointed it out. I would have fought whoever came my way with a kite, but after a duck or two I cut Selwyn's kite and brought it down, so when Selwyn start crying like a kunumunu we began to fight in truth, rolling on the ground and tearing and kicking at each other till Ma came running and chased Selwyn home, still crying and trailing his bust-up kite.

Despite such regular commotion, though, the house grew still when letters arrived from Judith. She had a clean quiet place to stay with a decent landlady, unlike what others had to put up with. Some passages Brother only read aloud when Ma was out the room. A West Indian student Judith knew had been given notice but had not found anyone willing to rent a room to him and the police had been called in to remove him from the old room, for trespassing. Other students had protested but the authorities dismissed that as a native rebellion. Brother also skipped the part about a student who took ill in a student facility that refused admission to a coloured doctor. However, another letter described people in class with her, *three good friends: Cecile, my Naps friend, Jo-Anne from Barbados, and a fellow named Jeremy Teemul, whose father was from Trinidad . . .* The Indians from India didn't seem to think much of those from the West Indies, so she didn't bother with them. Mostly, though, she got on with everyone.

So the days without Judith passed and the weeks became months. A new baby, whom Judith had never met, took her first steps in awkward dancing movements and chuckled heartily. Tessy hardly moved without dancing and skipping, and she inevitably tripped over her own feet, so Andrew had called her Dizzy Tessy, then Tizzy ever after. Andrew, indoors with his books, played with her most. It was Mark that I wanted to be with even if it ended in a scuffle.

Mark lived through each week to get home for Ma's food. Every weekday after lunch, he said, he bought bellyful, a hefty sweet-bun that tided him over to the mingy little dinner provided by the old woman he boarded with – always, he said, with she face set up for rain. Mark had to study frantically before nightfall, when Miss Cassie put out the light he was *wasting*. Yet he was doing well. Brother would grab him in a ferocious hug. "You see" – he grinned – "you picking up speed and you not stopping so in third place, you know." Brother pointed up at an imaginary kite. "You're watching those two fellows above you and after this you moving like a zwill." He flung back his head laughing and plopped his hands on his knees. "Cut them down, man." He grabbed Mark's hand and crushed a few dollars into it.

"I glad to see you, boy," Ma said. "You bring little fun in the place. Timmy does be so serious – you barely say two word to he and is like you raise a nest of marabunta."

I can remember how my heart sank as Brother glanced away from Mark, eyes narrowing. Brother cocked his head as if he couldn't believe his ears, and crooked the forefinger. "Eh? You're miserable to Ma? Who do you think you are?"

"Yes, boy," Mark said, "you see that opening? Things not looking good for you." He made violent flogging movements with his left hand, but without success. He never diverted Brother's attention from me. And even if he had been laughing at me, Mark was no one to jeer. By the last Sunday evening of school holidays he had become more and more fractious, playing cricket in the September evening that grew dark quickly and coming in with a bold stare at anyone who questioned him.

"You have you mother worried here," Pa shouted. "You don't know you expect to come in before dark?"

"Yeh, well ent I come now?" It was always the same. The end-of- vacation madness was on him and he shrugged and turned his back to Pa and swaggered off, and Brother exploded and drew his belt and fired a lash at Mark, big as he was, but Mark only made it worse by goading him.

"That is the best you could do? That is how you does hit? A big man like you?"

By this time, though, Brother had more on his mind than Mark; on evenings he consulted Pa about the plan for his own house. Yet night and day the boys still felt his unwavering gaze. "I say he would ease up, now he in love and thing," Mark grumbled, and Luke said, "Nah! You crazy?"

One day Ma drew Brother aside when Luke was out of earshot. For what would Luke *do*? Even Mark grew serious when they pondered Luke's crooked walk and unsteady step. How could he board in San Fernando, cross the stream of traffic to the school gate or hustle for a taxi on Fridays. Despite glowing school reports Luke remained in the village even when Andrew left for college. Then, the girls who smiled shyly at Matthew and were beginning to laugh with Mark glanced away from Luke. Brother and Pa talked to Chacha and he was sympathetic but raised his palms and said it was such a sad thing.

One day Mark and Luke were playing cards when Luke hauled himself to his feet, throwing down the chair, limped to the top of the steps and stared out past Ma's plants. "If is not wall is fence," he said. "Wood and galvanize, border plant and chicken wire. And what it have in Mission besides the rumshop, except bush and more bush?" Luke drew a long sobbing breath as if all these things were crushing the air out of his chest. "So what it is? This go be my whole life?" Mark's hand rose almost to Luke's shoulder, then dropped as Luke swung away and pushed haltingly past the crotons, away from the house. I could see Ma standing in the doorway and when I made to go after them she shook her head.

The next day she dressed with care and went into the village. By evening she reported to Brother that she meet with a mister who was running a new school. Brother said he had heard there were classes in typing and bookkeeping, but what was she thinking? "I did thinking bout Luke," she said. "Is a type of work he could sit down and do. The mister say he could come to class Monday, please God, but I don't know how we go pay for that now."

Brother was quiet for a long time, his arms clenched round her. "Aaha," he said at last. "You remember Judith's last letter? The little job in the library is paying her rent. The money we save might almost cover the fee for Luke."

Tizzy was riding Andrew's back. "Who Judith?" she asked, sliding down.

"Your sister in England." Brother smiled at her and rumpled her hair, and she spread her arms and wheeled around, bouncing and swaying.

"So if she gone England, then when she come back she go bring ting for we?"

"Only for you and me," Andrew said. "You cutting or what?" He and Tizzy linked their small fingers and the bargain was sealed. "Is you and me alone who must get the ting from England, right?" And she laughed and whirled again, round and round, her skirt flying, till Ma said, "That nuff!" But Ma was smiling too, her arms laced round Luke's shoulders.

*Gran-zafe*, the neighbours said, that is what it would be. "Ent, Madam Jai?" Teacher is a big man so it have to be a big wedding – at last, after an engagement of one year to allow Brother time to build his house, then a postponement of four more months. Only a room on the side remained unfinished and that was locked off until they could afford to complete it, so he had actually moved his things from Phuwa's to the new house. Judith wrote in distress about being unable to come home, and she wanted every detail. *You are all so bad at relaying news. When I have a sister-in-law who knows what is important I suppose I'll find out then about the decorations for the church and the style of the cake.*

In no time at all Brother had to write her back.

"Tim," he said, "get them together, because it's from all of us." He read it out before he sent Matthew to post it:

*February 27, 1959*

*Dear Judith, Yesterday I went to cricket with Pa and Israel, and we took the boys. Perhaps we should not have gone because Pa was not feeling well to begin with but he insisted it was the best thing for him. Then the pains became severe and we had to bring him home. It was a good thing we had Israel and the boys to carry him from the stands and it was really Matthew who was able to help me get him in the car. We sent for Griff and he tried the usual injection but this time it did not help.*

*My dear, you know now what I have to tell you. This is the hardest thing I've ever written.*

*Pa died early this morning at 3:30. Griff stayed with us to the end and is a constant support with all the arrangements. The funeral is tomorrow. By the time you get this it will be over so it is not worthwhile to spend the fare. Do NOT come home. Stay and study. I am sorry to think of you alone with this over there. Here at least we are together, but in my mind you are here with us.*

*Your loving Brother*

*P.S. Ma is holding on. I'll do what I can. Pa would want you to <u>stay where you are</u> and work hard. Brother.*

Brother sent Matthew to post it and when Matthew paused in the doorway Timmy saw for the first time how big he was, filling up the frame. "Brother," Matthew said, "you don't think Juds will come? Really?"

"How?" Brother seemed surprised. "I told her not to."

Luke whispered to Andrew that that was never straightforward, telling Judith what to do, but I insisted she would do just what Brother told her. "And what money it have to bring she anyway?"

Brother rested his head down on his arms. I remember flinching, but when Brother raised his head again he was not crying after all. His eyes were dry and he peered outside as if the immediate terrible loss yawned on something else, something unimaginable. His face clenched in pain before which I ducked out through the door.

On the way out I passed Mr Israel, directing the men setting up the tent. As they worked, the other men exchanged views on the death. "Boy, is a hell of a thing. One day you does be working good and the next – *baps*, you fall down. Basil bowl you out." Pa? I could hardly grasp it was Pa they were talking about.

It was hard to keep track of what was real. A man called from the street asking if it was true it had a dead in the house, and whether he could come and see. He walked on peacefully when Brother refused, but he was back that night for the wake. He came for the freeness, and when he got rowdy Israel and old man Lezama put him out. Then he was furious and began to pelt bottles and curse. Next morning Phuwa said, "Watch! It have bottle all over the road."

Brother said we had to clean it up at once before people burst their tires, for everybody from all about would come to the house. He paused as Mahal steered past, carefully negotiating his way amid the broken glass. Then Brother warned us about the funeral. "No loud bawling. You understand?"

The next morning he surveyed the dejected group sternly, dressed and waiting for the hearse to arrive, then his eye rested on Ma. "I know, Queen." He folded his arms around her and she seemed suddenly very small, but she just shook her head.

"Nobody doesn't know nothing," she said quietly.

It was true – what Brother said about everyone coming. Of course there was Chacha and his family, but also relatives of Ma that most of us had never seen. They came in carloads from Couva and bustled forward to make themselves known. Then, not only close friends like Griff and Israel but the entire village – the Alis, the Lezamas, Miss Beharrysingh, Warden Green and old Teacher Mangalsingh – even an ancient neighbour from Quick River Trace whom no one had seen for years and who was supposed to have died long ago.

Amani Manniram and her family arrived early, but after greeting them Brother was so occupied that they drifted to seats near the side of the tent. Ma noticed at once. "Boy, if rain come Amani parents and them will wet," she told Luke. "Bring them up near the front." He was fourteen now and doing so well in the bookkeeping course that he was bursting with confidence. Only a few days before, he might have risked heckling Brother about Amani; but everything was different now, unthinkable – a day to survive and to get Ma through. When the hearse coasted to a stop in front the gate, Brother hurried over and tightened his arm around her before going to help with the box.

"Oh God, Jai. How you could do this." She said it almost under her breath, and that was when I realized that in all my ten years I had never before heard her call Pa's name.

Later, against the Reverend's preaching, came a shuffle and scraping at the back of the tent and a woman I did not know wavered beside a row with a few empty seats. She wasn't old, yet was shaky on her feet.

"Get her out before Dada gets here," Brother whispered to Chacha, and Chacha replied, "That go be real trouble, boy, but how we go send she away?"

The woman's voice rose. "No. Move from me. I doesn' belong back here." She shook off a hand put out to steady her and tightened her orhni around her face. She was drunk. "What, nobody know me, or what? I does know me mind. I doesn' pretend, just because I never skin and grin to married." She dropped heavily into a chair, scraping it on the stony ground, then, in a moment, she was up again clumsily, still pinching the cloth over her face. Everyone was looking. Only Mahal paid no attention, involved in manoeuvring between the drain on one side and the mango tree on the other.

Mr Israel gripped her arm and steered her towards the back. "Quiet. Mind youself. You better leave quiet."

"Madam Jai, what happen? You is not like dem little boy. You could pretend you forget me?"

As she became boisterous, Israel dragged her off more roughly. They could hear her shouting outside but the words were blurred.

"For once is a good thing Chaitlal still in the rumshop," Madam Beharrysingh whispered audibly.

The voice rose outside more clearly. "You tink you could advantage me. I come here with my good mind and you get on so." But then the words were lost again.

After the service Ma asked to speak to the strange woman, but no one could find her, and I, for one, saw no reason why anyone should have tried.

When they had left the cemetery and got back to the house, Ma stood for a moment at the gate.

"What really going to happen now?" she whispered.

And that was when we saw it. The house was still mainly of wood and Pa had repaired it when we first moved in and then from time to time, but years of weathering had left the roof patched with galvanize that had rusted, leaked and been patched again. As soon as Mark finished school and found a job, he and Matthew were to have put together with Pa to build the brick house, so few repairs had been made of late. Boards warped or swollen in the rain bulged out, edged with mildew, or shrank so spaces gaped between. One of the handrails Pa had sanded so smooth Ma had stroked it lovingly and said was like Tizzy face – one of these same handrails had taken up wood ants and hollowed at the base so Pa had wired in a length of PVC, temporarily. Moss was creeping up the outer wall and lower steps. Only the fretwork remained stubbornly intact, though the paint had mottled and peeled. Ma stared past the rust and wood rot at an emptiness impossible to comprehend.

"This man could really gone and leave me here?"

The issue of what was to happen next was a separate thing and sank in more slowly. "I suppose we go sell a cattle," she said. "We go sell ting, one one."

That evening while Andrew lay wretchedly on the bed beside Ma, Brother sat at the table before a few books. Mark came in and put down the bowl of chow, caught my eye and slid over to sit close by me in the corner.

"What you writing, Brother?" I asked after a while.

"I write to clear my thoughts," Brother said. He spun the book and put his head down on his hands as if he was tired in a way he had never been in his life before. What he had written stood out starkly from the page in his careful penmanship and it was the language of the Bible but not a verse I recognized: *Then shall deliverance arise from another place . . . but thou and thy father's house . . .*

"But what that means?" I asked. "What it has to do with us?"

"That is what I am trying to work out." Brother looked tiredly at it, but went on writing, and I tried to leave him in peace by opening a book on my lap. Mark made no such pretence but sat there unable to be anywhere else.

A week or so later Brother shaved his head, although we were not Hindus and did not have to observe Shradh. Oldtime people believed it helped the soul on its way, he said, and Pa might have expected it. At the back of his head curled the tiny lock they left after the ritual.

"You shoulda tell me," Israel said. "I woulda shave with you."

"No," he said. "I didn't tell the boys either. They might have felt they had to, and then get harassed in school and that sort of thing."

Luke, Mark and I exchanged looks, trying not to show relief, but of course Andrew was the one to pipe up, "I coulda shave too, Brother. I don't mind."

Later that evening I had fallen asleep briefly but woke up in the brief twilight to Ma's voice, raised, arguing with Brother. This was unheard of and when I rolled off the bed to see what was going on, there were Luke, Andrew and Tizzy clustered wide-eyed in the doorway, with Mark and Matthew leaning over them. Ma had finished kneading the roti earlier and put it to soak, but it was laid out now on the hot tawa, and her hand paused above it.

"No, boy. How you go do that? How the girl will feel?"

"She'll understand completely, Ma. It's just for a year more, to . . . stabilize things here. Most of the boys are still in school and Tizzy is only now ready to begin, but by next year Luke will be qualified, and Mark can start working even sooner."

"When Judith know what taking place she will come."

"Judith must not know. By the time she finds out it will be too late to do anything but waste the fare."

"Lord Father, no, boy. What this girl father and mother going to say?" She stared at him and the sada stuck to the hot iron of the tawa. The unaccustomed smell of burning roti rose and lingered, infusing me with a sense of life as I had known it gone up in smoke.

The days tightened round us, seeming to speed the warping and mouldering of wood and to crush even the lives in the unsteady house into disrepair. As the limited but steady trickle of money dried away, Ma dug up provision, gathered dasheen bush and cut seasoning for the bhaji. But we boys grew difficult and wayward. Even Chacha grumbled about it when he travelled from Moruga to see how we were doing, but what possible solution could there be?

"I too worried bout your ma, Teach," I heard neighbour Ali remark to Brother. "How much longer she go live there with the old house falling down round her and the bandon land filling up with bush?"

Some months after Pa's funeral, Phuwa had brought word in hushed tones. Amani was marrying the pharmacist's son who had studied in England and returned to Trinidad three or four months ago. Her parents had pressed her into it, or so Phuwa declared. I glanced at Brother in shock but it was clear he knew already for his expression did not change. He pushed his bare feet into the white shoes he had bought for his wedding and went out.

Phuwa attended the lavish ceremony and reported that the dress was pretty pretty, if you see, but the girl face look like she di' dress up for she own fineral. In the village, respect for Brother prevented anyone except Lezama from breathing a word like *tabanca*, but there were glances of sympathy against which he visibly steeled himself. Into Ma's loss and fear lanced this new pain, all the sharper for being Nathan's. Their silence tightened the tension in the house. "Don't bother bout macocious people," Phuwa told her. "Nathan go find another girl. He go find one nicer than Amani."

Brother never referred to it. He told Ma that Pa would have wanted his brothers consulted about the future and that was all he was prepared to talk about. Dada having come directly from Manny's, no one could understand what he said, but Chacha was eager to help.

"Boy, you just tell me what I could do for all you." Chacha would have handed over money gladly if he had had it, Brother said afterwards, but knowing Chacha had none to spare, what Brother really needed was advice. Then he told Ma he had decided house repairs must wait while he saw the boys through school.

He rounded on Mark. "And you see you? You now write A levels and you think the evening is to ramajay in saga clothes. Cruising on the corner to pick up girls – flagrant nonsense. After you play your little windball cricket on Saturday, then find yourself here and help Andrew with the Physics. The boy is finishing Form 2 and you harrassing him calling him duncey instead of explaining when he's willing to learn. In fact he *one* is trying to do the right thing. Timmy now, barely get into college and shouting out 'fens' when he's supposed to be learning Spanish – busy pitching marble."

"And what bout Matthew?" Ma put in. "Coming in with he head bad from the rumshop. What example he really giving?"

"You don't understand, or what?" Brother raked a furious eye over the lot of us. His jaw clenched as he reached out tight fists and then tugged them to his chest as if reining in hog cattle about to pull his cart off some steep track. In the quiet that had fallen, his voice, low and strained as it was, seemed to thud into the deep places of our hearts. "We have to pull together." And it came back to me, that night of the burned roti – the jolt that went through me as the future swerved out of control, noiselessly as Brother's life changing track to intercept it.

We gathered closer, wide eyed and dumb, till Matthew said, "Brother, you just tell me what I must do."

"I must always tell you? For the rest of your life?"

Matthew dropped his eyes. "All right." He blurted it out. "It have a job as messenger in the Warden Office. I go start teacher training next year instead, and see if we catch weself over the next few months. What about that?"

But Matthew did more. Before and after work at the Warden's Office he hoed, forked and cultivated the land in Balata Trace so Ma could reap and sell produce. At the end of the eight months he postponed teacher training for another year. It was Matthew who wrestled the land back from the bush, a rough physical grappling with weeds, vines, insects, squirrels, birds. Only his constitution could stand it, for he was tougher than the rest, more like Pa in body, but bigger and more muscular, able to absorb the shattering recoil of the hoe on drought-hardened soil, to drag down new bamboo and hoist it up to replace the old poles that had rotted and no longer led water to the plants, to hack and prune, and to cutlass the edge of the land where the forest tried to edge back in.

Like Pa too, Matthew had stories to dispel the darkness. Some were from Dada in the old days but more were from Pa. Some were from men Matthew hunted with. At night Tizzy demanded the stories, but the rest of us gathered around him too when he took a seat in Pa's chair to recall the ones Pa had told, and add his own embellishments. "If you suffer for me forty days and forty nights, said La Plus Belle, I shall be yours and you shall be mine."

When he was done he walked away from them leaving Tizzy sleeping where she had conked out on the floor beside his plate and mug at the foot of the chair, and he went off in search of a drink at Mr Manny's. When I grumbled, Ma said, "Leave he. He does wok overhard. Pick up he cup."

Sometimes Matthew cooked. He could curry goat, duck and common fowl, and, these being unavailable now, he set off into the forest with his gun. He cleaned lappe or manicou and seasoned the meat with garlic and pepper and bandhania while the younger ones stood round breathing it in until he called, "Come then, come then. Taste it and tell me what it want." And nothing was ever wanting. Once or twice a year he would get up early on a Sunday morning and tell Ma to stay out of the kitchen, and while Brother marched the rest out to church, Matthew would draw out saltfish he had bought in the market the day before and knead flour to make fry bake and buljol, but for the most part he cooked only meat and only on special occasions.

He grumbled too. Having postponed teacher training repeatedly he announced he had put it out of mind, only to say now and then that he had given everything up to work the land and so missed the opportunity to qualify himself like the others. Then again, he would seem content. "What? A set of little children in class to mind? Nah." He would say he didn't have that kind of patience. Yet he had put up with Mark's goading and my temper and, later, turned out to be infinitely patient with his own children. Matthew looked happiest outside with earth on his hands, moulding soil around the orange trees or digging out dasheen; it seemed to me he loved it more than he resented it. And when he limed in the rumshop or with hunters in the forest, he gathered the stories and brought them home.

But the months passed in one small wrenching loss after the next. The rains and a strong wind left the house almost in ruin. Water poured into the kitchen and almost everything that could be sold was gone. The last cow left was Beauty.

Beauty was a pretty calf we had all petted and played with and she had remained a favourite. Beauty's milk, Ma would say later, was the best milk. But the time had come when there was nothing left to sell and Ma took Brother's hand and spoke with her lips hardly moving as if she was in pain. "Boy, you know I don't like to always ask." He was absolutely still and squeezed his eyes shut, his chin pressed down to his chest. "No, no," she hurried, "is all right. All right, child."

"Nothing. Nothing left. I've spent the money from my next salary. Uniforms, school books." She put her arms round him and he sobbed like a child. "Ma, I'm so sorry."

I was frozen because for Brother to cry like that it must be the end of the world, and later, when Ma told us Beauty was going to live on a big farm not far away and we would see her sometimes, I knew. At the time Tizzy screamed and threw down her cup of cocoa and it spattered the couch. Andrew said, "Don't beat her, Ma. Is just how she going to miss Beauty. Wait, Ma, wait." He flung himself in front of Tizzy, who had thrown herself sobbing on the ground. "Beat me. She will feel sorry and wouldn' do it again, and I could take it." Ma shook her head and slumped into a chair and said, "Nah! Nobody getting no licks tonight. Get up, child. See if you can wipe up that for me."

When Andrew left for school on Monday he would not be coming back until holidays because of the fare. Soon enough Tizzy missed him so much she stopped asking about Beauty, and later, when I enquired, Brother confirmed it expressionlessly. Beauty had been sold for meat and gone to the slaughterhouse.

In between the shadows, though, were patches of light. Mark's examination results were outstanding and he found a teaching position in Mission High almost at once. "Just for a couple years," Brother said. "Then you have to get into Training College."

"No," Mark said. "I want a degree. I must be able to get a scholarship."

And Brother nodded, well pleased.

Matthew introduced us to a fair-coloured, sharp-featured girl he seemed to think pretty, and she told us at once that her father had died and her mother re-married, and that was how her name was Hemlee – from her stepfather, who was a dougla. At first she seemed withdrawn in a superior sort of way, then she opened up. In fact she was soon able to pass a cutting little remark about knowing Dada from seeing him in and out the rumshop opposite her house, which was true enough but, as the slight lift of Brother's eyebrows conveyed, out of place. Mark came in just as she left with Matthew, so the rest had to fill him in. Her name, Brother reported, was Maydene Hemlee, and Mark lost not a moment in renaming her Mayhem.

This turned out to be prophetic. Maydene remembered Judith from school and talked about her with the authority of an old acquaintance and someone now close to the family. "Degree what?" she was reported to have said to a friend in the village. Judith gone away because of some boy she like, so the family wasn't taking *that*. Maydene passed this and other misinformation on as confirmed fact and it all came back to us through Madam Jasmine, who no longer did ironing because her health was failing so she would sometimes *take in* and be visited by Phuwa. Phuwa had sold her house to supplement her own dwindling income and moved in to become a constant help to Ma, as well as a source of village wisdom.

Meanwhile, Israel came on weekends and did what he could to mend leaks and reinforce walls and he reassured Ma by reminding her she was supposed to have a son called Israel. Griff approached Nathan with a loan that would carry Ma and us boys over the next few months. Having no collateral apart from his own unfinished house on which money was already owing, Brother could not transact any such business himself, so it was Griff who took the loan and I only found out when I overheard Ma expressing her thanks.

Two years of grinding effort and self-denial passed, in the midst of which a woman came calling at the door. "Please, I want to speak to Madam Jai." It was the woman whom Israel had escorted out of the tent at Pa's funeral. She clutched her orhine close over her face and after a brief exchange of words and even briefer rustle of paper slipping from Ma's hand to hers, she was gone.

"Who that was, Ma?" I demanded, quite rudely as I remember. How could I believe, after all we were going through, that Ma would give money to a stranger, especially to a woman who had come drunk to Pa's funeral.

She brushed me aside. "Boy, you too fast with youself." Tizzy's stomach was griping her and she needed medicine. "She have bellyache," Ma said. "Must be something she eat."

Still, after her experience with Judith and Luke she had called the doctor immediately. Griff was away on a course in New York, and the new doctor at the clinic examined the child and told them to give her fluids because she was dehydrated. Ma explained that Tizzy was bringing up whatever she drank, but Dr Mitchell said to give little sips often. "All of you must help you mother," he said to us. "Keep giving her little sips." No, it was not time for hospital yet, he assured Ma to her relief. They could hardly have managed the fare to get there, let alone doctormedicine. Dr Mitchell gave Ma a bottle of pink stuff and gently silenced her promise to pay.

That was when Judith's next letter arrived.

*October 3, 1961*

*Dear Brother,*

*This is for everybody as usual and I know you will read it out. I've just written my last exam and expect to graduate with my Bachelor's in the next few months. In a while I'll need to start again to get the diploma, but meanwhile the library has offered me a full-time position, so at last I'll be able to send something home. Yes, I know how well you are doing from your last letters. I'm sorry I can only manage it now it's no longer necessary, but at least use what I'm enclosing to buy some little thing for Ma and the children.*

*Now I have other news. I've told you about Jeremy Teemul so you may be half expecting this. Jeremy and I are getting married in July. It will be in the Catholic Church – I told you Jeremy is Catholic. I think it's better we stay here and have a quiet wedding than spend everything on the passages, so meanwhile I'll send something every month and come for a visit when we can. Brother, I am sorry to read about the Federation. I know you had such hopes of it . . .*

"Visit?" Ma said. "Son, she say *visit?*"

Brother seemed not to hear, his eyes distracted as if he were casting a vague glance inwards. I used to wonder if sometimes Brother found himself looking for some other Nathan, one with time to himself. Perhaps a lone clergyman immersed in meditation and community work? No. Children. Children learning all around him. His and other people's children, deep in their books. Soon he came back to us.

"Best thing for her," Brother answered. "Education and a good job. It's an opportunity, and if she's marrying someone living there – well."

"Visit?"

"I wanted her to stay and finish her studies. She would be here with us if I hadn't kept writing that we were doing well." He glanced around. "Don't worry, fellows. Your chance is coming." He rumpled my hair and gave Luke a playful cuff on the chest. "I'll see to that."

"You going up for the wedding," Luke said. It was more a statement than a question.

"No."

"You mean because it's Catholic and thing?"

"Oh Lord, no, man. I'd go. But the fare is a little hot." He passed his eye over broken windowpane and faded couch. "They will come when they can, and she's right – she can help more from where she is."

We all knew that Brother wanted to go to England more than anything. He never talked of going to India like Chacha did. Especially since it was Judith's wedding, he would have gone if he could.

Andrew seemed to hear nothing we said. He was home from San Fernando for the long weekend and sat by the bed staring at Tizzy uneasily. "Ma, how Tizzy breathing so funny even though she take medicine?" He laid his hand down beside hers on the bedsheet yet she didn't stretch for his fingers. You could see the fear stalking through his mind like a mocojumbie.

"Visit," Ma mumbled, turning back to the room where Tizzy was tossing under the net. "I here, popo."

At first, in the days that followed that heart-rending lowering of the little coffin, Andrew had nothing to say to anyone. He seemed engulfed in fury. He walled himself off from the rest of us and huddled down in some pit he had dug in his mind.

"We can't blame the doctor," Brother insisted in the aftermath of the shock. "Mitchell's young. He did his best but he just graduated a year or so ago. How could he have the same experience as a man like Griff?"

Something in that ignited Andrew. "But he *did* graduate. Not so?"

Absolute silence fell. Any voice raised at Brother, let alone now and in Ma's hearing – it was unthinkable. The outburst stopped Mark tiptoeing across the room and halted Brother's hand passing Limacol over Ma's face, which was pale and gaunt against the floral pillowcase. Matthew darted forward, locked one hand over Andrew's mouth and dragged him out of the room with the other arm. He pushed his face close to Andrew's. "I have to take you out the house, or you can shut you mouth?"

"Let him go." Brother had followed them out and now grabbed Andrew by the front of his shirt. "You trying to kill your mother? You have no idea what she's going through?"

It may have been that – why Andrew snapped. Griff said so later. He had come to the house straight from the airport and walked in while Brother was holding Andrew by the shirt. "Nathan, man," he said, and locked his arms round Brother, drawing him away to the gallery.

They talked for a long time while Matthew and Mark drifted off together and Luke sat with Ma. Andrew went outside where Ma's machete leaned in the corner and and walked across the yard to a croton that raised thick bunches of bright green speckled with gold. I could not believe Andrew was chopping at it, even when the bunches of leaves dropped, leaking their poisonous milk, and even when the hacking went on till the bush was strewn dismembered on the ground. I started up when Andrew turned on the Ixora. The flowers jolted and scattered and he went on hewing a line of jagged branches, slashing the buttercups, which oozed their white blood until something out of my range of vision gripped Andrew's arm with such force that the machete fell, inches from his feet. I dived toward the door and saw it was Griff, who kicked the machete away, grabbed Andrew tightly in both arms and raised him off the ground as Andrew struggled and shouted and eventually collapsed in exhaustion against the doctor's chest.

Behind me came Matthew's outraged whisper. "Must be mad."

But Brother said, "No. No, we never noticed what was happening to him. Andy was closest to the child."

"Who the hell have he to study?" I wanted to know.

But Griff waved us away and settled down with Andrew on the bench outside the kitchen door, ignoring me on the pirha just inside.

"Your brother says you're angry with Dr Mitchell." Griff paused. "Mitchell's a serious chap, you know. He'd have done his best. The medicine he prescribed is what I'd have given." A mutinous look from Andy stopped him. Griff continued. "Right. Why wasn't I here? It's as much my fault as his, Andy."

"Don't worry. Brother won't think that."

"No, I know he won't."

"And he won't think it was Ma's. He won't wonder whether she shoulda take better care of Tizzy."

"You wonder that?"

"No." Andrew whispered it. "But it have no danger of him blaming anyone, right?"

"Actually there is." Doc's voice thickened with pain. "He blames himself. He says he was supposed to be taking care of all of you, and he should have seen the danger."

"It was so dangerous, really?"

"Gastro?"

"Don't people get better? How she could die just so?"

"Dehydration."

"Brother wasn't even here."

Griff was beginning to sound impatient at last. "He can't always be here. He was in school. He was working. Even in the holidays and on weekends, he works. He never stops."

"No, I mean it wasn't his fault, because . . . he wasn't here." Andrew's voice sank so low I could barely hear it. "I was here."

SEPTEMBER 10, 2010 – 6:05 P.M.

*They say htis is only chance to write and dont ask more time someone else willl buy if you dont pay fast but no police or oh god uncle htey say will cut off my haed Please ucnle can't you*

PART
2

# UNCLE

## *(damaged)*

### Nathan

What was there to be afraid of in the old days? Not like now with bandits and kidnappers and druglords. Nowadays, oldpeople say that then it was only hard time we had to struggle with because people di' live together good.

But they delude themselves.

One night *he* was at Phuwa's door cursing and howling, his usual display of murderous grief. Another night a man stood bawling outside my door. "Teach, you have to come. Oh Lord, Teach."

When I opened the door I saw he was barely out of his teens and he was crying. He said, "Oh Jesus, Uncle." I had never seen him before. I hired a car and it laboured along as far as it could up the Mission Hill Road, then I made the driver wait while I walked the rest of the way.

In the clearing the same young fellow helped me fold the girl in a sheet without touching the bad side. One of the neighbours brought the sheet, perhaps the lad's wife or mother. The girl stopped screaming and fainted by the time we lifted her down to the car. She regained consciousness on the long drive to the hospital and screamed again, then fainted once more. Lying there with the side of her face to me that was unharmed, she looked so much like Judith my heart went out to her all the more. If only I could have kindled something in her, I thought, an interest in schoolwork that could have carried her beyond his reach. I always thought she had it in her. But he smothered it. When she tried to get away, he tricked her into returning to his house, doused her with kerosene and threw his cigarette.

When the hospital was ready to release her, I had a car drive her wherever she wanted to go. I told no one but of course news carries.

Phuwa said, "Nah! He wild, but he woulda never do that. How people could say so mucha wickedness?"

Don't mind how it opened its jaws to swallow us up time and again – poverty was joke to what we had to fight.

# CHAPTER 10

# LESSON PLAN

## Elroy

Nah, we were never close in the old days. You crazy or what? What I feel now is nothing I could have imagined when I was that age. At ten years old I had nothing in my head but keeping my skin from licks.

I see the letter my father write, but it didn't mean nothing to me then.

*August 20, 1975*

*Dear Principal Deoraj, This is to tell you. I living Guyana years now and come back. Now I well sick doctor say is cancer. It have no estate again Papa Jacques dead he family don't know me and the chilren mother die two years now. Dr Griffit advise me to write you and say he will carry the letter heself. What I have to say to you is. My daughter grow up and married is OK but one son I have Elroy not doing well in school. Please help him there is no one else.*

*Yours truly,*

*Reds de Jacques*

Nobody really expect he because the postman don't bring mails out where we di' living, so Pa never hear nothing back. The funeral home done send and pick up Pa body aready when Sister hear the knock and tell me to open back the door. Like anybody else, I know Principal Deoraj by sight, but he look bigger to me. He was tall already but now he take on size and fill up the doorway, and everything fall quiet.

"You are Elroy de Jacques?" He study me, then see Sister. "Accept my condolences."

What the hell we could do with condolences? I ent know what my father call he for, much less why he come. But Sister and he talk anyway and agree I going change school to Mission Presbyterian and I suppose to reach one hour early and stay another hour after school for lessons. I never have no choice because Sister is a big woman twelve years older than me, and she husband, Sinclair, hate me tail; and if I don't do what they say I wouldn't have nowhere to sleep now Pa dead. So, after that, if I don't get out the house early o'clock is licks because they have no child yet only Elroy to study; if I don't reach Teacher lesson on time is worse licks. So I reach. Of course some morning I never prepare. I say, "Chut! I go give he the lesson extempore." But it never work. Licks for so.

All the other boys call him Sir to he face, but when they talk about him they call him Teach. I never call he anything but Principal.

The only thing me and the Principal ever have in common is we di like black pudd'n. How I find this out is one day I get a couple piece of money and I go to buy pudd'n and I see him there buying pudd'n for so – and he friend Israel ask him if he planning to sell it and he say no. He brothers come for the weekend and he buying pudd'n for the whole of them and plenty for heself.

Everybody in and around Mission know everybody life history and what they don't know they make up, so I hear longtime that Principal have small brothers like peas. When I say small I mean younger than he for they all done grow. Matthew working for the past ten years in Sanchez, but he still live in he mother old house by the Junction with he wife, Maydene, and they child, while the Principal and them building a new house next to it on the same land. The next brother, Mark, study in Jamaica and he and he wife teaching San Fernando. Timothy teach Maths in Mission Secondary till he and all get scholarship, and after he come back with the first degree he gone again and do master's in the States. These two fellar, Mark and Timmy, have a set of children and everytime you see any of them all the children together so you can't know who belong to who.

I hear it have a brother name Andrew but I never see him because he do Medicine in Jamaica and gone to England to study more again, so I can't say nothing bout he. But one of them, who never study nothing much that I hear about, make more money than the rest put together and he walk funny, kinda twist and hold on, but he have business all over the place. Sister say that Matthew madam, Maydene, tell one of she pardner how Luke did get damage from in he mother belly and she sure is licks the mother used to get, but it have a set of other people say that is pure wickedness and they know the boy when he was born good good and stay good until he get sick with a ting they call polio.

It have people like to say the boy and them had three sister – one married and living England, but she husband dead; then another die as a little child; and a older one, nobody seem to know where she end up. But what really happen is that the big one wasn't the Principal sister at all but he uncle child, the uncle name Chaitlal. Principal and them di call he Dada. They had a younger uncle too was a cool fellow, they say – everybody like Ravi – but he must be die longtime. Anyway it turn out the Principal end up with a set of brother and the one sister who never live here, and the Principal heself don't have no children. I always want to know why he ent married and get some child of he own to beat.

Is not to say me one was getting licks, and some of them well look for it. When Kenny tief Boysie shoes – the rich boy, Boysie – and Kenny see he going to get ketch and he stuff them in my bag, I nearly dead with fright because I say I going get expel and my sister and Sinclair go kill me. But the Principal say, "Nah. This boy Elroy is lazy but he's not a thief." And he look round and see Kenny pants bulge out on the side and he say, "What you have there, boy?" And he grab him and pull a socks from he pocket. And he say, "Boy? What you doing with socks? When last you wore shoes, let alone socks? Like you expecting shoes?" And he shake Kenny till the fool start to bawl and talk everything.

Next thing, Principal say Kenny father is he friend, Israel, and he owe it to Israel to straighten this boy out, so Principal give he some good licks. And everyone say Kenny go get expel and Principal say no, because that does destroy a child. Some of the teachers say Principal shoulda send the child home because he rotten and going spoil the rest, but Principal say no. He want to leave the child with a future. But you think Kenny ever thank him for that? All Kenny know is he get one set of licks and he lose a pair of shoes when the rich boy coulda well spare it.

The rest of we say, "Weeeei." Principal have eye in the back of he head in truth, and he never take that eye off us. But one day Principal cancel class – a thing that never happen before – he cancel he class to go look at a house in

San Fernando. They say he finding it for he sister who di' living abroad, Miss Judith. She husband dead and she decide to move back from England with she child. "Principal nephew must be bout your age. Anselm, he name," Sister tell me a day I was working on a box cart. "Perhaps you will make friend and ting." I ever ask to fren with any of them? Like Principal going take me home with him to eat pudd'n? But I never say nothing because Sister husband watching me like I kill he white fowl.

Like Principal di' want to finish the house they rebuilding near the Junction in Mission before he sister get back, but every day something keep it back and that make him extra irritable. Like he hand itch him if it don't have tambran switch in it. Before he come to class he would go to watch how the house going up, and sametime he looking out for the workman and them. One day he get away with he brother, Matthew, for that. Matthew agree to take food for the workman and with one thing after the next Matthew leave late. So when the Principal see midday pass he get blue vex and start to get on with Matthew for treating people like dawg. Anyway, Principal would run out when we eating lunch and go again after we leave school. Was the mid-seventies when I get in the Common Entrance class and the house nearly finish build.

"Nearly finish build?" Principal stare at me as if he couldn't believe his ears. "And you're writing the exam this year?" So he grab at me with he left hand. Oui foute!

"The building is nearly complete." I cry out fast, and I dodge him.

"Come, boy."

I inched forward and stopped just short of him, standing very straight, a little to his right. "The building is nearly complete, Sir," I pronounced.

"That's better. Sit down."

When that house was built, Principal Deoraj went on living on his own, a three-bedroom place including the long room on the side for lessons and another room on the other side that wasn't finished. The land had some portugal trees and a few struggling crotons they say his mother had planted, but no flowers, and the grass was usually overgrown. His mother moved into the new house and he went every day to check on her, but since he had never bothered to finish his own house I wondered why he didn't just live in the big place with his mother.

Everybody knew about him because he was a big man in the community, and he knew every child in the school. If you missed school two days, Princi-

pal would land up by your house to find out why, and your parents did whatever he said because he had taught them too. (Nobody father was coming to
tell he nothing.) Now and then his brothers would argue though, and I would
know because I was in his house for lessons day in, day out, weekend, holiday,
you name it. Lessons in my skin. What would cause real trouble was one of
the brothers charging for lessons in CXC Math and I hear when he and the
Principal get away over that. Now that don't mean they don't get together
and pull good – just sometimes they get away.

When the sister called Judith came back to Trinidad she took her son to
live in San Fernando, near the college where they wanted the boy, Anselm,
to go to school. So I never had anything to do with him.

Was only a little after that I got through Common Entrance and passed
out of Principal Deoraj's hand's into big school where no one bothered me
anymore. A set of teacher say is up to us if we don't want to do the work
because they get they degree already. Some of them give lessons, but I had
no money for that and they would hold back part of what they had to teach
for they lessons class, so although my head wasn't bad it woulda take more
effort to keep up than I was ready to spend. Is that same why the Principal
dead set against lessons for money, because he never used to charge for anything he teach before or after school. Don't mind how the young brother
insist he give free place to disadvantage child, and how he don't have people
from his school class in lessons because he cover the syllabus in class, and
how he say lessons only for children who teacher never cover the syllabus,
still, the Principal swell up and say the fee is a bad thing, so they get away
again.

Whether Anselm take lesson or not, people say he was doing well. I never
take it on. The little I see of he, my blood didn't take him. Anyway, when he
pass CXC with one set of distinction, the Principal say they must have something for that. They call the Reverend as usual but they get a priest as well
because they say Anselm remain Catholic like he father. I self get a couple
subjects at CXC but it didn't have nobody to study that.

Same time I di like a girl in a next village use to breeze off on she gallery
just when I was passing she house. But I didn't have no money, and the cut-
eye the mother give me – I don't know how I never bleed. So next thing the
girl mother drive me like fowl from in front she place, and then she turn
around and announce it to the whole trace. "I tell him, if he come to married,
talk. Otherwise don't heng round here. Don' come here with you stupidness.

I done talk I very serious. Two month you come here, you see me daughter, you talk to she, you don't talk no sense. So what you father thinking? If I have a son and he can't tell me why he going down the road to talk to people girl-child, he going to have to find a next place to live. Friend? Say he just a friend? Wha' dat? Boy and girl could be friend? Well, I tell she that stop right there. Friend does carry you but they doesn't bring you back. Friend? But what the arse this?" Bredda man, watch me. I say she pelt me bucket and stone.

Meanwhile Anselm write A level and early in 1984 I hear he gone away to study Law. I say, is the Law? And I look for a job as a police. But that never happen right away. For months after I leave school I couldn't get nothing. Dem was ketch-arse days, pardner. When you see I get that job – *if* I fête? I fête for so. But after that I hear Principal voice in my head, say, *Elroy, boy, you better keep that work*, and so I begin to take it serious. After a while I hear he nephew, Anselm, never like Law again and he study History and Sociology instead and decide to teach after all. But like he decide to teach the whole country, because he writing all kind of thing in the paper bout justice and equity for children, and I say when I was a child who ever think bout justice and equity for me? But I say never mind, at least he make a start. Better late than never.

I never see the Principal for years, till the brother after him die of a stroke. Matthew, he name. I did always hear he suffer from pressure and the Principal friend, Dr Griffith, say this man refuse to take it on – Matthew only eating doubles and pudd'n and other thing with endless salt and fat and he wouldn't take the tablet regular neither. But was more than that. It seem like he put what money he had in International Trust and when that collapse and the government take it over is only a little bit people get back and this man had wife and children and he well take it on. One day a senior man in the force call me, say, "Watch. It have a man fall down in the road," and when I see was Matthew Deoraj self I send for the Principal, for the school just a few steps up from the station, and we get him into a car to the clinic. But Matthew never make it. Afterwards I get to hear from the same officer who call me that was the Principal did give me a reference why I get this work.

So, boy, like it or not is so you half-brother Lennie and me end up as pard-ner. And watch how thing does come round, for allyou father, Israel, and the Principal is real friend – *that* is pardner. And, watch. Is not because he friend Israel is Kenny father too why he didn't expel him, you know. For stealing the shoes, I mean. Nah! That is just how the Principal does move.

I hear he and all get piece of the quenk Lennie and Kenny catch the first time Lennie gone hunting with the set of them? That was must be twenty, twenty-five years now. Of course I hear bout it – how Teach eat it up clean and take two Scotch and start to sing, *Take me down to Los Iros – but don't let me mother know*. When Lennie give me that joke I say to him, "You see what I tell you? So we have to just hold onto this work and see if we could move up in the ranks, don't mind the bobol and victimization, we go teach them who is man – we ready for them. I tell you we ready or my name not Elroy de Jacques. And you see them two nice girl we have?" Because those days I almost say I would settle down. I tell him, "Watch me. Make we take a song fe dat. Leh we call on the Birdie, man."

Now I look back on the two of us belting out the words of Sparrow's "Salt-fish", I find it hard to believe we were ever that young.

# CHAPTER 11

# DEEDS

[Copies made August 12, 1951]

THIS DEED OF CONVEYANCE is made on the 3rd day of April, in the year of Our Lord one thousand nine hundred and fifty Between Richard Sawh storekeeper and Nathan Deoraj teacher. . . .

THIS JOINT TENANCY DEED is made on the 20th day of June, in the year of Our Lord one thousand nine hundred and fifty-one Between Nathan Deoraj and John Deoraj and Matthew Deoraj and. . . .

## Chinksie

I don't know why they expected to get anything out of me. I got to know what I do by keeping my mouth shut. Even my friends don't learn anything from me that could help them identify each other. Besides, the surest way of getting out of this is to know as little as possible about what went on.

It's like I told Cerise a good few years back: Some people stop just so and know everybody's business. They don't ask questions; they keep quiet and let the rest talk. You see when you look cool cool and go about your business? People tell you things they don't tell their closest pardners. When they stop noticing you they talk to each other as if you aren't there. Don't watch them and they don't see you; stay quiet and take it in. It's nothing you mother would teach you.

"My mother look like she have anything to teach me? Hear nah, Chinksie, my parents wasn't right here, you know. And Maamie say, 'Cerise, if it wasn't for my brother, Elroy de Jacques, I ent know.'"

According to Cerise, her Uncle Elroy was taking care of his sister now she was so sick with the sugar, even though she had been miserable to him when he was young. He said Sylvie was the one who kept a roof over his head when their father died, whatever her husband had to say about it. Cerise said, "I can tell you, my mother don't stop here." But Cerise felt it was mainly her father's fault. Sinclair would harden anybody.

This Sinclair was openly unfaithful. "Heself would tell Maamie to she face not to expect him home because he have a wok to put down." Cerise understood such things good good. "My parents and me living in one room and when she gone to work he coming in there with a woman and tell me go sit outside a little. How I could not understand what go on? And it have crack in wall?" But her mother never took it on till she got to hear these other women were living better than she and her child. "But she never say nothing for months. Is that why I tell you my mother have a belly of iron."

Cerise was a bridesmaid at her older sister's wedding, and the reception was in full swing when Maamie told the MC she wanted to say a few word to wish the couple well. Then, in front of all the people Sinclair worked with in the post office, not to mention Dr Griffiths and Israel Lee (my grandfather) and even Principal Deoraj, who had taught both Sinclair and Uncle Elroy – all *big* people – she unpacked the seamy history of her marriage and especially of her husband's miserliness, alcoholism and womanizing. "She leggo the whole story, so my sister wedding just mash up," Cerise said.

Cerise's sister and brand new brother-in-law moved away as far as they could and left for America once they had their green cards. They never contacted anyone in Trinidad again. "And I don't gi' she wrong. My father leave too, gone Arima, but, as people say, he make worthlessness a virtue, so we never miss he. Only, last year Maamie get sick till she nearly lose she foot and no one to see bout neither of us, because I doesn't know how to watch bad foot much less clean it."

Cerise's Uncle Elroy came for them. He was short and thick-set with curly reddish hair and strange eyes. Different. Grey. There was regular food now, which compensated for Cerise having to go back to school. She told me, as her best friend, that he was well fast with heself to tell her what to do, but he could real cook and he bought medicine for Maamie so she didn't get on so miserable. He would even talk to Maamie. That was how Cerise learned about a case some woman wanted to bring against a set of other people – against Principal Deoraj and his family. "And the Principal and them don't even know yet that it have a quarrel."

Holi Payne was the woman's name, and she was the sort that spoke proper English in her sleep. "Nah. I not making no joke: she does fart in sentences." The two of us giggled, and Cerise explained how miserable the woman was, according to Uncle Elroy. "You only walk near she and she does get on like poison bat bite she. But most of the time she does keep she face straight like she don't see you." The family she had taken on were big people – teachers, doctor, businessman. This Holi Payne said that when Jai Deoraj died his older brother, Chaitlal, who was her grandfather, should have had part of the land where the widow still lived. She had waited for Chaitlal to dead, because she wasn't fighting no case for he. Now she insisted that she was the only legitimate child of this man's only legitimate son, and she was suing the whole of them for her fifty per cent.

Now, this woman, Holi, was nearly as old as Cerise's mother, but everybody where she grew up remembered her as a child. Uncle Elroy said, "She was hardly older than Cerise here when the whole village was talking bout she."

In the first place, Holi was so bright in school that she managed to make the teachers look stupid. Some of them said she was mad and others that she was bad, so it was as if she said, *Leh we give them something to talk about.* She put up a jhandi for Kali and a black flag, and when the neighbours asked her what she thought she doing she said she making a puja to bring down her pumpkin vine family. The Shouter Baptist on the corner denounced her, shaking and prophesying with her robe flying white and purple, while the neighbour who was an elder in the Presbyterian Church called her a dain, for the whole street to hear. In school, even the children said Holi was a demon and the more knowledgable began to call her Hollika.

Holi ignored them and finished school with straight As in eight subjects. She married a Syrian boy from QRC whose family had money and who left her well provided for when the marriage collapsed. So now she had the means to take on the whole Deoraj clan, who, she said, had taken possession of her rightful property.

Irritating as Cerise could be, she was at least more entertaining that Aunt Annette and the set of boring people she idolized.

"Aha," Aunt Annette said. "I see the white shoes. Teach?"

It was Principal Deoraj, and he said he had not come to see Chinksie's grandfather, Israel, but to ask Annette to curry a duck for him on Sunday. "You know Chinksie, Teach?" Aunt Annette dragged me forward. "Kenny's daughter." And after the usual small talk they went on to exclaim about the recent coup and to finalize arrangements for the duck. Aunt Annette watched the Principal walk down the steps holding the handrail, and when he paused at the gate and turned to look back and wave, she waved too. She stood very straight and patted her hair in place proudly, as if she had had a visit from royalty.

"He was my teacher, man, and then your grandfather, Israel, was his good friend, so I grew up knowing Israel's two boys. They were in school with me, even their half-brother who left early. When your father gave me a hard time, Leonard would say, 'Oh Gorm, leave she nah, Kenny.' Leonard was a kind fellow from small. And, you know, when we got married Teach gave the toast to the groom's parents, and he said, 'Israel is a brother to me, and I rejoice to see him get a daughter-in-law like Annette.' When I tell you, I felt tip-top. And it's not to say I would have got anywhere if it hadn't been for Teach. I certainly wouldn't be a teacher myself today."

This reminded Aunt Annette of something she had meant to tell me for some time, about watching friends, like this Cerise who her little Chinksie seemed to be getting close to. She was the type to carry you down. Aunt had heard all kinds of things about Cerise breaking away from school to hang out in Gulf City Mall and changing in the ladies room into sexy clothes.

"Put more flour, sweetness," Aunt Annette said, on Sunday morning when we were making the roti. "You can never tell how many will be there today. If they drive down to see the old lady they bound to drop in on their brother."

You have to wonder how these old people think. Aunt Annette take it on herself not only to set me up to carry duck and roti (with a little channa and some pumpkin) to the Principal's house, but to stay there till they had eaten and to wash up for them. "The least I can do," Aunt purred, just as if she would be the one doing it.

Listening to the Principal and his sister talk was pretty dull, but better than reading a book as Aunt had advised.

"So you and Timmy vex? Brother, no."

The Principal insisted he was not vexed, but he couldn't stomach the boy charging money to help people's children with schoolwork. Miss Judith pointed out that even if the giving of extra lessons had grown into a racket, Timmy wasn't charging children who belonged to his own class in the college where he worked.

"So he says he can't work out the rationale behind your objection to a fee."

"To hell with rationale," the Principal shouted. "You hear me? Tell the boy I say, to hell with rationale." His sister reminded him that "the boy" was a man past forty and she changed the subject hurriedly to some great new scheme in which their brother, Luke, was investing for a rate of interest two per cent higher than the bank was offering. The Principal calmed down as the talk floated from one family member to the next.

"But Anselm is doing better now?" He sounded anxious.

"Yes, the blackout was a mercy. It forced him to do the tests and take the Glucophage."

"And the diet?"

"Still in denial. I wish you would speak to him. I have to contend with this hardened posture that, deep-fried or not, doubles is a sugar-free and nourishing breakfast."

"Don't make joke." The water drumming in the sink drowned their voices, but once I turned it off I heard the talk surging on. "Refused the principalship? Of a major girls' school? Turned it *down*?"

The tone of his voice made it impossible not to peep around the door at them. He had placed together the tips of his forefingers on both hands and held them there, waiting, his eyes piercing.

"Brother, don't get vexed now. You see, I want to study some more." And she burst out laughing as if that was an old joke.

"Again." He closed his eyes and moved his fingers to the temples where the hair was greyest but not so thin.

"Okay," she said. "So I'm fifty-two, what of it? UWI accepted me for the doctorate, though they insist that the title is impossible." He opened his eyes and they were bright with anticipation, waiting. She raised her chin and announced it: "Committing Fatherhood: Interrogating the Political Incorrectness of Paternalism in the Classroom."

"Oui Papa." He flung his head back and howled with laughter.

"I beg your pardon – I'm quite serious."

"I don't doubt," he gasped, "but I needn't be."

A minute later they were still hugging up and grinning.

That was when the gate creaked and a man walked up the drive, handed the Principal a letter and turned away.

"What?"

He seemed not to have heard his sister as he turned the letter over in his hands. He looked stunned. "A lawyer's letter, dated August 12, 1990," he said eventually. "A woman named Holi Payne claims to be Chaitlal's grandchild and she's asserting her right to half the value of the land at lamp post 31, et cetera, east of the intersection commonly called Mission Junction, and other assorted property, and she is prepared to take Nathan Deoraj and all others connected with the matter to court."

"Eh? But what nonsense is this? Who?" Miss Judith snatched it and held it out at arm's length, then fumbled in her purse for her glasses. "I never heard of Dada having any child but Doolarie."

"No, he was married before. I remember Phuwa saying the first wife had run away, back to her parents. And I think . . . there was a child, a boy. But I was a child myself when I heard them talking. Good Lord. This would have to be that boy's daughter. Holi Payne, Chaitlal's grandchild."

"So the land is partly Dada's?"

"Not a bit of it. Pa and I paid for that and I made sure we put the boys' names so Pa could . . . relax and know there was some security. It was early in the fifties when his pressure was acting up, and I think the chest pains had started, but we didn't understand." He reached for her hand. "My dear, what can I say? In those days, you know . . ."

"Certainly I know. I also know educating girls was not the obvious thing to do either. You gave me something of greater worth than land."

"Well, well. Never mind that. The deed then, and, down the road, lawyers and wrangling."

"What could this woman want from us? You know, Brother, she's some cousin or something, and what have you ever done to them?"

"What have I done *for* them?"

"When? Why? They had a father, or a grandfather at least. Dada died just fifteen or so years ago."

"But I knew what he was. For years I lived on the edge of what he might unleash."

"Like something that messed up my computer recently. Got in files I didn't even have yet. Brother, don't touch this! Put the stupidness in the hands of a lawyer and out of your mind. How could they do this to you?"

"*Oh Father, have mercy*. Ma always said that."

"Indeed. I thought you'd have said, 'Who does she think she is?' The effrontery."

You keep absolutely still and take it in. Little by little it comes together.

"That is what Uncle Elroy say," Cerise confirmed. "Boldface."

He had been surprised to see Holi Payne calling on the law, and when he saw the line on her file that read "nee Deoraj," he had to notice, even though she wasn't one of the set he knew. With those connections she had that he *did* know about, he was surprised she drew attention to herself at all.

This was the sort of thing he said just to have something to talk about with his sister, Cerise's mother, who went nowhere and knew no one, and so could be depended on not to pass on sensitive information. "Eeh, that remind me. Chinksie, you remember when you daddy take Uncle Elroy with him to hunt? He tell you anything about a camp? I hear Uncle Elroy say he and Kenny come to a track in the forest and you father say not to go that way because the hunting not good, and Uncle say why, and he smelling smoke so he continue on the track and reach this clearing with a camp and people in it moving like soldier training." Kenny told Elroy to turn back if he didn't want to get hunt down himself, and Elroy said to Maamie later that he mighta get shoot in truth if Kenny wasn't with him. "You don't know bout it? It have all kind of thing I wouldn't talk because I don't want to cause him no trouble, but you see I could tell you because your father is a police too and know about them thing."

It seemed safest just to say one's father wouldn't normally talk about things like that at home, and Cerise was willing enough to continue. Her Uncle Elroy had said that when he saw the camp he never knew what it was about, but then, when he was sent on a raid to another property and found a set of long guns and other things (about which Cerise was infuriatingly vague) he began to wonder if there was a connection with the camp. So he decided to talk to someone he knew in police headquarters. And that was why Uncle Elroy took up himself and went to Port of Spain. "How you mean? He gone, I tell you. That is how he was there when the thing start." Approaching headquarters he glimpsed the fellow he was going to see, but while he watched, the man was shot down. "He say bullet like rain." Cerise voice rose in the excitement. "Before Uncle could reach to do anything, a car drive up and people jump out and run and the car . . . blow up. When he get there people scattering and bawling out."

In the midst of it he glimpsed the same woman, Holi Payne, running for her life like the rest; and later, when they questioned people who had been there, she said she never knew it would be that day and she had gone to the Red House for a paper about her land.

"Hear nah, Uncle Elroy say it have all kinda thing does be taking place and we doesn't know. He say it don't matter how he try to tell people about ting he see and hear, nobody want to know. He boss and them say they busy dealing with the coup and ent have time to take he on. 'And I tired, when I tell you I exhausted.' That is what Uncle say, and he box he cap off the sofa and throw himself down on it.

But he must tired, because how he does ever relax? He TV so old it have snow falling over every picture. And is because of his own attitude. He too lame to take a new TV when TV was sharing out in Port-or-Spain. If you father could get TV new bran, after the coup, what happen to Elroy? But he harden. He say, 'I working night and day, I tell you. I ent in no curfew fête: I chasing murderer and looter. And every time I catch myself and say it coming to an end, is a next thing. And now Holi Payne want to bring big court case against Principal Deoraj when her grandfather is the Principal uncle, and she posing there like she alone ever suffer in this world."

Here nah, Chinksie. This Holi had a grandmother, Dhanmattie, who dead when Holi small. They say the old woman head turn bad so she end up in madhouse at St Ann's."

Cerise knew how that had happened too, and she explained how Haresh, Holi's father, had never got over how his own father treated him. It was Maamie who had said everybody hear how Chaitlal spit on Haresh in the street. So when Haresh wife dead having the baby and the baby live somehow, his mother, Dhanmattie, call him and say, "Haresh, son, look what you can do for this child, boy. You is all she have. I getting old, boy, and I have a hard life, I can't do no more." Maamie said that everybody from Mission to Piparo knew this thing. The old woman told she son, "Come. You is a father now." And people say that word *father* – like it work in he brain like a acid and when he get home he drink Gramoxone. So he dead and he mother take it on and end up in St Ann's.

Some of the neighbours insisted it was spirit lash, how Haresh died, but others said no, "Was do he do for heself." Either way, Holi grew up with an aunt who made sure to let Holi know that when they first show her to her father he drink Gramoxone same time. "See here. Like she say it have nothing on this earth going to hurt she again; she go hurt it first."

Uncle Elroy had his eye on Holi Payne for all sorts of reasons and even speculated on whether she was some relation of his as well. Sort of. "You know T and T, nah."

Had he told Holi that? I rarely asked questions, but Cerise was such a fund of information. "Nah, Uncle Elroy never speak to her. He ent have to tell she nothing. Nah, nah. Is to pass she in the street straight. Chinksie, all like she ent want to know any of we; we can't carry she nowhere. She is a socialis – I read she longtime. But I say where she come from no better and no worse than where I come from, so let she haul she tail."

CHAPTER 12

# MEMO

## Holi

Not everyone has something to look back to. (Or forward to, for that matter, but let that go.) So what was it that made her mother extraordinary, gave her that edge that propelled her forward but also helped her hack into herself, gifted as she was? On a sterile white-sheeted bed in that strange flush of maturity forced on by illness, Amy had little else to do but clinically analyse those around her, and no one else but her mother, Holi Deoraj-Payne, held her attention.

Only Amy had seen Holi's closed, tense face open and animated, and her mother connected directly with no one but herself. Not that they lacked family, from what Mama said, but there was no link with them. Holi seemed like that lady in fairy tale, looking out from a high tower on a cliff – not some high-rise town house but some vaguely foreign dwelling far from human habitation – a fairy lady too dangerously different to release. Amy played games of all sorts in her head and sometimes she re-plotted their lives, reinventing her mother by juggling words she had learned for a recent test, fishing out syllables, and toying with alliteration or assonance: *alien, alone, aloof.*

The doctors they had consulted did not understand Mama. *Impassive* was how one described her, even cold in her cut-and-dried responses. They questioned the mother about herself rather than her child, curious about the perceptions of a woman who operated at the rarified upper level of the business world. They pointed out a sort of flatness in her view of the world, a reductive

169

vision that missed nuances; they probed into how she ran a business such as she described. They talked about Amy as if, already, the child did not exist.

Two years ago, when the tiredness had begun but before Holi had noticed the bruising, Amy had unearthed one of her mother's old school reports, which described Holi Deoraj as arrogantly inattentive to instruction. "So it's not new, Mama?" Amy teased, leaning her head lovingly on her mother's shoulder and easing back into that fusion of their minds that so relieved her. When Holi shared her memories with the child there seemed to be some she suppressed, but once there had been a nightmare and she screamed out, waking Amy. Just a dream though, Mama said, about something that had happened long ago when she was a child herself, or should have been.

There had been a small unsteady house of damp-darkened wood and at night in the rainy season the smell of mildew tightened her throat. In the morning she would run to see whether the mud volcano around the back had got bigger. A grey-brown expanse of shining mud was setting, drying and riddling with cracks at the edge but heaving slightly around little vents in the mound that was growing behind the cage in which the dog whined and pawed day in, day out. People had carefully plugged what vents they could as if they could subdue an upheaval in the belly of the earth itself, but new ones had opened and cracks ran away from the mound. A mess of slippery brown oozed and puddled like diarrhea. Beyond the mound and its surrounding mud a gap in the grass and low bush widened where the earth had parted and the mango and plum trees had fallen, but that did not worry her. What kept Holi awake in the night and jolted her out of sleep again and again was whether the mound would remain a small thing burping and farting harmlessly forever or whether it could swell into a real volcano like those abroad, those they heard of in school, the ones that exploded in molten rock and fire – whether that was what they had growing behind the house.

The aunt she lived with was not someone who answered questions and Holi had hinted to children in her school that she was part of a large rich family and could go and live at the big house anytime she liked, so she could hardly ask them now what they thought about the mud belching behind the tottering wooden house in Piparo. She told her teacher she had heard there were mud volcanoes in Trinidad and asked whether they were different to the one in the reading book.

"Best *you* teach we about mud," Miss jeered. "Watch mud halfway up you foot self. You look like a expert in mud. Is *so* you mother send you to school nasty?" She steupsed. She had more ambition than to waste time on backward children in the class, like Holi Deoraj.

"Miss, after Holi don' have no mother," a girl in the class called out helpfully.

The next day Holi did not go to school because during the night the creaking of the old wood rose to a groan, rending, crashing, the dirt floor giving way in slush sliding beneath her with such force it tugged her out of the wreckage before that flattened completely, so she was swept along into the mush that ended in a pile of refuse and wet leaves. Someone screamed at her, to her; later she realized it was her aunt but she was so accustomed to her aunt screeching that she paid no attention. She made up a story in her head to account for the collapsed house and the shambles of her whole life and she cleaned herself off at the water drum, which was still standing beyond the place where the house had been. She was neither glad nor sorry when they got her aunt out of the debris, and only vaguely relieved when they moved to a place called Mission some distance away. And that house too soon became just another rotten wood shack – but all that mattered was that she got out of it, first through her mind, through alternatives she constructed for herself, little stories that helped her hold together, as she explained to Amy. Then, she worked hard in school and passed exams and made herself what she was today, a successful entrepreneur without the slightest need of a past.

As childish physical pastimes became impractical, Amy had learned more and more about the business her mother had built. It was really over the past five years that the interests of Payne Enterprises had expanded and diversified, attracting admiration in the business community. Experts on financial affairs observed how Payne leveraged sympathetic organizations to achieve a level playing field for home-grown businesses and especially for e-commerce. Her mother explained it all to Amy and pointed out the buzzwords. Holi had always spoken to Amy like one adult to another and their voices were becoming less distinct.

Payne Enterprises, she said, had developed a remarkable infrastructure for local, regional and international communication, and through their electronic gateway they forged synergies between different types of business. Amy grasped at once that Payne had eliminated stupid bureaucratic delays in processing movements of funds, and that the firm was a model of prompt response. More than that, at the award ceremony that Holi described to Amy, the Minister of Trade and Industry praised their transparency. Only, Holi was so alone at these ceremonies. There was no one for her to introduce to the Minister and no personal acquaintance to cheer her on. When Amy was old enough to attend it would be different, her mother assured her.

Holi's face and words might not display emotion, but, minds locking, heart to heart, she and Amy cradled each other: *I am the child of a devoted mother; I am a devoted mother.* No mother and daughter had ever been closer in feeling or thought, but none of it showed in the working world. Amy's doctors remained unconvinced about Holi as mastermind of an organization, perhaps because they saw no public flashes of talented entrepreneurship, but Amy saw it all: there was no question in her mind that her mother was a genius.

Certainly, Holi was a brilliant mother, attuned to every change in her child, and when the first doctor recommended vitamins for Amy's recurrent fatigue (in an offhand way to the mother who had dropped in to see him without bringing the child) and the next specialist considered the possibility of hemophilia, Holi moved swiftly to a third, asking about the blood tests that prompted a bone-marrow sample and then a spinal tap. The outlook was positive, according to preliminary discussion with an American specialist. Based on the statistics, he felt quite optimistic.

Amy had an excellent head for Maths and understood percentages well enough. Despite the time lost in illness she had achieved high scores in the SEA examination (although the administrators had contrived to lose her records, which hardly mattered when she was confined to bed in any case) and she easily worked out that if eighty-five per cent now tended to live for five or more years, and since her treatment had begun two years before, the outlook with a raging fever and red spots was limited. The bone-marrow transplant had not worked magic. But her mother, networking oncologists and hematologists, would find a way to draw her back. Lying among her mesh of tubes and monitors, Amy knew her mother's day was long and densely packed as ever, even as Holi sat beside her bed, the iPad askew on the dressing table with the big mirror.

Their eyes searched each other's and the firm ran on autopilot. Understanding her mother's face as she did, Amy knew that what others might see as a lack of interest in what went on was really a preoccupation with processing it, with instant distinctions between core issues and peripherals. Holi ran the business from the coldly sanitary room where she and Amy talked more and more about the thriving operations of Payne Enterprises. As part of a transnational industry, Payne bought and sold in a global market committed to satisfying its external stakeholders. A model of entrepreneurship and inno-vation, the firm had captured a niche, with what university lecturers in man-agement and consultants from other institutions were hailing as *competitive intelligence*. So Holi explained it. All this admiration had market value too; she flashed a rare smile, almost unnatural, but only Amy was there to see it.

Holly Deoraj-Payne, a quietly spoken woman in her fifties, had achieved success through unflagging work and decision-making that was unmuddled by sentiment, which accounted for everyone except Amy writing her off as a cold fish. Her staff whispered that she probably wore a business suit to bed – if she had a bed – and she laughed with Amy about that too. Holi whispered to her that it was only her darling girl who stood between her and the Furies. Not a good outlook for Mama if one did the Maths – the thought flashed across Amy's mind occasionally – so it was as well the firm was there (depend-ing on whether the business would provide distraction when it happened, or would help Holi to self-destruct).

Perhaps it would save her. Amy knew how protective her mother was regarding the firm. Payne Enterprises focused on transport services, and a misunderstanding in this area had once made Holi livid, a brief scandal about tours underpinning escort services. Mama said it dried up when a lawyer's letter went out warning about defamation and stating the company's deter-mination to spare no expense in the defence of its good name. Image was crit-ical. Mama said business success had as much to do with perception as with reality. Mama cultivated even Amy's perceptions, busying her mind with choice insights into the organization, including fiscal issues which Amy did not yet understand – her mother insisted that they still use the word *yet*. The legal and financial expertise that was part of the company's infrastructure enabled such sidelines. "Almost everything has a spin-off you can make work for you," her mother explained, emphasizing the *you*, as if Amy would indeed grow into the partnership, and Holi pointed out how these smaller operations, like an employment agency and a security firm, fitted in the business value chain that meshed back into a wide, strong network.

Amy knew why Mama was doing this, but she was grateful for these details that busied her mind as she lost mobility, and made the future seem real. Amy and Holi did not read *Harry Potter* or watch *Friends* on TV or play X-Men. The business was their unfolding drama. E-business, that made prompt customer service possible, was better than a game - the sort of electronic game that appealed to young people of Amy's age – for this was real, this tracking and manoeuvring among the branching networks of transport, employment and entertainment agencies.

With her quick mind, Amy followed Mama's voice when her face blurred, the child clinging to the words that spun out operations of the firm, in the cold room that smelled of disinfectant and whose walls were no longer visible to the shrinking form on the bed. Customers appreciated Payne's fast tracking of orders and payments, and that was what had encouraged Holi to develop robust systems for *electronic funds transfer* and *heightened processing capability*. The phrases lodged in Amy's brain, glowing among other darker things and lighting up all that she could have been as if it could still happen. "You'll soon see how all this, in turn, enhances market liberalization," Holi said bracingly.

Amy was proud of her mother's cool, almost offhand penetration and unfaltering account of the systems that kept her fast mind operating while she remained aware. At this late stage she discovered that her mother cared not only for her after all, but for strangers. The growing technological capacity Holi had contrived was not only indigenous but socially responsible. Payne Enterprises not only proclaimed concern regarding cyber crime but funded international research projects to explore it. The company's practical concern for the community expressed itself in job opportunities for the underprivileged and in a hotline for reports on destructive exploitation of the environment or of local groups and individuals. A social worker with strong qualifications in psychology was available to concerned callers and ready to interview victims of reported abuse.

All this accounted for the firm's cadre of staff – customs brokers, drivers, lawyers, guards, financial advisers and IT personnel; for arrangements in place for every contingency – police support, fast-track printing, emergency medical and ambulance services, personal bankers and, when required, a phone call from an appropriate senior government official to move along a shipment. The network hummed and sparked in Amy's mind even when Mama's voice faded in the distance, for there were connections with similar organizations abroad, specialists in the Caribbean diaspora, gophers in Ministries of Trade and Industry, Foreign Affairs and National Security, and in pertinent NGOs. The child's concept of the enterprise glowed vivid enough to maintain some level of consciousness in periods of static that intervened in her connection with her mother. Sometimes the static came when her mother was crying inside, or so Amy thought even when Holi said there was no crying. (For look at what she had built. She *had* built it, and how things turned out were up to her in the long run.)

A few people in the firm caught a rare remark from Holi about a sick child somewhere and conceived of Amy as little more than a vegetable, but most had heard nothing of her at all. No one imagined Holi Payne having a private life. Her subdued clothes, the absence of her husband and the rumour of a child dying somewhere – agreed to be a sad business – had prompted the workers to nickname her the Black Widow. Holi dismissed it comtemptuously. She was accustomed to injustice.

Naturally enough, Amy had wondered about her father, and Holi had concealed nothing from her. Eric Payne had begun the business, his mother's Syrian background inviting expectations of grand success. That was the stereotype operating. It was Holi herself, his East Indian wife, who built it, expanding on Eric's pharmaceutical imports in the eighties then, after his departure, founding and building on the transport company throughout the eighties. Holi and Eric had so little in common, though, that their life together became a loveless desert into which they had somehow strayed. A child could be their only common interest and contemplation of her sparked some tenderness, not for each other but at least in common. So Holi and Eric settled into a cooperative but neutral relationship, an absence of actual dislike that passed for friendship. Still, Eric complained she seemed hung up on ancient grudges that had rankled for years, and eventually declared himself tired of her dark moods and silences.

He said Holi left no space for a father in any child's world. He said she made it all up, their world, and that she freaked him out. That was how he put it: Holi freaked him out. One day he took a plane and left her with the house and the business, took himself off to Canada and never contacted her again.

Since he had the makings of a considerate father, Holi spoke well of him to Amy (as of a decent man now deceased), but she was not sorry to have the child to herself, gathered soley under her eyes. Eyes Amy had watched grow distant from everyone else, their depths easily mistaken for emptiness – or perhaps that was what it was, their dark bottomlessness. Amy had discerned, while her mind still functioned in its original sharp analytic way, that her Mama had not learned love early, as she had. Holi had grasped the principle of taking care of herself, making the most of almost nothing, building something marketable from anything whether that *anything* was worthless or beyond price, but she had concluded she was to be utterly alone forever.

Only, then she contrived a time when the child filled her heart, so she worked out what it was to have within her gift everything she had never received, never known, yearned for with only a vague concept of what she was missing. Now it was hers to give, even as the child faded away in the glimpse of it. And the dry-season wind rattled through her heart leaving a parched cracked terrain in which nothing else could grow. So there would be nothing else to fill the day but the buying and selling, the accumulation of property, the business she built to substitute for a life. When Eric had left, Holi hardly noticed, but Amy's fading was different: this was desiccation.

When Amy began to hallucinate, Holi located herself as far as she could in the child's mind, to stay close to her up to the end, but then it came swiftly. Prying reporters outside the house where the private funeral was conducted barely caught the image of the bereaved mother, Holi, a shadow in that shade of grey tinged with brown that people called *oyster*, a suit of elegant cut, high necked, long sleeved (exactly matching the frames of her dark-tinted glasses), hiding the festering wound in her mind under a face that seemed a world away. "Numb with grief," they would report (so she constructed it in her head), clueless as to the workings of a mind seeking to anesthetize itself while hacking away every remaining shred of feeling and diverting itself by collecting and processing data, sorting connections to be stored in shimmering bytes of information, holding aloof from human connection and suppressing every throbbing memory of feeling. *There is a spider climbing up a wall*, she crooned distractedly to Amy. Then she remembered.

Sometimes when you make it up you do it so well that the story takes over and develops a life of its own beyond your control, and to be true to the story you have to sacrifice characters on whom you have gambled all your passion and even if they were all that kept you going you give them up to be true to the story and you go on without them, knowing everything of value is lost, and you try to find your way back to where you were before. Only, if you weren't anywhere, then that is where you find yourself: nowhere. With nothing to do but to construct a new story and new characters.

And it wasn't worth it. The recognition overwhelmed Holi with nausea and she heaved over the sink. All the temporary relief these inventions brought was nothing to the agony of deprivation. Alone in her mind she watched the walls curve in and the floor tilt, dislodging the structure and sweeping along with her thoughts sliding about helplessly in it. In the long run it was all mud. Inside her head the ceiling caved and she closed her eyes and flung her hands across her face.

There was no one; no one would come. There was perhaps one person who might have made a difference, once. An uncle, or cousin or . . . or something, but neither he nor anyone else came for her.

The day after the workers in the travel agency heard the rumour that the child they had never seen was dead, the more heartless of them chuckled that at least now Holi really was Payne free. But that wasn't true. Even if Holi was just shuffling the names of her characters, putting one down was an obliteration of whatever version of herself she had adopted in order to survive the past, and it was excruciating to let go, however unruffled she appeared on return to work.

She would never do this again, never make up another (less-alone) self and certainly never invent anyone to love and lose. She rocked wordlessly over the sink in her private bathroom. In fact, she would never expose any part of her mind again to anyone real or imagined. As for the doctors, they were useless. She cancelled her next appointment.

Somewhere the thought nagged on that perhaps, if she did not exist as far as her father's family were concerned, she was in fact somehow not there at all – that her life was a sort of misconception she had had, and from which there seemed no way out. Nevertheless, now she had relinquished Amy, Holi circulated a memo that she was resuming her maiden name, Deoraj.

Yes, let me be myself. What have I to lose? Long before the press, the police, the rival gangs, my sources pick up the news of missing children, even before their parents know. None of this is new to me. I too have lost a child, real or not. I was that child, real or not. Lost a childhood.

Love her all you like. I wouldn't lift a finger for you. Yes, I could restore her if I chose. But I owe you nothing.

# CHAPTER 13

# PASSPORT

## Judith

Anselm was about that age when we came back in 1975, or a little younger – much like me when Pa and Brother were talking about sending me to high school in San Fernando. But, for my boy, moving home brought greater upheaval.

To Anselm, London even at its most grey and grim had been at least serious – a real place, somewhere to be reckoned with. Bone-rattling cold flowing through cloth and flesh as if one's body were insubstantial, and the air so wet, he said, that it was like breathing water. What was it like, he speculated, to be a fish, to stare through water, the medium that was strange to others taken for granted in that unblinking gaze? I can see him now, hanging there, warm in front of the window, his eyes on the swirl of water over glass, not needing to stir, ever.

In London we had window boxes that Jem used to call Mom's Garden and that he cleaned scrupulously on Sundays after mass. Anselm's father, Jem, had finished his degree in economics and worked in the business department of a chocolate company, and I would ask if it didn't bother him – what I called the dark history of chocolate. For it was built on child labour. Jem said, "Bitter sweet, eh? Better stop using sugar too, then? Better bitter?" He knew I loved playing with words as much as eating sweets. And I would laugh and tell him to go along and stop his stupidness, but make sure he bought chocolate cake on his way home.

When Jem fell ill and stopped going out to work he would still sit and take care of the window boxes (he called it pottering in Mom's Garden) until Father dropped in after mass to see him. Then one day when Jem was gone and the window boxes were taken over by chickweed, I had not glanced their way for weeks until I looked up unsuspecting and there was this riot of red and gold without a weed or dead leaf. I could feel the blood drain from my face, caught the glimpse of myself grey in the mirror over the mantel, felt my lips frame "Who?"

When I spun around, there was Anselm watching me, at first hopefully but then his face fell at my reaction and I grabbed onto him realizing all he had taken over, almost as much as I had, and just as wordlessly.

"Jolly good then," I whispered.

Outside, things went on as if nothing had happened. And why ever not? No one in the Bates Road area of Finchley knew who lived or died next door. You only saw what went on in the road and you fixed your face as if you hadn't noticed. Well, sometimes not. The fellow across the road had parked his shaggin wagon proudly in front the door and people nudged each other and peered through the curtains or pointed at the sign that said, *If this van's rockin', don't come knockin'*.

By then the plastic vials and smell of medication were cleared away, although I suppose the child could still hear me crying at night. Afterwards he said that in his mind my tears mingled with the water swirling on the windowpane. But the house, empty as it had become, was not uncomfortable. Although I could no longer bear it this was all he knew, peaceful in its muted colours, the rooms marked out by warm areas from which the glow faded to the three cold corners farthest from the heater, and even the fuzz of the frayed rug was comforting under one's socks.

"Weren't you going to buy the new rug after all then?"

"Not now we're moving," I objected. "No point putting a new rug for tenants with young children."

"Moving?"

"Going home," I said. "We're going to Trinidad." But that was holidays as far as he was concerned. Trinidad wasn't a real place, to live in. What would happen about school and church and the museum and Brighton in the summer? "You've got better than Brighton there. You've got Mayaro. And it's home."

I suppose it truly did come out like a sacred word with a sort of pause after it, like how Father pronounced the word *cup*. And how could Trinidad be home?

"Home?" He dragged it out eerily. "This is where we live, not some stupid little island. If we've got to leave here why don't we go to the States?"

"For what? Think. I leave my job here and go there – to start again?"

"You started here, didn't you? Besides, we won't know anyone in Trinidad. I won't have any friends."

"You'll have family."

"You did it again. That voice for celebrating mass and stuff."

"Lots of family," I continued. I suppose it seemed relentless. He said afterwards that the word *family* inched round him and began to close in. Every time it came up it squeezed tighter. At the time he just argued about waiting till the end of the vac. He had thought he was going to have the one last real summer. "You'll have it there," I insisted. "It's always summer in Trinidad."

"That's why it never is!" he shouted, and I glared at him.

It didn't matter how I explained that we needed time to settle down before school. "Time to get the house together," I insisted, "a much nicer house than this one."

"Fab. So we're going to be with all these people I don't know. The whole set of nerds?"

I tried cooling him down by explaining we'd be living in San Fernando where there were only a few.

"So where are the rest?" he demanded.

"All over the island."

Not comforting. But after a while it was all he would talk about. "So when do we float?"

"For goodness' sake speak English. Your uncle will wonder whether you've been living on Mars." He didn't bother to ask which uncle, although in his view he had all too many. He knew that when no one was singled out by name, "your uncle" could only be the big one. "Be a good chap and give me a thought," I snapped at him.

"Once we know this is just about you."

"Oh, sit on it, Charlie."

Thank God it was his Uncle Mark who met us at Piarco Airport, stared at Anselm's back-to-front head gear admiringly and pronounced, "That is one *bad* cap." And against all odds the child's eyes betrayed what might have been a flicker of hope.

The house in San Fernando eventually fitted us, so well that nothing came of the plan to build a bigger place on a lot I had bought overlooking the sea, even though I had safeguarded the plot from the inroads of the Gulf by bringing in an engineer and ensuring a strong retaining wall. I had no intention of watching thousands of dollars slide down into the sea.

Some twenty-five years later I went on to declare that I had no intention of taking on worries like building construction in my early sixties, by which time, as a grown man with his own frailties, Anselm no longer cared about such things. The property would have appreciated when his own child was old enough, and she could work out what she wanted to do with it. But at the time he was merely having a look at the land to confirm that it was no point selling yet. He stood on the building site next to my lot and looked out to sea. It was a stunning view, he reported later, though I knew that already. The workman must have noticed him when he drew back from the edge as a wave of mild faintness passed over. Oh for chocolate, he admitted thinking before he pressed back that yearning with a familiar line, *what sweet in goat mouth* . . . The salt breeze revived him quickly and he glanced back again at the mass of bush and rubble dumped on our property by the woman responsible for the structure growing around him. He took note of how her driveway swerved across the corner of our land, tearing through my retaining wall in the process.

"Who is this lady?" he asked the workman.

"Ent is you family?" the man responded in surprise. "She name Deoraj. Ent you mother was Deoraj before she marry? Ent you mother is Principal Deoraj sister? I born Mayaro, and, as I hear the name and she land right beside yours, I say is allyou family."

" I've never heard of her," Anselm told him.

The workman showed Anselm around.

It was a massive structure, four storeys with an open-air patio on top, bedrooms on each wing of the third floor and a wide porch looking out to sea, as well as bedrooms on the second floor. The main entrance was on the second floor, the driveway swinging in to a wide garage at the back and a vast living and dining room with glass sliding doors for the view. Below was a garden patio with benches, a pool designed for the mirage of water pouring over the edge towards the sea, bar, shower and bathrooms, Jacuzzi, servants' quarters and storage. An elevator for the four storeys.

"Big family then?"

"She one," the workman said helpfully. "I hear she did have a daughter, but like she sickly. I never see the child yet. I think maybe it pass away."

"Sad."

"She one going to live here." The workman regarded him slyly. "Is not you family in truth?"

"Never met or even heard of her."

"Deoraj."

Later, when Anselm told me that her full name was Holi Deoraj and I realized this was the woman who had tried to take Brother to court over Ma's house, I was even more annoyed with her. Still, as I had never mentioned to Anselm the whole travesty regarding the old property in Mission, I had nothing to say to him about Holi Deoraj. It would have meant digging up stuff about Dada that was best buried with him.

Anselm was the one who arranged a meeting with her to discuss her intrusion on our land. They stood on the border of the two properties and he searched her face curiously. She showed not the slightest interest in his.

"Your workman asked if we were related," he began pleasantly, "and it made me wonder."

"Presumably not, if we've never met. What did you want to meet about?"

Taken aback by her manner, he tackled the main problem. "The retaining wall. We wondered how you intended to address the damage."

She met his eyes with a blank stare. "There was a wall built across the entrance to my property. I suppose the road had to pass." She looked away, out to sea.

Something about the movement of her eyes was familiar, he told me, but he could not place it. It was impossible to have a conversation with someone who behaved as if you weren't there, so he decided to leave it with a lawyer. It was clear that she understood the value of retaining walls, for hers marched rank on rank up the rocky slope and she contemplated them with apparent satisfaction.

Anselm described Holi Deoraj as older than he was and now, even if she had been sturdy once, as slight figured, almost wraith-like in the fierce curve of her body braced against the wind on the unfinished porch, her mouth clenched with some implacable resentment. Miserable old bat, he summed her up. Assumes she can walk over everybody because she has money and a big house. But there was something familiar about her, he said, methodical in fortifying her property against the inexorable sea at its edge, against water runoff and landslip. He even entertained the thought of some resemblance to me, but then he thought no, not at all. For how could there be a relationship when he had met everyone within a few months of the return from London. He had never even heard of a woman named Holi.

The Saturday in 1975, after we arrived in Trinidad, the whole family had gathered. Anselm had met a few at the airport, but after the long, boring flight and unending drive over bumpy road in pouring rain, he could not distinguish one from another. And more and more of us poured into the house near Mission junction, my brothers, their wives and children, their children's husbands, wives and children. Even the occasional in-law.

"No, I'm Timmy's wife's older brother," one corrected me. "We're on holiday from Toronto with Tim and Jenine. Our boy is the same age as yours."

More and more family, he said later, looking alike and blurring instantly. Yes, Uncle, thank you, Aunt.

Everyone trailed in to kiss this old lady in the front bed room.

"Ma." I hugged her and glanced back. What was he hesitating for? "Anselm, kiss your nani. You don't remember?" He did not, or she was not the Nani he remembered. Not as old as he had thought at first glance, he later said, but very still, with a faraway gaze, inexpressibly sad. When he leaned near, she seemed, in a way, to wake up.

"Anselm?" she whispered, her smile faint from sheer effort. "In truth?" And she began to cry.

I drew him out of the room hurriedly. "She suffers from depression," I told him. "Right now she's in the midst of a bad bout."

"Wasn't seeing you after all this time supposed to cheer her up?"

I felt like slapping him, but all I said was "It doesn't work like that apparently." Then, more to lift my own spirits rather than anyone else's, I added, "She comes out of it though."

All he seemed to take in for most of that day was that his mother was occupied, talking, talking to everyone about people he did not know. "The Lezamas still live in Quick River Trace?" I glanced at Anselm when he tugged my arm. "Darling, all these cousins to get to know. What *is* the matter?" I glanced aside again. "And where's Brother all this time?"

"Next thing the car shut down on the road again," said Mark and a general groan rose. One of the others made some joke about it that did not take, and Mark raised his arms from his body and said, "Tickle me, tickle me," so they would all know he needed help to laugh at the stalejoke.

Then, suddenly, as Anselm described it later – a lull. One of the children had run in from the porch. "Uncle reach." Now faces turned towards the steps, looking in the same direction, same expression, same noses or mouths or eyes, or tilt of the head. Apart from his Uncle Mark, whom Anselm recognized now, only one was immediately distinct, that thin fellow with a bent frame and a wry twist to his mouth worn by pain rather than ill-temper, because he was full of jokes and even burst into song from time to time, some old calypso in a fine mellow voice. Yet even he had a look of the rest of them. I caught Anselm's anxious glance at me, as if I was the same yet not the same any more now I reflected bits and pieces of people he did not know

Footsteps sounded on the stairs, before the voices broke out again. "Here you are!"

He was sorry to be late; he had classes. "Saturday, Brother?" someone asked. The tall, broad figure, with hair greying at the temples and thinning on top ignored the question as his eyes searched the room and fastened on Anselm. They were lighter-coloured eyes than mine in a fairer-complexioned face, but, as Anselm often said, the same appraising gaze.

"Anselm. Good morning, man."

Uncle. Uncle what? So many uncles, so many names. This one had a name no one used to his face. *Brother*, we called him.

"Uncle Brother?"

The face above him broke into a wide, delighted smile. "Come sit with me, man." Anselm perched awkwardly beside him on the sofa while the talk flowed on.

After a while Brother turned to me. "And tomorrow, Judith? What about church?"

"What you mean? We'll go with you."

"Didn't you say he used to go with his father? And went on going to the RC church until you left. Not so?"

He looked down at Anselm with a swift penetrating glance from which Anselm pulled away, his lips tightening mutinously. I knew that deep, almost beyond his own reach lay an emptiness from which a draft gusted up when he least expected it.

"Young man, you'll have a bit of a wait in the morning," his uncle warned, "because the RC service is half an hour later than ours. We'll have to drop you off and go to ours, then come back for you. But you won't mind that, of course."

It was a statement rather than a question, but something more Anselm could not quite define, something unexpected and precious, something of his father not quite lost.

He must have put out his hand, because now his uncle was crushing it while nodding in response to my glance, which was thankful yet fleeting in the midst of all the talk surging on – talk of house-hunting and of cloth for uniforms, of arrangements for lesson plans and a cleaner once or twice a week – in this mesh of many voices where once there had been just three, then two. Only it did not seem to be so intrusive now, now his dad was not so . . . so gone.

"Eat some wild, boy," Uncle Mark called to him. "This is the one they call lappe. Your Aunt Leela cook this for you to taste." Soft, juicy like pork. We watched his face and laughed as he gasped over the pepper, but reached for more.

Afterwards we dropped Brother home, his car being incapacitated somewhere, as suspected. No, someone else would see about that, he said. What? Oh, some one of them, nah.

"Nobody wouldn't steal *that*," Mark taunted, drawing no more than an affable nod.

Anselm traipsed after me into Brother's house and halted, confused by its absence of signs. It was sufficient to come back to after work – comfortable enough chairs with a good reading lamp, the house of a man who lived alone, one to whom a house, like a car, was a basic utility, its details of little import. Apart from a large sobering family photograph at the airport, the pictures on the living room wall (the Last Supper, and some English garden) appeared to have wandered in on their own, or to have been brought and put up by others. Later Anselm told me his first thought was that this was not Uncle Brother's real home. Even then, he must have begun to realize that Uncle Brother lived, essentially, inside his own head.

"Are you listening, Anselm?"

He was startled. "Sorry?"

"Uncle says we're going to Mayaro next Saturday."

"Cool. I mean, yes please."

Afterwards, on the road back to San Fernando, he was full of questions. "He lives there by himself?" He knew it was an empty question, even as he blurted it out.

"Where else?" I reflected. "He says when he sits in his rocker on that gallery with his book and a cup of cocoa tea . . . oui, Papa." But the boy's attention had shifted again.

"It's dark," he exclaimed, still unnerved by the swiftness of nightfall.

By the next weekend he no longer noticed. Saturday brought a family outing to Mayaro. It was after ten o'clock when Mark and Leela drew up the station wagon before a wide, long expanse of cream brown sand, edged with fallen coconuts and ragged palm ends on the land side and ruffles of white foam on the other. Much later, in the afternoon when we were packing up leftover food and washing off sand, Brother sighted Griff making his way over. Griff insisted that by ten o'clock the boy would have missed the best part, and he promised to bring Anselm out early another morning to see the fishermen drag in the seine.

The morning Griff, or Doc, as Anselm called him, was to collect him for another visit to Mayaro, Anselm was up and peering anxiously from the porch till the car coasted up and he ran downstairs, shouting to me that he was gone, and everyone in earshot calling back to warn him not to go in the water. I walked out to remind Griff that the boy was not to swim, and Griff laughed and said he had been told by Nathan, several times.

"The child needs to learn though," I said, "to swim, I mean," and Griff flashed a look of admiration.

"You are a radical thinker, young Judith," he said.

As usual Anselm replayed the whole excursion for me that evening when we settled down for cocoa before bed. Doc had led him between the palm trunks that slanted above them and along the shore to a huddle of men with grey-brown nets and children jumping around to catch fish that flipped and wriggled away. A patchy brown and white dog crouched just beyond them, shifting its head rapidly to keep in view the little flashes of silver. Doc pointed out the boats and reeled off the names of different fish and details about throwing and drawing in the seine. He paused with a grin. "You wonder how I know all that." Anselm nodded, and Doc went on. "My father was a fisherman." He told Anselm about his old man bringing in a shark, how much they had sold, and how much he, Griff, had eaten with hot bread and pepper.

"How come you're a doctor if your father was just a fisherman?"

"Just? He was just the best fisherman in the Western Hemisphere."

"But not the world?"

"Perhaps not. St Peter was a fishermen and he was your first Pope, wasn't he?"

"You're Catholic?"

"Nope. Hindu." He grabbed a wad of sand and flung it at Anselm. "You feel I can't be Hindu because I'm creole? Actually I'm agnostic. You know what that is?" Anselm shook his head. "Then don't ask, for now."

Yet Anselm's incessant questions endeared him to Uncle Brother, as he gradually discovered. He knew better than to insert questions into conversations that went on in his presence, but later he would nose out interesting details. One of his strengths was in the wording of them. He never asked why Uncle Andrew hadn't been to Trinidad for fifteen years; he asked where he lived. Brother stopped rocking and turned his full attention to the boy sitting on the gallery beside me.

"Rhode Island, son. Do you know where that is?"

"No, Uncle. You have a globe?"

"I have a map." He slipped on a battered pair of rubber slippers and signalled Anselm to follow him inside.

Over the map on the dining room table, once they had confirmed the location of Rhode Island, Andrew asked, "You ever went to see him?"

"I'm afraid not. He always invites me though."

Anselm waited politely and when his uncle turned away from him, to me, I could not keep the sadness from my voice. "So she's never thawed towards us at all, eh?" Only, as Anselm pointed out later, my voice fell, betraying that it was not a question. I knew the answer.

"His wife is not altogether to blame," said Uncle Brother. "In fact, not at all. There were unfortunate comments on this side." And that was all he said. For years.

But Anselm could wait. Brother observed him with a gleam of amusement, and said he recognized something of himself in this lad, but he divulged no more about Andrew. There were references, occasionally, to a phone call. A rare note by mail accompanying a clipping about Andrew's research passed from hand to hand, for Tim was in regular contact with him. Eventually, though, Anselm's Uncle Andrew must have faded to that periphery of consciousness where family abroad whom one had never met naturally belonged.

One day years later, school ended as usual with the maxi taxies pressing close to the school gate, vying with each other to attract passengers, and the afternoon prayer coming up on the school PA system goading the taxies into blaring their music, pounding it louder and louder till the bass rattled the school windows and in nearby cars the waiting parents mopped their faces and swore – every day, same stupidness – and Anselm glimpsed me straining through the car window and signalling him to me instead of to the maxi he and his friends were rushing to board.

"What?" he said irritably when he jumped in, because it wasn't as if I was going to let him play his cassettes in the car so he could actually hear them.

"We're going down to Mission," I announced. "Family meeting."

An hour, even an hour and a half on this road. "Lord," he groaned. The roti and sweet drink helped, but *oh Father*. And when we reached there, no one seemed sure what it was about.

"Get on with whatever homework you have," I directed Anselm. "Don't wait till you get home tired." I could see he stopped himself just before saying, *Who tell you I not tired aready?* But still I added, "And *don't* give me that look."

An hour later, we were all still waiting on Brother's arrival.

"How he taking so long to come and he living right here?" Timmy grumbled, reaching for fry bake in the Styrotex box. "Saltfish and tomatoes chokha? You know how long I don't eat that?"

"Saltfish get expensive now. Like is a wildmeat." Mark knew nothing could regulate Brother's movements or timing and so (in accordance with Brother's own approach to problems) had fortified himself and was cleaning his plate with the bake.

"Must be the car." Luke shrugged. After the usual wave of complaints about Nathan's battered Hillman, Mark cleaned up at the washbasin behind the dining table and prepared to go forth and find him.

But then there he was, wading into their midst with a preoccupied smile and the odd pat on whatever head presented itself near at hand and, yes, yes, the car, and he sat just anywhere, not at the head of a table or in any special seat, yet still the room reoriented itself, around him. He glanced across, met Anselm's eyes and said his name, stretched out his arm and shook hands firmly, holding the boy's eyes in a glad steady gaze as if this was the face he had waited all day to see. Sounding Anselm's name again as if it was music to him, he sat down again.

Anselm settled at the dining table to the back of the group and opened his books; I could see he was working steadily against the talk but without missing a word.

"When do they arrive?" Brother asked.

"Wait, wait. That's definite?" Luke was irritated, as if a matter to be discussed had been settled high-handedly.

"People don't need our permission to enter Trinidad," Timmy snapped, and Brother clasped his hand and squeezed it.

Timmy continued more calmly. "Andrew told me on the phone they were thinking of coming for a few days in the summer and I asked him for the travel information one time."

"And who tell you to do that?" Luke demanded.

"One minute." Brother forestalled the inevitable eruption. "Timmy was right. The question . . ."

"I don't know about that." Luke glowered at them.

"That is why I am explaining it to you," Brother said with studied patience. "As I see it . . ." He paused for the flurry of stifled laughter to settle. "As I see it the question is how best to make them comfortable."

"Well, I suppose I have no business in this." Maydene shifted stiffly in her chair so as to stare out through the door to the gallery and towards the street. Our brother, Matthew, had died before I moved back with Anselm, and Maydene lived in the house with Ma and Phuwa, steadily conveying that she knew herself to be a burden.

"No of course you must say what you feel, Maydene. Everyone's thoughts are welcome."

"I believe in respect for our elders and remembering all they did for us and the sacrifices they made. That is all." Maydene raised her chin so that her eyes were fixed above the gathering, on a higher truth.

"Go on."

"Is only a few years ago we sit right here when we hear about this marriage and your uncle, you own dada, say right out what he think about it. That was your father brother who talk. Was like your father voice on the matter. And he say this woman Andrew married is not our kind of people and that is that. And if Matthew was here now we wouldn't be digging up this question again. I can't believe we going to disrespect we own parents so."

Anselm was riveted now, and I suppose my own fury was only too clearly etched on my face. But Brother responded with a mild, almost depreciating gesture of his left hand.

"I remember. Yet I would be reluctant – with respect to this issue, or indeed almost any other – to bow to Dada's moral authority."

In the little wave of discreet, almost shocked amusement that rose, then dissipated among them, I felt my face relax. "I'll meet them at the airport," I said. "They'll stay with me. Listen." I turned back to Maydene but glanced around to include the rest. "We grew up playing with everyone around us; we went to school together, our parents passed food over the fence. Allyou forget who you build kite with and help chook down mango for chow. The boys and their marble pitch – it was everyone. What we cared about all that nonsense?"

"We were children, Judith." Maydene's air of stern but wounded dignity gave way to one of impatience. "As we get big we learned where to draw the line. We didn't grow up and married them." She ran her fingers through her hair with a sort of frantic despair. "Watch me. How I going to go to work and sit in that staff room when all you bring down this family I find myself marry into? Eh? What people going to say about me?"

"I imagine they will feel sorry for you," I returned swiftly. "God knows I do."

Maydene surged out of her chair, hand probing the folds of her bosom in urgent search for a handkerchief. "You see *me*?" she said. "I go sit with Ma. I go do what I can to cherish we parents and what they stand for as long as we bless to have them." She passed out of sight, blowing her nose loudly.

"Andrew?" I couldn't help muttering. "What has *he* ever done us? Matthew's the one who saddled us with this unspeakable woman."

"We are straying from the issue, I think." Brother was as benign and courteous as ever. "We haven't heard from you yet, Mark."

"I was thinking to get a lappe and some common fowl."

"Aah. Now that would be most practical. Yes, Luke?"

"That spare room has been used for storing all kinds of rubbish for years. It's going to need work and Maydene obviously won't be lifting a finger."

Brother studied him thoughtfully. "And you'll see to that?"

"I suppose the first thing the boy will do is come to see Ma, and it must be possible for them to stay even if it's for the night. I don't know what allyou plan to do about Maydene mouth. You know the letter that went to Andrew that time, claiming to be from Matthew on behalf of all of us – it could only have been written by her."

In the long pause that ensued Brother surveyed the faces turned towards his, then got to his feet. "I believe we may have been overlooking how important it is to Maydene to remain in this house," he reflected. He strolled unhurriedly towards Maydene's door with the calculated calm of one undertaken to defuse a bomb.

But nothing untoward developed along lines one might have foreseen.

Arrangements proceeded cordially by phone between San Fernando, Mission and Rhode Island. Two women from the village scoured the spare room and Israel's daughter-in-law, Annette, ran up new curtains. The helper left in a huff, but before anyone could object, Brother hired Audrey who had worked there in the past. He declared that someone should be living in the house and looking out for Ma anyway.

"Impossible." I was dazed when Mark reported it. "What possessed Brother?"

"He says Audrey's had a hard life and needs the work."

Anselm said he vaguely connected the name with a light-complexioned woman he had seen *helping* with Phuwa during her illness, and he was right. Phuwa had recovered from her stroke and would sit dreamily on the gallery, smiling and waving absently to whoever looked her way, then she would get up and limp about dragging a duster over the furniture or turning roti on the tawa. "What is that big wad of ghee for?" Anselm had whispered to me, and I could only raise my shoulders in agreement.

Gradually I confided to him that Audrey had not always been large and slow, although for an East Indian woman she was unusually well-endowed behind. And it was not only in name and shape but in demeanour that she had diverged from any expectations we might have harboured. She had earlier been given to tight clothes that did justice to her gifts and was of a modern turn of mind that prompted her to play mas at carnival, wearing tights and shiny beads and shimmering all over as she moved – so much so that the younger fellows, Mark, Timmy and even Luke, had renamed her Sugar Bum.

In the light of this name, in which of course I never indulged, Anselm tried to reassess the generously expanded figure he had later encountered in his grandmother's house, not bustling like the usual rounded middle-aged woman but conspicuous by her inactivity. Sugar Bum had watched Phuwa from her position on the sofa, which she seemed to overflow with her soft belly and great breasts, and now and then she said, "That good. They has to move about, you know. Is for the circulation." Anselm had developed a loathing for the woman spread out immobile as a frog, her eyes following me under heavy lids but bright with malicious interest.

"And Uncle Brother bringing that woman back? What Nani needs her for?" Anselm demanded. "Is true Nani was low when we got here first but ent she got better, in the garden and ting? So why she back in bed? Depressed about what? Allyou ever take her to a psychiatrist?" I stared at him, then swept him into the car and to Brother's house where I unfolded Anselm's proposal while the boy listened in horror (because, he said later, "Now the whole of you going to feel I calling you mother mad"), and Brother listened politely and thanked him. Anselm assumed his uncle was humouring us both till, weeks later, we learned how a car had been hired and Ma taken to Port of Spain, Brother conducting her back and forth to appointments for weeks, and coaxing her to swallow medication for clinical depression.

They had just thought it was old age, Luke said. And he cried, Luke did, actually cried, because he said it was as if he had given up on her after she had so refused to give up on him, and where would he be now if she had? And look, now when Andrew arrived next week she would be her old self.

And indeed Ma was transformed, so much so that a memory of her from Anselm's early childhood rose again, and he said now he recalled her deliberate step and that glance glowing with delight as she held out a cup of chocolate, or opened out roti too hot for other hands.

"'Zlem?" she said. "I too glad you come back to us, beta."

"And you to us," I put in.

We exchanged glances of disbelief and happiness.

So Andrew and Cindy arrived and stayed with us – Anselm and me – which is to say they slept and breakfasted there before some other branch of the family whirled them away to another house, to Toco or Mayaro. But it began with the drive to Mission and the steep climb up the steps to Ma.

"How much years I waiting, boy?" she said, giving Andrew a resounding slap and enfolding him again, then, "You move now." She turned to Cindy. "Come, beti."

Andrew turned from her and flung himself into Nathan's arms while Griff leaned back against the wall, waiting his turn with a flash of perfect white teeth and deep boom of satisfaction.

And in no time it was over, the reminiscences and filling of gaps, the assembling in house after house and in between the balancing of dishes with hot curry on the back seats of cars, the minute instructions from Brother, the gifts for Cindy (for only I managed to select clothes that fit perfectly on people I hardly knew), the calls and messages for mending unravelled years. Timmy and I waved from the departure gate at Piarco Airport, content that all was healed.

Meanwhile, now Ma was doing so well, no one needed to take care of her.

Faced with the prospect of assisting with domestic chores instead, Sugar Bum took in with her nerves and stayed away, to Maydene's dismay, so nothing more was heard of her for a while, although a rumour started (traced back to her) that Brother had a whole illegitimate family hidden away up north – Arima or somewhere, nah – that accounted for the condition his mother had been in. Was that same, the story went, why the old lady did be so low and crying all the time.

"Good Lord," I said. "What next? But I wonder if all that was from Audrey, for she and Maydene were so thick."

"Sugar Bum good for sheself," Mark agreed, "but you right not to under-estimate Mayhem." He turned matter-of-factly to Anselm. "Boy, see what you can do to help me with these doubles." He opened up an oily brown bag full of soft warm packages that gave out the smell of curried channa.

When Anselm graduated from UWI and had been duly celebrated (for his uncle said, "We have to have something for that"), he landed a temporary job teaching History, then spent his first salary to buy me an outfit I would have admired in the shop window but never bought for myself, a lavender and yellow jacket with white pants. I was delighted, but instructed him to put the next paycheque in the bank, raising a forefinger he said was exactly like Brother's, but on my right hand. By then, he had learned the family, although there continued to surface things from the past so utterly unknown to him that he said they seemed to have happened to other people, to strangers.

Deeply embedded in the family now, he would hear Brother and me unearthing shards of this earlier life.

"Amani? No," Brother said. "I glimpse her in passing. Of course she was not to blame. It was all my doing."

"She could have waited." I levelled a look at Brother. "She *should* have waited. Didn't she have a mind of her own?"

"She had a mind of wonderful subtlety and a voice I . . . I did not listen for enough . . ."

Brother had drifted to another place in his head. It was something Anselm pointed out to me that he did.

I eventually told Anselm about Amani, the woman for whom Brother would have laid down everything – except his family. No one else could have done for him, I had to admit, feeling my way through vague memories and chance remarks Brother or, more often, Griff might have let fall. "People say she had some gift for, I don't know, for reconciling people. In the staffroom, in her own family, the sort that made peace. That would have drawn Brother." Yet perhaps Amani had some subtle intransigence Brother had not recognized. I wondered whether Amani had set a deadline in her head, a deadline that Brother had not kept. Amani would never have articulated it and how could he have dreamt of such a thing, having always been the one who set deadlines and never the one bound by them.

"You make him sound like a despot." Anselm grinned, studying my face.

"I suppose he was a . . . a sort of benevolent dictator, and still is at heart. I'm sure we made him one."

But I was more concerned with Amani's accountability, and I had raised the subject that day the opportunity presented itself.

"Amani has never really been happy, and I am responsible," Brother said sternly, then his face relaxed to its customary, more reconciled cast.

"Do you never wonder whether you did the right thing?" I asked, startling myself with my own directness – but he was not offended.

"I can never be certain, for you were not the only ones whose lives hung in the balance. On one level I'm sure I did not. But I know I did the only thing I could." The subject had obviously remained delicate and he said little else. It seemed the scattered renewals of acquaintance had only become more awkward after Amani's husband died.

"And of course you went to that funeral," I said. "It must have been difficult."

"No. At least, there was unpleasantness – the man's family. One of them." He went on to describe the gathering at the house before the rites began. The pundit was late and as family assembled on both sides the tension grew. "Then a scream I shall never forget." The dead man's older sister shrieked and collapsed over the casket. "And on and on, this loud wailing and sobbing and accusing Amani (Amani, who had nursed the fellow selflessly through the cancer, mind you) accusing her of neglect and abandonment and I don't know what not."

"Good Lord."

"On and on, I tell you. This shrill tirade of pure . . . venom. And the unseemly bawling, and she would be sliding out the chair and some daughter would come and fan her and put Limacol and squeeze her head. Hmn."

"So they walked with their Limacol too," Judith remarked. "Poor Amani."

"She was utterly dignified. I suppose it was beneath her notice."

"So the connection between you remains . . .?"

"Fraught with . . . excessive delicacy. And entirely overtaken by time. Why, I wonder," Brother mused, almost under his breath, "why have I been, at crucial times, so . . . so inopportune?"

"You were well in time to intervene in our lives. You were before your time in putting mine on a course altogether – "

He broke in almost impatiently. "Don't deceive yourself. This reputation you ascribe to me for . . . gender equality, is it? It did not work across the board. I made every decision. I never consulted Amani, probably never even explained my intention for us to marry the following year. I assumed she would wait. And, perhaps . . . if her parents . . ."

"Exactly." I swooped down with what Brother liked to call my ferocious loyalty to thrust aside the possibility of blame on his side. "She should have waited."

But he looked away, and reached for a book on the table beside his chair as if inclined to step out of this one of his lives into some other. He took a deep breath, something he did on beginning to read, Anselm had pointed out to me, as if his uncle were inhaling a new world before actually setting out. It was how he had built himself, his mind enlarging exponentially to arrive at this extraordinary self-cultivated scholarship that his own loathing of vanity prevented him from recognizing. These contradictions amused Anselm, who noted that his uncle was studious but not retiring, respectable yet never austere, almost recklessly generous and without extravagance.

"Next time, we must buy a ham," Brother announced one day.

"Next time what?"

"When we get together. Next *time*."

"I thought you said you were going to fast," I protested.

"So? I wouldn't fast forever. When I break my fast, I mean to break it with a vengeance." His eyes gleamed with delight. "Understand me. I respect self-denial, but I'm not given to flagellation. You follow me, 'Zlem?" He shook with laughter.

But Anselm always said that no sooner did he feel he understood this uncle than some glimpse revealed a mind vaster and more complex than he could fathom. Brother gestured away his own individual disappointments along with whatever pain had attended them. There was a bigger scheme of things, he argued, in which the significance of personal loss was swallowed up, and whenever he could he turned the talk to this larger framework. This pursuit of meaning was where Anselm liked to go with him, for you could introduce a radical idea and Brother would pounce on aspects that had not occurred to you. Sometimes it was not so much the idea itself that interested him but how you arrived at it, how your mind worked. Only insincerity threw him into a rage – itself astonishing because he never shouted or cursed yet his controlled fury was more devastating than the ranting of others, and so feared that no one dared provoke him.

It was true we all tiptoed around him, every one of us, suppressing what might vex or worry him, but rarely able to hide anything in the long run. When it came out, he inevitably seemed to have known it all along from the most insignificant clues.

Anselm gradually worked out that the family as a whole protected each other by a sort of selective silence – before strangers, obviously, but even to some extent among themselves. It was Anselm who actually put into words for me operations I had always taken for granted. As usual men shielded many of their thoughts from the women, but he was more aware than the other men (perhaps because the two of us talked with unusual freedom) how much the women hoarded their own secrets from the insensitivities of men. Fascinated, he observed how both the men and the women of my generation censored what should pass to their children even when that generation was grown to adulthood. So information that was not shameful but simply private or, at worst, open to misinterpretation that could be damaging, fell through generation gaps and was filtered out of the known history.

Nonsense like Maydene's had always been an irritant rather than a danger because no one who mattered believed her. No one of any authority could have anything really negative to report because Nathan's strong grip had maintained the family's respectability.

By the time Anselm was grown, he could divine how his uncle's steadfast overview of the family's operation has brought some members into sharp relief and caused others to fade from view. Certainly Anselm could imagine my pa with more clarity than Dada. Whatever system there was for flushing away undetectable impurities in the family history had evolved into a state of moral hygiene that wiped out the more unpleasant odours of the past. To leave it at that, though, was to undervalue his uncle. Anselm knew that morality in the family was not just a result of manipulation to achieve a socially acceptable impression. Nathan had hammered in the values that framed our understanding of whatever life sent our way.

How? Timmy grumbled that pointing out the moral behind even the most mundane occurrence was a wearisome habit no one could shake out of Brother. Yet Nathan's own subtlety of mind overtook and fenced with those same platitudes. Anselm perceived that the universe his uncle had engineered was strictly ordered but not rigid, and I and all my brothers had been able to locate ourselves in it without petrifying – while the sterile existence fate seemed to have had in store for us had been replaced with fruitful lives.

It amused Anselm that however we muttered about some of Brother's methods and about his lingering tendency to govern, our reverence for him reinforced that very aura of authority. He pointed out that every one of us – the boys and I – remained blissfully confident of being the most like Brother and of being, secretly, his favourite. Timmy argued that Brother understood him, hot-tempered and impatient of nonsense as they both were, while Mark ridiculed Timmy out of that playful streak Mark said he shared with Brother, and Luke dismissed both claims, recognizing an echo of loneliness in two men whom domestic bliss had passed by. If Tizzy were here, Mark reflected, she would have pointed out how Brother loved to dance as she did. But the stories of Tizzy ended in sadness and Anselm never pursued them.

But Anselm did insist that a sheltering silence blanketed any events that would better not have happened. Eventually there was no fear that children of the next generation (now grown and passing on apocryphal tales of their elders) had anything unedifying to reveal or suppress. And there must have been such things, Anselm argued as I grew less talkative about some thread of family history. "But there's no handle for taking up any such thing with Uncle Brother," he reflected. Brother occupied himself with exalted ideas of teaching as a ministry and church ministry as education, blurring the line to envisage a common responsibility for lives and souls. He propelled events that remained within his reach as a matter of course and remained superbly oblivious to the borders of his authority, treating Mark to a repetition of rigid scruples regarding the observance of hunting season by expressing his horror at a family member having frozen wild hog in the freezer after the season had closed.

But when Anselm first arrived thirty-five years ago, such tantalizing subtleties had been invisible. There was just the giant we called Brother, palpable and powerful, crediting his own parents and teachers with every success in the family.

"What were they like?" Anselm had asked him shyly.

"'Zlem, boy, what were they like." It sounded like an exclamation rather than a repetition of the boy's question. Probably Anselm thought his uncle was going to tell him some of those stories, but instead Brother talked about what he had felt when he heard stories of his old people, how they swept him along. Then he lent Anselm a book called *The Cloister and the Hearth*, the same copy he had lent me twenty-five years before, and said when Anselm had read it they would talk again.

## Nathan

When I awoke a moment ago it was with a start, to the feel of a small smooth hand slipping through my fingers, yet I am not the sort to let go of a child. It was no easy thing sending Judith away to school; how far San Fernando seemed. Until she left for London – grown, yes, but still in my heart I felt the child of eleven holding fast to my hand. But she came back at last, and brought Anselm.

This Anselm was utterly unlike the others, which should not have surprised me – Judith's son, after all. He was, from the first moment I saw him, set apart. Yes he was in this new place, and imagine coming to Mission from London, but he was also . . . unanchored. A tall boy, thin and a little pale but strong-boned and active, he was back and forth from the gallery to the back door, his movements sure but urgent, his eyes quick, inquisitive.

After a while I began to see myself in him, the boy affecting not to listen while he took it all in, stocking it up to pull apart and reassemble later. After a time he began to ask me polite, indirect questions; and I thought, here we have an interesting fellow. It seems he developed a curiosity about me too, and an affection – I don't think I flatter myself too far in saying that. Uncle Brother indeed.

Judith was better at letting him find his way than I could have been. I've always taken the approach that young people need to be told what to do (and I have been right), but perhaps Anselm was different. Certainly I never lifted a hand to him, and not only because my notions of discipline had changed but because he was not wayward, just propelled by something he was not properly in touch with yet. And then, he was not held in place by all the same ideas and beliefs we had. But he could listen. Watching him I remembered how I had wanted to account for everything that had brought me to where I was, and how I had this sense, as a boy, that fragments of a past peculiarly my own lay partly buried, waiting to be exhumed. Judith calls me a romantic at heart, and certainly I peopled the spaces in my head with characters from near and far, medieval knights and eighteenth-century lords and ladies and revolutionary mobs mixing with the Lezamas and shouldering their way between notable characters in Mission like Mahal or Capital K. Judith being so much of my own mind I suppose it was inevitable Anselm would become a sort of son to me.

He questioned me about members of the family who were gone before he came. "What about Matthew? Is it true what Uncle Mark says? That he could hux coconut with he teeth?"

"Not that I am aware, but one or two of the workers on the land used to say so and no doubt Mark is happy to quote them."

Matthew had been popular with the men, because of all sorts of mysterious exploits I was not supposed to know about but also because he drank and hunted with them. His wife complained incessantly but made excuses if any-one else criticized him. In the long run Maydene's self-absorption and pre-tensions were unsurprising. When Matthew died and Mark and I took over the education of the children and they did well, no one was surprised at May-dene preening herself, and even exulting over Timmy's son having failed Maths. I'll hand it to Tim and Jenine – they just steupsed. It was in one of those periods when my mind was so exhausted it ached. I had seen Maydene for what she was from the beginning, but hoped Matthew might guide her somehow, and I thought, let me at least be sociable. I tried exchanging a few words with her, but she looked at me like a child being forced to listen to something that is not entertaining, and whatever topic I tried, her concentra-tion wavered quickly and even the show of attention flickered out.

What could have attracted Matthew, Mark always asked. "Even in the wedding sari," Mark said unkindly, "yellow and lumpy like phulouri in chut-ney, and by no means as delectable." Mark. Glib, versatile, exhuberant, but thank God he has outgrown his follies, for look what he did for Maydene and the children, even after that letter to Andrew that drove a rift of years between us. Mayhem indeed. She even undertook to issue advice to Judith on Anselm's upbringing – as if he could ever be a problem, devoted as he always was, first to his mother, then to the little girl he married.

Natasha. She was so young, Anselm's wife, too young, and in every way fragile. I watched her with a premonition of disaster although she was bright and sweet and idolized Anselm. He was a hero to her, with his projects in orphanages and halfway houses. And he was a fine teacher, although he insisted that was not his vocation. "I don't know whether I'll ever find it," he said. There was something indefinable about him, in every group in which he found himself, setting him apart and fitting him in at the same time – whether he found himself in the roughest area accompanying home some child from his class who was afraid to return to his parents, or on market day at Mission amid a blaze of colour and the cries of vendors, the carts and hooves and fenders and the odd drunk tottering through it all. Everywhere and with everyone Anselm was at home, and he was alone.

But he was one of those people you could talk to, even without seeing his face. We talked on the phone about books everyone had read and they were new again. *The Man in the Iron Mask, A Tale of Two Cities, The Count of Monte Cristo* – all of men breaking out from some prison and about loyalty, self-denial, persistence. Anselm would insist the stories were about resistance and redemption, and go on to talk about Toussaint and Gandhi and Mandela in the same breath as if they were all from the same work, some larger volume. Then he would produce another book I had never heard of and I would return from that seeing my own world with different eyes. In teaching I engaged with other minds, while Anselm had this impulse, a compulsion in fact, to reach out into the lives of people he did not and perhaps could not know. In the long run it seems to have been the world outside that moved him most.

For me the invisible world is just as real, real as the tangle of bush under the citrus trees that shine with the glitter of rain on dark leaves. So, we are perhaps not as alike as I thought? For what was I at Anselm's age? Not Anselm. Was I lonely and, on some level, deprived? Sometimes it occurred to me that I was, but mostly I was too busy hurtling along the course of life. Yes, in the hard years I felt sorry for myself a few times, languishing after a few drinks, for example, and when I look back on it now a little maudlin perhaps, occasionally, at Mr Manny's.

Because of Amani? The subordination of passion to duty (or, was it, in truth, to a different passion?), the suppression of all that, did not make me unfeeling – how could it? Now I think of it I was all the more sentimental for it, the more emotionally fraught. Sublimating my . . . my dreams, then, to practical necessity only intensified the poignancy of the vision.

Amani's husband was a dull man, I used to think. There is a difference between serious and dull. That man made every setting a morgue. No, not just because he married my bride (yes, of course because of that as well) but more importantly because she deserved better. Judith's recent reference to Amani went through and through me, throbbing not with the intensity of the early days but shaking me with a reverberation of forgotten sensations, with remembering what it was to see my future shrivelling to dust.

I have missed – what? I mean, besides a wife and children of my own, education at a university (for UWI came too late for me), travel and exposure. I have missed the opening of many doors inside my head. Like the chance to appreciate fine art. Painting, sculpture – I only know how they look through pictures. Pictures of pictures are all I have of them. The architecture and landscapes of faraway places. Which reminds me of Judith in the gardens. It was a brainwave, I thought, when the child recovered from the fever. It was beyond anything we had expected, for she had no concept of a garden laid out on the principle of beauty, a dream landscape she told me afterwards, that reached into her and reordered her inside yet made her look again at what was real around her, how trees and bush really behaved when left alone, how Ma negotiated with the land for food. What if I could have seen other, stranger and grander gardens, English and Japanese.

Most of all, I think, I have missed the opportunity of interacting with a range of other minds, one lifelong and deepening and others transient but cultivated in various ways. Fostered in their own disciplines, perhaps? Lettered, is it? To have encountered their turns of phrase and even thought. For sometimes when directness was required I paused too long. I recall that evening I was tongue-tied – fluent enough about the family situation and what I must do, but I got out only such delicately veiled hints of what I felt that the almost overpowering ache I was working my mind around remained unspoken. And that calm postponement of our own happiness must have communicated a lack of urgency and, worse, a shallowness of feeling.

All of this would come back to me in the green solitude among the portugal trees and the fragrance of fruit picked and eaten straight from the branch. All of this would meld with the passion for fruit trees and bushes that bear food of every sort. The scent of crushed grass and blossoms and of the wet earth itself rising from beneath my feet lifted and calmed my spirit at the same time. And she could have been there with me. The thought of strolling under those trees with Amani ravished me and imbued the place with a sort of magical loveliness that even her actual absence could not destroy.

The fact is, I have come as close as I could to having a son of my own. Anselm's combination of vibrant physical energy and mental, almost mystical fervour made him interact naturally with everyone. He was vivacious with Mark, genuinely so, and with me subdued, searching. Yet it was never an inconsistency, just an unfolding mystery, and what he would become remained a fascination to me. Anselm did not precisely flit from one interest to the next so much as process, as if each was a logical step to the other, and when he decided once and for all, I recognized it was the inevitable outcome.

And the premonition? Aah. We had a terrible blow and an inexpressible blessing. Yet neither explained the premonition adequately. Anselm's wife, poor Natasha, really as fragile as she seemed, experienced a terrible pregnancy, increasingly hypertensive as it turns out. Judith at her wits' end, Anselm too devastated to eat or sleep, fainting in the hospital because of the diabetes. And all the while, at the same time – Ma.

Nineteen ninety-eight. A time of emergency on every hand. Ma had been in bed for years and for a couple weeks stopped speaking, then refused all nourishment. Of course I went every day, several times a day, to coax her into sipping a teaspoon or two of eggnog, but by the time I realized I was only disturbing her, she slipped away. How can I explain my surprise at this, when she had been fading so long, so obviously? I assumed the required calm, indeed I felt it, yet the shock of deprivation, of the inconceivable – a world without Ma – buffeted me inside. And then. Barely had we laid her to rest when Judith called that Natasha had gone into labour early and that her pressure was dangerously high. So we were swept along, swept along into a new catastrophe.

Maydene prophesied that both mother and child would be lost – she had assumed her funeral voice for the occasion – and although hers was the last opinion I would have sought, she echoed my fear. Indeed, by the time I arrived, much of it had come true. The screens were drawn around Natasha, pale and straight on the bed in the maternity ward. Anselm, who had forgotten to eat and fainted, seemed barely aware, when they brought him round, of anything but the loss of his wife. He seemed not to notice the IV being administered to him, or his mother's haunted face and hurried movements to and from his side.

I had almost forgotten the rest when Judith called me outside. I must sit down, she said, and I was flustered – by her commanding me but then at once by the fear of something more, some new terrible thing still to be revealed. "Anselm?" I could hear my own voice tremble.

"Oh no. He's out of danger. Such a blow I don't know how he will recover, but he has to, because . . ." She turned back to a nurse holding an armful of soft swathed cloth and took it from her. "But I have to arrange . . . arrange . . . Here."

And into my arms was passed a sleeping newborn infant in tumbled pastels (I had never in all my seventy years held one so, so new), skin so delicate my breath caught in my throat, and a feel and smell altogether unlike anything I had felt before overpowered me. Anselm's child.

The terrible days passed in observance of loss. Every day I had a driver get me to San Fernando to Judith's house and I sat with our boy, Anselm, wordless for the most part. But then there would also be the unfolding miracle, the tiniest pink crumpled hands filling out to exquisite roundness and eyes opening on the world. This was real, I was real. I glowed with the sense of being a participant rather than a spectator. She looked up, bright pupils at first unfocused, then searching our faces, lips puckered around the sliver of pink tongue tasting air, and there was something of her father, something almost ethereal yet tenacious (for here she was) that radiated and enveloped us.

Filling me with warmth and sweetness like a cup of chocolate at twilight. And I, suspended by the feel of her in my arms.

Shanti.

SEPTEMBER 9, 2010 – 4:08 P.M.

*Hi UB! See you home soon. LVE Shanti*

PART

3

# UNCLE BROTHER

## खोया

*Note: rough translation, frag of old book in Ma's possession, possibly from her aja. Prose introd., translated (through kind intervention by Prof Beharrysingh) by Mr Amandeep Gowda, Temporary Instructor (and poet) in Hindi, from Indian High Commission.*

Baap should have known: there are things you do not utter.

I survived despite him – because of my eyes, some said, but also there was what they called a gift for words. It was more than that (and less than that) but I was a child and did not understand. Hauntingly beautiful, they assessed me when I was brought in, and a hypnotic voice for one so young for, yes, I write this verse they admire and read aloud.

Where did it begin? There can be no beginning to some stories. The place I come from was so old, so inscribed with holy legend and embroidered with heroic deeds, a world so prized among the ancient kingdoms as to have been a gift (so the scriptures said), a mark of gratitude between divine brothers. Ayodhya, they say it was called before Mughal rule, and then Awadh.

When we, as children, began to hear about the British that may have been 1857, or '58. Now, it seems a lifetime.

At first we heard how fortunate my father was to have been granted a position in the regiment, but then he came home with these incredible tales. He should have been silent, but Baap was a talker, and my brother and I, who were tied by more than blood, more than our twinness, and as always huddled together out of the way in the shadows near the door – we heard him telling the other men how the Nawab, Wajid Ali Shah, the poet, was cast in prison, that our people were enslaved (so he put it) and vile strategies had been devised to destroy their spirits. The cartridges they had to open with their teeth were greased with the fat of hogs and cattle. He said so, and the men listening groaned in disgust. Later I learned there had been more to it, but at the time we were little children.

When the fighting broke out and the Nawab's son, Birjis Qadr – a boy about our age – was to be thrust on the throne, one of these men to whom my father spun his tales killed a British officer, and because our house had been a gathering place for talkers the investigation followed swiftly to our door. Baap was afraid for his life (or let us even say for his family) so he named this man and led to his execution.

But there was a brotherhood, and they turned on us.

I remember the torches and the firelight flashing along the blades. The two of us, hand in hand plunging for the door almost under the hooves – I do not know how it happened. I know they had my brother, then they . . . rolled . . . it . . . rolled *it* in through the doorway and as my legs gave way, they reached in and grabbed me. They pulled me up by my hair and the horse thundered away with me and I never saw my mother again. I heard my father died that night also but I do not know how and no doubt it is as well not to know. In any case there was no one to come for me when they sold me to the kotha.

Here I was meticulously taught. I speak Persian and Arabic almost as fluently as Hindi and have acquired some English, cumbersome and uncivilized as it is. I rather immerse myself in our own voices, even the ancient writings saved for us by Naval Kishore who promises to publish my verse when he has finished with the rare manuscript he now has in hand. Meanwhile I entrance the powerful, the wise, the artistic – they hover around me, are singed but drawn in, closer. A writer of fiction proposes to tell my story, but why should he speak for me? My voice at least is my own.

Yet I remain bound, for who was there to deliver my body. I may have been eleven when I was brought to the kotha – so little remains of that night, that night that severed me, for who was to restore, to suture? – I did not even speak for weeks after coming there, or so they said. I recall becoming aware of it though, thinking it was a school, until the first time. By then it had become all the home I had.

I had danced the mujra as they had taught me, and they were pleased. I smiled with pride when they counted out the rupees, but when I had been led away to that inner room with the drapery and soft lights, I screamed because I thought the man was holding me down to chop off my head.

And then I wished he had – just as swiftly, cleanly.

Now I have a son, but I have sent him away from me where he can be brought up without disgrace, and I shall never know his children. My name will be lost to them and, meanwhile, all he will have of me is this book of my verse, bound in paper patterned with cloud and wind, which he may never read. But I hear he has my eyes that reflect the flame and the glint of the blade.

*This is where our translator stopped. I've preserved it as a sort of testimony. It makes me reflect on all that our older heads passed through, on how far we've come.*

# CHAPTER 14

# SESSION NOTES, JULY 2008

## Shanti

Coming here – it wasn't my idea. My folks . . . hold on. How far back should I go? Just start with my dad? Cool.

So here's his latest to the papers, see? May 2008. Granma J and Uncle Brother and me – we'd always cut out what my father wrote to the papers, but this one I keep in my wallet, "Half-way Caring". It's about shelters for women who run away from men who beat them up. Father Dads says the shelters aren't equipped – like, not enough beds or food, and they don't protect people. This is the part about the girl whose husband came for her and dragged her away. She was real young and when the lady managing the place called the police they said they couldn't interfere in a marriage and when the manager tried calling the girl's parents her father said, "Ent she run away with the man? She make she bed; let she lie in it." See it's all here. The husband hauled her into the car and drove away and the manager says the girl's arm was broken from when she came to the shelter in the first place.

Can I, like, have that back? It's the sort of thing I mean. None of the other kids had fathers anything like him.

Granma J – that's J for Judith – always says she was at her wits' end with Anselm from he was small. She christened him Nathan Anselm but they all called him Anselm – not to mix him up with Uncle Brother, she said, but, hey, who calls UB by his name? Anyway, Granma said Anselm was the most loving child but always running in the other direction to everyone else and talking about stuff no one else would think about. She said it was awful for him when his father died, but once they got back to Trinidad it wasn't so bad 'cause, you know, he got in with Uncle Brother and they were real tight. UB liked listening to him talk, though it's usually the other way around: people listening to Uncle Brother. Granma J says they're all *in awe* of Uncle Brother – she and the other brothers. But I don't find him awful; fact is – he's kinda cool.

Anyway, Uncle Brother was the one who calmed everyone down when FD – it's just easier to call Father Dads *FD* – when FD went on the march. I mean our family is real quiet and proper, right? At least the older ones, and there are lots of those. Because – hello? – it's vast. *And* not too adventurous: a trip to Mayaro is this wild excursion, getting your legs wet as far as the knee and Uncle Brother goes ballistic if you look like you're *thinking* of immersing, which doesn't bother me 'cause I'm just as scared of water. But they're not into anything exciting, see? Let alone, like, public. Not a set to jump up or get something and wave in a carnival fête even when they were young, or to bawl into a mike at some political meeting or anything like that. Okay?

I mean they argue over politics, because Uncle Luke defends Basdeo Panday no matter what and hates Ramesh. I mean he loved Ramesh then he hated him then he loved him, but now he hates him again. All depends on how Ramesh feels about Bas. Once they start talking politics Uncle Luke and Uncle Tim end up glaring at each other. But no one's going on any platform – though there was this rumour once that Uncle Tim was gonna run for PNM because he was so anti-Bas, but Granma J says she thinks she knows who started that one. Some gossipy lady who used to take care of *her* mother. Some Audrey.

But so it sorta freaked them out a couple years ago when they heard FD was going on this march. Granma J said she wasn't interfering with Anselm because, look, it was a march protesting crimes against children; then Uncle Brother said he'd have been there with them if he were ten years younger. Course, once *UB* said that, everyone figured it had to be okay.

Yeh, Uncle Brother's real old, but he's pretty tough – you'd be surprised. He still drives to church, everyone waving and getting off the road till he's passed. Hey, Uncle Mark says even the old guy who used to totter along *thinking* he was driving a car and doing his hands in front of him like he was steering, he'd swing his arms left and get up on the pavement and salute, then get down again when Uncle Brother had passed. I don't know whether I remember that old man; probably I just heard about it, like half the things in my head. Some things don't change though. Like, Uncle Brother stops to offer Mr Israel a lift even though that old guy is going in the other direction, to his own church.

"Going my way this morning?" Uncle Brother calls. "I'm still driving."

"Driving is for old men, man. I still walking." Mr Israel waves his stick at UB.

"We taking a drink for that later then."

"Not me, pardner. Washed in the blood of the Lamb." Old Mr Israel's standard response.

Then the two of them laugh like anything and go on their different ways. Every Sunday same ole talk. Mr Israel's granddaughter, Chinksie, works at my school, holding on in the library. Her father's a policeman in Princes Town and Uncle Brother's not too keen on him – says he hears all kinds of *unsavoury* things about "that Kenny" – but Chinksie's cool. She says I can call her that because we're tight. She's small and looks like a teenager even though she's, like, twenty-something. "Petite" is what Granma J would call her if she liked her, but no way. Granma J says "all that Wonderbra and tinted hair isn't appropriate to the workplace." Old people just freak out over nothing. *I* think Chinksie looks good, and that smooth kinda chocolate-brown skin she has really sets off those highlights.

Chinksie's not really a teacher although it sounds so when she says she's got a post in the school; she's holding on in the library while Mrs Ali's on maternity leave, and she knows the sort of stuff I like to read, fantasy and sci-fi and stuff. Only not vampires, right? I told her vampires *don't* turn me on – I just think they're gross. Chinksie and I chat all the time. She's hardly taller than me and passes for one of the girls if you don't look sharp, and the teachers are kinda mean to her when she needs people to like her, or even see her – hey, she just, like, wants to make an impression. They get hyper about her saying things like how she gets high on risk, but that's talk. You know? She's cool.

Except for the Chinksie issue, Granma J and me do real good together. Course she retired ages ago, from I was born I guess, so we cn do stuff. Sometimes it's just to drive up to Mission and spend the night with Uncle Brother. That's when we might go to church together. It's always good to get back to his house and come out of the car alive. Then, first they trash the sermon, which is okay 'cause it's usually a disaster. Uncle Brother heaves this great sigh: "A singularly tedious address today." Yeh. He really talks like that.

"Unfortunately not too singular," Granma J says. "Not like the old days with the missionaries."

"You see, some of these young people don't prepare. It's *laziness*." He kinda drops his voice when he says it, like it's a cuss word or something. "This fellow has no business in the Church."

Granma J says, "One has to worship somewhere." Usual story.

It's just a few people you can actually, like, listen to. Most of the family, when they want someone to run a prayer meeting, they just call Uncle Brother. At least he reads up and figures out in advance what he means to say and when he's done he stops, instead of putting us to sleep.

Sometimes Uncle Brother borrows Mr Thompson from Uncle Luke and gets a drive up our way. (Mr T's some sort of relative of Mr Israel, a son or something, a big big guy who looks like a policeman but he's kinda cool.) But more often we go to Mission and Miss Annette cooks curry common fowl and then something else, kinda different, like conks if she meets up with some fisherman she trusts. Miss Annette is Mr Israel's daughter-in-law and she helps Uncle Brother out a lot, like when he's getting together this group of his friends about what he calls community issues and she's gotta track down chataigne or halal goat or whatever.

When Uncle Brother and Granma J get together on his gallery, he plants his bare feet on the parts of the rocker that jut forward at the bottom and she pats his hand while they *analyse,* so I get to know all kinds of stuff they don't realize I'm hearing, which is cool. Then they remember I'm there, and Uncle Brother calls me. "Darling?" – I'm the only one he calls that – "When you going to let me taste your hand?" But I'm not interested in cooking. I tell him I just like to eat and he throws up his hands and slaps them down on his knees and he shakes with laughter. Course he and I talk too – we're tight – and he has this voice (not that he can sing or anything, though he likes to). It's how he talks. Like, after he's done you can still hear him.

Anyway. So now you're wondering whether I have a mother and I don't. Granma J sort of stepped in. She'd have given me some name from the Bible but FD said Shanti was the name my mother wanted. My mother died when I was born so all I know is what they told me, something about her blood pressure, which nearly killed both of us – but I made it, which doesn't seem quite fair, but I'm okay with that 'cause it's not to say I knew her. But it was hard on my dad (FD, you know) and a couple years after she died he – he was Catholic like his own dad – he went into the Church.

Yup, he's a priest. Father Anselm. So, why did you think I call him Father Dads? (Hey, did that sound rude? I don't mean to be rude – I'm just talking like you said.)

Anyway, so FD was about as different as he could be at those parent–teacher meetings. Like, how many of the other children have a priest for a father, attending PTA? And he sticks up over the rest of them, you know, he's real tall with black black hair (well, pretty black still) always out of order. But he's thinner than he used to be, and sort of pale, except for the shadows round his eyes, only his eyes are . . . have this . . . they kind of hold you. You know? Actually he hasn't been so well recently, and sometimes I had to really buff him to take his pills or follow the diet, and then he would put down his head and say, "Yes, Mama." Granma J laughs at that because she says when she was little her father used to call her "Mother."

Course there isn't much money. Before he was ordained he gave Granma J just about all he had, for me, and she invested it or something. But he'd come by every day, even if he worked late, and we'd play checkers and hopscotch, or he'd do schoolwork with me while they were figuring out how to deal with the dyslexia thing. We made a kite and he wrote my name on the yellow part and showed me how to fly it. All my friends, cousins, the kids at the school – children just followed him around.

Chinksie never met him, but then she's not a kid and isn't into family much. She asked me once if I had a boyfriend or what and of course I didn't, I didn't even want one, but it was kinda nice that I looked as if I might. She used to say she felt sorry for me because my grandmother had lame old ideas, and she said one day she would take me out with her so I could see what it meant to have a good time. Can you imagine what UB would say? Even FD would've said no, though he's always been real cool.

He used to have a backpack – you know, the collar, the Bible and stuff, and then this backpack – and it was, like, full of snacks. Because when he dropped in at school to do prayers there would be some child who had no lunch, or when he went downtown there would be a character begging by the traffic light, and on the way home there had to be a stray dog. Granma J said he had Pied Piper blood in him but it was from his father's side, not hers. Look. One Old Year's he decides to invite in the garbage men. You know? He stops the truck at the gate and calls them in and shares out ham and hops bread, and cake and stuff, because he says, who else is gonna treat the garbage men? And when they're leaving he gives them extra bottles of soft drink and the only bottle opener in the house. Typical.

And we did stuff. I have this dog I got from Uncle Mark. Uncle Mark's dog was *not* a pitbull. Someone in Mission made up this thing about him having a pitbull that had bitten off a child's face. Of course Uncle wouldn't have a beast like that – she was a real friendly dog and I had a pup from her called Road March, and Road March went all over Trinidad with FD and me. I was, like, *all* over the place with FD. Okay? We went fishing, hiking, all up in the hills and wherever. FD was real fit then but he wasn't strict with his diet or even the pills sometimes. But very cool. I had this real old old aunt my folks called Phuwa, who used to say, "The world have all kind of father in it and all kind of uncle." I guess I just lucked out.

Course the whole family is Presbyterian back to the beginning of time, right? Okay, I guess they must've been Hindu before and some folks have married Hindus since, so – Hindu Presbyterian, usual thing. So this Catholic priest business kinda stuck out. But they didn't mind or anything. In fact they'd call him if they needed something blessed and Uncle Brother couldn't make it. There's always something new somewhere – house, car, whatever – that needs blessing, and with so many of us in the family, it was kinda hard for one person to keep up with, right?

Oho. I just remembered, Uncle Brother says not to say "right" and thing too much when I talk or it will spill over and spoil my essay writing. And what with my crapaud-foot writing and the spelling madness, I gotta watch that, right? Shucks, I did it again. Granma J says I better do well in school to get a good job, for one thing I don't have to look forward to is any inheritance.

Not that we're that badly off (though Chinksie's got it into her head that we're rich, which we aren't) and the rest of them are pretty okay. Uncle Luke is well off, they say, investments and other stuff I don't know about. It's a lie about his money being from some inheritance he got dishonestly. No one was ever rich in our family before him. Uncle Timmy seems to be okay too, he has a swimming pool and thing, but his isn't from swindling anyone either – he just gives the best lessons in South. But he and Aunt Jenine have their own children to leave stuff to. Uncle Mark was doing pretty well but his wife had surgery recently and it cost a bomb so he's being pretty careful now in case Aunty Leela needs any follow-up. Anyway, Granma J and the uncles all say they'd have been nothing without Uncle Brother. He's their hero.

But he kinda freaks them out: Granma J says, "Brother's a law unto himself," 'cause he won't, like, listen to anyone. He goes around on his own all over his land, picking portugals and carrying this big bag to the house by himself. The folks get real hyper about that. "Suppose he has an attack out there all alone and no one hears him?" I mean, you cn see why they'd fret. So they bought him a cell phone. He never turned it on and it disappeared somewhere. They got another and he dropped it in the bush, probably under some citrus tree.

So I said, "Buy one and *I'll* give him for Christmas." They said it'd be waste because he'd just throw it away, but FD said, "Listen to the child. She's the one to sort him out." So Christmas Day comes and we drive down to Mission and I sit on Uncle Brother's knee like when I was small. And I hand him his present and dial from my own phone and his Christmas gift starts ringing. And I say, open it and press the green button, and he does. And I say, "You gotta carry this and answer every time, because I could be asking you some grammar something for an essay, right?"

And he looks at me a long time with his face serious and his eyes squeezed up and, like, shining, and he says, "Mamaguy."

And I say, "Yup, why not."

So he agrees, and FD says, "See? I told you."

FD has always figured that he knows Uncle Brother best, though every one of them thinks that. I don't bother to spoil it for them. See, Uncle Brother and me, we talk by phone all the time now. I call him or he calls me. I showed him how to text but he won't. He reads it when I text him though. He doesn't use the phone for anyone else and if it rings he knows it's me. And what he kinda likes is how it vibrates first, before he hears the ring.

"These modern gadgets," he mutters. "And you know everybody has them now?"

Just as well. 'Cause that's how, the other day, we were able to call him from the shelter.

What happened was so gross it's almost impossible to talk about but, you know. We never did anything wrong, so what's to be ashamed of? Right?

FD used to visit the shelters – like this one in the clipping – all the time, to counsel the women and see if he could help them find jobs. Or lawyers, 'cause a couple of them went to court. One stayed and worked at the shelter. She had needed this retaining . . . no, a re*straining* something, so her father couldn't follow her there to take her back. She was, like, just a couple years older than me and in her case it was the father who beat her and did all kinds of other stuff FD wouldn't talk about. So he found a lawyer who helped her for free and got the restraining thing working. And the reason they could do it was they had evidence, like the report of the doctor FD brought to see her, and the picture of her with the cuts and bruises. He and the doctor agreed they had to have the photos because the legal thing might take so long she would be healed by the time her case came up.

Once when FD and me – FD and *I* – were going to Gulf City Mall, we took a shortcut (he knew these crazy shortcuts to Gulf City that took longer than going through the traffic and even went way past Gulf City and turned back) and he pointed out the shelter to me. That's how I could find it.

'Cause one evening when I was doing homework, FD calls Granma J from the shelter and says some man has made a report about him and police were at the shelter questioning him, and the man was waving his cutlass and accusing FD of hurting his family. I didn't hear the man, only what Granma J said.

So Granma J didn't want to take me there, but how long could this stupid thing take to sort out, right? And there was no one home and no time to drop me anywhere else. On the way she phoned Uncle Luke and he called Mr Thompson to drive him, but he didn't want to worry Uncle Brother. So we're hardly there before the rest start to show up and one of them has a lawyer. Which was just as well, 'cause the police wouldn't let any of us inside except the lawyer. And every now and then Aunt Jenine or one of them would point at me and say, "Shanti should never be here." But no one was leaving to take me anywhere else, so I got to stay. Which was a pretty good thing because Uncle Brother was at one of his meetings with his phone on silent, so I sent a text, and see, Granma J hasn't a clue how to do that. Then Miss Annette drove him up from Mission herself because she said it was too much stress for the old gentleman to come all that way on his own.

The manager of the shelter said FD had been counselling a woman who had come in with her baby but left her other two children home in the house with her husband, and by the time FD got to talk to her she wanted to go back for the other kids, only she was afraid her husband would kill her. And the girl (the one who had been there from before and got the restraining order) tried to convince this new lady to stay at the shelter, and showed her the photo and stuff with all the bruises and told her how her case was going to court. But all the same, next day when the husband comes to the shelter, the woman with the baby just goes back home. Only, then, the husband goes right back to the shelter and starts smashing it up because he says FD is getting women to leave their homes and promising them jobs but getting them into bad houses and people must be paying him for each one he delivers. When the police come he tells them FD takes indecent photos of women and he brings out this one of the other woman with all the cuts and stuff and . . . her body. You know.

His wife must have pinched it somehow from the other girl.

All this time none of us knows that this guy has called the press and reporters turn up now and start to take pictures and the police go to our house and search it and find FD's camera with pictures of us at Mayaro and the old VHS I used to have for watching *Chipmunks* and *Lion King* and thing, and old albums with baby pictures and stuff, so some of them say there's no evidence and another says the family threw out the evidence – even though we were right in the shelter all the time and no one was allowed in the house while they were searching it up except for Uncle Luke, who went with them even though his legs were hurting like anything and he took the keys from Granma J and let them in and they walked around with big guns pointing at him and everywhere.

Meanwhile Uncle Brother arrives and the whole of us are outside, near the shelter. More and more folks had got there, Uncle Timmy and one of his boys, a daughter-in-law of Uncle Mark who drove him because of the slipped disc, and others, because word spread, you know, and some of them stayed in their cars not to be in the way and Uncle Mark lay flat on the back seat and others stood up in the rain or, like, under a tree because it wasn't really pouring, and they waited. Granma tried to see FD but they wouldn't let her in, and a police-woman who kept coming to the door and looking at us hard told Granma she better teach her grandchild not to watch big people in they face like that – she meant me – and everyone was standing around just hopeless. Only Uncle Brother kept watching the road.

Then he said, "He really came." He said it kind of quiet, but everyone stopped and watched, and he went up to this car that drove up and and a guy in uniform comes out, oldish, may be in his forties so, but much younger than Uncle Brother of course (but so's everyone else in the world), and Uncle said, "Elroy, boy."

And the guy grabbed his hand and said, "I don't know what I could do, Teach, but I here."

So in a while this same Officer de Jacques told us how it was, for at least he got to go in and out. He said the man accused FD of using his visits to the shelter for all kinds of stuff no one would explain to me (but I'm not stupid, you know) and that even though the search turned up nothing, he might really have to go to court because this fellow had lodged an official complaint. Elroy said people knew about FD's work in the shelters and how many women and children he had helped, and most of the police felt the story was a lie, but one said, how a man would make up a thing like that involving he own wife. And, whatever Officer Elroy said, the same officer told him that he knew the Church was going try to cover it up but he ent taking that because a man have a right to protect his own family.

Anyway, Officer Elroy calmed them down and they said FD must come and give a statement in the morning, and the man they called the plaintiff had to go home. Officer Elroy insisted the police keep the cutlass – can you believe they were going to give the cutlass back to this guy whose wife thought he was gonna kill her?

So then at last the police let us leave, but FD said someone should drive Granma J and me home because all this was too much for her, and he would come on in her car. Miss Annette was going to take Uncle Brother back home but they dropped us off first. When we left, FD was looking pretty sick because he hadn't eaten, but he said it wasn't far so he would manage.

Only, the sugar, you know, so he blacked out and ran off the road by the waterfront there into the sea, and we sat home wondering where he was and the next thing we heard was they had found the car in the water and he was . . . he was inside.

Next day it was all in the newspapers, all twisted up, and one had a picture of a woman's back all cut up and bruised. Some papers just reported the accident but one of the papers had this headline: PRIEST IMPLICATED IN PORN RING DROWNS SELF.

I wasn't interested in going back to school but I went anyway. Granma J said I'd better stay home a couple days, but I felt like if I didn't go right away I never would. You know? And I was okay. Everyone hugged me and said FD was the kindest man they ever knew. My friend Chinksie stayed close to me in lunchtime, and after school she walked me to the car. Granma J can be a bit standoffish and she says Chinksie is too old for me to be friends with but I think it's that Miss Annette warned Granma J about Chinksie, which isn't very nice to say things about your own niece behind her back, and besides, who I'm friends with is my business and I love Granma J and I know she means well but she should butt out.

See, I don't care whether Chinksie's father, Kenneth, is a bad cop or not. He's Miss Annette's brother-in-law so I guess she cares. It's got nothing to do with me. Whatever it was about bags of ganja and cocaine missing from a twelve-million-dollar drug bust, it wasn't Chinksie involved, so I'm not on that. Officer Elroy told Uncle Brother he had kept away from Kenny after the coup because of some camp in the forest. Whatever. He said all he knew about Kenny's girl, Chinksie, was that she had been friends with his niece, Cerise. All that matters to me is Chinksie's my friend; she came and kissed me at the door of the church, then stayed away (I figure it was from Granma J) for the rest of the funeral. I think. I can't really remember it all. I was all right but I don't remember, okay?

I guess the service was packed all the family, four or five generations of us – I don't know. Even Uncle Andy flew in, though he has problems because of the recession. Officer Elroy sent to say he was on a job and couldn't get away or he would have been there. The family filled most of the church and then there were all the friends, the priests who had worked with FD, all kinds of people he had helped and we never knew, women from the shelters, parents from my school with their children. They stretched outside under the tents and into the street and they stood under the mango tree across the road. The man with the violin played "It is Good with My Soul", which was all very well for I knew it was, but I'd have preferred to have FD back.

But, you know. People die. I'm okay, even though all the family and friends and parents and people cried and they were, like, wild, but it didn't change anything. Uncle Brother seems to think he should have done something to keep FD safe or just set the record straight, and he kinda freaked out when he found he had no control of anything. The insurance people investigated and said the accident was an accident. The police agreed there was no evidence of his having done anything that man said, but they wouldn't change the record because the accused was deceased anyway, and the newspaper wasn't interested in any of that stuff.

"They told me retractions don't sell papers," Uncle Mark said. "It makes no difference to them what impression people are left with." And he was just crying and crying.

Like, I don't know. After the first madness I didn't feel to cry. Like, I hadn't a tear left, I guess I kinda dried up. But they can't believe I'm all right.

Granma J didn't say much. She's just, like, fixated on me. She carries me about everywhere. Her old foreign-used was destroyed by the sea water and thing so she bought a new car because she wants me to be safe, but I keep telling her I'm okay and she just doesn't hear.

I mean, somewhere the woman who said this thing so her husband would-n't kill her is keeping quiet, and he might still kill her anyway. Somehow their kids are growing up as if none of this happened. It's like sci-fi. You make up this . . . this world, right? And people in it do what you make them do 'cause you made it up. Only then it spills over into someone else's real life, but you just go on with your own story, you know?

Course it nearly killed Uncle Brother, but he's recovering and they say there isn't much damage to the heart. It was a mild attack, so at least we've got him.

The family says I need to talk about this with someone, so I'm here, okay? Uncle Luke got Mr Thompson to bring Granma J and me to Port of Spain and on the way back we'll pick up Uncle Brother – he's been on the cardiac ward but they're discharging him – then Mr T and Uncle Luke will get him back to Mission once Granma and I get home. But right now Granma's just outside. Could you just, like, tell her I'm *fine*? And I'd like her to tell Uncle Brother that.

Hey, don't move that! (Please.) That's FD's. I got to keep his backpack and I take it around with me all the time even though it looks pretty battered by now what with all the watermarks and thing.

> (In supplying these records for reconstruction of an account relevant to an open case, confidentiality is hereby breached under conditions of grave emergency relating to a minor. Please return to this office as soon as possible.)

FEBRUARY 10, 2007 – 6:40 P.M.

*Testing texting. Won't know if you get this ulness you reply. Call later. Wish youd try txting. Don't be lame. Lve Shanti*

# CHAPTER 15

# ACCOUNTS

## Thump

How I got into this when I am just the guy who drives the Principal and them sometimes? It goes back forty years or so to when I was a little fellow in Mission and they called me Thump. They called me that because the "th" in front my name was not supposed to be pronounced and when I said it as if it were spelled "Tomson" they laughed at me and said, "*Thompson*, boy. What happen to you? You so can't speak English you don't even know how to call you own name? Say 'thomp' or we go 'tump you."

This was highly unlikely, for I was tall and hefty for my age. "Nimble and quick-witted," it said on my school report. I was a big boy, with not an ounce of fat but well developed, for I ate *real food*. I was not a boy others of my age would attack, so I refused to call my name the way they say I had to and we reached a compromise. Everybody called me Thump, and I answered to that right through school. Fine, I said, once they stopped trying to make me call myself *Thhompson*.

Eventually a few who did not know the story assumed the name, Thump, celebrated some famous blow I had delivered, so further respect accrued. I understand it was unanimously agreed I would go far. Teacher Deoraj thought so too, long before he became Principal, but based on other considerations. I must be the only fellow in Mission who passed through Teacher Deoraj's class and never got licks. I used to say, I wonder what I missed. I know it wasn't licks, because all the teachers used to beat in those days and I got my full share from the rest.

No. My extended contact with the Principal arose through different circumstances altogether.

My family was not badly off. In fact, from all accounts they had had more money to start with than any Deoraj had seen in the old days. My grandfather had had a dry goods store in the village and it did well. He could not read, but that was all right because he had employed a young fellow named Israel Lee to do his pen work, and the boy was honest so the store thrived. The old man was fervently religious and attended church not only on weekends but on weekdays, so he used to say God prosper he business.

When my grandfather died, his oldest daughter, who was my mother, took over at just about the time the fellow, Israel, was thinking of leaving and opening his own store. The new owner asked him to stay on because he knew the business so well, and what with one thing and another, my mother and Israel got married and they did very well together – only I learned afterwards that Israel refused to take any money from the store for a long time.

Now my ma had been married before but this man had run off and left wife and child when I too small to have any memory of that father at all. My mother reacted instantly, seeking divorce for abandonment, and while the law took its time she sold the house her father had settled on them (in her name) before the man even knew what was happening, and she moved back in with her old man. So when she married Israel, I may have been four years old or so. Tell you the truth, I can't remember a time when Israel wasn't my father. Of course we didn't resemble, for Israel was this slim-built brown-skinned man while I couldn't be more black and eventually turned out to be a foot taller. Probably a foot wider too, as Israel himself would say with his big grin. The store did well except for a few years after my half-brothers entered Mission CM School, and they found themselves attending barefoot as their elders had done.

These two sons Israel had with my mother, Leonard and Kenneth, grew up in Mission and they were in Teacher Deoraj's class after a while. By that time I had spent a year in the class of the head teacher, who did not like me for the simple reason that I used to pick up errors on the blackboard and point them out. But I was always polite about it, eh? That is one thing: I was always polite. Now I was a good few years older than my half-brothers so I was high up in the school when Leonard was coming in and just a year or so from School Leaving when Kenny began. At twelve I was quick with figures and for a few pence a week the people in charge of the school office let me help after classes. I was eager to do that because Israel was like a god to me – I wouldn't lie – and when I could take home even a couple coins to help I felt like a big man.

One day, the head teacher found me in the office in front the open desk drawer with money in my hand. So the office staff checked the cash pan and what was missing turned out to be the exact sum in my hand. The head teacher called the staff together and said he would have me expelled.

And Teacher Deoraj asked me what happened.

The head teacher was scandalized. He asked Teacher Deoraj what he meant by such a question, for hadn't he, head teacher, made it clear he caught this boy with his hand almost in the cash pan. But Teacher Deoraj said he still wanted to hear the boy say something, and I told them I hadn't taken the money. I was bringing it back.

You can imagine the reaction, laughter from one or two and a steups from another. Teacher Deoraj paid them no attention; his eyes fixed on mine as if he was looking through them to the inside of my head. Where were you bringing it back from, boy?" he asked me.

"Sir," I answered him after a long pause, "from someone who took it, sir." But I wouldn't tell the name.

The head teacher said this little thief was not spending another day in the school, but Teacher Deoraj argued that expulsion would be the end of young Thompson. When Nathan Deoraj saw he could not convince them to keep me, he persuaded them to at least let me leave on my own. And that was what happened. I just dropped out of school and nothing about any theft went on my record. Teacher Deoraj was good friends with my stepfather, Israel, so the two questioned me, and when I still refused to give them a name they called Leonard and Kenny. But they learned nothing more from my half-brothers. Teacher Deoraj said he knew the child was protecting someone and he told Israel not to beat me, just leave it alone.

So I helped in the store for a while until I could be apprenticed to an able workman and later found employment as an electrician. Then I went to T and Tec, moved up through various supervisory positions and retired early on account of a stomach ulcer. It was after that, when the ulcer cooled down and boredom set in, that I heard Luke Deoraj needed a driver, and I started to do that a day or two each week. It got me out the house.

Driving Luke and then others in the family only confirmed what I had sensed even as a child. Most, including the Principal, were not completely situated in the real world – not because they were escapist or snobbish, nor had it anything to do with intelligence. It was something I sort of glimpsed that awful day in front of the cash pan in the head teacher's office, what with my mind reeling between what Teacher Deoraj would think and what Teach might say later to his pardner, Israel.

When the head teacher pronounced expulsion, Teacher Deoraj winced. It was like a ripple of . . . anguish, too brief to catch unless your eyes were on his face, and in that instant I realized that even if I *had* been guilty, Deoraj would have resisted expulsion. His eyes might go through you like a knife but inside him was a softness, like he couldn't believe anyone to be . . . well, irretrievable. Sometimes I've wondered if this softness could cloud his vision. A brilliant man, yes, raising people and inspiring them to raise others, but I don't know if at the core of this very goodness was something a certain type of person could exploit. Long ago one's immediate circle was closely bordered, but now . . . Now is not like longtime.

Over the years, the old Principal and his family have bought their newspapers and sat in front of TV6 and BBC news, confident they are keeping in touch with what is going on. Every now and then they wonder what the world is coming to, while every schoolchild knew it ent coming to anything; it done get there. Not that Trinidad is worse than other places: it's in many ways better, which was why I never moved to New York when I had the chance. But as to God being a Trini – one of them stupidness people say whenever obvious disaster looms – I don't see God as that partisan.

Hear me. Evil has crept in, and there are those inside here who have invited and fostered it. And some of them export it. That is the type I give a wide berth, though some of them are old acquaintances. And all that may not seem to be an obvious explanation of how I come into this – but take my word.

## Judith

I suppose we have to look back at everything that might have a connection. Some things are just random, but one never knows. That day . . . No, Mr Thompson was not with me for I'm perfectly capable of driving around San Fernando in broad daylight.

A year or so ago, I was edging through the market to get back to my car on Mucurapo Street when I came face to face with this woman who had a small child gripping her skirt. "You is Mistress Teemul," the woman said. "Father Anzlem mother." It was more a statement than a question.

I nodded. "You knew my son?" I answered quietly, because I still can't always control my voice when I talk about Anselm without having had time to prepare.

"He di' good to me." The woman glanced over her shoulder, then down at the child, and dropped her voice. "I was sorry to hear," she whispered. Her eyes filled with tears. "I never wanted nothing to happen to he."

It was as if someone was choking me. "Your husband. It was your husband?"

"Father Anzlem di' only want to help everybody. Nothing so shoulda happen to he."

"Happen? It didn't *happen*." Now the words were bursting out of me and I couldn't make them stop. "And you stand there and cry? Crying is all you're good for? You lie to save yourself and when confusion comes down on a good man you keep quiet and now you stand there and tell me you're sorry?" I shoved her out my way so hard I nearly threw her down. "Lady, keep away from me. I pity your children, but you . . . I can't pretend I feel a thing but disgust."

"You don't know what it is," the woman cried. "You see, to be afraid for you life? I can't even sleep at night. I doesn't know what the man might do me when I asleep or do the children to spite me. I does only lie awake and watch."

"Well, my son is dead I have none to watch. Get away from me."

The woman cringed aside and whimpered.

But she was too pathetic to have breathed a word about that meeting. It must have been the child who was with her. The child was probably too afraid himself not to report on his mother. The next Saturday at the market a man was waiting by my car when I returned to it. His voice was thick, hoarse.

"I know you car, you bitch," he rasped. "I know you house. I know you school where you does work. You open you mouth to my wife or my child another time, you open you nasty mouth and say anything bout me and I coming for you."

His eyes blazed red with drink and darted such venom I was paralyzed. The realization of who he was froze me in place.

"Priest come to meddle in my business and, Teemul, now he dead, he family and all . . ."

But Anselm's name in that man's mouth unleashed something in me and I was suddenly not afraid, just impelled by . . . by rage. I shouted, "Don't you say a word about my son that you killed." I know I must have shouted it because the people clustered around the citrus vendor nearby stopped haggling and stared. I yelled at them. "He killed my son with his lies, and now he's threatening me." And I swung back to face him. "They've all seen you. Watch!" I pointed at him. "All these people can identify you if you do me anything." When I wrenched open the car door and jumped in, I told him, "I'll make my own report to the police now."

But as I turned on the engine, he stepped up close to the window. "Police." He spat the word back at me. "Before you leave the station they done forget you longtime. I go wait. And I don't have to do you nothing, ole woman. I ent even going touch you self. Watch. Ent you have more family to lose?"

## Thump

Yes, occasionally I would drive one of the others besides Luke – not only the Principal himself, when he was ill after the death of that nice young man, but the Principal's sister taking her granddaughter to the doctor. That was usually over long distances or when they had to go out at night. The tragedy was over a year ago and they seemed to be settling down now, but it had been a cruel blow. Old Principal Deoraj had always been strong though.

In the old days Teach would work for incredibly long hours because he used to keep class after school for some of the children who needed help. Right after I left the school with those teachers thinking I was a thief, Teacher Deoraj made me come to his house early every morning before school and before the shop opened, and he taught me arithmetic as if I was still going to take School Leaving.

Once I was old enough to leave home, I did, and it hurt Israel that I wanted to and that I would not say why, but Teacher Deoraj said he believed he understood. Of course, he never took anything for teaching me, and when I asked if there was anything I could do, anything at all, he made me take over the church accounts. After a while I got that job in T and Tec and moved to San Fernando, but the little experience with the church accounts stood me in good stead when I became a regular church member myself and ended up as treasurer.

I was driving Luke nearly a year before he discovered how good I was with figures and offered me a different job, but I told him it was more relaxing driving about the countryside – not that I wouldn't help if needed, but for free. (What? Charge the Principal's brother for help with figures?)

The funny thing was that by that time, apart from myself, there was probably no one alive besides the Principal, Israel and one other person who knew the story of my leaving school, and the Principal and Israel knew only a fraction of it. I've never had any regrets, though now and then I've kind of wondered what I would have become without those two old fellows and their sense of what glued the world together. Now I watch a different, merciless world unfolding in dimensions way beyond their view and I think perhaps I'd have allowed myself to be recruited into projects that have come my way and now I might be rich and powerful. And dangerous. Or, perhaps I would have yielded the name in the first place and the right boy would have got to finish school.

No. Probably I would not have interfered regarding the money to begin with, and all sorts of things would have taken a different course.

# CHAPTER 16

# TEXT

## Nathan

It surged and sucked me under, then swelled beneath, buoying me. Light glimmered far above and I floated up, breaking the surface. Then it grew so blinding I couldn't close my eyes. Balancing barefoot on rock, the water tumbling round (if only you could throw *me*, Ma), but hold, hold her up, rice swirling and a wall of black ocean rising, curling over. Close it out, Anselm's hair floating behind the windscreen. Block Dada's fist, press it back into the box with the uniform. I forced my eyes open.

A nurse studying the monitor glanced up, her lips moving: ". . . awake."

Submerging again, the child pressing his hand over his ears. The lagahoo, beat it to death. The soucouyant, she, no sometimes he – for even as one builds lives, another sucks them away – beat it to death. I couldn't stretch myself to reach them all. Elroy I caught, but . . . so many. Dada spat one out somewhere out of my sight and one or two perhaps slipped through into the void that would have swallowed us all.

So much was wrong those days. March, boy, and write your columns. And Shanti, all light and mischief and the liberties no one else would take – but I am not a holy relic, eh, Anselm? *Anselm.* Aah. How not to think, to unthink two years, but the candles now are birthdays. Ma too. Too ill to tell her about Matthew when she asked for him, but Dada's was a death she could bear, only she whispered, "Never take you eye off the child," calling Dada a word I didn't know, from the old language.

How had I come here? Two years ago that first attack was understandable . . . but why now? And then again, why not? Eighty-two, after all – but made of old iron, the doctor said.

I recall Timmy's hand clamped on the wheel. "They have drive-through pharmacies now," he said. "Nah, don't worry about no money. Mark is stretched, and Judith suddenly a child to raise in her seventies, but Luke and I will take care of it. Don' mind you and me does always get away over stupidness – all that is nothing. Watch. I retire just in time to see you through this thing."

Later, the voices, lapping softly. "Can you hear? You've come through. The operation was successful." Drifting in white sheets until another voice. Ma. No, Judith. ". . . soon be well enough to . . ." *Keep my footing. Hold. Hold her.* The room settling, walls forming to hold up the white ceiling.

"Shanti."

". . . soon you can . . ." Judith colours her hair but the edges gleam white where light shines through. Why, when she is beautiful anyway?

Ma never knew Shanti, but the same eyes. I couldn't stir as she stood by my bed, but in my mind I put my hand in Shanti's and her glance held me – *I am alive.* Bright fiery eyes. "Take care of yourself, darling," I said. The last thing I remember.

Try to disconnect, was what Timmy advised. You can't bring Anselm back and you mean a lot to his child. Don't you die on her too. Another time he said, "Get your mind back to good days – further back, before you were responsible for everything. Try to relax and allow other people to take care of *you.* Get yourself in a positive frame of mind for the procedure."

I forced myself to look out through the car window as we hummed into Port of Spain. *You are eighty-two but made of old iron.* I caught the eye of a well-dressed young man with a rasta hairstyle tied back with a thin black ribbon, and he nodded with a smile of utmost gentleness to the old man I had become. When did this happen? At the traffic light, alongside the car a woman made her way, about Ma's age as she was when Tim was a baby. Things were hard but still the bake was hot and soft and the saltfish cripsy. In the drizzle the quiet-faced young woman hurried by, her hair coiled tight; only the back of her jersey read *Don't piss me off.* I remember how disappointed I felt, irrationally angry, as if I had dishonoured Ma through the brief comparison. Then children in school uniform distracted me, running in and out of shops on the street during school time like crazy ants – but what was this at all?

It was a relief to turn in at the entrance to the hospital. Inside, they were all there, or getting there, except Matthew. Even Andrew was on his way, despite the recession (and he may lose even his house). I had told him not to spend the fare, but Judith said, "Leave the boy to decide. Let go of the responsibility for every breath we take." She added in a whisper, "Or don't take."

So I waved. "Ready for them," I called, and at once it was true.

I settled down and closed my eyes, swept back, back to those days. Children by the grappe – that was what they believed in. Pa set down his enamel coffee cup on the yellow plastic cover for the table and pulled out a paper, untwisting the ends, the children crowding round for red mango. *Tell us about hunting in the forest.*

"One day you will come with me and Dada, boy." But I was afraid, as if I were the one being hunted – or Ma. Her eyes bright, sharp, watchful, as she turned the handle of the jata, grinding finer and finer with an intensity that bewildered and frightened me, her orhni gathered around her, clutched against her throat. She never lowered her guard unless Pa was around. She tried to keep Doolarie with her but that was not her child. If Ma was going out with me she took Judith, and Dada might say, "Leave Doolarie. She is a company."

Ma branched above Judith, delicate sprays of pink samaan blossoms holding on against the wind, hoarding their secrets. Little. I was little. I was at school when the spots came out, measles, so the teacher sent a message for someone to take me home and Phuwa came. As we walked she picked some samaan blossoms from a low branch on the track. When we got near the house I saw a machete stuck in the ground near the door and boots caked with mud. I was at the door before I heard Ma's voice, shrill, "What you doing here? Get away!"

"Ma!" I screamed, letting go of Phuwa's hand, "I coming, Ma."

When I burst in, she was unhurt, standing with her head flung back against the wall, and I could not see all of her face, her arm up, the hand clenched and the sun reflecting from what she held, dazzling, straight in my eye so my head felt it would explode, then the sheer bulk colliding, throwing me down. Phuwa and Ma lifted me from the ground and the samaan blossoms scattered, and they put me to bed. Ma's face was like a mask. Afterwards when I asked her about it she said it was the fever, the fever mix up my head. Was I confused because I was ill, or was it the other way around? I held onto Ma and shuddered for a long time.

When I was better I wrote in my prayer journal, *Lord, please, Lord, don't let Ma ever look so again. Like how animal in the forest must be look when it see the dogs coming after it. Please, Lord.* That is why I could never hunt. Even when I grew up I said, *Lord, for Pa's sake I will help Dada if I can, buy medicine, tell the police I don't know where he is. For Pa. But I want Dada to go away.*

Judith's voice broke in but she was safe. Far from his devouring gaze. "But your face is not relaxed," she said. "Whatever are you thinking? Focus on something good." Calm. Like Ma's face most days. Like Amani's voice. There is a quiet place in my mind where pain has mellowed to a sort of haunting wonderment about how things might have been. Now the tartness of one loss or the other intensifies the flavour of the past and draws me back to it again and again. At times I can almost feel again . . . Amani's lips. And what is wrong with that when this sense of her lingers from before her marriage. A stupid fellow too. What could he have had to say to her mind?

"Something that brings you unalloyed joy," Judith said, her hand squeezing mine insistently.

Right. Whatsoever things are of good report. Pa whetting his brain on a cup of coffee. Whatsoever things are lovely. The generations unfolding. Shanti's hair tumbled around her face and her eyes, what eyes. Flambeaux in the night. She is brought up to move at Anselm's pace, fit and swift. Safe from evil.

Thank you, God, for taking Dada away. If Pa had been alive he would have cried for his brother and I would have stood behind him with my hand on his shoulder and cried too. But I would have been crying for Pa. Around me, the whispers spread like fire in the cane. "After all these years as a hunter, to get shot in the forest, his own gun – you tink that could happen so?" "He interfere with somebody girlchild again," another one muttered behind my shoulder, "and they do for he. That good." I didn't say so though, only, oh Father, that is over.

Doolarie had come to us as a child, little more than a child when she left. She was not there when Dada died. Or perhaps she was gone by then as well? Pa would have said she was worthless, her own father dead and she foot never cross the door, but Pa had passed by then. She came when Pa died and we got her out before her father arrived. He was drunk, Dada was, but people understood; that she was drunk was unforgivable. She sat quietly at the back in the service for Tizzy though she had never known the child, her eyes fixed on Ma, and she cried and cried. Ah, Israel, between the memories of cocoa tea and old talk and laughter the past hunts us sometimes.

There was another woman I never knew, Dada's first wife, and I never saw their son or knew he had a child. The case she brought went nowhere because I had all the papers in order, but one day when the lawyers were talking, I suddenly stopped hearing them and I remembered an essay someone sent. It was a teacher from another school who said I had a niece or some other family in her class and the teachers there thought she was . . . I forget. . . . They sent me something she wrote. Troubled, that was what they said. I was tired – so many children – and it was a day I felt sick. I remember because I am never ill. I threw the essay in the bin, then snatched it out. But I couldn't follow it up. Those years after Pa's death, even eight years later, we were barely keeping afloat. Sometimes one of them is out of reach; let him see about his own children. Sometimes, sometimes when you are tired you, you lose hold and things slip through, things you wonder later if you should have held.

Israel's son was in trouble and I caught him. Not like the first boy – Thump, they called him. What he said was true and I barely stopped them finishing him – but this other one, I held him all the same so he could get through school. The reference for the job too, just like Elroy. One doesn't always know where to draw the line. Kenny - now they say all sorts of things. All the time emergencies coming at you; decide fast. Don't throw away this child. Quickly you turn it around. Then another I didn't know. I had eaten some bad wedding food and was barely getting through the day and they wanted me to read something. A child in another school, *she say she is you family*, but my stomach was heaving, I couldn't make it.

And then Anselm. Gone like that, such a beautiful young man. And wanting only to heal, one vocation into the next, the torture and exaltation of caring about . . . And you did your best, Elroy. I read the lesson; the eulogy would have been too much. *Though the waters roar and foam* . . . But afterwards I fell down. These two or three years since would have been unthinkable if it were not for Shanti. (No, darling. I want my own house. Why don't *you* come live with *me*?) In just a few years she will be Ma's age in my earliest memory and even now she looks at me through Ma's eyes.

Sometimes I thought I glimpsed myself walking another path, along corridors in the vast library of a university, or sitting in a study lined with books and lit by reading lamps over every chair, and my children passing in and out, hovering over me and going again but only for a little while, grown now, successful, with their own families, grandchildren clustering, dancing, asking for stories, and in another chair her face hidden, bent over her own book – aaha. There is music, and we dance. I sing too, not in my own poor voice (nor Griff's, nor Luke's) but the voice I find myself with in this other life I might have had. I have always wanted to dance, I mean dance well (take lessons, you know) but the opportunity did not present itself. A pity. Young people should dance.

Amani? Very well off. She would not have had all that if she had stayed with me. She would have married a man with a whole extra family of children to raise. What if she had? Sometimes the other life I could have had runs through my mind – a wife filling my arms, we could have talked in the long evenings, sons growing up doing well, doctors, engineers, civil servants. I would have done my degree too, theology or literature. Or the law? Perhaps I would have been gone into the clergy. No. Never anything but teaching children. But Amani was rushed along a different track. *Drink to me only with thine eyes.*

I believe I have had many lives offered me and in my mind they play out at the same time along alternative paths that sometimes intersect. I look back fifty years and Pa's dying was such an intersection. One path washed away and I set off along the one without Amani. Every morning that I woke without her was a little death. And yet I wake out of that too, glad to be alive. And she came, did she? When I was asleep. And sat by me a long time. Is that so? I felt it, then thought it had been a dream.

What does it mean? I ask this often. At times there seems to be a band playing, yet beyond the voices and notes I can pick up no melody, no lyrics to grasp, no steps to follow, just noise and gyration. I remember dark trackless nights my mind groped through and an occasional point of light, a star penetrating the tangle but too distant to light the path. Only a sign of which way was up.

Shanti said, "Cell phones are just cool, Uncle Brother. Get with the programme." I was propped up with a book open on my lap when she came yesterday, and rested it on the crisp white hospital sheet to just look at her. She wanted me to watch movies as well as read and she said, "I see I'll have to straighten you out." Her eyes danced and the corners of her mouth twitched, and I couldn't help it, I laughed, throwing up both hands and slapping them down on my knees so the nurse had to come and connect the drips again, though I hardly need those now, thank God.

When I get out, I thought, I shall take up my prayer journal again – I was a child like Shanti when I began it – and later I thought of pulling all the other papers together too, but now I suppose . . . Or has it its own life, unfolding us all along? The light widened, taking in the whole room. Someone. Andrew, aah. He leaned over and kissed me, his eyes filling. "You're all right." His voice broke with relief. They come and go, Luke holding the door frame to support himself, his breathing a little laboured, his hair whiter than mine (what's left of mine). When I woke up properly and made them out they smiled and said, "Look. He's awake. Doing well."

Light, shade and quiet. When finally I breathed easily the equipment was rolled away, the last tube gone. Judith brought me a Dickens I hadn't read, *Little Dorrit*, and she said it was her turn to bring books. Shanti called me on the phone I keep on my pillow. Wheeling away from Intensive Care I rejoiced that I would be able to see her more often, and soon I could leave for the green quiet of my own gallery and the smell of portugals and the sweet Mayaro breeze that heals body and mind.

"You will be home soon," Judith said. "Only, then you must take it slowly."

"It what? What will I take slowly, what will I *do* while getting better?"

She sat gazing at me, through me, into the past. "What about the book," she said, "what you said once, when I was little, about writing a book."

"Ah, no. Wasn't it that I thought I had a book inside me?" She waited for me to explain. "Like the sculptor I read about, reaching down into the stone for the form waiting there. I used to feel there was a book like that writing itself inside my brain."

"About what?"

"Pa, Ma, all we've . . . our lives, you know."

She studied me in surprise. "That doesn't write itself." Then she leaned forward. "You did that."

Her intensity jolted me. "What are you saying?"

"You wrote our lives – or there would have been no story. You wrote us with your blood." She saw I was overcome and she stopped, kissing me. "Too soon to talk seriously. Rest now. We'll see you in the morning."

Thoughts. Dreams. Relivings. Difficult to distinguish. My mind had become a habitation for those gone before and a repository for their voices. Once I asked myself what would remain for me when I was finished taking care of them all, one after the next, and I smiled wryly when it came to me, the word from old-time people: *macafouchette*. Mine is the leftovers of other people's lives. In the same instant, I glimpsed a deeper truth – mine a cumulative life, every one of these others extending my own along myriad different paths. Loaves and fishes infinitely reduplicating – I am a guest at a thousand banquets.

The decades blur into a space I gouge out of darkness. It is formless, then takes shape, the space for each of them, so I too might become. A tune hammered from discarded tin, steel into melody. In the space I defined, perhaps, some version of this story lingered in the limbo of the unsaid, awaiting release.

Every day I grew stronger, with less pain. I would live a little longer after all, I realized. I might even see Shanti grow up. Take care, darling.

At last, well enough to go home. Friday, they promised, September 10.

Not to take me home though. I relive it, their gathering silently round my bed. See again how terrible, this thing they came to say so reluctantly. But there was no other way. I looked into Judith's eyes and although hers are dark I glimpsed Ma's, against the wall, flashing above a blade. I drew a deep breath – feeling, almost wishing, it might be my last – and gave them a look of consent, permission to unloose words like knives.

*Shanti has disappeared.*

I flinched from these words they would have held back if they could, if they could have spared me. Disappeared?

It must have happened during school break. The note was in rough upper case letters:

> WE HAVE THE GIRL. $200,000 BY TOMORROW 2 PM IF YOU WANT HER ALIVE. THE BIG UNCLE MUS CALL HER CELL. NOBODY ELSE TO CALL NO POLICE OR SHE DEAD.

Her face quivered in my mind as I dialled the number, her mouth tightened to hold in the cry she had never uttered at the service for her father. Judith leaned her head near mine, close to the phone.

"Hello?"

I heard a crackling and Shanti's voice trembled so I could hardly make out the words.

"Uncle Brother – ?"

Then, at once, another voice, muffled.

"I can't hear you." I spoke sharply. "I'm an old man and my hearing is not good." Instructions as on the note, and the money to be taken up to the lookout on Lady Young Road. "I am an old man in hospital just out of heart surgery and I have no money," I began, but the voice chopped through mine, menacing.

"You have big family. Ent you brother is the businessman? Talk to you small brother come from America, the doctor. Beg them the money if you want you child alive."

How can they know everything about us? "I'll never get all that by tomorrow, I can't find half of it that fast." I held my voice steady, stern. "Don't be ridiculous. You must give me time."

"Shut up, old man." His voice sharpened. "You ent my teacher. Hear me. How she young and pretty, you better pay fast and get she back. We don't do her nothing yet. But she well nice so don't leave it long. And, old man, don't call no police unless you want to hear they find she head in a bag on the road. When we done wi' the rest – " He rang off.

Judith's face was faded to grey, hollow like the voice in which she began at once to talk about the money. She knew all I had in hand went on the tests and medication, and what little capital Mark could spare after Leela's surgery and chemo had been tied up in my treatment too. But Luke . . . Whatever the mix-up with the real estate investments, this sum was nothing to Luke – the only question was how quickly he could lay hold of the cash.

Luke's colour drained, leaving him deathlike, and his body slumped against the wall. "CLICO," he whispered. "I didn't want to upset you, Brother, so I said nothing at the time. It was only Timmy I told, because he had to take over the full cost of the bypass." I could only stare at him blankly. "It have no time to explain now," he said. "I don't have it. We must get it somewhere else."

Timmy? Tim shook his head. When Luke came to him, Timmy took over the balance of payment for my operation, the sum I did not have in hand – because I could convert property to cash and pay him soon enough.

All I have spent my life building shattered around me. What we needed to save Shanti had been tied up to win a few more years or months for an old man.

They had put together what money and jewellery they had, and showed me there was a bag of cash and fine gold chains and a couple rings. I pulled Ma's thin plain gold band from my small finger and gave them to throw on the pile. The whole of it totted up to a paltry fraction of the sum.

"Griff helped me contact Superintendent de Jacques," Judith said. "He won't come right away in case they're watching us, but he's started work on his own. Then, Griff says he's trying to arrange more money. But from where?"

"Ring them back," I said firmly. "More time." Time to collect my thoughts, which were plunging, racing toward too many dead ends. Rein them in. I called her cell again, but before I uttered a word the man rasped, "Twelve noon. Yeh. Is two hours less, so stop call us, get off you arse and find the money."

Faint under the sudden wash of cold sweat, I inhaled sharply, to stop the shivering, to steady my voice lest a tremor betray me on the brink of pleading, abjectly. Think, think. He too must have something to fear, something I could use.

"Let me tell you what." I whispered, but the chill in my voice must have held him on the line. "We will gather all we can and once we get her back safe, *safe*, it will end there. But if you touch her, if you harm her, we will come for you and everyone connected with you. All of us. And we have family in places you can't imagine. We will hunt you and kill you, but we will torture you first so you will pray to die . . ." My voice disconnected like someone else speaking into the phone, as if the assault has broken in and let out this other . . . thing . . . that shocked me with its ability to dispense with decency and humanity and every other concern except getting back the child. Every obscenity I had never uttered came loose and poured into the phone. "You'll get every dollar we can find," I said, "but be very afraid of touching that child –" I stopped and can't remember what happened for a while.

But I cut off so abruptly Luke thought I might be faint. He pressed the buzzer so a nurse hurried in and took my signs. These were strong, and although the staff set up the monitor again it was only a precaution.

"I cut the connection to assert control," I snapped, "not because I was losing it. We are wasting time."

"No," Judith said. "You are the contact. We cannot risk –"

"Get on with it," said Timothy.

Hours later we had traced every cent we could, read and reread texts they subsequently allowed the child to send, and agonized over each word. Then, who would drop the ransom? It must be Mark, I said. (I thought Timmy might do something rash but didn't say this, and no one questioned me.) And there was nothing to do but wait. Mark said he had to walk a bit to ease his back and the rest went with him except for Luke and Judith.

"What happened, boy?" I asked Luke, and his eyes flooded instantly.

"Oh God, I let you down." From 2001, he said, he had put in a million TT dollars for nine per cent, and two years later he thought of taking out the principal but it was going so well he let it all ride. In a few months he added another million. By a couple years ago he had eighteen million in Colonial Life Investment Co., and began looking around for other options, real estate and so on – we all knew that. He invested a good bit on the town houses. What with the crime situation, everyone wanted to buy into a gated community and it didn't matter about tying up capital because he could pull what he wanted out of CLICO anytime, and it wasn't to say he didn't have money in the bank.

Then last year he saw from the financial slide in the United States that he should spread it out. Only, the sales on the town house project slowed and it was taking longer to make up for the building costs, so he took a loan from the bank using the property as collateral, but then the sales ground to a halt. Yes, it would pick up – but when? That was the thing. And now, while the building project dragged, the costs were going up, the overexpenditure mounting – and that was what forced him to draw the money from his own account, but it was still all right, because of the money in CLICO. "I mean, how was I to know?" he whispered. CLICO was no little fly-by-night investment company. They were into the most lucrative ventures in the country – petrochemicals, that methanol plant. They owned half of Republic Bank, for God's sake. Luke had planned to diversify, but he didn't know there was any rush and the town house thing had become pressing.

None of it made any sense. "What are you saying?" I insisted.

"Brother, you must know CLICO lock-down," Judith began. "No, of course you don't. While you were preparing for the surgery you shut out all the madness going on. You stopped reading papers and watching news."

"What is there to say?" Luke threw up his hands, then ran them frantically through his thin white hair. "They themselves got into investments that didn't work out, but there was more to it than that. Now we hear all kinds of things about the chairman being a one-man board and people close to him drawing in vast sums for their services, or making huge claims they approved themselves." Luke could not explain it.

Mark had come back in followed by Tim and Andrew, but they stayed quiet till Luke finished.

"It mightn't even be true," he said tiredly. "I only know what I read, and who knows the truth of what one sees in the papers? I can only tell you I've worked hard all my life and made . . . a fortune, and I can't get my hands on two hundred thousand dollars."

Where else to look? The room hummed with our frenzy. I could see it, them, the cell phone, all of it, only through the blur of Shanti – bouncing up and down with the tendrils of hair flying like Judith's when Pa put the baby deer on the ground in front of her to stand on slender legs splayed out under it, quivering, Tizzy whirling, Shanti's bright, bright eyes. *Uncle Brother, watch me, Uncle Brother.*

It was almost six o'clock and we had not got the full sum, so it ground down to whether we could get them to accept what we had and return her, or whether to bring in the police. And my yearning to retrieve the child was so infused with rage, I thought, what if this muddles me and puts her more at risk, and how, *how* to deflect the edge of this steel in my heart, so as to think? I forced my mind back to the money. Father Almighty, the money.

The tap on the door was so light I thought I had imagined it, but Timmy sprang up and opened it. Amani stood there supporting herself on a walking frame.

She seemed so frail that Timmy helped her over to my bed. Griff had had his grandson drive him to her daughter's home in Cascade, Amani explained, so he could tell her what he knew. She had been lying down when she heard his voice, and got up at once.

"I know you need cash desperately," she said. She laid down her purse and took my face in both hands. "Everything I have is yours. But they must give us time for me to arrange with the bank. They must. You have to convince them."

As I reached for the phone it tingled in my hand and there on the screen – the words, crowding, darkening, crushing my voice so I could only turn it toward Amani:

SEPTEMBER 10, 2010 – 6:05 P.M.

> *They say htis is only chance I have to write and dont ask more time some-*
> *one esle willl buy if you dont pay fast but no police or oh god uncle htey*
> *say will cut off my haed. Please ucnle can't you*

# CHAPTER 17

# HEADLINES

## Shanti

Nope. Nobody'd see it from the road through the bush and rusty galvanize. Granma J and I passed this place a hundred times, and stopped too, to buy goat meat, only I looked away so as not to see the goats grazing there, waiting. But this was way in from the road. I'd never seen it.

The concrete paving stretched maybe six feet from the post I'd been tied to – for, like, ages. Throughout most of the night before. (Gotta keep track of time, of everything. Uncle Brother would say you never know what'll turn out to be important.) It was, like, forever – this thick post, knotted so I couldn't even lean on it. I tried rocking it but it didn't budge, sunk in the ground, rigid – in concrete, I guess. In front, that was one huge tree cut down but it must've been years now, by the look of the stump. I could sit on that: it was, like, three or four feet wide. There wasn't anywhere else, nothing to drink either. My throat was dry though there had to be a pipe somewhere 'cause there was the hose coiled up that at first I thought was a snake hiding in the brown grass and old rubbish.

I thought of my uniform, if only I had it on, for people would notice a kid in school uniform on a Saturday. But it was stuffed in FD's backpack somewhere in the car because the men made me change into these other clothes they'd brought, dark green and kind of baggy – who knows who had them on before and I just hoped my underwear was enough to have in between; but then, who gave a crap about clothes?

That man who hauled me into the car the day before was the meanest. He was the one who shouted into my phone at Uncle Brother. He jerked his head at me to move farther into the shed, and I backed in but didn't take my eyes off my phone. First I hadn't known how long it would keep going; then they charged it in the car. I never had a car charger but they'd thought of everything. *So they knew what kind of phone I had?* That's the sort of thing that ran over and over in my head, along with the texts they let me send and whether I would get a chance to text again. The first one went early the evening they got me and the next later, I'm not sure when.

It had been dark for a while but I hadn't slept. I didn't, hardly, all night. The mattress on the floor was gross and just sitting on it I was afraid a rat would run over me or something, and when the man grabbed me I forgot rats and the mildew and the dog crap in the corner, and when his weight crushed down the scream choked in my throat, but the bigger man heard and flung himself at us shoving and cursing. I thought they were going to fight and then, *good*, I thought, *I'll run*. I was ready to, but they stopped arguing, and it was after that they tied me.

The big guy who shoved off the other one insisted on waiting in the shack with me. When the thin one came back with the food, they gave me water and Crix and unwrapped the doubles they got for themselves. The smell of peas and curry and oil made me feel sick so I only took little breaths. The shelter was open all around, some broken-down shed, so I could hear them talking outside plain as anything.

"Ratchet, watch me. When day come and you see I leave here, don't touch the girl."

The thin dougla was Ratchet, then. At least, he could be dougla. I couldn't tell for sure what with his close haircut and clean shave.

"You don't tell me nothing," Ratchet said. "Don't try that."

"I say, if we get the money and give she back safe, we go just move on to the next wok. Best we don't make no trouble."

"Hear nah. Counsel, is the last time I telling you: don't tell me nothing. I say shut you arse."

So the dark heavy guy with the plaits was Counsel.

They had let me send the next text before Ratchet went for the food, and after they ate they brought my phone again, but they stood over me studying every word I wrote. Then, right after the third man came and collected Counsel, I got to send another message. Some of the stuff they wanted me to say made no sense but I had to get through to Granma and Uncle Brother any chance I got. I wanted to use my phone so bad it hurt. Like a cramp in my belly.

All morning, once I was on my feet, Ratchet looked jumpy, but I figured I'd better stay out of the shed and I'd just sit on that tree trunk again. The surface of the stump was wide and hard, tough like iron, but it had rough lines cut into the surface and they criss-crossed each other in this pattern I knew, but I couldn't place it. It bruised my bottom through the cloth, but inside the shed I'd have had to stand, or sit on the ground in the dirt. I wasn't ever going near that mattress again.

"I going long out this rope, so you could sit down." He pushed a sack towards me with his foot but he was trying to catch my eye. "You could lie down too." His voice had this smirk in it. He's tall with long arms knotted with muscle but his face is skin and bone, his hair trimmed close so his head is like a skull. When he grins he watches me hard and his hands open and close tight.

I reached out in my head for Granma J and Uncle Brother and I got up and walked as far away as the rope allowed, keeping my eyes turned away from his, but I could feel them, this greedy kinda stare boring through me, and I was glad the clothes were baggy but it was like I could feel him on my skin. I'd stand, that's what I'd do – stand. Easier to run if I got a chance, and I could keep turning round so he never got behind my back. He sat on the big stump and fixed me with this hard hungry look, and that was when I remembered I'd seen him before, through a car window as the car passed the school, him peering in at the schoolyard with the expression people have when they're window shopping.

Then he was up. Maybe bored, I thought, as he walked over to look at the bush. But I realized it was just to pee. He paused while he was opening his pants and looked at me. Slyly, like he wanted to see if I was watching. I turned away just as the light flickered through the bush, what with the breeze shifting the leaves so the sun sort of slanted in suddenly on the cut-off trunk, and then I saw it . . . a chopping block. A curved handle stuck out at the side.

Oh God.

It's for the goats, I tried to tell myself, tried to draw a deep breath but it came in these shallow gasps. The goats. And tried to get my head around around how . . . how to watch everything for a chance to run or, or I don't know. Make a call, make a call. But the man had my phone. *Uncle Brother, you gotta hear me. You gotta tell me how to get out of this. Right? I'm listening, but I'm not hearing you.*

"How you no call?" The man, the shopper – Ratchet, they called him – he was talking on another cell, not mine. "No, Chinksie don't hear nothing. No police come by the school yesterday." Chinksie? Chinksie at school? "Next thing no money nah drop." He cursed violently into the cell. "Watch me. Counsel, I say shut the . . . I say if we no hear soon we have fe clear out. What we doing with she?" He was quiet for an instant, then he said furiously, "What difference it going make? After nobody going know the difference by what leave." His voice changed again. "Alright. Make sure the two of you reach the Lookout onetime."

He stuffed his cell in a back pocket and turned on me, snatched up the sack and yanked the rope off the pole and hauled me forward. Then he slammed me against the block.

"You see this bag?" His face was inches from mine; I could feel his breath. "Is to move you in." He pointed to the axe handle within arm's length and said, "You getting in it quiet or we must carry you piece by piece?"

I stumbled into the bag fast, and before he pulled it up he made me write another text. He stared at it closely, pressed send and grabbed up the axe, and the scream stuck in my throat again as he swung it, but he was only dumping it into the car trunk. He yanked the edge of the bag over my head and jolted it so I dropped on the ground, and I was dragged, bumping over dirt and stone and sliding on grass, then the stones again, my knees legs battering and scraping, and then I was lifted. He pushed the bag so I fell onto the car seat, then he stuffed me down on the floor.

"Get down." Shoved down tight against the seat with a blow hard on my leg. "Squeeze up you foot." I curled up tight in the sack, tucking in my head in case he kicked again, but the engine started almost right away. "I don't put you in the trunk because I want you where I seeing you. You understand? If police stop me and you make a sound, if you move, I putting a bullet in you head onetime. You feel this? Is you head that? Okay, is a gun you feeling."

*Catch your breath and lock down the scream. And listen. Don't even stop to pray; keep your whole mind on him.* The car sped away, bumping over every rut, battering my elbows, knees, my head pressed under the glove compartment, the floor hotting up under my skin and even my mind squeezed tight. I guess I was losing it and kind of whimpering to myself 'cause none of them knew where I was. And someone always had. *Where are you now?* Uncle Brother would ask when I called him.

So I needed to figure that out, or how could I tell them when I got a chance? I had to pay attention to what the car was doing. I could feel the way was north from having gone up and down to see Uncle Brother since the operation. The steady run was along the Hochoy Highway, with less traffic on the weekend. When the car began to stop and start, that was the Uriah Butler and the roadworks. It felt like hours before the sharp swerve that meant we had swung west and hours more to the steep curve of the overpass to the Lady Young. It probably wasn't one hour, but it felt longer with the air hot and thick, and the glove compartment thumping my head over every bump. I tried not to pass out, but got to thinking perhaps it would be better, only then his cell rang.

"What take you so long?" His voice was heavy and sour with distrust. "But it look 'nuff? Is all cash or it have jewellery? What sort of chain?" The car still climbing, the engine changing pitch, my stomach growling, my mouth drying out, and the heat overpowering so it got, like, unreal – a nightmare that had got hold of me. "Where?" He shouted and I jumped and thumped my head again, but it was just Rachet, still on the phone. The car swerved, then braked abruptly and the door on my side opened with a brief rush of air. "Where Ladoo? Whe' the bag? What you do with Ladoo and the money?" But some-one else stuffed himself in, landing his shoes against my ribs, and I cried out.

"Shut you mout. Drive, drive." The man who had just got in was out of breath. Counsel. The car jerked and screeched off. "Don't make so mucha noise. Ratchet, hear what I tell you. Swing round here."

"Where Ladoo?" Ratchet screamed at him. "Whe' the money?"

"Police," Council gasped. "They hold Ladoo and he try to run 'way. They shoot he down and take the money." The car swerved out of control, the driver cursing loudly and Counsel bawling at him to pull himself together.

"We going have to find a place to get rid of she," Ratchet said. "We have to dump it and split up."

"Not yet."

"What bout the teacher at the school, that girl Ladoo was frenning with. Next thing she talk. We have to done this before we get more deeper . . ."

I saw him again in my mind. He sat in the back, behind the man who was talking with Chinksie through a car window. She was talking to the guy I couldn't see except for the back of his head, his hair scraped back to a ponytail.

She turned and smiled as if she was laughing at me, and I thought, *She's teasing me for being shy and not coming over.* Chinksie, my friend.

My stomach churned so I could hardly swallow. I wanted to spit out my saliva but it would be there in the bag with me and that was gross so I swallowed somehow. Counsel was arguing that they couldn't assume the family called the police. "Police must be di' looking Ladoo for that other job last month. When he run they shoot him down. If they was looking for the child they would try hold him and question him."

"You don't know that."

"Ratchet, watch me. Let we hold her and call the family again. Tell them the money gone. They not calling police for we to kill her. They going have to come up with it again."

They drove on and on, wrangling over me. "I tell you, best we drive into the forest," Counsel said. "They go know Ladoo from south. They not looking for us in the east. We go take the turn-off into the forest."

The car bumped along. After a while they stopped and tugged me out and pulled off the bag, then they pushed me on the back seat. My legs were too cramped to straighten out and I crouched there while the feeling in my feet needled back like a million fire ants. When I could raise my head to peep outside I saw we were off the highway, driving uphill. I grabbed the handle but the door wouldn't open, and Ratchet flashed a savage grin at me in the rearview. They had a child lock like what Granma J used to have when I was small and I wouldn't be able to get out unless they stopped and opened the door, but the quieter the road got the more frantic I was to get out and the more afraid of them stopping to open the door. Fewer and fewer houses flew past until even the vehicles passing were few and far between. The car slowed, climbed, trees lacing their boughs overhead, blotting out the sky.

The road fell away on one side but branches reached up from the depths and stretched across to tangle with those from the other side. My head swam, and if I fainted, then what? What? I thought what Uncle Brother would say and I tried to pray but it only came in little screams inside my head and I couldn't concentrate in case I missed something the men said, and I sat upright to keep from falling asleep. *For your chance will come, darling*, was what Uncle Brother would have said. And then Granma: *Keep your eyes open.* On the right hand side of the car the mountain towered above the road, rock and fern, tree roots locked into the stone and the limbs lifted far out of sight above. I knew this road. I'd been on it, but I still couldn't tell where I was.

They stopped to eat, and made me get out the car and stand beside it. Then they handed me a hops bread and cheese with a plastic bottle of warm sweet drink, but I needed to pee so I didn't take more than a sip. Uncle Brother would've told me to eat. I forced the bread into my mouth so I won't faint but the smell of the cheese turned my stomach. I wanted to drink the Chubby but there I was from one foot to the next as it was, so I pushed the little bottle of soft drink in the big pocket of the baggy pants and pulled the zip.

"What difference it going make what we do with her if we not giving her back anyway?"

"Shut up."

"But I say what difference . . .?"

"Shut the . . ."

*Not giving her back anyway.* Ratchet's words tumbled over and over in my head so I couldn't hear anything else. The wee-wee almost got away and my feet kind of gave way so I slid down the side of the car onto the mossy ground.

One of them jumped up but I didn't want to attract their attention.

"Just tired." I managed to blurt it out, leaning on the car door, like I was falling asleep. Because all I could think was, I gotta get out of here, gotta think how to get away. I talked to Uncle Brother in my head, to figure out how to move. I tried to open up my mind into his to work out what he might say, how to get away.

It was easier than I thought. They figured I was too scared to move, and in clearing the food and crumbs out of sight, they turned their backs . . .

*Run!* And I was gone. Slid off into the grass and big leaves, behind a rock, over a bank and rolled down among the vines of christophine and under the mesh cover blanketing one hillside after the next and protecting the christophine crop that climbed on and on. I ran zigzag through the propped-up plant, the hard fruit bumping my head, the tangled vine and cluster of dark and lighter green, and crouched among bags of manure and rolls of mesh and wire and then ducked under the wire and dashed across the road again into fern and broad leaves that climbed up the trees and tumbled down again over the banks. And I lay there, lay dead still under a huge dark green leaf that spread its fingers over me until the shadows began to spread and swallow up the forest, and me, curled in its belly.

## Elroy

"Call this number, Chip-Chip," I told them as they trailed after me from the parking lot into the hospital. "A lady name Miss Judith going to answer and I will tell you what to say."

"Y-Yes, Uncs."

Well, I was really their mother's uncle, but I'm the one they knew from they were born and the one who stayed with them. Before she died their grandmother was always telling them how their mother, Cerise, pushed them out into the world and then the worthless girl rode out without looking back. In truth, Cerise never bothered herself about keeping track of them. My sister, Sylvie, who was their granny, would say she, Sylvie, could never have managed it by herself even before she lost her foot, and don't even talk about that waste of skin, Sinclair, the husband who had left her so as to move on from one younger woman to the next after taking the best years of her life. If it wasn't for her brother Elroy, Sylvie said, the twins wouldn't have had anyone to see bout them. "Then crapaud woulda smoke allyou pipe, oui," she would say.

In the Westhaven parking lot I told the children the message they were to give Miss Judith, and one of the twins dialled and handed over the phone for the more fluent one to do the talking. We didn't realize Miss Judith was slumped in a chair right there in the hospital waiting room with the Black-Berry squeezed up in her hand, as she'd been dropping off for ten minutes here and there from sheer exhaustion since the kidnapping. So by the time the twins got through the door, she was right there, a straight-backed, broad-shouldered lady with all-seeing eyes, who could only be a teacher.

It took me by surprise until I thought about it, but when she reached out her hand to me I squeezed it hard without asking what she was doing there. Even if she had been prepared to drive down the highway at night, going home to San Fernando was unthinkable because the kidnappers were only communicating with the Principal, and then there was the matter of how long the old gentleman would bear the strain. So really, there was nowhere else to be. It was still early anyway, not much after 7 p.m.

I headed up the steps right away, two at a time, not learning until a little later that when Miss Judith reached the foot of the stairs, a harassed nurse asked her if she was the one who would be watching out for the twins.

Twins?

"W-we it is who c-c-call you, Miss . . ."

"We never know you was here already."

She looked properly at the two of them for the first time – small, slight, coffee-coloured, indistinguishable, their voices interlacing seamlessly while the identical pairs of grey eyes studied the tense frame and shocked face of the elderly lady in front of them.

"Uncs give we you number and say call you because we can't stay by weself in the house, and we must . . ."

"D-do w-whatever you tell we."

The nurse pointed out that they could not be left on their own in the hospital, nor were children allowed upstairs on the ward.

By now I had reclaimed my cell phone from them and must have silenced it to go on the ward, so I was not answering, and Miss could hardly walk away from children left in her care. The children told me later that she began making frantic calls on her own phone, the minutes ticking away till someone she called Griff responded. Shortly afterwards, a man in a well-pressed shirt and a tie came out of a door with a sign that read ADMINISTRATION, and said his uncle, Dr Griffiths, had contacted him. Young Mr Griffiths said Miss should take the grandkids with her anywhere she wanted, and he hoped she would forgive the inconvenience.

Miss called the children after her, kindly enough, but she had a dangerous light in her eye by the time she got them up to the waiting room outside her brother's ward, where I was talking on my cell. Once I switched it off, she turned on me.

"How could you walk off and leave these children? The hospital has policies. What were you thinking?"

"Once I get to hear anything I might have to leave onetime," I warned her.

"But what about the children?" Miss Judith demanded. "You're not expecting me to watch children at a time like this."

I raised one hand to silence her (which made the twins open their eyes wide), pressed a button on the cell, listened and said, "Go ahead." Then I turned back to her. "What happen is this: my sister, Sylvie, die last week and I take leave to make arrangements for her grandchildren and them, but it have nothing in place for weekend. Now I just rush out my house when I get to hear this thing, and I dragging these little Chip-Chip round with me all day. They don't give no trouble – once nobody separate them. Watch." I lowered my voice with a glance at the door to the ward. The Chip-Chip kept their eyes fixed on my face. "You see the longer this thing go on, the worse is going to be. From today noon when Mark drop the money, nobody don't hear nothing, so we can't brakes now. I get to know that Mr Israel granddaughter, working right there in the school – she look like she involve. Police catch one of the men – well, they shoot him, and when he fall they hold him and they well beat he, but before he dead he talk a little."

This young woman in the school, Chinksie, had been working with her father. "Someone shoulda stop that Kenny years back," I went on. "I know him from he was a child and, remember, is years he work in the force too. Yes, same Kenny, Mr Israel son. So I drive from Princes Town, where I living, to Mission, where I lose more time again waiting outside Israel house because he still have the set of hunting dog and nobody couldn't hear me over the noise until Miss Annette see and let me in. So then I have to tell him (one) how he pardner family in this situation and (two) how is he son involve. I so sorry to drop this thing on him that I find myself promising that Kenny not going to get hurt, and it have no way I can control that – apart from the fact I mad to shoot he myself." Realizing I was running my hands over my hair, a thing I did when something unsettled me, I took a minute to cool down.

"I didn't like to trouble the old gentleman," I told her, "but I couldn't do better. Mr Israel tell me everything he could, all the place to look for Kenny and people to ask, and I feel was too much for him. He in one state there now – he son in this thing, after all – the truth is I ent know if he go make it."

"Poor Israel." Miss stared at me and gripped my arm. "Don't tell Brother about Israel's situation now."

"But I would never do Teach that. In fact, is that why I talking to you before we go in. I call Doc Griffiths and he say he go sit with Israel while the young fellow (Dr Seepersad, he name?) do what he can. But you can see how I might have to leave here anytime, once I get a lead on Kenny. I prefer talk to him before the daughter, for I feel this Chinksie connect directly with one of the kidnapper. And remember, they say, *no police*." I thought a little, then went on. "Of course, the press have their connections in the force, so don't be surprised if it reach papers by tomorrow. I feel Kenny might talk to me. Remember he brother and me, Leonard and me – we was good pardner. Ent you remember Lenny and Kenny? Right. Years now I keeping away from Kenny, but when I can't help meet up with him we talk good, so I might get something out of he. Hear, nah. I know you ent moving from here, so is that why I say you go see the children for me if I need to run out."

She nodded, but her face was so pale and stiff, the children whispered later that it looked like a wildmeat I had in my freezer before the season closed. The phone vibrated again and I went with it to some notes on the table near the window, while I signalled the Chip-Chip over to her.

I caught sight of one of the brothers, who looked like Miss Judith except his hair was grey and receding from his forehead. He had been standing on one leg with the other propped back against the wall on the other side of the waiting room, looking miserable, but now as Miss Judith flashed a stern look around the room he dropped his foot from the wall and hurried over. Others sat on the few available chairs in the narrow space, asking no questions, just waiting, but you couldn't mistake them. Most had phones in their hands, and I had a good idea of how many others there were in Port of Spain, San Fernando or Mission, landlines jangling, Blackberrys vibrating, connected through Judith.

Now she shepherded the children gently to two padded seats and patted their heads absently. They nodded at her reassuringly.

"It's okay, Miss. We . . ."

". . . g-go s-stay

". . . right here."

She plunged her hand into a roomy bag that looked as if it should have copybooks and whiteboard erasers and she came up with two brown bags, each with a doubles. They accepted them reverently and said, "Thank you, Tantie."

She turned to her family. "The girl they're talking about? Same young woman Shanti calls Chinksie, whose father is Kenny, the policeman Brother always said was, well, dirty. Oh Lord. Israel is indestructible but, Mark, he's Brother's age, eighty-two."

Mark smiled a little sadly. "Washed though," he said. "Blood of the Lamb, and all that. Might still make it."

The children were trying not to stare at an old fellow who had something wrong with his legs and was shifting his weight painfully from one foot to the next.

"Sit down, Luke," Mark suggested, but Luke shrugged him off fiercely.

"I heard all that about Kenny already. Annette called as soon as Elroy left there," Luke said. "She says Israel has taken it badly. Griff had just walked in, but Israel is low. Don't tell Brother, though."

"How many years we try not to tell him things? Makes no sense," Mark said.

"You mad or what? He shouldn't have to know any of it." Luke gripped his sister's shoulder. "I should have been able to do something." His eyes were red.

She leaned forward and kissed him, then waved away a food container thrust forward by another, younger-looking brother.

"It's just a little wonton soup. I told Mark you wouldn't eat doubles," he said.

But she patted his face and turned away. The twins trailed her with their eyes as she walked back towards the door of the ward. She paused there with a slight shrug of her neck and shoulders as if she were pulling on a shirt or a covering, but it was a calm she was drawing over herself so she could live through this trouble. The Chip-Chip glanced at me, then at each other thoughtfully and nodded. Cool lady.

When I turned with her into the room, they scrambled up to follow, and I had warned them so I knew they were bracing themselves for a pale flat form on a bed with tubes going in and out, like on TV. But the bed was raised at one end and although the man propped on it had white hair around a high bald dome, he was broad and solid and swung his head vigorously towards the door, thrusting out his hand to me firmly. He swept his keen eyes over us all, eyes that still seemed to penetrate deep into the far corners of one's mind, to thoughts of which one wasn't fully conscious.

"What word?" It was the same voice, quiet but deep, filling the room.

"We don't know . . ."

"Wait." He held up his left forefinger. "The issue is, what *do* we know? We know they have the money and have not returned her. I know she's alive. Perhaps they're holding her for more money, but we've heard nothing from them. So she could have escaped, in which case we can be sure of one thing – she is hiding."

"And we have to find her before they do." I pondered a bit. "But if she's escaped and is keeping out of sight . . ."

"Then she g-go . . ."

". . . try and reach allyou."

The Chip-Chip had thrust in their thoughts uninvited, but the look Teach shot them was appraising, then lit by a sort of dawning respect.

# Shanti

I couldn't tell how long I'd slept but it seemed quieter, the shadows longer, the forest alive with strange noises. *Stay still.* The tiny needles like ants biting from the inside of my legs were unbearable but still I froze there and the jhunjhuni grew maddening. But, right, no sign of anyone. I could crawl out and make my way alongside the road. There it was cool and shady at first, then dim, and in no time black under the trees, so I clung to the edge of the road. A car flashed by and I hid, then nothing, so I eased out again. Because of the high rocky bank on one side and the steep drop on the other, I had to cross the road sometimes to be sure of shelter to dart into on the way downhill.

Far in the distance I picked up the grating of a heavy engine that could not be their car – a van or something – but I drew back into the bush again till it eventually rounded the corner towards me, and as it came up, the light inside showed the driver wearing a green scarf on her head.

A woman. The relief brought me out to the road under the headlights and I flagged it down so the van screeched to a halt and the woman jumped out holding the scarf under her chin and she was tall and her arm sinewy, the scarf whipping away as she let go of it to grab me, and it was Ratchet grinning at me with a hard fierce grin like a skull's.

"You want a lift, eh?" His hand crunched my arm just below the shoulder as if he would rip it off. "Change of transport, you little bitch."

He shoved me through the back door and Counsel reached round the back of his seat and grabbed, flinging me down on the seat. Ratchet pushed his head in so his face almost touched mine. "You better don't give no more trouble, seen? Or you wouldn' worth keeping alive. Like you want to dead? Don't play with me or I go teach you a next game before I chop you skin."

That snapped something inside me, like a cord that was holding me back. I flew out of control, struggled wildly, biting and kicking till the side of his hand hacked down –

Swimming in my head, Counsel's voice: "You is a fool or what? She no good to us dead." Then I drifted away and other voices swirled round. *Find her, find her.* The clamour and pounding. A nail driving through my temples.

When the hammer slowed to a throb I turned, and the pain was a torch at my neck, sending the burn flaring along my arm till it broke up into sporadic electric shocks down to my right hand. After that I shifted my head a tiny bit at a time, the pain blazing along my arm each time but more briefly. Paper rustled and the men were searching through bags on the back seat as if I didn't exist. This couldn't be happening to me, I thought. As the pain dulled I remembered Granma J watching an action flick with me and giving the hero advice under her breath: *Don't provoke people who are dangerous. Watch them. Learn what you can.*

"You shoulda buy more. It mightn't have no parlour where we going."

"Don't study that. We go get food. Nobody know we here. In south, they know bout Ladoo."

"Ladoo did use to say he school teacher looking quiet quiet you see she there, but *that* is woman for high wind. I wonder how he Chinksie go take the news." Granma never liked her. "But you sure he dead?" Pause. "Eh, Counsel. What happen to you?"

"I studying whether you hit the girl too hard. She small, you know."

"Nah. She could take more than that."

"Lef' that, I tell you. Come. Out the cigarette inside the car. Don't leave no burn mark or rubbish on the road."

After a while they turned off the main road and a while later they backed the van carefully off the track onto a hard level place that curved behind a thick stand of bamboo. They wedged fallen branches and palm fronds round it while they talked about walking deep into the forest, but this time they tied me. While Counsel wiped out the inside, Ratchet fiddled with the knobs till the radio came on with a newsflash, an update on the kidnapping. It threw them into a bitter argument about how the information got out and what happened at the Lookout.

"The news say a tip from sources inside the police force," Counsel said, "but that don' mean the family call police. Like Ladoo didn't dead right away and he talk first; the report say he die of injuries sustained in resisting arrest. That mean they must be beat him to say where he get the money, but the news never say nothing about no money." They switched to another channel and the announcer said the churches had been asked to pray for the child's recovery. Police were carrying out inquiries in the Arima area and would begin searching Blanchisseuse Forest first thing next morning.

"At least they make we know." Counsel stared at the radio like he couldn't believe it. "Eh, eh! Is police fool so, or newsman is we friend?" He laughed.

They pushed some bush aside and sat in the van a bit, running over their choices about what to do with me. One was some . . . some deal. Big business and a lot of money, but dangerous, and they wanted it but were afraid. Counsel wouldn't tell Ratchet much. I could see they knew each other well but they were not friends. *Uncle Brother* (I talked to him to keep my thoughts straight), *that's gotta be a weak spot, right? But where does it get me?*

From what little Counsel said there was something in a clearing under a tarpaulin. If they went there they could get a lot more money for me, or something else might happen.

"Nah," he said. "Not even from plane how the bush thick. It hide, I tell you. Camouflage. Mostly women and girls it have. A few boy."

"How they finding it in the dark? When they get them out from there, where they taking them? How they move them? How it does work?"

Counsel shook his head, but later when Rachet asked again, he shrugged. "Nah van and truck? Container. Boat. How else it go work? It have a man not from here," he continued, "but he can speak English, and then it have this woman. She speak Spanish good, like one of them. She educated, rich."

"Old?"

Counsel refused to say any more. It was not safe to talk about the woman.

"It have food for morning, right?" Counsel asked.

"Ent you just eat?" Ratchet watched his partner sourly. "An you studying breakfast? You shoulda buy rum steada papers."

"You forget police get we money? It have no money for rum yet and we head have to good if we go pull this off."

It had women who came here from away, for the work. He self deal a Venezuelan, Luz, come by boat a year ago. Man in a suit did stop Luz on a street in Venezuela and say he from a employment agency. He offer her a job as waitress in a upscale restaurant with a room of her own and all she could eat. You going work your way up, he say. You might get manager job in the service industry. But now she here like she in jail.

"Nah. It have plenty woman do that from choice."

"This one get ketch and she say is like a jail," Ratchet insisted.

"Then she a fool to talk so with you," Counsel said.

"She run 'way from them."

"They go catch she and beat she. One like that was a Guyanese, oui. Beat she to death."

"How much they would give for one like this?"

Counsel raised his shoulders.

"What they do with them?"

Trade, according to Counsel. Coke, gun, woman. It had man from Colombia and all. But the real terror was this woman.

"You going try make the sale?" Ratchet persisted. "You know which part to find the place?"

"Ent is there I was taking you?"

"What the boss woman name?"

"How I go know that? Like I want to dead?" Then Counsel stopped talking altogether, just slid out of the van holding the light low and began to clear away the bush they had packed round it.

"How I know was Ladoo that really have the money when police come?" Ratchet demanded.

"You see me come in the car with any bag?"

"You coulda hide it. Watch me." Ratchet turned on Counsel furiously. "You and Ladoo think you smart or what?"

"I tell you police have the money. You expect to see that in papers?"

"Let we make the deal and dust it out of here tonight," Ratchet urged, untying me roughly without taking his eyes off Counsel.

But Counsel hesitated. "You see them people who run this thing? If police hold them and get the child, she can describe we real good." They stopped talking and stared at me and in the cool damp of the night I could feel my body turning to ice. "And as how we take she there," Counsel continued, "the woman in charge go say we lead police to she people. Police never going touch the woman who run this thing – but she go send after we. She have a big operation. Is we go get squeeze."

Standing there beside the van with me in between them, they moved straight into another argument it was hard for me to follow even though it was going on over my head. Then Counsel summed it up. "Leh we say we stop now; we getting nothing outa this. And if police find she dead, that going force them to look for we. Watch me. I know the bush, but we can't live in bush forever; and once they put they mind to it they going to track we down. Otherwise, they mightn't bother with one more kidnap case. Leh we keep quiet a little, then contact the old teacher again. If that don't work we could make the next deal, so we still have a sure money. But first we have to find a place to lie quiet." Suddenly he brightened. "Eh! Eh! I have the place. Exact."

They cleared away the fronds and branches they had used to hide the van, and Counsel shoved me in the back but not hard enough to hurt me. *Take note of that.* Counsel is middle height, broader than Ratchet but less muscular, his dark face quiet and watchful, as if this is just about a job to be done. As if there is nothing personal in it, whether he sells me back to Uncle and Granma J, or to the woman he is afraid to talk about.

Ratchet, now – Ratchet is different, powerful, wound up tight. Grinning his death's-head grin.

CHAPTER 18

# LOOSE LEAVES

## Holi

It was late at night before I heard the news, and I thought, Good. About time they lost one that mattered to them. Then, as far as I was concerned, I put it out of mind. But I tossed all night. The same dream. Always the same.

It is the sixties and I am in Form 1 or 2, my second-hand uniform neatly pressed, every pleat steamed straight as I always did it – for who else would be doing anything for me – walking briskly from my aunt's house (which is broken down and hitched back together in its arid yard of dust and leftover rotten wood and irrelevant rusty pans) towards school, squeezing back my toes, which are sore in the outgrown shoes. I can hear her calling after me.

"Holi! I know you hearing me. Holi!"

I ignore her. A dull, sickening pain presses down at the base of my belly. I walk very straight so no one will know, a little weak because this morning I felt too sick to drink even the watery tea she left grudgingly for me on the counter. The bread, carefully wrapped in a paper, is low in the bookbag so the other children will not see, and by the time I get to it, it will be squashed.

In the bookbag is a copybook with my essay. I know the teacher will not be pleased. I did write it the first time as she would have liked. Everything she wanted to hear. Then I felt what I had written like a brick in my stomach, and I struck that out and flung the other sentences at the page.

I have to pass in front the house and try I not to look, but I cannot help it and the old woman is sitting as usual on the gallery in a rocker with a small child on her lap. It is a big house, the front of the yard a riot of colour, brilliant leaves and flowers spilling over towards the road. On either side a small space between walls and fence reveals lush green, a bush bowed down under tomatoes but, above that, and even rising above the house itself, trees bearing breadfruit, mangoes and other things I cannot make out, trees burdened with fruit.

Suddenly I realize I have stopped, as I always do in my dream however hard I try to avoid it, and I glance up. The woman on the gallery peers down and smiles, her eyes sparking, and she holds the child's hand to make it wave. "Watch, dou-dou. Anzlem, see? It's you friend. She does always stop and watch at you. Wave to she again." She kisses the child and pops something into his mouth. Leaning back in her chair, she reaches for a glass with some chocolate drink, swirls the ice and takes a sip. She strokes the child again and juggles it on her knees, then puts the glass to his mouth.

A hot gush of feeling turns me aside and drives me on, hatred churning in my belly. I loathe them for sitting there idly plastering themselves over each other and nibbling this and that. Fury propels me forward to a time when I can wreak justice on them one day, one day I will come back I will rip it all away, one day I will have it all. All. Although they don't even know my name. They don't know it's the same name as their own.

Aunt said I was born February or March. No one remembered precisely, only it was during Phagwa, which some people called Holi, so my grandmother said, "Best we call this child Holi." The contractions began when my mother pushed through the crowd trying to find a car to take her home while people around her splashed abeer on each other and it spattered and ran down her face, staining her clothes. It took a long time to get home and when she did no one was there. When her mother came, shocked to find her huddled on the red and pink cloth, it was mostly abeer rather than blood; but it was only the little scrap of life that survived, the baby itself that was bloodstained and with all this my grandmother eventually said, "Call she Holi, nah? For the timing if it." But at the time she just bawled and bawled over my mother's body, bawled that she child dead there by sheself. She picked me up and cried out to anyone who might hear, "Oh Gawd, O Gawd! See if anybody could find the father self." My aunt was there and saw the whole thing.

At school most people pronounced my name Holly and when I tried to correct it the children sniggered and asked if I really thought I was holy, and in between squeals of laughter one of them said, "Nah, but she get the *ho* part right, ent?"

I wake and the emptiness remains, even though the cold void filled gradually with poison seeped up from the past and with all I accumulated as I laid hands on more property, more money than the whole of them were worth put together. After a while I drew on the employment agencies I had set up, so as to network the firm's capacity for recruitment and extraction of girls from Venezuela. So now the unprotected children were all mine; I could make them into whatever suited me or ship them away as I liked. In my mind I flung them back in time whether to mines or chimneys or factories for pesticides, to brothels or rich households as child brides. But in fact I owned and distributed them as I pleased. I expanded the business to include transport services for supplying labour. We churned out the very containers of all sizes, from those for heavy equipment to smaller ones for large pets like Labradors, and I dispatched shipments to Latin America. I draw all this up in my head whether I'm in my bed or at my desk or driving in traffic. I just draw it up.

But I was lying down exactly like this when it happened, when my aunt's house fell. Afterwards, the mud sliding me away from under the splintering wood, I crouched there in shock and no one came to see where life had dropped me. I waited and waited till long after it was light, but no one came.

When I eased my arms and gradually my whole body out of the mud and grass and debris and cleaned myself, washing out the taste of mildew from my mouth, I walked around the deep sink in the land into which most of the house had slumped. I found my aunt sitting on the neighbour's step sipping lime-bud tea and contemplating the cave-in, and she looked up and watched me contemptuously. Then she steupsed.

"But everywhere this child find sheself – is confusion. Watch how she mother dead making she, and she father do for heself. You could say she kill she two parents. You could say that, oui. I see she on the bed bawling after my sister dead. Then she grandmother, too, gone madhouse. Is my mother, and I see she in the madhouse, and I know when she dead same place. I tell you this child is confusion. No wonder my house fall down. She is a blight, I tell you."

I built my life on my own. I did it all by myself. I fed the entertainment industry with personnel for sex tourism, while the printery churned out staff evaluation forms and business reports, and between them passports, birth and marriage certificates, visas, and drivers' licences. I built a culture of strong work ethic and insisted on the firm's participation in social action, so I could penetrate antislavery groups and, through the hotline, intercept complaints and reports. I fostered police cooperation and paid for competent legal advice so as to block legislation, protect the privacy of our end consumers and officially deny the existence of human trafficking. That is how I did it. Innovation after innovation contributing to the transformation of the country into a hub, a transition site. First I did it all in my head; how much of it is outside of my head now – well, that's my business.

But in those old days all I had in my head was my aunt's voice: "You bring this down on us. Is you. Get up make tea and go school make something of youself. Perhaps you will find a wok and do something for me for a change. Get you tail out the house."

*Make something of youself.*

The business community cheered when Payne Enterprises won a prestigious award for innovations in human resource development and expansion of traditional marketplace rules, when Payne funded the award of a special postgraduate scholarship for researching HIV risk in the transhipment of human cargo.

And I am Payne.

I fight sleep but sink into it struggling, drowning in the dream that surges back and closes over me again. The rotten house in Piparo is behind me and the mud washed off and in front of me is the big upstairs home that is not mine, and I walk on away from that house too with the old woman and the baby boy and my mind slashes out at them, but for the present (this present I have gone back to) I can do nothing have nothing am nothing, and this crippling nothing of my life gapes like the empty wound of my belly.

This was what I had felt when I rewrote the essay for that day's class. Using my ruler I drew a neat diagonal line through the first essay, about the day in Mayaro with sliced ham and potato salad, and I put in the new one. It wasn't anything as long as Miss would want it to be, one paragraph really (an un-essay).

> Assignment: Write an essay ending ". . . so I will never forget that holiday with my family".

> *My family is a large rich happy one and they all stick together because my big uncle, Principal Deoraj, took care of the others when their father died. The family celebrates birthdays and Christmas and weddings, and holidays are fun. My*

*grandfather spends his days and nights celebrating, and my big uncle and his sisters and brothers and their children often meet at one of their houses. My mother and father and grandmother are all dead but I have enough family members to make up for that, only I am not inside the family but outside and no one knows I exist. So because I have never had a holiday with my family I will never be able to forget that holiday with my family.*

After a swift glance back at the gallery I trudge on, knowing everything that child has should be mine, feeling the bellyache sharpening. Then. An instant of realization. It is more than hunger – I've lost count of the weeks. I search my mind frantically but I have nothing I can use, no washrag, nothing I can fold and put in my underwear, the ragged panty my aunt handed down and I knotted at the waist to prevent from sliding. I wake, and I remember the essay was real and the teacher brought the ruler down on my hands and asked me if I thought I would pass a test with that. And she said she knew Principal Deoraj because he had taught her and she would show him what I had said. Then I fall asleep again, and again the decades drop away and the dream resumes. I'm almost at the school gate with the impossible essay and the bellyache knifes me in the gut and it's coming down. Over and over I do a mental inventory of my bookbag for something absorbent and I come up with nothing.

Except the bread.

# CHAPTER 19

# QUOTATIONS

## Shanti

They had driven for a while after hearing the newsflash and quarrelling over the next step. By midnight or after, they had gone well past the sign that said BRASSO SECO and turned the van so it pointed as if they had been going to Blanchisseuse. Then they stopped and opened the bonnet, fiddled with something, left the van on the side of the road and walked downhill on the bank (wherever there was a bank) with me in between, keeping under cover as far possible. Counsel laughed over the idea that police would be searching the forest, find the van and waste time, while he and Ratchet were getting farther and farther away with me.

"But what if they done find the car already?" Ratchet grumbled. "Like you never think bout that."

"Nah." Counsel was sure of himself. "Ent they woulda tell we on the news?" Granma J would've called him cocky; and she'd have been right. Again. Ratchet glared at him, his thin mouth set in an unyielding line. They were walking with me behind Counsel, and Ratchet following. An hour or two along the dark road and overhanging bush they came to what looked like a rock jutting forward under vines and leaves and stuff, and when they hauled aside the branches it was the original car.

"O ye of little fait'," Counsel said boastfully.

That was just so gross, them quoting from the Bible.

"My family will kill you." I couldn't believe I said that. It was crazy but it made me feel free again, and strong.

"What family you have?" Ratchet said. "Set of ole people. You don't even have no father."

"Don't talk about my father."

He looked at me, eyes narrowing, mouth tightening. "You father was no better than . . ." He didn't finish because I lunged at him, screaming, "I'll kill you, I'll kill you. Don't talk about my father."

But Counsel grabbed me, his fingers biting into my ribs. "Shut you mouth. You forget where you is or what."

And my body slumped down, I couldn't help it, it was like someone else's body. I fixed my eyes past them at the trees but I could hear myself whisper, "My big uncle will find me."

Ratchet went very still, and grinned. "Oh yes?" He pointed to the car radio and hissed, "Uncle dead, baby girl."

"No."

"Ent he was in hospital? Intensive Care. Right. He get a stroke and dead. Was on the news earlier this evening when you sleeping. Well-known Mission Principal dead of stroke."

*He's lying.* But then, I did fall asleep for a few minutes. How do I know?

"And the other one, the rich cripple, like he ent care too much bout you. That mean we going have to collec this money from you grandmother. So tell we: Granny have jewellery?"

"Not much." All I could think of was whether Uncle Brother could be dead.

"So what she spend all she money on?"

"Books. She has no money; she's a teacher."

"Granny can't help you?" He threw me a look of disgust as if I was worthless and he was sick of me, and something in my belly turned over.

"Yes," I said. "Yes she will sell things, everything; just give her a chance."

He looked more interested. "What she have to sell?"

"The car. The house, the land. She'll sell it, she'll sell everything she has to get me back. There's money my father made over to her before he went into the Church, what he put aside to get me through UWI."

A long steups, and he shoved me aside, but Counsel steadied me and pushed me into the car. That might have been one or two o'clock. I was in the back again as they headed on down until they came to an intersection and turned. It was just darkness and bush flying past till, eventually, the forest opened out, and after a while I could glimpse the sea for the sky was clear. Counsel kept nagging Ratchet because he wanted us to get where we were going while the weather was good. Then the road seemed familiar again and of course in the end I could hardly miss the lighthouse.

We left the car while it was still dark, and they hid it again, this time on a path that curved round behind a small house Counsel said was empty because the man had gone to Venezuela. They hauled the axe out the trunk and used it to chop bush and conceal the car in case anyone bothered to follow the rough driveway, and they tore down a few leafy branches to brush out the tyre marks in the dirt. Once they heard a car approaching on the road and they flicked off the torchlight. Soon they were ready to walk again. But I had to reach Uncle Brother, even if for an instant.

"Can I send one last one?" My voice was thin and raspy so I could hardly recognize it. It's what happened every time I saw them with the axe. But if I could just write him something I knew my throat would stop clenching up.

They handed me the phone and watched me write. My hand shook so I could hardly press the buttons.

SEPTEMBER 12, 2010 – 3:45 A.M.

> They let me send one more raelly last one Uncle Brohter they have me ereh . . . help me Ullni they say money no police or they willl do it like htey said they have an axe

Counsel read it again and nodded, so I pressed send.

Uncle Brother will find me. There are some they never find. But Uncle Brother will find me. Uncle Brother takes care of children. I am all that is in his mind now and he's thinking and thinking and he will . . . he can't be dead.

They walk on, forgetting I still have the cell, and I know I have to do something with it fast or this will be the last text. Really the last. They haven't charged the phone enough.

Then it goes.

"What?" Counsel looks back sharply.

I must have made a sound, a sob or something. "Dead. My phone's dead." Ratchet snatches at it and flips his hand in disgust. They walk on, one in front and one behind, watching the path, and my hand cramps round the dead phone. I push the back with my thumb and slide out the chip but I can't see what I'm doing in the dark with my hair falling over my face. I stick the phone under my arm so as to box the fringe back and clip it all up tight with the chip inside, using the same grip Granma J bought me at the school bazaar, but I can't tell whether I got the chip in safely or if it's dropped out. *Granma J? Uncle Brother?* I kept feeling around for them, in my head.

As we walk on, the mangroves cluster close around and the ground gives soggy under our feet in places, so Counsel makes us go carefully to avoid leaving tracks. He's been searching for the way and Ratchet is getting irritable again. After a while the ground hardens, firm but uneven, and the mangroves fall behind so there is only hard dry bush. Now Counsel has found the path he wanted, and they shove me along faster, Counsel with the sack they moved me in earlier (only now he has other stuff in it), Ratchet carrying a bag with food, keeping the light low to show the surface and sides of the trail.

"Out the light," Counsel says.

Now we can see our way in the grey light. The steep rough path has brought us to a point where Counsel leads us down, climbing and holding bush and rock, to this shore with the water pounding the edge, and the sun is coming up so a small island just across the water looms dark against the sky. But, in between, now it is lighter, and a strange pale line of tumbling sand and stone under the water leads from the shore into the sea. They push me towards it, but I stop as the water sucks at my feet. Ratchet shoves me forward.

"No," I whisper. "I can't swim."

"Watch," Counsel says, taking the phone from my hand and throwing it to Ratchet. "This not going reach above you waist. We can take you back and leave you with the set of them in the forest. That is we backup plan. But if you behave youself and you family send the money, you could get to go home. If that is what you want, we cross here and stay quiet."

"Can't go into all that water. I can't."

"Is shallow. We go walk over. Move." He pushes me hard, towards the waves surging forward from both sides and meeting over the place they want me to walk, but that's underwater and the waves smash together, stones giving underfoot and the foam swirling, the sea stretching away each side, deepening from pale to dark, stretching back forever, tearing in and along the shore, crashing on the rocks, boiling, sucking, ripping forward, churning the loose stones under foot, sweeping my legs from under me.

# Elroy

Most of the others had left the hospital the night before and I was alone with Miss Judith in the waiting room when the old Principal shouted, "Oh God!" That was when he got that last text, early Sunday, long before daybreak.

Luke had taken a room in a hotel nearby and I had sent the twins with him, so they heard it all on the phone when Judith called because Luke had mixed up the buttons and had it on speaker. He and the children get to the waiting room just as we are coming out of the ward.

"He's stable," she tells her brother, "and calm. He knows he has to hold on. They've been able to take off the drips again." Her back is straight and her voice firm yet something in her face makes her look stretched thin as if only a little more pressure would make her transparent and a little more again might make her vanish altogether. "What does it mean, Elroy? The child is writing as if they're still waiting on the money."

The question I had been hoping she would not ask. "Leh we focus on how to find her," I said. But Judith has no other lead to offer. "It had some altercation recently with that fellow who accuse Anselm?" I asked. But we have nothing to connect that with the kidnapping. "This child keep a diary?" I persist. "She make up stories? Anything so?" Judith has searched her laptop, her essays, everything. But I keep probing. "It have a teacher who would have more of her work? What the child hand in and don't get back yet?"

"The youngster she has this year hardly sets work." Miss Judith lifts a shoulder at the work habits of a new race of educators. "Her form mistress is excellent but teaches Maths, so that won't help you. It's Brother who has been guiding Shanti with her writing." She turns back to the ward with me. "He sees some on weekends and the rest she reads him over the phone."

"You have them, Uncle?" I ask the Principal.

"Naturally. Send in Tim or Mark." He gives exact instructions regarding boxes of papers and the youngest brother leaves at once. "Meanwhile," he continues in a level voice, "we start finding money again."

"I already spoke with Amani," Judith answers.

# Shanti

Light, even through my closed eyes, a reddish glare. Someone carrying me curses and I jolt to attention. The sun is higher and the waves crash around us, sending a shower of salt water over my hair. I can't help squeezing my eyes shut in the spray, and the darkness seals off everything for a moment except their voices.

"I tell you this thing not working. Is not looking good. Leh we get rid of she and dust it."

Two hundred thousand, Uncle Brother, can you get all that? How, when you're in hospital? *Listen, I am just as afraid as you are,* Uncle Brother said once, *but that is why Granma says you must take the swimming lessons. You won't need to be so afraid if you practise in Uncle Tim's pool.* But this is not a pool smashing together from each side. On the school outing Miss pointed. "Where the Caribbean meets the Atlantic," she said proudly, as if she arranged it herself. We laughed at her then but now I wish with all my heart she was with me.

My face, flopped over his shoulder (it is Counsel carrying me), sways above the water that races forward from each side and clashes together hurling foam into my eyes and nose. My stomach heaves but I force it down because if I vomit the man might drop me. I groan and try to keep my eyes open, swallowing hard. The water surges forward again and swamps me. In the dizziness my stomach heaves and darkness rushes up.

Shade, sand and a smell of salt, and waves battering rock. A shack with bush surrounding it. Beneath me is sand, not concrete, and in the clearing there is no block. The flood of relief makes no sense; they don't need a block to . . . to . . . As my mind clears I see the shack itself is only a shelter of coconut boughs on a rough frame fixed between almond trees.

My clothes stink. I must have vomited after all, perhaps as I lost consciousness. The axe leans on the wall; they brought it all this way. Even if the money is paid, will they . . .? I edge past it to the corner where there is a bag of food and my backpack with the school uniform, and I manage to slip into the cleaner shirt. Then I walk out from under the shelter and they stare at me.

"I want to wash my face in the sea." I say it to the trees and the sky, not looking at either of them.

"Nah. Take a bath, young girl," Ratchet says in a soft creepy voice. "I go help you."

"I'm just washing my face." And Counsel says, do what I want. There's nowhere I can go.

On the shore where the waves swirl up I sink down at the very edge and soak myself, clothes and all, keeping just my hair out the water. The sun is hot now, drying me off while I try to look as if I'm paying no attention to them, sifting the sand through my fingers, and picking out the tiny shells of minute creatures. Once in a restaurant Uncle Brother ordered chip-chip cocktail made from these and I tasted it from his spoon.

We are far from everywhere so the men argue boisterously. "Once she get back safe it go cool down. But if they don' get she back *then* they go study come after us."

"Watch me." Ratchet's voice is a snarl again. "You fraid the old teacher?"

"You is a fool or what? You don't see the whole country raise up? Police can't drop that so."

Ratchet starts up as if something in what Counsel said reminds him. "You tell the man to carry the next note?"

"He getting it drop tomorrow." Before Ratchet can explode again, Counsel says, "By tomorrow Monday, when they ent hear nothing today, all day, they going be so glad to get that note they go pay fast." He considers. "Let she send a last text. You think it go have signal out here?"

"How many last text she go send?" But in the end Ratchet agrees. He had the phone last and searches his pocket. "Must be drop in the water." Then he remembers. "It didn't have no charge anyhow."

My phone. Floating, sinking. Granma J and Uncle Brother drift farther and farther away. I had been terrified before but not quite lost. Now . . . . Counsel stares at Ratchet as if he cannot believe his stupidity. "The girl phone? Hear me. You throw away the phone?" He is boiling over, but manages his voice. "So what going make them feel she alive now? Hear me," he continues, keeping his voice level. "Once they say she dead it have no money in that – only police. Of course, it have police and it have police. Chinksie father done arrange for a crackhead to drop the next note."

"So he text you? Why he never text me?" Ratchet fidgets more and more as the sun gets hotter and the breeze dies down. "How long you think a man going sit here with nothing to do?" He flicks away the sweat pouring down his forehead and glares at Counsel. "Why you don't contact the Spanish man and done this thing. They don't quote no price?" They begin to compare figures, but my mind hitches on the idea that the people in the clearing are more likely to keep me alive. Only then I may never get back.

Back. No one will come for me here.

I sit on the edge of the sea, the light dancing on water, and it occurs to me that I have to get back across it somehow; unless I stay here for my whole life I must cross back, and can I be sure of blacking out again so they carry me. *Unconscious? In their hands?* But at the thought of physically walking across on the submerged path I cannot even make out in the play of light my stomach lurches and I crumple, emptying everything from it and straining until only a rush of acid floods my mouth. Suddenly my insides settle down and I can think. *Listen.*

"But how you know bout here?" Ratchet is asking.

"Nearby I grow up. Hear nah, is me find food last time. You have to go across just before night and come back tomorrow evening."

"You mad? Where you expect me to sleep?" Ratchet is furious but not as frightening as when he smiles.

"You is a child or what? Watch me. Is evening to walk across if you don't want people to notice. Then place go be close for the night, especially since is Sunday. Time they open back is bright day and anybody watching can see you cross. You have to go tonight, buy tomorrow, come back tomorrow night. Simple." He brushes aside the money Ratchet pushes on him to go for the food himself.

Eventually Counsel says they can go together because it have nowhere for me to run except into the sea. Why has it taken them hours of wrangling to work that out? With the afternoon wearing on, even under the almond tree I have to close my eyes against the glare, and I cn just see the whole thing, see them crossing, accusing and cursing each other the whole way till they are out of earshot. And now the sky is overcast and no change in colour marks the way any more, as far as I can see, only the spray and foam of water meeting and falling back. I back away and huddle in the shelter.

I'm . . . I must have slept. But I'm drenched in sweat. A dream so horrible I cannot . . . think it. Much less say . . . tell . . . I seem to have been choking, and struggle to draw and catch breath, suck the air in, painfully, as if a hand squeezing my throat has just relaxed. A quarrel and scuffle – they are always quarrelling, more and more, but they never actually fight, only scream nastiness at each other, never actually take hold of each other like this, and they're wasting time, wasting it when they have no choice but to go and buy the food.

This time it began with Counsel losing his temper. "Barbeque? What the arse you think this is? Ent smoke going announce it have people here? Meat, you say you want. Meat is what go leave of you when police come and shoot you up like they shoot up Ladoo."

"What it is you say?"

Counsel can't stop. "They should bust two shot in you head for true, make me collec the whole money." And the other man's face hardens; his eyes turn up and his hands twitch, open and close. Wrong answer.

Now Counsel cannot turn back, he has gone too far; those words are the edge of the blade that severs them once and for all. Ratchet lunges at him – he is fast – but Counsel is heavy and pushes him back. They grapple with each other until Counsel pitches Ratchet to the ground. They fight brutally as if one must finish the other, and the sun sets, blurring their thrashing arms and legs. In my dream they tumble on the sand that grows red in the evening till it turns dark and everything is still.

I cower in the shelter as their silence seeps out around me and listen for Uncle Brother. *Whatsoever things . . .* Till I must have fallen asleep for, when I open my eyes again, everything is peaceful and I see they have left me here alone on the island.

# Elroy

When Tim turns out the box on the table, I set the twins to work using my regular formula.

"Come here, you little Chip-Chip, and chip in," I tell them. "The girl family pay the ransom but they don't get she back yet, so now we looking for anything it have in the Principal papers about the girl, where she like to go and who she talk to and everything." I tell them how when the Principal was my teacher, every essay had to have something in it from real life. "So children does write down all kinda thing."

They start at one end of the table and I start at the other, and everything I read, they read over again.

"Weei, watch at paper it have here!"

"You s-see this? It g-go . . ."

". . . take all night. What she name again?"

"Sh-Sh-Shanti."

# Shanti

Night crowds close with its strange sounds and silences. A bush crackles near at hand and erupts as a bird flaps away, but what disturbed it and what else is here and how it will be if they do not come back? Or if they do. Get rid of she an dust it. But what if I get left alone on this little pile of rock and bush? With the one packet of cheese balls and the Chubby soft drink. Alone with the water all around. What if they don't come back?

A few coconuts lie there beyond the edge of the shelter. It was different for Tom Hanks in *Castaway*: he had a real island with rivers – fresh water, not half a Chubby. In the school outing my Teacher pointed to the crash of sea and ocean – we could see it even in calm weather – and perhaps if I wave frantically when day comes, a piece of palm or my shirt or something, someone might notice. But no. Term has just begun; no school outings yet. From inside of my head among all sorts of stuff Ratchet's long sidelong stare rakes me and his lips twist into a grim smile, and I am more afraid of him than of the sea.

My head swims again, the dizziness building to nausea. They will curse and fight each other again and this time one of them will win. Inside my head the darkness swirls and a hot gush down my legs shocks me with my own helplessness. I am too big to wet myself but I couldn't stop it, couldn't, it just came down.

I've been squeezing even my eyes shut and now I open them and I am lying on the sand and the sea creeps up and washes down my legs. How did I get here? It's early, sky, sand and water streaked with red, and although I don't know when I left the shelter or if I saw them go, I know I am alone. I must work it out: it is Monday, the third day since they took me away. And I might never get back.

Some things you try to lock out your mind. *No. Try to look at them.* Only one way: to walk across. By myself. Before they return.

But what if I meet them coming back for me, coming back to take me to the Spanish man, to the terrible woman. Or coming back because I'm worth nothing after all. What if they meet me on the way and throw me off into the deep rough water, or pick me up and bring me back? What if Ratchet comes alone. *Uncle Brother, say something.* The thought of the path under the waves swirls in my head but I must must steady myself for already the sun is moving higher. I'm not under the shelter any more – I don't even feel as if I'm under the sky, for now when I look up away from the sea there is only emptiness stretched over me, and when I turn back to the sea, clouds are gathering above it so even the sky churns and foams. Now the water is sullen grey. Uncle Brother would understand because he is afraid of water too.

I squeeze my eyes shut and search for his thoughts in my mind. *Eat something.* I can't. But look at the sun – past noon already. *Swallow something and put the rest in your bag.* I nod even though my head swims when I open my eyes. I hear him reading the lines rushing in and out of my mind, like the waves, in and out, *'Twas vain: the wild waves lash'd . . . 'Twas vain: the wild waves lash'd the shore . . . Return or aid preventing . . . The waters wild went o'er his child . . .* My eyes sting, tears welling and blurring the lines I try to pick out, as I wander, back and forth, to and from the edge of the water, finding my bag and swallowing bits of stale hops bread and putting away the rest, back and forth. How long have I been back and forth along this shore, searching the sea for the path of pale stones that will get me home.

# CHAPTER 20

# SCREENS

## Elroy

Jammed up tight with me, the children have gone through the stacks of paper Tim brought up to the waiting room.

"Oh Gorm. How one man could keep so mucha paper."

From back when old Teach self was going to school. Set of old book with no cover; must be too mash-up to keep on the shelf. Inside one was written *A Tale of Two Cities*; another *The Cloister and the Hearth*. One so breaking up more when you touched it, and it had writing nobody could read. खोया

Then letters from Andrew, thanking Brother for roti that reached London and money for books. Papers like that were crumbly and spotted brown. Then things Teach had put together: *Lesson Plans. Fireside Tales. Jokes for Wedding Speeches. Prayer Journal.* And another set of papers: *Medical: Luke; Judith: Letters from London; Essays.*

"I think I'll rest while you do that." The Principal closed his eyes early in the proceedings, businesslike, as if sleep and wake come under things he could decide on for himself.

While I pull out everything that has the name Shanti, the twins jump at a sound behind them and realize the Principal is snoring.

"That is the man you dealing with." I shrug and go on drawing out more papers with what anyone can recognize as the girl's handwriting.

Soon I have the pile narrowed down to about twelve papers, along with copies of the messages she sent since she went missing. The children huddle close by, reading over my shoulder that last one that came in in the wee hours of the morning. *They let me send one more raelly last one Uncle Brohter they have me ereh . . . help me Ullni . . .*

"Uncs, who name so?"

"That text send to her Uncle, but she have a condition that affect how she spell," I explain. "The stress and thing would make it worse again."

Luke has been watching irritably as if he expects that the children will somehow distract me from what I have to do.

"Children pick up all kinda things we miss, ent?" I toss the idea to him gently and he relaxes a bit.

I scrutinize the other papers, the children now sitting aside and working on a package of salt prunes Mark produced. Judith has drawn up what record she could of everywhere Shanti has gone for the past six weeks – every visit to Gulf City Mall, their dentist in Chaguanas, the vet who was treating Road March for mites, the neighbours' prayer meeting that Shanti had rebelled against but ultimately been forced to attend.

"Parent-Teachers' meeting and all?" I ask.

"How was I to leave her at home?"

The twins argue on by themselves.

"But w-why she s-spell it so?"

"They say she does spell funny," the other one said.

"But is *not* s-so she does s-spell."

I lift a hand that halts Judith's parallel conversation about Shanti's movements and raise my eyes from my notes to focus on the twins. They chatter on, ignoring us.

"No. She have a reading problem. She bright but she have a way . . ."

". . . she does sh-shift l-letters but . . ."

"You mean, where the *n* and the *c*?"

The old teacher props himself up in the bed, his eyes riveted on the children, but they tug at my arm.

"Uncs, how you know this not . . ."

". . . a n-name?"

"I know it's not her uncle's name," I tell them.

Now they pick up an essay. "This have her name, but is not her writing." Across the top was written, "Essay by Cell."

"Teach's writing," I say right away. "I could never forget that handwriting in my whole life."

"I help her with her essays," the Principal says. *"By cell* means she read it over the phone and I took it down." Which explains the perfect spelling. It was about a school outing to a national monument, and Teach had written "Fine use of quotation" at the end but it was good right through.

*We drove and drove through the mountains, then along the coast. Then we began to walk. The track had thorny bush on each side and the sound of water pounding the rocks.*

In the other essays the spelling is odd, like the spelling in the text messages. Not just wrong, but strange. The twins read the one Teach took down over the phone, to the very end where Teach had noted "good use of quotation". They exchange glances and nod wisely.

"That is because it have . . ."

". . . a p-poetry."

"*'Twas vain: the loud waves lash'd the shore.* . . ."

And I interrupt them, continuing, *"Return or aid preventing.* . . ."

The children stare at me as if I am suddenly talking in riddles, but Teach had made me learn that poem when I was their age and had shown the class pictures of purple mountains and lakes big enough for storms.

Judith closes her eyes and she too draws up the next lines from some deep place. *"The waters wild went o'er his child. . . . And he was left lamenting."*

And suddenly Teach is bolt upright, his face alight. "Toco."

The whole of us stare at him, lost. Judith pronounces, "Lord Ullin's Daughter," but she is still puzzled.

Then it breaks, blinding bright like sun on galvanize, the child with the stammer wasting no time trying to get the word out, just pointing at the mangled spelling in the text message: *Ullni.*

While I grab my phone, I shoot a glance at Teach for confirmation. "Toco she went to for the school outing in the essay?"

While I dial, the Chip-Chip nod triumphantly.

"Wasn't no spelling of *Uncle.* Was *Ullin* she mean to write."

"*Lamenting.*" Judith fixates on this one word.

"Don't study that," I say to her. "What this means is that your child is alive." I catch them up and sweep them along. "This means that last text is genuine, nothing they could just make up to get more money when they done kill her." I stop to answer the expression of dawning horror on Judith's face. "Oh yes, that was very possible. All that time she could very well have been dead. But she was trying to tell Teach something – I know a smart child *must* try to send a message." I rub the head that has burrowed under my arm to peer up into my face.

"Where to l-look, ent?"

"I have people on the way there now," I assure Teach. He grasps my hand and I remind him, "Is these children insist it was a name."

"Thank you," Judith whispers, while Teach closes his eyes in relief, or maybe prayer, and the Chip-Chip settle down on the floor.

"You t-tink Teach go be all right?"

"I ent know, nah? But once dem line on the monitor don't get flat is okay. Nurse say he might make it."

"Me f-foot cramp."

"Stay quiet or they go put we outside."

The nurse is glaring at them.

"Quiet like a mice," the one without the stammer promises, and the other just raises a finger to closed lips.

In a few minutes old Principal Deoraj opens his eyes again, bright and clear but etched around with worry. "Nothing yet, boy?" he asks me.

"Too soon, Uncle."

"I knew she was alive." He regards us sternly, like children in his class, then his face eases as if he's listening. "I feel for her in my mind and I am certain, certain . . ." His voice takes on a steel edge. "When they find her I will know why *I* am alive. But afterwards, how do we lift her out, past this?"

"You were always able to do that. Look at the Lezama boy."

"He still didn't reach far, poor Francis."

"I don't know. He devoted himself to his children, and look – now Francis's daughter has been appointed ambassador to – "

Teach looks up, startled.

"It's true," Judith says.

"Francis was never a bad fellow," he says. "Now Kenny was always shady . . ." Suddenly he seems tired of pretending not to be thinking about it. "Elroy?"

"Uncle?"

"Maybe something is left in Kenny that we can appeal to?"

"Watch. N-now he ha-harassing heself again. SHH!" Teach sweeps a haughty stare their way, then relaxes, wafting his left hand at me. "When this is over, we'll address that stammer."

## Judith

The text early Sunday morning had brought unimaginable pain, but this new day dawning without a word was excruciating. Then the note arrived.

The nurse who brought it said someone thrust it at the security guard at the front entrance, got back in a waiting car and sped off – a half-stupidy young boy, the guard had said. Elroy read it with me till my legs gave way, and he steadied me as I sank onto the chair he pushed under me, my hand pressed over my mouth, the heavy, black uneven print chopping at my brain:

> WE STILL HAVE YU CHILD BUT POLICE TAKE THE MONEY THEY WON'T LET SHE TALK DONT CALL POLICE THEY GO KILL SHE. WAIT DIREC-TION TO DROP MONEY AGAIN.

As the others press forward and read it, Luke whispers, "You can't tell Brother."

"But is his phone the texts coming to," Elroy objects. "And if the men call is Teach they talking to. He has to know."

As I turn back into the ward with Mark, Elroy says almost to himself, "We better pray them text keep coming," but I cannot stop to take it in.

Of course, when we tell Brother, trying to shield him all we can, he is the one to comfort us. His fingers wander over my brow, tracing the years I can almost feel etching themselves deeper by the hour. My eyes roam the room and I see the twins have not gone to school. When I ask, Elroy says, "How they go work?" They are locked into this thing now with the rest of us. But what can they know of it? What could I have imagined at their age?

This is not a pain like other pain – nothing medicine, surgery or death can end. This is cold metal through heart and brain, severing the spirit. Not pain for the dead, whom nothing more can touch, but anguish for the lost who could be anywhere, undergoing anything. Not grief, but terror and bewilder-ing helplessness, for now when the priority was to keep the child safe she has slipped through my fingers into the hands of . . . What hands!

The years. Jem's death carved my life apart, yet Anselm, the car filled with water, have mercy, my boy, my one boy – and Shanti, only Shanti left, having gone through so much already.

And Brother, now eighty-two – however hard it may be to accept that I must lose this father-brother, as I lost my husband, my son . . . I *cannot* accept, sweet Jesus not . . . not her.

# Thump

Watch – the last person I expected or wanted to see this afternoon clutching the door of my car, begging me to unlock it so he can get in.

"This man, Elroy de Jacques, have he people hunting for me all about," Kenny whines. "And that other set worse again." His face puckers on the verge of tears. "You did always look out for me, boy, Oh God from I small. You go turn you back now?"

"Tell me what you do now before I let you in," I tell him, "and who it is really looking for you that have you in this state."

I have to rev the engine and begin to pull away with Kenny clinging to the door handle before we make any progress.

"Wait," Kenny bawls out. Then he drops his voice. "I get in a little trouble with some pardner and I ent know how they go take it." My stepbrother stares pleadingly at me. Again.

"What sort of trouble?"

"Two, three fellow I know hold a young girl and ask for some money. They get close to her through my daughter."

"Go on."

"I bring in a couple pardner on the force and they well beat the fellow who collect the money for the girl, and he dead."

"So why they vex with you?"

"I holding the bag of money he collect, and after I turn it over to them they get to feel it suppose to have more in it."

"So where the people who have the girl?"

"I don't know. We lose touch."

"Not for long, you know. Not really."

Kenny stares at me, startled.

"They asking for you all about." I manage to regard him calmly.

"What you saying?"

"They say is you bring police in this thing why they friend dead."

Kenny watches me in disbelief, then horror.

"They asking for you," I affirm. "It have anything else you need to tell me?"

I keep the lock on and Kenny tugs at the door mechanically.

"It have a woman," Kenny whispers. "She does give good money, and one of my pardner on the force – the one who feel I take out the money – he saying it go be all right between us once we get back the girl because he working a deal with this new set of people . . ."

"Yes?" I try to sound encouraging.

"He make the deal but I lose touch with them fellows who take her and I can't say where the girl is to turn over to this new group that waiting on delivery. I say she dead. Mus' dead if she disappear so. It have a woman in charge, in the traffic . . ."

I unlock the door and Kenny scrambles in and collapses on the seat.

"I hear this woman and all looking for you," I tell him. A wet patch appears on the front of Kenny's trousers and widens, and he begins to cry. "It look like the best I can do for you now is to give you to Elroy." Kenny nods but a sob escapes him as I put my foot down on the accelerator. "Elroy promise the old man to save you life if he can. All the same, I feel that promise good just so long as the old man last."

Kenny's eyes widen. Questioning.

"Israel get sick when he hear you involve," I explain, "but Elroy de Jacques not a violent man. He go just turn you over to the first one who ask for you – " I am interrupted by my cell phone chiming. "Thompson here." I take the rest of the call in silence and say, "Thank you," then end the call and turn back to Kenny.

"Tell me something. You have any idea what they do with the girl? Because that is the only way I can see for you. It have police like de Jacques who make it their business to operate lawfully."

Kenny nods sourly. He knows the type.

"If you can lead them to the girl – " I begin, but Kenny cuts me off.

"Forget about she. She dead longtime."

"You know that?"

"Must dead. She could identify them and lead back to me. They was to build up a set of message to show she was alive, collect the money and get rid of her."

I swing the steering wheel hard towards San Fernando instead of taking the Port of Spain exit. "Elroy wouldn't need you then."

"But ent he promise Pa – ?"

"The old man just died. Two forty. That was Annette. She said, 'Israel gone to sleep, boy. Kenny can't hurt him again.'" Passing a hand quickly over my eyes I grip the wheel hard again. "And the next thing is, this child is the

Principal's family." I can see him pondering the relevance of this as I swing off the bypass at the roundabout.

"So what we doing?" Kenny's eyes shoot back and forth between me and the road. "You going help me, right? Is you always stick with me. Ent?"

"But it was always for the old man," I reply quietly, pulling hard to the left in front the police station. Before he can gather his thoughts I lean across, press the door handle and shove him out hard onto the asphalt before tugging back the door and swerving off.

In the rear-view mirrow I can see Kenny crawling on the hot pitch, the feet of curious policemen gathering in a circle around him.

# CHAPTER 21

# LINES

## Shanti

Uncle Brother, you'd be just as scared but you'd do it somehow, for now I remember what you said to Granma J once, 'cause she told me, *If I perish, I perish*. She says it turns out right for the good people.

There's nothing to stay here for – bare shore and the land torn away so all that's left is bush and stone, then the shelter collapsing. On what? Some island broken off of an island. Remember you taught me what *al fresco* means? This is jail al fresco. Lighten things up, is what FD would say. But he was good and look how that turned out. Some things you can't lighten up; it's gross to try. Wait. FD blacked out because of the sugar, and suppose . . . Does that get passed down? 'Cause there's nothing to eat. I've searched for anything to stuff in the backpack. And it's a jail all right – only this line of churning water out of here.

Uncle Brother, what about if I listen and you talk me across. You gotta tell me if you see them coming, for the other side is not clear like it was earlier and they could be in the bush, on the cliff with the lighthouse, watching. Way off on both sides is dark water tugging, fizzing. Step into the swirling and walk like it's the driveway to your house, right? Rain? No. Not rain too! Cup my hands and drink some; the Chubby finished hours ago. *Water is good for you, darling. Drink it instead of Coke.* When the sun rose I made out that light green streak of shallower water between the shores and I thought: I can do this. Only I should have gone before the rain. *Drink it, and go now.*

But if it rains won't the sea get rough? In movies with storms at sea, when it rains the waves heave up like mountains all around. *Go before it gets rough. It's no distance.* Surging, clashing, sand spreading underfoot and giving way so my feet slide, my face goes under, my mouth fills – *spew it out.* Back on my feet and the water stretches away to the sides, there, look, that side reaches the sky. Grey screen, like a spoilt TV. *Look ahead.* But the shore looks far whatever anyone says, now it has this curtain of rain between me and the rocks. They rise up hard and dark, but there was a beach, at least a strip, for that's where Counsel found the path. Now with the rain pelting down hard all at once there's no lighter coloured water, no sign of that spine of higher, firmer . . . although under my toes the pebbles crunch down and at first I think it's the bones of the sea strewn knobbly under my soles. It showed pale through the water in the early morning sun, yet now I'm here it's all pitted grey – and how do I know where to put my feet?

Stones, it comes back to me, stones swept together in the current, sliding under my feet before I blacked out. Wait. There, a stone hard underfoot but shifting, worried by the water, and I press my soles down on it till they hurt and the pain that is the proof of them is a comfort – I must be going a little mad. *Feel for them,* don't stop to think or look at the nothing out there or even the rocks nearer now for there the waves smash in and throw up water higher than the tangle of overhanging green. Forget the bag, it's on your back, and balance, elbows raised, feet inching forward along the strip of stones, face the shore, this shore. *Come. Come back.* Another step and the water clutches and yanks my legs. No, don't notice, only shuffle one foot, now the other. *Not far.* Ease forward again.

That palm. A palm overhung the place where they pushed me in. I was afraid a coconut might drop. Hold it in sight, keep the stones underfoot though it is rougher here. Forget the sting of sand and crash of water, then yawning grey, tumbling, legs splaying, and jolt of dark rough rock. Clutch it and drag myself, only keeping my face out of the waves and their arsenal of pebbles, hauling out my legs that the sea tries to suck back. Roll onto the flat rock, then sand. I'm across. Above me looms a whole wall of rock, but bush too, and the palm overhanging. I twist from my back onto my stomach to push myself to my feet.

Slammed down. A shadow hurtling. . . .

# Nathan

Gone. Thompson brought the news himself.

This is what happens when you live too long: shred by shred everything that has made you is stripped away. And not even time to mourn – after all Israel has been to me, to Pa, to Ma, how he propped me up time and again when I felt on the verge of collapse. And now. *Now*. Yet the horror of the rest deflects it.

For now they are questioning whether the child is alive. Yes, up to when the Ullin message came in, but since then – nothing. No further text after so many following fast on each other. Amani has put up the cash, but no further directions have come. I've told them all, and Judith utterly agrees: *We must entertain no doubt that she is alive, that she will be found.* We must hunt on. Elroy's people are scouring the area around Toco.

But then, suppose, *suppose* he has some further information and is . . . preparing us. My uselessness tugs me under like a current and I am wondering whether I should bother to force my way up, when Judith's hand grabs mine. *For such a time as this.* Did she say it or did it come to me – for what would I have left to give?

"Be here," Judith insists. "She will stretch out and feel for you."

But suppose. *Is* Elroy breaking something to us gradually? *No.* Then where? The two surviving men of the three that took her have disappeared, he says, and Kenny too. None of them traced, dead or alive. The girl, Chinksie, has been charged but turns out to know little. Then the talk of another option, some gang or . . . to do with trafficking. One reads of such things, but here? How could they avoid the police in a country this size? No. It must be those same men, the kidnappers. But days? And nights. This beautiful little girl. Dear God, a nightmare only Israel can talk me through. Aah.

No. Now my mind is for Shanti alone. *Darling, in between trying to pray, I listen for you,* I whisper to her. I can hear from her at any time, I repeat to myself so my heart can beat on.

# Judith

But when I open the door a crack and look out at Elroy to see whether he has heard anything, he beckons to me with his face down as if he is unable to meet my eyes. Mark is with him. I shut the door gently behind me, although

I am certain Brother is wide awake behind his closed eyes, and I force my feet in Elroy's direction.

"Something," he murmurs, looking away from me still, "something has been . . . found."

"Not . . .?

"They can't say. Can't tell." The remains are female. About the same age. "But there is no evidence," he says hastily, "no evidence that it is the one we are looking for . . . at this time." After a while he adds. "We need to identify . . ."

As I stare at him, dumb, Mark says, "No. Let me. Don't ask that of her."

"Before anyone goes through that . . . anyone," Elroy says, "we're working with dental records."

Oh Jesus.

In the corridor, a bench. But I cannot sit. I stand near the door through which Elroy will come back to us. The boys are somewhere behind me. They tried to make me sit down but I cannot. I cannot meet their eyes and the reflection of my thoughts in them. I stand with my eyes to the floor, which spreads to the walls and the walls to the ceiling. The corridor is a long box I cannot contemplate and I turn instead to the closed door and stand facing it, my forehead almost touching the surface. Cold. My skin and the shudder beneath my skin and the ice creeping between flesh and bone. I notice a distant faintly irritating noise I cannot place, an uneven rattle. And I realize my teeth are chattering and I cannot make them stop.

"Not your child," Elroy repeats, leaning over me. I am lying on the floor and I don't know how I got there. "Someone's. But not yours."

Back on the ward I intend to say nothing about it because for once we have managed to get through without Brother knowing. When I reach his bed he stretches for my hand and takes it in an iron grip without opening his eyes.

"Alive," Brother says. "Never question it."

## Shanti

It must have been the rock. I guess it was a wave upended me. That hard slap I thought was Ratchet's hand. And no blade rising and crunching down, only the stone jutting out where the water tumbled me. Then the nightmare, prowling, not quite faded even now I'm awake. Am I? My eyes are open.

But how long have I been lying here in full view?

No one's come. Is it true, then? Uncle Brother's dead? For he'd have called Officer Elroy; he or Granma J would've done that. Only the men said *no police*, but my folks would have found some way and Elroy would come. I remember how he grabbed Uncle's hand at the shelter when the police questioned FD.

I gotta move, not lie here and roast. But wasn't it overcast, raining? Blazing hot now although its gotta be four or later. Get off this rock and under the bush. Drag my legs in and draw them up tight. *Yes. Stay out of sight.* Lie still.

But the dream edges around me, the sea turning to blood in the sunrise, shimmering like the sweat on their skin so they couldn't grip each other, just lash out – then blows raining, and my voice squeezed to silence so as not to call attention to hands reaching, gripping the coldness. And I know the end of it in that deep timeless pause before the hot gush of terror and the relief of waking up.

It is cooler and quiet when I open my eyes, evening perhaps, but I don't know where they are – they must be close, waiting for it to get dark so they can cross back. The bush on the side of the path up to the lighthouse has cruel thorns, I remember. On the other path, where the class went on the outing, one of the children stumbled into the bush and I could not look at her leg – but still, if I must, I will dive under it, into it. So watch for little openings to hide in.

Listen. Is it . . .?

Two pairs of feet crunching, voices grumbling, cursing, paper crackling. No. Nothing. Still, wait a little. Granma J is sitting beside the phone. Uncle's on his pillow; he is listening for me. They will get Officer Elroy to help.

Slip again to the next cover and listen. *Be thankful. The water is behind you now.* But now that I'm here, Uncle Brother, aren't they? Somewhere? Every step's getting me closer to them 'cause they're headed where I'm coming from. Every corner of the path they're round it. No, not this time. Slide behind this. Watch.

But can I trust what I see? When things are, like, jumbled? I can't figure out the way now that the path is flat, or if I passed here before or if they're behind or up ahead. Waiting.

Wet hair in my face, push it back. Wait. No, the clip is gone and the chip from my phone too. But still. . . smart is what they all say. *Smarter than all the rest of them*, Uncle Brother said. But how to . . . I mean, it's not like *Lost* and stuff, on TV, or some game you just power off.

I can't make out the ground, and it's as if the thing that happened messed up time so I don't know whether this light is dawn or twilight, or even if the path is still . . . the path. The rock underfoot tilts into the darkness, and if I step forward, with the sea roaring so loud might it be the edge, and the next step . . . And I'm not sure if . . . if it matters. After all the blood and thing. *Keep going up. Not to the side.*

Easy for you to say, what if it was you hounded by these big – you know – strong, so you couldn't fight them and they figured out this price for you and the path was under water, through macca bush, branches scattered, chopped limbs. And if I could just get back I'd never, never again, oh please I'm a little girl and never going to pretend I'm big again, all right? I mean not even my first bra. *Listen. Don't think, don't stop.* Okay, suppose they'd run you down to the absolute edge of . . . of . . .? What would be *your* next step? Talk to me, Uncle Brother. Talk.

But he can't hear me – I mean, get real. They even said he was dead. But they're liars. I sent text after text, but did he get them or are they lost? My fingers spread in front me, the blood gone from them now, but they're like ice and trembling the way they did last time I pressed the buttons:

. . . *or they willl do it like htey said they have an axe*

The lighthouse looms up straight and tall beyond the bush, disappearing into the night sky, so solid that I find myself crying with relief. I dry my eyes to peer from the trees and bushes around the space at the base of the light-house, out at the deserted picnic area. A form leaps out but darts aside – a stray dog searching for food. Food? On the nearest table a shallow box of chips with half a hamburger juts over the edge. Break off the bitten part and eat the rest of the bun; throw the meat, the dog'll find it. Circle the open area in the patches of shadow under the trees, then stay close to the clumps of bush following the road that led us uphill. Head down now, hugging the side and darting between them.

Dark. And silent except for the sea. Even this wider road is rough, and after the long walk down, the soreness under every step and my legs almost giving way, the roadside is scraggy grass and low bush with no shelter. Only a cart stands on the roadside. A police car cruises oddly, crawling. Searching for me?

Counsel or Rachet said something about police not wanting to find me alive. Run before it turns back. The cart is full of grass and close now, the spokes of the wheels thick and within reach, a foothold to clamber up. I drop inside and creep forward in the tray, banking the grass behind to hide me and putting my face on the backpack to be near FD, Granma J, Uncle Brother. Blue light flashes through my blanket of grass and I squeeze my knees tighter to my chin. Limbs coil and scramble in my head and a hand opens and clenches. *Force that out. Whatsoever things . . .* I gather Uncle Brother's voice in my head, sink deep into it.

The bed jolts and it is the cart moving, lurching along. Here is water in the Chubby bottle I don't remember filling. The old hops bread is mushy with sea water, but once that's scooped out and the grass and stuff brushed off, the bag slips comfortably onto my back again. My stomach has stopped groaning and only squeezes and jabs at me now. In the grey light of early morning a police car coasts by in the other direction and I burrow down in the cart. The road runs parallel to the sea for a long time before turning away uphill. It doesn't matter where, once it goes as far as possible from the shore, the island, Ratchet, the police – swaying, carrying me along over a steady thud of hooves. Rocking like when I was little, sitting on Granma.

A shout jolts me, and the branch of a massive tree passes overhead. When I peep out there is a track to a small house, so I haul myself over the other side onto the road and sprint for the dark line of forest. The bushy slope takes me farther in, deep as I can if only for a soft bank like one I knew before, though it is hazy now, but I remember a huge leaf that was my friend and there must be another like it somewhere in the whole forest.

The thing is, as I huddle here, rocking, the thing is how to work out where the dream begins and ends. Ratchet's arm reaches under my leaf to grab my shirt and rip it off, only a thick vine twists viciously round him and I hear his arm crunch. As I roll deeper under the leaves a woman leans over me smiling, her clothes glittering in the dim light till she draws back her jewelled high-heeled shoe and inches forward the other foot, cocking her hoof with a shriek of mockery. None of which can be real. And yet, from what I overheard between Counsel and Rathet there is a woman who owns a forest of lost people, buying and selling. Lie very still under the tangle of vine and leaf and shadow. *Granma J and Uncle Brother are real*, I tell myself.

But as I relax it comes on me again. The dream I cannot get out of. Counsel and Ratchet struggle furiously and scream at each other words I've heard on the street or seen written in toilets. Locked together, they struggle with faces set, teeth clenched. One must must bring down the other and *one* I cannot be alone with. The thought of Counsel being killed stops my breath. I strain for air, my throat squeezing tighter. This is not like them arguing along the way. No chance of their cooperating again. I'll be left with *one*.

They thrash on the sand, arms writhing for a murderous clasp, Ratchet is wilder, as if nothing matters but to kill, whether or not he dies too; even though his knees slam on the ground and stones tear him bloody he doesn't care once his fingers lock on Counsel's throat.

The thought of being left with Ratchet sends icy needles down my spine.

*Take care of yourself, darling,* Uncle Brother said. How? Counsel is weakening under those iron fingers. *Do something.* Counsel's heels drum the ground and his hands slide uselessly on drenched skin, his body arching in the struggle to breathe, then sagging, his fingers opening.

One hand reaches for the axe. It has been leaning there for hours, years it seems, as if it followed us of its own accord and lay in wait. The shoreline tilts and the sea swerves, the horizon askew. The axe drags, scraping on the stones. Heaved up, barely under control, then drops heavily. Grabbed again and hoisted. A crunch, bone splintering under parting flesh; and a pause in which the wind stops, leaves hang hang still, and the sea stills, a new smell rising above it, salt too but not of water, blood everywhere. Splashed wide and still pulsing out red-hot. It is not, cannot be, and knowing from experience this is a nightmare I look away back at the sea, and of course that comes and goes as usual, only the waves meeting and clashing open again along the line of turbulence that marks the submerged path back, and I close my eyes so as not to see those pale stones under the surface.

When I open them, all I want is to forget these men, the woman who would buy me if she could, the man who terrorized his wife into lying about FD, then carried her lie to the police – which has nothing to do with all this, except that FD is gone. Except that the girl who comforted me, Chinksie, pretended to be my friend when I was nothing to her but some favour for her boyfriend, something to sell like meat, like in the market, only that is too close to the dream and I must not let it start again.

But now I am quite awake, wandering among the trees, and suppose I walk the wrong way and meet the woman with the stolen people and they keep me, there with Luz who knows Ratchet and who Counsel said they would have beaten to death. Or, suppose I meet no one to ask for help. No longer safe to assume a woman will help – perhaps only a child. Except the stories say there are dead children in the forest not quite dead but unable to live or die, thrown-away children. Do not let them lead you for their feet turn always backways. Or am *I* one of them now? Or suppose the men killed me after all and, like in a movie, I don't know.

Uncle Brother? Are you dead too? *Don't believe people you can't trust. Don't follow them. Say your prayers then make your own path.* Now I open my eyes and a track winds up to disappear into the trees and down to disappear into the trees, but across the way a valley opens out and the land folds back hillside after hillside, dimmer and dimmer, blue grey in the distance. Am I trying to hide or to find help, for how can I do both? And why doesn't someone come for me? *Uncle Brother, aren't you all doing anything about it? If you know so much why can't you find me?*

*Darling,* he once said, *anger is no good. It doesn't work.* What works? I whispered to him after FD died, and he sighed. In *the end, they say, forgiveness – but it's hard. I hope to live long enough to grasp that.* But maybe someone forgave Ratchet once too often instead of wiping him out – did you think of that? *Hold onto the ones you know, the ones you've known all your life.* But they're not here. And if I give up on strangers altogether, I can't get back. Sometime I'll have to risk one.

But not yet. The forest thickens uphill. Green cocoa leaves splash around the base while the ground yields with years of fallen leaves. Cocoa? A red pod hangs barely in reach, and I grab it, but when it lets go of the stem and bursts in my hands, what do I do next? I never looked inside one before. Granma J said people would dance cocoa to polish the beans, so I pull one out and rub it clean and taste it. But I spit it out and hurl away the pod and I could scream because it's supposed to be chocolate and instead it's nasty.

Aah. A pool among huge rocks with ruffles of green toppling out of crevices and hanging over the water. I could drink that because the green is only a reflection of the bush; in my hands the water trembles clear and cold, but then that film of red moss might not be good. Refill the Chubby bottle, for later, and slide it into FD's backpack.

A snap and crunch whirls me round. Only a branch. The noises are sudden and startling but there is no one. The bamboo creaks, its feathery plumes dipping as the stalks groan. The corn bird flashes by, an instant of hard yellow-eyed stare, its call lost in the rest of the whistling, peeping, chirping, twittering, grating, tweeting. Overturned roots grope and behind them pink plastic-looking torch lilies rise among stalks that shoot up twenty feet. I could live here if there was food, live here with the birds fluting, chattering, squawking, darting through – electric blue, dull brown, grey, gold-capped, or red-throated, or sometimes a streak of metallic green lost instantly in the bush.

Oranges? An old sour orange tree furred with moss and the occasional fern frond and wild pine bears fruit that are still hard and green. And there, berries I know nothing about. At least cocoa isn't poisonous. A yellow pod dangles in reach and it opens more easily, the pulp all over my fingers as they pluck out the beans again. I brace myself against the taste and, absently, just to clean my hands, lick off the pulp and – the relief! It's not nasty at all, sweetish. I gulp it down and here is another pod, yellow too. If the forest can hide me perhaps it might feed me too.

I know the names of plants because of Granma J – philodendron and heliconias, but that deep purple red creeper spilling from the fork of the old tree is a stranger to me, and those long tresses of green are not garden plants, not tame. The woodpecker raps furiously on the uncaring stump and nothing feels anything for anyone, like stone impervious to the water channelling it century after century. The little drops of moisture do not care for it or hate it but just pass over it to find the easiest way for themselves. No. The forest will not help me.

Find my way down to a road, to a house with children playing, regular children. Ask them for their mother. Every step rubs the blisters on my feet to sticky raw flesh, sharpens the ache in my legs, and throbs where the thorns gouged my skin that is closed back tight and shiny.

A clearing, and a track leading away from it. Perhaps to someone with food. The track widens to a rough road slashed through the trees.

And at last a woman, unmistakably a woman and old enough to be my mother. Older. She pauses where the path opens on the road a kilometre or so beyond the clearing. The clearing had tarpaulin shelters with guards around it, and I edged back into the trees. A little past it was this wider track, flat and hard enough for a car or van, and I just walked along in the middle because I was fed up of tripping over roots and vines. And just around a bend there was this big SUV idling in the way. The woman peers at me through the windscreen, then slides out from behind the wheel and stares. The sea soaked me all over, and washed my legs but what it didn't clean away has dried on me. Her eyes search my stained clothes, my face, my feet. Then her hand (almost as if she is too shocked to control it) motions me away. But I can't move, only stand staring back, trapped in her gaze.

She gestures vaguely, not just shooing me away like a nuisance, but as if she is rejecting something huge, looming above us both, so I look behind and above me but can see nothing.

"Go," she says tiredly.

She might have been beautiful once but she isn't now, for her face looks as if she has been tired and angry and hungry her whole life, and when I turn away I realize she can't have been real because . . . wouldn't she have helped me? Or sent me into the clearing under the tarpaulin?

*Run,* says the voice in my head. *Run before she changes her mind and sucks you dry.*

Was she there, or did I dream her up?


## Holi

I know a real child when I see one.

Perhaps no one did know I was really there, since no one ever came. They say *he* caught up the rest of them, one after another. But not me. I waited and waited, and no one came.

And now I could take you away and keep you. I had Amy once and I thought I could keep her because if she was one of myselves what could go wrong – but it was not like that. I could have you for myself. But no. For I lost Amy and it was . . . was agonizing, so you know what? You go. I can keep you from them and that is all that matters in the end – that I can.

A child wandering alone in the forest, old enough, well formed enough to pack in with the rest. So much like Amy though, as if she had materialized. Somehow, in her lostness there I was at that age, like in the mirror tarnished by rust-brown spots. Only the fury was drained out. Like how they found me near my mother's body, not even crying any more, tangled in the cloth stained with abeer and blood. Alone.

A vast tiredness overwhelmed me and, and I thought, what was one more or less. As she backed away, the longing welled up and I suppose I gazed more closely at the stains on her clothes, even her skin, the bruises on her legs, but her eyes flinched from mine and her arms raised, warding off – no, as if struggling in a current and being swept backwards.

I knew who she was long before the news report. I had waited all my life on this chance to strip them utterly, and now the key to it had fallen in my hand, and I let it go. Now she can tell anyone who finds her about the clearing and *my* presence on the road to it. I could have called the guards but she was *me*, yet so unlike me, so treasured that something drew me, though I fell behind and found myself looking for traces of her and stumbling on nothing except under this tree, older and wider than the rest, and its twisted roots gathered me in. And sitting here in this nook, gathering up the spilled contents of my purse, the cash and keys and even those tablets I carried in case Amy's pain grew unbearable, carry still, I begin to think I can tease out the child again, the one I wasn't and never had, that was not found or looked for but only frittered away. In the play of shadows the bush whispers to me what I am, its incantation rustling through my brain, thoughts scattering like little white pebbles, pills, patches of light from between the leaves. *Douen. Little douen. Bring them into the bush, the clearing, the emptiness.*

But now I think perhaps I will not stray from here. Not any more. Just not move.

## Shanti

Someone searching for me rends the darkness and a woman's voice echoes in my head, not Granma J's, a stranger's. "Get out of here," said the woman by the SUV. "Fast. As far as you can." Uncle Brother, who was that? *Just come home, darling.*

Downhill, downhill. It is overcast, and dim under the trees, which throw down lianas, not like Tarzan's vines or Mowgli's but hard, rootlike, and spirals of wood, and the roots and vines interlace on the uncertain path between dark mush or stones. Earlier where I could see better there were light brown dry leaves perforated by insects and now noises are sharper than before, insects whining, chirring, and an anxious fluttering of a bird disturbed, so I spring aside and freeze. A 'gouti darts past with a twitch of curly ears, glossy sleek brown melting into the shadows.

Downhill, down. A flat rock and big wide leaves. Rest. I sleep more and more, more carelessly too. I roll to the side, under a trumpet tree with its white bells tipped with peach, curling tight and drawing my legs and arms deep into the clothes that seem even bigger now. I pull a leaf I have broken off over my face to keep off mosquitoes, but most of all I try to shield myself from sleep, though I must lie down, I must, my feet so raw and puffy, only try not to sleep in case the dream comes back. But I lose hold.

It never happened because nothing like that could happen, but it is real every time. "What you dream is what is in your head," the therapist will say, for if I get through this they will make me go to her. "Your thoughts and wishes present themselves in disguise." Only, don't tell Uncle Brother about the dream; he mightn't be able to stand it. Yet Uncle Mark says tell him everything because it always turns out he knows anyway.

A smell disturbs me. Perhaps it's me. I smell like raw meat, not clean and washed with limes, but left sitting in the kitchen or the sun, or like if you had your period and didn't bathe. No, there was water tearing at me, and the blood was not the curse. It was the other thing.

They screamed filth at each other and all I knew was that the one I would be left with would be the more relentless, the one with the secret grin and whisper, for he was the one pinning the other to the ground, and Counsel's feet kicked uselessly, his hands opening, fingers going limp. I could get it to him, I thought, if it wasn't too late. There's the hard clench on the handle, the imperfect swing and sick thud, and night darkening the sand. All I can remember of the sunrise is dark crimson staining the sand, and when I turned my back quickly and ran to the shore even the water broke red around my feet.

Then it is gone. The island and the sea are behind me, and damp leaves brush or peel away as I scramble again, one raw foot before the next, the trees giving way to lower shrubs. And there's a sound I know, surging and breaking, not behind me after all. I am afraid of it but more afraid of the woman's voice, lest she call and my feet carry me back to her. So I break out into the bright beyond the trees, and across the road a beach reminds me of the other shore and look, there, footprints (are they mine?) leading backways to the sea and at the thought that I am going round in circles I am turning to run lest I find myself back on the island, only I have slashed it from my mind, hacked it from thought, and when I look again, it is not the same place where we crossed to the island, no hard steep rock but an expanse of sand and the sea, gentle, barely rippling on the shore, and at the edge of the sea there is a bent old man on the water's rim.

A twisted almond tree reaches above him and scatters its shadow on the water. Slowly, for I am not certain it is safe, I cross the road and peep around the tree, legs throbbing, feet raw and swollen but poised to run. But this isn't a young man, or a woman who might be Chinksie, or Ratchet in a scarf, or a demon of the forest, but an old, old man, old like one I have loved since I was born, only thin, sun-blackened, bent over a seine as late afternoon cools toward evening.

He stares at me stumbling towards him and I falter because my feet are too torn and bloody now to put down hard on damp leaves, let alone this sharp gritty sand. It is drizzling again lightly and water runs down his face.

"Child! Where you come out from?" Astonished, he straightens up but his shoulders are still stooped from years of bending, of mending nets as he is doing now, yet muscular from years of throwing them arcing over the water where he is so at home. His eyes are piercing bright under thick white eyebrows, against skin baked black over the years.

"Child, who you belong to?"

Only I have not spoken for two days. Four? I don't know.

"Child?"

"Uncle." It is the only word I can find and perhaps he can't hear for my voice is little more than a croak.

"Child?"

I search for my voice again. "I'm lost, Uncle. I need a phone. Please, where I could get a phone?"

He turns to his worn bag on the sand behind him and reaches in. *You don't notice everybody has a cell phone nowadays?* Uncle Brother said that. The old man hands it to me and watches a little anxiously as I try to press the buttons, not sure if my fingers will work after everything. He peers more closely at me.

"You hurt youself, child?" he asks. He puts his hard rough fingers softly on my face to lift it and I am not afraid of him as he runs his eye over my clothes and drops his hand. "Oh God, what happen to you, dou dou?" And the sea sighs beyond him and creeps up to curl lovingly round his feet.

As I press the numbers they blur with water. Rain or sea spray, tears. The rain soaks my shirt and darkens, dripping down onto the sand like an old wound opened and bleeding again. I turn my mind from the dream that threatens, and press the ruin behind me deep into my head, sending my thoughts out to those who are looking for me – those who know there are tales impossible to tell or acknowledge as true, too terrible for a little girl to listen to even in her own head let alone replay. I try to leave it behind, that other . . . that damaged, destroyed, that not-me.

I am one they are going to find. A bright space lights up in my head and they fan out in it, Granma J and all of them, in the hospital waiting room, on the benches outside the hospital overlooking the sea, in the roti shop nearby and outwards all over the island, at work, at home, the old ones beside their landlines and the younger ones fingering their cells. And Uncle Brother holding me firm in his thoughts and searching for my own. Whoever I call will come for me, but this is a prepaid phone and who knows how much money's on it. I've gotta call just one number, and I listen for a voice in my mind.

*Again, darling. You have it in you.*

I knew it. I knew he couldn't ever be gone. A raised forefinger stills the other murmurs in my head and I brace myself to steady my hand so my fingers press the buttons right, and my mind forces back the red tide.

Because somewhere, I know, in a hospital room, an old man's eyes are flashing to the cell phone on the pillow beside his head, for it is about to ring.

# AUTHOR'S NOTE

This is a work of fiction. The character of Nathan Deoraj is to some extent drawn from life, inspired by a remarkable man with an unwavering commitment to family. There is a factual basis to the account of a father's death followed by a brother assuming the care of his siblings. The rest is invention. Brief mention is made of actual persons such as political figures (peripheral to the story), but the characters with whom Nathan interacts in the story (Dada, Shanti and the rest) are all imaginary.

CPSIA information can be obtained at www.ICGtesting.com
Printed in the USA
LVOW11s2022231014

410227LV00004B/5/P